PRAISE FOR ANDREA BARRETT'S
SHIP FEVER

"The seven first-rate stories and the exceptional title novella making up Andrea Barrett's *Ship Fever* are a magical wedding of the truths, the ways and means, of science and storytelling. The result of this happy marriage is a brilliant and highly original book."

—George Garrett

"*Ship Fever* ranks with the best of the new wave of historical writing—Nicholas Mosley's *Hopeful Monsters*, Jeanette Winterson's *The Passion*, and Charles Johnson's *Middle Passage*.... Barrett courses back and forth over the history of science and the science of human relations in the nineteenth century, giving us the people behind the history—doctors, collectors, inventors, and women—in a glory of passion, ambition, and love. This is just simply inspired writing."

—Douglas Glover

"Andrea Barrett explores the scientific soul—its solitude, its animating curiosity, its baffled despair when discoveries are elusive or misinterpreted. This is a mysterious and beautiful book."

—Joan Wickersham

"In these wonderfully original stories, the great explorers of mind and geography seem to enter the room, and history feels more immediate than the present....Andrea Barrett does not flinch from large subjects, yet her uncanny investigations into human curiosity are sensual and soul-enhancing, and always underlit by splendid intelligence."

—Howard Norman

"In these extraordinary stories, romance is saturated with material detail, scientific curiosity corrupted by passion, and history intimately connected to our contemporary lives. An inventive and elegant collection."

—Joanna Scott

LUCID STARS

ANDREA BARRETT

Delta
Trade Paperbacks

A Delta Book
Published by
Dell Publishing
a division of
Bantam Doubleday Dell Publishing Group, Inc.
1540 Broadway
New York, New York 10036

ISBN 0-385-31943-6

Printed in the United States of America
Published simultaneously in Canada

September 1988

10 9 8 7 6 5 4 3 2 1

BVG

For Barry

Contents

PART ONE
Penny

And God said, Let there be
lights in the firmament of the heaven
to divide the day from the night; and
let them be for signs, and for seasons,
and for days, and years:
And let them be for lights in the
firmament of the heaven to give light
upon the earth: and it was so.
And God made two great lights;
the greater light to rule the day, and
the lesser light to rule the night:
he made the stars also.

—Genesis 1:14–16

Orion, Mighty Hunter in the Sky
(February 1955)

★   ★   ★   ★   ★   ★

Bellatrix.

Betelgeuse.

Aldebaran.

New snow falls on the ground and sparkles in the blue light of the winter stars. Cones of snow cap the posts of the ski racks, empty now; the wind sends snow devils swirling across the Vermont plain. Inside the ski lodge, two men slump in armchairs near the fire, their boots resting on hot stones and sending up occasional puffs of steam. Penelope Webb, nineteen years old and usually called Penny, slices a lime and considers telling the men that they're warping the layered leather of their soles. Before she can open her mouth, the older man snaps his fingers at her and calls, "Hey, honey! How about another beer?"

So much for his boots. She sets a bottle on the table silently and then, although it's ten below zero and although these two men are her last chance for a decent tip and some company, she puts on her coat and tells Harry she's taking her break. Harry will understand, she thinks. He's a decent bartender; certain things he always understands. Maybe not the litany she recites to herself to keep from snapping back at those men: Rigel, Pollux, Sirius, bright stars rising one after another in the sequence her grandmother taught her. But a break to get some fresh air? Sure.

Outside, her boots squeak against the snow and she drinks in the cold, trying to clear away the skier's rude fingersnap and return to the dream she was hatching while she quartered limes. She runs through this same dream every night, while she hauls trays of hot rum and Irish coffee and eavesdrops on her customers' conversations. She listens to the ski instructors and ski patrolmen who come here after the lifts close, the Austrians arguing with the Swiss, the Swiss bickering with the French. They have accents and yodels and fancy foreign equipment, and each thinks his skiing technique is the only valid one. Penny can't tell which of them is right—she's taken lessons from so many of them that she's gotten confused. She's been told to lean gently, to dive forward, to unweight from the hips, the knees; to rotate into the hill and to tilt away from it; to shape a perfect snowplow and not to stem at all. Despite all this, she still can't ski.

In her dreams, she skis like a bird. What she was dreaming when that skier snapped his fingers was this: that she, Penelope Webb, newly dropped out of college on the occasion of her grandmother's death for the express purpose of learning how to ski, now slashes through the bamboo gates of a giant slalom with her arms just brushing the poles and powder rising in an icy spume behind her. On her chest is a racing bib; on her feet, new skis and new boots. At the edge of the trail, cheering her on, are the same instructors and ski patrolmen she watches from the windows of the bar.

She skis faster than any of them, with perfect, graceful technique, flying when her skis lift off at the bumps. Flying over all the obstacles before her—her lack of money, her unfinished education, her own inability to decide what she wants from her life. She, who in one year changed her college major four times, from math to history to art to ancient languages, now thinks: Travel. See the world, maybe; try a little of everything, the way Gram did. Raise hell on skis, hang out in high places. She was soaring when the man in the bar brought her back to earth.

Now, pretending she's on skis, she leaves the lights of the lodge behind with a few gliding steps. She punches her arms forward one at a time as if she's planting poles, and she throws her body into exaggerated angulations. Like a racer, she thinks. Like Fritz, like Franz, like Rudi. She was born to ski, she knows; has known since last winter when six Dartmouth skiers gave an exhibition that made her realize that she, never athletic before, was meant for this. Only some technical trick, some disagreement among her instructors, holds her back now. A good teacher, she thinks. The right teacher for just a week, someone who could teach her skiing as clearly and carefully as her grandmother taught her stars. That's all she needs.

Instinctively, as she always does whenever she thinks of Gram, Penny tilts her head back and finds the Big Dipper, following the line from Dubhe and Merek, on the outside of the bowl, to Polaris. Polaris is where it always is, and from Polaris she can find anything. The stars have a logic that's lured her since childhood, since those wartime nights when the houselights in Brattleboro were shielded with blankets and the streetlights were painted black. Then, while neighbors scanned the skies for enemy bombers that never came, Gram bundled Penny into a plaid overcoat and took her outside. They sat in the snow behind the house, near the leafless hedge and the crisp, tan balls left hanging on the viburnum. With a star chart spread across their knees they named the constellations, plotting routes between them as Penny grew older and then, as she grew older still, escaping from Penny's parents into nightly starwatching. Penny's father might sit aloof, drinking beer and fretting over his hardware business; Penny's mother might fuss upstairs over asthmatic Mick or over her own imagined illnesses. "Be a doll," either of them might say. "Get her out of my hair." And Gram, in whose house they lived and on whose money they depended, would take Penny out through the twin glass doors of the porch to which she'd been banished with her dark, fragrant cigarettes and her dusty souvenirs. Scarves, vases, bits of lace, medals, crumbling letters, relics of old lovers dead in earlier wars—things Penny loved but which made Penny's mother sneeze and sent her younger brother into choking spasms. Penny used to wonder if her parents were foundlings, slipped in to substitute for the real daughter and son-in-law Gram was meant to have, the real parents meant to be Penny's. Gram, and not her parents, taught Penny everything, and Penny can still hear that patient, lightly accented voice. "We start here, with Polaris, where my mother started me when I was a girl, back in the old country . . ." Bit by bit, each fact building on the one before it.

Penny carves her way around a fence post as if it's a slalom gate, trying to shake off a prickle of fear. After six months she still wonders if leaving school was the right thing. Gram always meant her to finish, but within a month of her death the house was gone and the giant garden and all the bits and pieces of Gram's life, vanished when Penny's parents moved to a subdivision nearer town. Penny was left with only her sense of the night sky and the feeling that she wanted something different. Not school but skiing or, if not skiing, some other wild life full of the dreams and huge reversals that marked Gram's before she finally settled down at forty to have her one disappointing daughter. Twenty years, Penny thinks, gazing into the night. I've got twenty years anyway. Every tangible reminder of Gram is gone, but Penny knows she's kept what's important—she can still recognize Orion, who hangs low in the southeast. She still can't see a bunch of stars without grouping them into patterns. Gods, birds, beasts, fish—Orion looks like a bearded man with a jeweled belt and a sword, fending off the mighty Taurus. A hare crouches beneath his feet and to the west, just waiting to rise, lurks the scorpion who killed him.

Penny's dreams are broken by a noise from the slope above—a steady, rhythmic rasp of skis on snow that makes her think for a second she's dreamed a pair of them into existence. The slope, unlighted, shines pale ash in the glow of the stars and the crescent moon. Against it, the dark lift towers climb like teeth. She sees no one, hears only the steady swish. Finally she makes out a man darting between the towers. The man stops, seems to pull something from the snow, rests the something on his shoulders. She watches, mystified, as he skis on, stops and pulls again, skis and stops and pulls. A bundle of something, long and light, is growing under his upraised arm. Ski poles? she wonders. Dropped from the lift? But there could never be this many. And then she remembers the practice slalom run someone set this afternoon, and she thinks, Of course—he's pulling the bamboo poles. But it's late, and dark, and she can't imagine why the poles can't stay until morning.

She hears the lodge door open, and then Harry crunches up behind her and taps her arm. "Honey?" he says, the word different in his mouth than in the skier's. Harry means well, she knows. "You coming in?"

"Sure," Penny says. "Just wishing those two guys inside would get lost."

"They're gone," Harry says.

Penny turns but then pauses and points at the skier whose poles stream behind him like a comet's tail. "Any idea who that is?" she asks. The figure skis, stops, and pulls twice more.

Harry laughs. "Benjamin Day, most likely—ski patrol. Likes to ski at night. Sometimes alone, sometimes with his buddy Otis Nelson. They ride the last lift up and then wait in the hut at the top until the mountain's closed and the moon comes out." Harry shivers. "Watch if you want—I'm going in."

"In a minute," Penny says. She, who can hardly ski in broad daylight, wants to see if this Benjamin gets down in one piece.

The swishes above her draw closer until she hears the lightweight rattle of the poles. Soon she hears breathing, then tips in snow; finally she hears the click of edges snapping together at each turn. She stamps her feet to warm them. Benjamin Day glides before her like a ghost, breathing as easily as if he's not skied down a mountain in the dark, not sat in a freezing shed for hours. One arm is curved around a pile of poles as thick as Penny's waist. She knows the poles are made of bamboo and don't weigh anything, but the bundle looks impressive just the same.

"Hi," she says softly, to see if he'll jump.

"Jesus!" he says, snapping his head around. "Who's that?"

"Penny. From the bar inside." She can't see his face yet, but she can tell he's slender and shorter than she might have hoped.

He leans the bundle against the rack and then glides over to peer into her face. "Penny," he says. "Don't you waitress in there?"

"Right," she says. "And you're Benjamin Day."

He doesn't seem surprised that she knows his name. Bad sign, she thinks—one of those men who expect to

be recognized. But he has light eyes sparkling with energy and a fine nose with a bump on the bridge, enough
to make her ignore that warning twinge. And he has
something else, some crackling aura of energy, almost of
power. He holds his head high on his neck, the way
Gram held hers, and his smile is as quick as fire.

He's waiting for her to say something else, but as he
waits he stares at her eyes until her tongue suddenly
glues itself behind her bottom teeth. All she can do is
point at the stars and stutter, "Look—Orion's out, and
Cassiopeia, and both the Dippers," fully aware that she
sounds ridiculous but unable to stop herself. Good, she
thinks, groaning silently. Thanks, Gram. She's not usually so awkward with men, but this picture she's suddenly formed of Benjamin Day sitting silently on the
mountaintop has pushed aside her own dreams and
thrown her off balance.

Ben looks briefly at the sky. "Just a bunch of stars to
me," he says, but at least he doesn't laugh and Penny is
so grateful for this that she invites him inside for a
drink while she finishes work. To her surprise, Ben
says, "Sure," and follows her.

Later, looking back at that first week, Penny will
wonder if everyone saw what was coming but her. She
was so busy thinking of Ben that she hardly noticed
when Cindy, her roommate, sniffed each time Ben ap-
peared. Penny ignored Ben's friends, who smiled knowingly when Ben touched her arm or shoulder in passing, and she paid no attention when Harry, never one
to interfere, told her several times to keep her mind on
her work. She didn't talk to anyone about her jumbled
feelings—she had no one to talk to.

"We're just friends," she told Harry then, knowing
that it wasn't true. No friend had ever made her move
like this, head up and shoulders back, aware every instant of the eyes on her. The boyfriends she'd had be-

fore were nothing serious, nothing like this, and when she thinks about it now (when she can think at all), she tells herself that Ben has hypnotized her. Perhaps it is his pale, sharp eyes. He looks at her mouth and her hand rises on its own to trace her lips; he looks at her eyes and her body stiffens. During her few clear moments, she's aware that Ben is hunting her, having chosen her for reasons maybe no more complicated than the fact that he found her waiting for him in the snow and wants to know why. She doesn't care what his reasons are. What she wants to know is what's going on behind his eyes, what he thinks about, dreams about, what drives his nighttime skiiing. In him, she can sense the possibility of some other life, as if he's a door leading her to another dimension, a secret world. He seems to hold the key to the life she left school to lead, talking about Chile, Colorado, the Himalayas, the Alps, all the places he means to go, about racing and drinking with strangers, bumming rides, sleeping outside. All the ways she wants to live but can't figure out how, and she thinks that if she can only understand what he's thinking she'll know how to live herself. But she can't, and when Ben, like any good hunter, finally moves just enough to draw the move he wants from her, she's so curious that she takes the final step herself.

He stays behind on Friday night, after the bar closes. "Mind if I sit?" he asks, sitting before she can answer. When he asks for a drink she pours him one and then another; she pours herself a couple too, while she's rinsing glasses. As she dips and wipes, Ben tells her about the coming Olympics in Italy and about the camp in Sun Valley where his friends are training for the trials in March. He talks about races and gates and tucks and turns and people she doesn't know, and all the time he talks he watches her.

"Why don't you go?" she asks him. She doesn't know much about racing, but she knows he can ski and knows he's better than anyone else on this mountain. She finishes her glasses and comes to sit by him, marking a paper napkin with a pattern of tiny dots as they talk.

Ben's face darkens at her question, her first clue that his life may not be as simple as it seems. He drops his eyes for just a minute, and then he raises them and says easily, "I could have. I'm good enough to go, but not good enough to make the final team. First-rate second-rate, someone used to say."

"Still," she says. "You could try."

"Not worth it," he tells her, draining his glass. "Besides, I'd rather do this. Get paid for skiing, have the mountain to myself at night . . ."

"Let's go for a walk," she says, because while he's been talking she's drawn a chart on her napkin and has made herself a plan, a way slightly better than casting dice of finding out who hides inside Ben. "I want to show you something."

"Sounds good," he says. His hand lingers on her shoulder when he helps her with her coat.

Penny stumbles outside and realizes she's a little drunk. It's snowed all night, and the drifts are unmarked and deep. She leans on Ben's arm and they shuffle to the base of the tram, where the big wooden shed shelters the tramcars for the night. They stop on the east side of the shed, away from the wind and invisible to anyone who might still be up, and Penny feels in her pocket for her flashlight and her chart. Before she can say anything, Ben drops to the ground as suddenly as if he's been shot. "Let's make snow angels," he says.

This is so unlike the Ben she's seen that she stares for a minute before she laughs and lies down next to him, spreading her arms and legs and flapping them to form wings and a skirt. The gentle swishing sound she makes might be owls in the woods; although the forest is quiet, she knows it's full of deer and rabbits and birds and mice. They make three angels each, and then Penny, who despite this interruption hasn't lost sight of her plan, says, "I made a map so I could teach you the constellations. Want to see?" If he can do this as well as ski, she thinks. Then perhaps . . .

"I'd rather look at you," Ben says.

Penny laughs nervously. When she unfolds the napkin and holds it over their heads, he leans in close and grazes her cheek as if by accident. But this is all right: Penny once sat near Gram this way, and Gram talked about her five sisters, long dead, while pointing out the Pleiades. Now Penny shines her flashlight on the map, finds the Big Dipper, and rotates the paper until it's in the same position as the Dipper in the sky. "See?" she says. "Over here."

Ben gives the sky and the napkin the barest glance. "Sure," he says, pulling her across the snow to him so confidently that she knows he thinks she used the stars as an excuse to get him here. "Pretty," he murmurs into her neck. "All those stars lighting up your hair."

Her head rests on his chest, and she knows she should stop talking now and wait for what's bound to come. Instead, she begins to babble about the celestial sphere, Gram's words, which she thought she'd forgotten, coming easily to her lips. "Not so many," she tells him. "Even when it's clear, we can only see a few thousand stars without a telescope, just a fraction of the total"— and here she gestures with one hand—"lucid stars. The ones you can see with your naked eye."

"Pretty," Ben says, but she doesn't know whether he means her or the stars. By now he is nibbling her ear. "They give just enough light."

Again, Gram's words return to her. "The light's not from them," Penny mumbles into Ben's chest. She's distracted by his fingers tugging at her clothes. She had a plan half an hour ago that didn't include this. "It's mostly from the stars we can't see, and from the dust between the planets." Hypnosis, she decides. That must

be it. Why else would she be babbling this nonsense?
Why else would she be letting Ben do what he is doing?

Ben laughs quietly. He unzipped her pants while she
was pointing at the sky; now he unzips his and guides
her hand inside. "Shh," he says. "Don't you ever stop
talking?" Her star map falls unnoticed to the ground.

When they get up, Penny brushes the snow from her
clothes and then pulls Ben away from the coat he'd
tossed under them.

"Sweet," Ben says. He pushes back her curly hair and
tucks it into her collar, then straightens her pants and
reties her scarf. She's waiting for him to do something
awful—laugh, perhaps, or walk off with a crude joke—
but he says nothing. There are questions she'd like to
ask him but doesn't dare. Can she get pregnant from
making love once? Has he done this before? Will everyone know that she has, just by looking at her face?

"Was I okay?" she asks instead. In the starlight his
face looks tired and drawn. She wants to ask him to
hold her but stands with her arms at her sides instead,
shivering as a cold wind streams down the slope and
pushes small rivers of snow before it. In the woods
some night bird chuckles in its sleep.

"You kidding?" Ben says. When he smiles his face
shines like the full moon and makes her wish everything hadn't happened so fast. She knows she's about to
forget what he looked like before she fell in love with
him. She should be counting stars or looking for nebulae, anything to keep her from losing her sight completely. This used to work when she was a girl, when
she used the stars to push her parents' indifference
away; she believes it would work now if she could manage it. Ben reaches over and squeezes her shoulder.
"Come back to my room for a while," he says. "Warm
up, maybe have a drink."

She nods, and he wraps an arm about her waist and

guides her over the snow. They're exactly the same height; when they turn their faces from the biting wind his chin is level with hers. She takes small steps, feeling dizzy from all she drank, and Ben says, "Did I hurt you?"

"Of course not," she tells him. "I'm just tired."

She's exhausted. They pass the main lodge, gone blank and dark; they pass the west wing where she lives with the rest of the female staff. No sound, not a light. If anyone's bent over a radio listening to Charlie Parker or Lester Young, they are doing it secretly. She wonders if Cindy is pacing the floor of their small room, waiting for her.

Ben's room is in a rude building resembling a barracks. The front door opens into a blazingly bright hall; while they stand there letting their eyes adjust, two ski instructors—Hans and Franz? Fritz and Rudi?—burst from one of the rooms holding wine bottles and laughing hard. "And then," she hears the tall one say in a heavy accent, "and then, this gorgeous girl, she bends over . . ."

He stops short and rearranges his face when he catches sight of Penny and Ben. "Pardon *me*," he says. His partner draws himself up and makes a small bow. They're all politeness, but as they pass Penny sees how they smirk at Ben and wink at each other. She supposes she looks like she's been doing exactly what she's been doing.

"Just ignore them," Ben says. "Sometimes it's pretty crazy in here."

He leads her down the hall, opens the door to his room, and holds it so she can enter first. She's not surprised to find it neat. Along one wall a ski rack holds four pairs of skis and an assortment of poles. One pair of skis is black and marked HEAD in yellow below the tips, and Penny knows just enough to realize that these are metal and very expensive. Ben's boots are treed neatly below his skis, away from the radiator. The room is small and has no closet; his clothes hang primly from an iron bar in the corner. A hot plate squats on an old black locker.

Ben gestures toward the single bed and says, "Why don't you lie down? I'll make us some hot rum."

Her pants are soaked through in the back and her socks are hung with ice balls. She'd like to take off everything, slip into bed, and fall asleep, but she settles for taking off her parka and her boots. Ben strips to his long underwear; the room is so small that she has nowhere to look but at him. She can see his body through the waffled wool, and this makes her curious again. After what they've done, she's amazed that she's seen only the skin of his face and hands, only felt that and a little more.

Ben turns the knob on the radiator. "It'll warm up soon," he says. "Give me your wet clothes."

She hands over her parka but sees, from his outstretched arm and patient face, that he means more. She turns her back to him and takes off her sweater and pants. Underneath she has on a turtleneck and long underwear like Ben's; despite these, she feels naked.

Ben smiles. "Under the covers," he orders. "Don't want you catching cold." The rum steams in the pot; the room warms and fills with the smell of wet wool. Ben hands her a mug and then strips off his long underwear shirt, revealing a pale chest punctuated with a wedge of blond hair. When he slips in next to her, he peels off his long underwear bottoms and tosses them out. Penny presses closer to the wall. She's not sure whether men wear anything beneath their long underwear, but she's afraid that if she touches Ben she'll find out. Ben slides his hand to her leg but then recoils at the wet wool.

"You still got those on?" he says. "You'll catch pneumonia. Take them off to dry."

Penny hands him her mug and then, keeping the cov-

ers pulled up, wiggles free of damp wool. Ben puts his
arm around her and returns her mug. They sit propped
awkwardly against the wall, Penny afraid to move.
Ben's arm is pale and corded and warm behind her
neck; his leg, against her from ankle to thigh, is hot. A
piney smell, crisp and yet warm, seems to cling to his
pale hairs. Penny remembers this smell from the edge of
Gram's garden, not at the center, but back, beyond the
Norway spruce. It is as purely delicious as the sun.

She wants to ask if he's using anything to keep her
from getting pregnant, but she's too shy to say a word.
Maybe, she thinks, he doesn't even want me again.
Maybe I'm reading him wrong. Even as he touches her
she thinks maybe he doesn't mean it, maybe he'll stop.
Possibly he expects her to stop him. She feels as stupid
as she's felt during all her skiing lessons, when her
teachers waited below her and waved her down and she
crouched above them waiting for them to tell her how.
Now, as she and Ben pass each turn, each touch, each
shift in position, she sees that it's here she should have
stopped, should have said something. Only when Ben's
inside her is she sure enough to speak.

"Should you . . . ?" she whispers. "Are you . . . ?"

Above her, Ben opens his eyes sleepily. "Don't
worry," he whispers back. "I'll take care of everything."

Three nights in a row Penny visits Ben's room. On
the third night he presents her with a box of rubbers,
holding them out on his palm as if they're a box of
jewels. "See?" he says. "Don't want anything to happen
to you."

Penny smiles and mumbles something that Ben can
interpret as he chooses; at the same moment she
squelches the odd, furtive daydream she's had these past
two days. An army of infants—triplets, twins—plump
in their padded snowsuits, shooting down the hill behind Ben and each other like a string of pearls. Ridicu-

lous. She's in love, and yet she's embarrassed by Ben's present. It means, she supposes, that he knows she likes what they do together and he assumes they'll keep doing it. He's a good teacher—when she's in bed with him, she feels none of the awkwardness she feels on the slopes. Still, she suspects she should be hiding more.

Later that night, after they've abandoned the bed for the bigger floor, she asks Ben if he'll teach her to ski. When he laughs affectionately and wants to know why, she can't think how to explain that she wants skiing to be her life right now, the first step in the new life she's trying to cast for herself. Once she can ski she can travel alone, can learn everything else she needs. When someone asks her what she does, she'll have an answer: "I ski." But until she learns she has nothing at all. She looks at Ben and says, "Because you're good at teaching me this."

"Skiing's harder." In the accents of Fritz or Franz he says, "Bend zee knees, two dollars, please." Gently, he pushes her heel toward the underside of her thigh.

"I know you could teach me better," she says. One step at a time, she's thinking. One motion, one movement, one turn, the way Gram would have taught me if she had known how to ski.

They make love again, and Ben says he'll teach her anything she wants. Through the window, Penny sees Orion sinking in the west and Rigel touching the horizon—a sign that it's very late, that she has to go. When they're done she gathers her things and tiptoes back to the room she shares with Cindy. She's not quiet enough, and Cindy wakes up.

"Nice night?" Cindy mutters. "It's past three."

Penny pulls the covers over her head, telling herself that Cindy's just jealous. Cindy's been dating Otis Nelson, but things aren't going well and she's taking it out on Penny. Just now, Penny doesn't like Cindy much

better than she liked her peach-sweatered college room-
mates. "We went for a walk," Penny says.

Cindy punches her pillow and rolls over. "Sure," she
says. "These guys are all the same."

"Not Ben," Penny says, reminding herself silently
that she has no way of knowing this yet. His present
stayed in his room. "He's teaching me to ski," she tells
Cindy, as if this answered everything.

"Good," Cindy says. "Of course that makes him
nice."

"Go to sleep," Penny says with a sigh. "We'll talk in
the morning."

But they never do. Ben takes Penny up the lift at
noon and points out the tiny tracks below them that
seem to start from nowhere and disappear as mysteri-
ously. "Snow snakes," he explains. "They hatch at
night, after a snowfall, and work their way to the surface when the sun comes out. You can't see them because they're white."

"Really?" Penny says. She leans over the arm of the
chair, hoping to see a snake against the snow. She has
very good eyes.

"Really," Ben laughs.

Penny blushes and says, "I knew you were only fooling." She stares off into the woods and sees, just as a tree
drops behind them, an enormous black and white bird
with a red crest. "Jesus!" she says. "What's that?"

"Woodpecker," Ben says, and goes on to tell her that
the snow-snake tracks are really made by tiny
avalanches. She tries out her yodel on him and he tells
her a dirty joke. By the time they reach the top she's so
relaxed she's sure her former clumsiness will melt
away. Her life, the life she was waiting for, is about to
start.

She falls getting off the lift. "That's all right," Ben
says. "Happens to everyone. You just weren't paying
attention." He holds her up, brushes her off, and leads

her to a gentle intermediate trail. "I'll ski down a little way and wait," he says. "When I wave my pole, you ski down using your best turns, and we'll see what we need to work on."

Penny agrees, but when she skis toward him her body feels like wood. She's sitting back, she can tell; her weight is on her uphill ski. Her shoulders are sometimes rotated into the hill and sometimes out. Her arms flap uselessly and she holds her poles too high. She can see all this with Ben's eyes, but she can't fix any of it. She falls twice.

Ben's face is grave when she reaches him. "You're a mess," he tells her. "You need work."

"I know," Penny says, hanging her head.

"An hour a day," he says. "Every day," and he sticks to his word. She has no time to talk to Cindy or to anyone else. All February and into March, they go out before Penny goes to work and on her days off. Penny skis harder than she has ever done anything, and it's fine, it's what she wants. Real work, she thinks. Really learning something, not like school. As soon as they reach the bottom they're headed uphill again, Ben lecturing her all the way up and shouting all the way down. "Plant your *poles*!" he bellows from below her. "Push your knees into the hill! For Christ's sake, use your *edges*!"

The more he yells the stiffer she gets. "You're not listening," he says. "You're not paying attention." She can't seem to make him understand that her body, on skis, doesn't seem like hers at all. This clumsy, unresponsive, inflexible object belongs to someone else, and during the day all she can do is apologize. At night she makes up for her clumsiness by being doubly responsive, doubly enthusiastic, but although Ben praises her extravagantly, this doesn't make him kinder on the slopes.

In the bar, throughout those weeks, her customers

wave her over and say, "Hey! Wasn't that you I saw from the lift? What a great fall!" She nods and smiles ruefully: What a fall. Before Ben started teaching her she fell occasionally, with gentle, sitting-down slips. Now she falls spectacularly—huge, sprawling crashes with her arms outstretched and her legs windmilling behind. She crosses her tips and flies through the air like an acrobat, fearing all the time that she's going to break her legs, her arms, at least a collarbone. At night, when she finally returns to sleep near Cindy, she dreams different parts of her body wrapped in plaster casts, her life careening offtrack while her broken bones heal. She mentions her fears to Ben, and he loosens the settings on her cable bindings, assuring her they'll release before her leg bones snap.

"Promise?" she says. She can't afford to break a leg.

"Trust me," he tells her. And so far she does.

The Broad Wings of Virgo
(May 1955)

★　　　★　　　★　　　★　　　★　　　★

Logan Rockwell, justice of the peace in Shelburne Falls, Vermont, is old and deaf and almost blind. Or so he appears to Penny on the May Saturday when she and Ben pull up to his little office on the square. Penny is three months pregnant but doesn't show. Ben knows; Otis and Cindy, in the car behind them, don't. Penny wears the pale blue suit Gram gave her when she was in college, and the too-tight shoes she bought in a hurry without realizing they'd make her taller than Ben. When she gets out of the car, Logan eyes her speculatively and then fixes on Cindy's flowered voile and white gloves. He walks up to Cindy and congratulates her before Cindy can steer him gently back.

Ben tries to smooth things over by introducing everyone. Logan nods but continues to look confused. "And your parents?" he says. "They've been delayed?"

"Sick," Ben says, and Penny sighs to herself. She could think of a better excuse sound asleep. But the fact is that Ben, for reasons Penny doesn't yet understand, hasn't told his parents he's getting married. And when Penny told her own mother she had to get married, Penny's mother told her father, Penny's father got drunk, and in the end they both refused to come. Penny got a small check Thursday, signed in her mother's jagged hand. A slip of paper from the kitchen pad was folded around the check; on it, as close as her mother could come to apologizing, was written "To buy yourself something pretty with." She bought her shoes with part of the money and saved the rest for this trip, knowing it's all she'll ever get. She can just imagine her mother's voice: *We'd send more if your father's business was doing better, if I felt better, if Mick didn't need clothes . . .* But it's fine, it's what Penny expected. It means that she's grown up. She wanted to be out on her own and here she is.

"Well, then," Logan says. "Well, well. Let's go in and get on with it."

Ben and Otis follow Logan; Penny and Cindy follow the men. "You nervous?" Cindy whispers. "You're so white."

"A little scared," Penny says, and manages a smile. She's pale because she's been throwing up—in the mornings she's had to rush to the bathroom without waking Cindy, who thinks their elopement is romantic. Cindy and Otis are planning a big June wedding, and Cindy pretends to be tired of all the fuss.

Inside there's an awkward moment while the men shuffle papers. Logan can't find the book he needs for the ceremony; Otis, for a minute, can't find the ring. And then, without warning, the wedding is underway. The words pass over Penny's head as if she's standing in a well. Capella, she hears instead. Vega, Arcturus, Antares. Cindy, next to her, snuffles and dabs at her nose. When Penny sneaks a glance at Ben she finds him staring over Logan's head at a framed picture of Mount

Mansfield glowing against the sky. She reaches her
hand out to comfort him, to comfort herself, but he
pulls away. She can't hear anything, can't feel more
than confused and numb. Ben stands perfectly straight
in the dusky office, frozen in the ill-fitting suit he borrowed from Otis. The green plaid turns his gold hair
mossy. He looks pale to Penny, and pinched around the
lips, and she wonders if he's thinking that he doesn't
love her. Doesn't know her? That too. Doesn't love her,
doesn't know her, doesn't want a wife and child. Wishes
he hadn't offered to marry her. Wishes she hadn't stood
at the base of the hill watching him ski down at night;
wishes, certainly, that he'd been smart enough to ignore
her.

Ben's eyes are dry and he repeats his responses perfectly. The night she said she was pregnant, he jammed
his head against the wool blanket and wept until Penny
did too, until they both stopped and he started muttering the places he'd meant to go—Portillo, Mont Blanc,
Aspen, Vail—the way Penny now repeats her stars. He
called a whole world of icy peaks and swooping winds
into his little room, and they both stared at it and then
shut their eyes. Ben said, "Would you even consider
. . . I have a friend who says he knows this doctor in
New York . . ." and Penny said, "No." Now that she
can imagine Gram's fire mingled with Ben's light, it's
too late to go back. "No," Ben echoed. "Of course not.
You're right." He touched her hand, and together they
watched their vision fly away. The next day, Ben made
Penny stop skiing so she wouldn't hurt the baby.

The room is silent but for Cindy's snuffles. "You may
kiss," Penny hears Logan say. "You may kiss."

She realizes this isn't the first time he's said it. She
turns to Ben and shuts her eyes, feeling his lips brush
lightly over hers. Neither of them manages to smile.
She waits for the cheers of her family and friends, for
the swell of organ music as she marches down the aisle.

She waits for rice, but nothing happens. Ben slips Logan a folded bill and they glide out into the sun. On the stoop, Penny unpins her lone gardenia and tosses it to Cindy. It arcs white across the sky.

They spend the afternoon by the side of a local waterfall. Cindy's brought a basket filled with chicken, potato salad, rolls and fruit and deviled eggs, and Otis has brought champagne. Penny's mood lightens considerably as the bottles empty. When Otis and Cindy duck under the spray, shrieking and splashing each other, Penny turns to Ben and whispers, "I love you, you know."

"I love you too," he says, and kisses her clumsily.

Perhaps if he doesn't mean it now he will in time. For herself, she's vowed to be affectionate even when she doesn't feel it. This is her marriage now. This is what she has. When Otis and Cindy come back, the women duck behind the trees and take off their shoes and stockings and garter belts. The men roll up their pants and sleeves and toss their jackets on the ground. As they wade together into the shallow pool downriver from the falls, Penny thinks maybe all of this will turn out right. "We should come here every year!" she calls across a rock to Ben. "For our anniversary!"

Ben laughs and agrees that they should. The afternoon passes in a sunny blur that dims only when they pack up and drive to the Cedar Branch Inn, which Ben has picked for their three-day honeymoon. He says the Saturday night band there plays good jazz. Otis and Cindy have agreed to spend the evening celebrating with them, and they smile when Ben signs the register "Mr. and Mrs. Benjamin Day." The sun is bright in the lobby, flashing down on great bowls of daffodils and Jacob's ladder and blue anemones. Penny has a headache from all the champagne, and the others are tired and drawn. For a minute no one seems to know what to do, and the clerk eyes them suspiciously as they hover at the desk.

"Well," Ben says. "Let's take a look at our place." Otis and Ben carry the bags upstairs—so many that Penny is embarrassed. The bags hold everything they own, down to the flat pink package Harry slipped her before they left the mountain.

"What you got in here?" Otis says. "Rocks?" He's carrying the smallest of Penny's bags, in which she's crammed all the baby books she could find during her one sly run to another town. Penny kicks off her shoes as soon as they get upstairs, thinking Ben might feel better if she made herself just an inch or two shorter. Even so, her eyes are dead level with his.

"Hey," Cindy says. "Aren't you going to carry Penny across the threshold?"

Ben groans but smiles at Penny and picks her up. "Jesus," he whispers in her ear. "Won't be able to do that much longer." He kisses her on the cheek so she knows he doesn't mean it.

"Why don't you rest up till dinner?" Otis says. "We'll go for a walk or something and meet you in the bar around eight. Okay?"

He smiles at Ben, and Penny knows he'll spend the time before dinner trying to get into Cindy's pants and thinking Ben is getting into hers. He doesn't know Ben makes love to her seldom now, and delicately, as if she's suddenly turned to glass. He worries he'll hurt the baby, as he worries about almost everything: what Penny eats and drinks, that she's smoking again, what she lifts. He would have made her quit work sooner if they'd had any money. In a way, Penny likes this concern of his.

Now they lock the door and undress slowly. Ben keeps his back to her and hangs each piece of clothing up as he takes it off. Penny throws her clothes on a chair. "I'm wiped," Ben says. "Want to take a nap?"

Penny nods. He's left his underpants on, as if he barely knows her; he cups her back lightly when they lie down, the way a man lost in a forest might hold a stranger for warmth. Penny leaves her slip on, knowing he won't make love to her now. He's tired, she thinks, excusing him. His whole life is changing and we're both exhausted. The ruffled white curtains let in too much sun, and a robin trills hysterically outside their room. Penny closes her eyes, times her breathing to Ben's, and falls asleep, dreaming that the baby in her belly is a fish. Blue, she dreams it. With red-tipped fluffy fins. She doesn't know how to tell the sex of a fish but she thinks, from the colors, that this one is male. The fish drifts silently over coral reefs, sea fans, starfish, shells. His eyes are near the top of his head, and he swims along the surface so that half of each eye sees the star-filled sky and half of each eye sees the water. The fish is sad because he has no parents, but some part of her dreaming brain whispers that fish don't *have* parents.

She wakes at eight to Cindy's tentative knock on the door. "You up?" Cindy calls. "It's dinnertime."

Ben sits up and says, "We'll be right there."

Penny's head is splitting and her stomach is queasy; she'd like to just stay there and sleep. "How do you feel?" she asks Ben. "I feel like hell."

"Me too," he says. "But they came all this way just to be with us—how about we join them at least for some dinner?"

Penny agrees. They put on clean clothes, splash water on their faces, and join Otis and Cindy in the hall. Cindy looks frazzled, and when Ben says, "What did you do all this time?" she looks down at her muddy shoes. Otis says, "We went for a walk. It's nice out back." He's flushed and sullen; Penny imagines the two of them struggling all afternoon. At every hidden place, every dark tree a few feet from the trail, she knows Otis has pulled Cindy aside and swarmed over her. Cindy has put fresh lipstick on, but a faint halo around her lips shows Penny where the last coat was ground into her pores.

In the lounge downstairs, they sit quietly while the band sets up. Their menus have singed, scalloped edges and are shellacked to boards; Ben mutters something about the prices and feels his wallet anxiously. Penny wonders if he has enough money to pay for dinner—her mother's present is tucked away upstairs and she feels guilty that she hasn't told him about it yet. The food is terrible, but their spirits pick up when the table is cleared and the band trickles onstage.

"I know that guy," says Otis, pointing to the bass player. "He used to play at the Dover Inn."

"Sure," Ben says. "I remember him." He laughs and orders a round of whiskey sodas. "Remember?" he asks Otis. "That time we went down from the Snow Bowl to that dive in Rutland?"

"And that girl?" Otis says. "The one with the curly hair?"

The two of them smile, exchanging glances, and Penny asks Cindy about her wedding plans so the men can trade old stories. She knows hardly anything about Ben's earlier life—only that he and Otis went to Middlebury and belonged to some fraternity there. They raced for the ski team their junior and senior years, but Ben said neither of them was good enough to make Sun Valley. They traveled together for six months before they joined the ski patrol, but this is only a fact and nothing useful. She'd like to know what their lives were like before she knew them. She'd like to know Ben's plans.

The band is hot. The room fills with people from town, drinking and dancing; the four of them draw closer about the table as the crowd jostles for seats.

"Where will you be living after the wedding?" Penny asks Cindy.

"New Hampshire, I think. Otis is going to work with some resort developers—they're planning a couple of new areas around Franconia Notch. Near Cannon."

"Yeah?" Ben says, and looks at Otis. "That deal come through?"

"It's not too late if you want to join," Otis says. "You want to? It'd be just like we always talked about. Of course, there won't be much money at first. But we could turn those mountains into something else."

They shuffle their chairs so they're closer together, order more drinks, and begin to talk fast and hard. Penny listens with one ear while she chatters with Cindy about furniture. She's not sure what the men are talking about, but she gathers that Otis, trained as an engineer, plans to do some sort of consulting.

"No, no," he says to Ben, and slaps the table. "We don't actually *buy* the mountain—why use our money when we can use theirs? What we do is get these big companies to front the real estate while we act as planning and design consultants. We're going to call the company Peak-Design, and we'll start with those two mountains south of Cannon. We'll decide where the trails should be, where the lodges will go, how many lifts there will be and where. None of this haphazard shit—we'll start from the beginning, from where the customer parks his car. We'll plan how to get him to the base lodge, how to get him up the mountain, down the mountain, into the bar and the restaurants. We'll *plan* it —all of it. We could build the kind of mountain we always wanted to ski."

"They're going to pay you for this?" Ben asks. "To ski and make mountains?"

"Not at first—they'll give me a piece of the action and I'll see money when we open."

"Our parents," Cindy pipes in, "are going to bankroll us for a while."

"Just for a year," Otis says. "Skiing is changing—in

twenty years you won't recognize this corner of the world. It won't be just us college goons trying to beat the toughest mountains. It'll be families, little kids, old ladies—it's going to be big business."

"Sure," Ben says. "But what are we supposed to do until the money starts rolling in?"

Penny tugs at Ben's sleeve and asks him to dance. He shakes her off and says, "Later, sweetie." There are big beads of sweat on his face and he seems to be drunk.

"Look," he says to Otis. "I had this idea once for how I'd make a mountain if I had tons of money." He grabs a passing waitress and asks for a pencil, and then starts sketching something for Otis on the tablecloth. Cindy says, "I have to go to the ladies' room," but no one looks up when she leaves. Penny sits very still while the men talk.

"No," says Ben. "The front should be facing near to south, so the slopes stay warm all day. We'd cut something broad here, something open and gentle right from the top that everyone would like. But in the back, on the north side, that's where we'd cut what you and I like. We'd have a separate lift system there, skinny trails studded with trees, minimal grooming. Powder." He and Otis grin at each other. "Rocks."

" 'Jaws of Death,' " Otis says.

" 'Kiss It Good-bye,' " says Ben.

"They'd pay us just to name the trails. How would we handle the crowds?"

"Excuse me," Penny says. "I'll be right back."

She's a little drunk herself, but not as drunk as the men. Neither of them seems to hear her; neither of them notices when she sails past the ladies' room and out the side door. It's warm outside and very dark—there's no moon tonight. She's trying to imagine raising a child in a shack at the base of a virgin mountain, trying to imagine the trails suddenly appearing as the trees are bulldozed down. Ben crashing through the forest in the cab of a huge machine, Otis in the underbrush with a chainsaw and an ax, birds shrieking, animals fleeing, a smoldering fire in a stump—is this what they mean? Probably they mean only to give orders to a crew. They'll sit in a neat office drawing plans while she'll be somewhere she can't imagine, trying to raise a child. It's impossible, but she's never seen Ben so excited and she hates to tell him no.

Her back aches above her kidneys. The parking lot is full of cars but free of people; she stretches out on the asphalt and leans against the wheel of a flashy Belvedere convertible. Craning her head, she guesses from the stars' positions that it must be past midnight. Virgo has passed the meridian and lies splashed against the sky, a hovering goddess with broad, folded wings. Between her head and Denabola in Leo is a faint haze Penny's grandmother said was a field of nebulae. Penny can just remember glimpsing these years ago, through a pair of binoculars. Spica glows white in the virgin's hands, an ear of wheat clasped in the hands of Proserpine.

Was that what Gram said? Penny struggles to remember the story. The girl was the daughter of Ceres, she thinks. She was walking through the woods one day, minding her own business, when Pluto split the ground and abducted her. Her mother tried to save her but managed only a compromise—six months, three months, something like that, the reason we have winter. Penny sighs. She feels rather abducted herself, especially when Ben blames everything on her. She knows he doesn't mean it—no sooner does he accuse her than he takes it back, apologizes, says he's under a lot of pressure. "Yeah?" she wants to say. "And how about me?" They dance around each other, each trying both to avoid blame and at the same time avoid casting blame. Penny tries not to remind Ben how he promised to take care of everything. And Ben? She can feel Ben trying not to say all sorts of things. The weight of what they're both not saying sometimes stretches the silence taut between them.

"Prosperity," Gram once told her. "Spica is the star of prosperity."

Penny would believe this more if she had any idea how they're to survive the coming year. "Let me worry about it," Ben says, when Penny tries to get him to make plans. "You take care of yourself and the baby, and let me worry about the rest. I'll figure out something."

She knows he will—but still, if she had this virgin's wings she would fly away. She feels seeds of some dark resistance sprouting in her as surely as ears of wheat, as surely as this hatching child. She digs a cigarette from her purse, although Ben has asked her to quit and she's agreed. And then she purses her lips and blows smoke rings toward Proserpine, who had to survive in the underworld for only part of the year. She decides she'll survive until the baby is born by a similar burrowing. But after that—and here she speaks out loud, as if Ben were sitting with her—"After that, I'm coming out."

When she returns to the men, she finds that the castle they've built in the air has grown into an empire. Cindy has fallen asleep in her chair; Ben's blond hair sticks up over his forehead where he's raked his fingers through it.

"That's a great idea," Otis is telling him. "I could sell this—I know I could. Why don't you come in with us? There's just the two of you, no responsibilities. Maybe Penny could even work for a while to get you over the hump."

He looks at Penny, who gives him a vague smile. Ben turns to look at her too. When he does, all the excitement leaves his face. She knows he's seeing bills, taxes, diapers, death. She knows he's seeing the fish that swims inside her.

"Too risky for me," Ben says. "We want to settle down."

"Settle down when you're old," Otis says. "Gamble now."

"You gamble," Ben says. "I'm going to dance with my wife." He takes Penny's hand and leads her to the dance floor. The band is playing "Heart of Stone." Penny holds him tightly and whispers "Thank you" in his ear, aware that he's given up something important. They dance as lightly as if they have wings, and yet despite this she sees with drunken clarity that their lives together may be only a long grinding down of dissimilar edges. Ben's eyes are closed, as if he's dancing in a dream.

She isn't surprised when he turns away from her that night and tucks his hands between his legs; she almost expects it when he doesn't touch her for the rest of their stay at the inn. It's only sex, she reminds herself. It isn't everything. They walk, drink, play cribbage at night in the library downstairs, but he's pulled into a private shell and is as distant physically as if he were the pregnant one. When she asks him about it he says he's thinking, and then he rolls over and proves it by not sleeping.

It's his sleeplessness that draws her from her dreams —not any noise he makes but a rigid, humming alertness that makes her feel she's sleeping with a reptile about to shed. She wakes with a start their second night and says, "What are you thinking about?"

"Nothing," he says, but when she presses him he turns toward her and tells her, in a quiet, wistful voice, what he used to do as a kid. There's an urgency to his voice, as if he'd never told her these things before, and in fact he's told her very little. He says he lived on Cape Cod; he had a boat; he fished and swam and dug quahogs. He tanned when he was younger but doesn't anymore. He drops these facts into the dim light as if they're pebbles, as if she could understand from them the texture of his childhood. He says his mother, not his father, taught him how to fish, and that his parents expected him to go into business after college but forgave him when he skied so well. In the silence between his sentences, Penny tries to reconstruct the boy he was. Against a hazy beach (she has never seen the ocean), she conjures up a white-haired Ben whose blue eyes blaze in his open brown face. It's not enough. Although the picture squeezes her heart, she can't get a sense of what he's missing.

"What about you?" he says. "Tell me something you used to do."

She talks about Gram, how she used to hack her way through the phlox and delphiniums wearing a skirt, stockings, gloves, and a hat.

"She sounds funny," Ben says. "She's who taught you the stars?"

"That's her."

Penny falls asleep again. When she wakes he's still lying there, staring at the ceiling. "You know," she says, as if they'd been talking all along, "I've been thinking about the baby's name. How about Webb if it's a boy?"

"It's okay," Ben says. "Strange, but I sort of like it—your last name and mine. Webb Day. Sounds like a lawyer."

"Doctor, maybe. Or a senator."

"What if it's a girl?"

She's touched by his interest, tacit admission that the baby is part his. It could be beautiful and smart—his blondness, her curls, his intelligence, her intuition. "I had a dream a few nights ago," she says. "I think it's going to be a boy."

"What if it isn't?"

"Could you live with Cass? That was my grandmother's name."

He's quiet for a minute, so that she wonders what he's thinking of. "What's it short for?" he asks finally.

"Cassandra, usually. Also Cassiopeia."

"More stars? I don't know—Cass, Cassie. I guess it's okay." He rolls over on his side. "I hope I'll be a good father," he says somberly. "I don't feel very ready."

"I don't either," she reminds him, and then she sleeps again. In the morning she wakes to find him packing neatly.

"I thought we were leaving tomorrow," she says sleepily.

"We are," he says. "But real early." He folds a sock into the toe of its mate and wedges it into a corner.

"Where do you want to go?" she asks. They've talked about several alternatives, but still haven't decided—with neither of them working, no place seems better than another. We'll just pick a place, she thinks. Park, look for an apartment, look for work . . .

Ben sighs and aligns the creases of his slacks. "Home," he says finally. "I don't know what else to do."

"Home like back to the mountain?"

"Home like to my parents' house."

For a minute she picks at her cuticles. This is something she hasn't considered—in all their talks they've projected themselves someplace in Vermont. Rutland, perhaps. Barre, Montpelier, even Burlington—someplace Ben could find a job but still be close to the mountains. He's mentioned that he might go into banking.

"You mean Cape Cod?" she says. "What's there?"

Her voice sounds hostile even to her, and Ben stiffens against it. "Don't get nasty on me," he says. "It's just for a while. We need a place to stay, and I need a job, and my folks will probably help out. They're in this big new house now."

"Great," Penny says. "We're going there and they don't even know about me." She tries, and fails, to imagine being presented to them. "My wife"—is that what he'll say? "My pregnant wife"?

Ben says, "I'll call them tonight" and after dinner he leaves her for the pay phone in the lounge. She spots him there on her way upstairs—he's fiddling with a mound of coins and has the receiver jammed into his cheek. She stops, waiting to hear what he'll say about her and how much he'll apologize. He waves her away impatiently.

She folds her dresses and underwear for an hour and more, but all he says when he comes in is, "Everything's settled. They're expecting us tomorrow night."

"Just point me," Penny says sharply, furious that Ben's made this decision without her. "Just tell me where to go."

"You might like it," Ben says. "If you give it a chance."

"I hate flat land. And I don't want to stay with your parents." She snaps her suitcase shut.

"Get some sleep," he says. "We'll leave at seven-thirty."

When he wakes her at seven she dresses sleepily and helps him carry their bags to the car. The trunk and back seat are crammed with their belongings; the roof is crowned with a rack and skis. Ben's ski boots are wedged between her feet.

The trip is lost on her. Ben drives the whole way, insists on driving, says she'll get them lost, and so she sleeps fitfully, with her head jammed against the window. Each time she wakes they're in another town. Rutland, Bennington, Williamstown. North Adams, Greenfield, Miller's Falls. Each time she wakes the hills are smaller and the air is hotter. Athol, Gardner, Fitchberg, through the river plain; Leominster, and they stop for lunch. Ben's eyes are red from squinting into the sun, and Penny says she's never been this far east in Massachusetts. Ben tells her it gets prettier.

She sleeps again and wakes somewhere near Taunton. The trees have shrunk to scrubby pine. "Where are we?" she asks.

"Almost to the Cape. Another hour and we'll be home."

She has never seen such desolate land. The earth is tan here, and sandy, not the rocky black dirt she knows. The houses are small and weatherbeaten, scaled for elves. Too much gingerbread, too much cute. They pass through Middleboro and Wareham on a two-lane highway lined with basket shops, bait stores, taffy stands, and restaurants marked by lobsters outlined in blinking lights. Clams, one sign says. The sign is a smiling clam with eyes and little feet. At the Bourne Bridge Ben stops to show her the Canal, which she finds beautiful in spite of herself. The sun is just beginning to set and the lights along the near shore twinkle. The water rushes by so quickly that it sings.

They head down the Cape on Route 28, turning off at the traffic circle in Pocasset. Ben drives through the narrow streets of the village, heading for the shore, and then he turns down a side road that seems to follow a point of land. "Wing's Neck," he says, when she questions him. She can feel him gathering his energies, concentrating himself into one small, hard point the way he does when he skis. This skill is part of what draws her to him, but she wonders, Why here? They park in front of a low, rambling house at the end of the point. A scuffy yard slopes down a cliff overlooking the sea. "Leave the bags," Ben says nervously. "Let's go in."

She smoothes her skirt and follows him, her palms breaking out in a sweat as he throws open the door and calls, "We're here!" His words echo in the hall; no one answers. He leads her through the dusky rooms and finds his parents drinking in the den.

Nothing is what Penny expected, and yet everything makes a peculiar kind of sense. Ben's brightness appears in his shrill-voiced mother as brittle sarcasm; the few expensive things he owns—good skis, good boots—translate here into veiled wealth. Ben's mother, Vivian, wears clunky jewelry made from some blue stone that's probably real. The sofas are soft, the paneling polished, the upholstery finely napped; the Scotch sits on a wet bar lined with copper and rimmed with crystal glasses. In this room, Ben seems an inch shorter, ten pounds lighter, five years younger—refined, polished, rendered small. The aura that first pulled Penny to him flares instead around Vivian, whose presence seems to drain and darken him. Almost as if the light and energy Penny loves in him, that glow that looked to her like life, is only a reflection. Penny pushes this thought away and tries not to wince when Vivian smiles tightly, lays her hand on Penny's stomach, and says, "Maybe it's not too late to fix this?" Penny shakes her head no and then smiles at Ben's father's neatness and thinning hair, at the flurry of meaningless chatter, at the tinkle of ice cubes and Scotch. She smiles and smiles, even when Vivian shrugs and says, "Well, you're part of the family now." As Ben explains briefly how they met and where Penny's from, Vivian makes a polite face that seems to hurt Ben and that tells Penny Ben has disappointed Vivian. How? she wonders. Just by marrying me? Or by not making the ski team, not traveling around the world, not doing something else? Penny smiles, but the voices around her fade away, and after a while she says that she's tired.

"Of course you are," says Vivian, with another of her smiles. There is something dry as stone to her, something mineral, and for a minute Penny thinks smugly of her own fertility. "Let me show you your room," Vivian says. She signals Ben to stay behind and talk with his father, but although the picture looks right—the two men talking seriously across a table, the two women in their bright clothes tripping outside—Penny knows this is only temporary. Ben's drawn-in concentration was for Vivian and, from what Penny can see, he'll need all of it. She shrinks from Vivian's hand on her arm and follows her to the door. Either Vivian is wearing a most remarkable girdle, or she's developed some new form of locomotion. Nothing moves when she walks. Deneb, Altair, Procyon, Penny says to herself. Among the lucid stars are twenty-one most bright. Six of these she has never seen, because they're below the horizon this far north; the other fifteen were the first stars Gram taught her to find, the first she means to teach Ben if she can coax him back. But already, Penny can feel Vivian wedging her away from him.

"We're putting you in the cottage," Vivian says. "Thought you'd like the privacy."

Penny nods, wondering what Vivian does to her hair. The uniform steel color might be natural; the rigid finger waves marching down from her part surely aren't. The cottage—small, gray, fifty feet from the house—is all one room, with a couch, two armchairs, twin beds. "It's lovely," Penny says. She has never seen a more depressing room. Everything is gray; all the wood is soft and damp and the screens are crusted with bugs. They have a shower and a toilet, but no place to cook. Meals with his parents, then.

"You'll probably want to rest," Vivian says, as if Penny is a child. She shuts the door behind her firmly.

No one has offered to help Penny with the bags. Back in the house, she knows Ben and Vivian are making decisions she'll have to live with, and yet she doesn't dare interrupt them. Just for a while, she tells herself. Just until we get set up, until the baby's born. She tries to tell herself that being dependent on Vivian won't be so bad—it's clear already that any money here is Vivian's. For a minute she thinks about running home, throwing herself at her parents' feet, pleading for help. No. But staying here is going to be tough.

Penny unloads the car herself, lugging one bag at a time and hoping no one's watching from the window. She unpacks her good clothes and hangs them up, and then, since Ben still hasn't come, she opens Harry's gift. She's hoping for chocolates—cordial cherries, perhaps, that she can eat right now. Instead, she finds a blue book with seven black dots on the cover: *A Field Guide to the Stars*. How did Harry find this? The pages are filled with maps of the constellations and descriptions of stars and nebulae. She turns to Virgo and smiles at the fanciful rendering—in this version, the goddess has complicated draperies and feathered wings. Penny closes the book and studies the cover again. This time, the seven dots resolve into the stars of the Big Dipper. Inside her, the baby leaps.

Cassiopeia Spins
(July 1959)

★   ★   ★   ★   ★   ★

Penny was to remember forever her first sight of that house. Three wings bent around the huge curved driveway, an enormous tulip tree centered on a broad green lawn, stucco walls, a rippled tile roof, a broken lattice fence around the trash cans. She held Cass in her arms that day, fresh from the hospital and light as a cat, and Ben held her elbow and told her how his mother had snapped it up for next to nothing when Devora Westfall took off for Greece, and how she was giving it to them. Still wanting to give her things then, he stretched out his hand and let the cool gray afternoon into the empty hall.

The hall is empty still. From the water the house looks like a castle, perched almost alone on a gentle hill and guarded by a sweeping porch up on pillars. But to her, inside, it feels like a boat. The huge windows open onto the bay, portholes gone wild; everything else spreads like a disease. Bedrooms—two on the kitchen

side, four more flung out in a separate wing—three
baths, living room as big as a normal house, kitchen
where, no matter what she does, she crisscrosses miles
of linoleum. And this doesn't even include the basement. The house was made for people with servants,
and it's not what she would have picked. Still, it's theirs,
and better than staying with Bryant and Vivian. Not
that it came free, of course: She's thanked Ben's parents
by entertaining them every weekend these past four
years. She's never grumbled about the broken roof tiles,
the sagging gutters they can't afford to fix, or the large,
damp stains creeping across the celery-colored mural in
the living room. And, because she knows she should be
grateful, she hardly ever mentions Paine Westfall, the
husband Devora left behind in the guest house six feet
from their kitchen. It's his small, stucco cottage that
keeps theirs from being the sole house on the hill.

She's not sure how Paine got stuck with this measly
settlement, although she knows he's the reason that
Vivian got the house so cheap. At this very minute
Paine hides in his shack, slumped down in a beach chair
on the porch that parallels theirs. Every few seconds she
hears the click of a stone from his slingshot as he tries to
murder the sea gulls invading his beach. As far as she
can tell, he spends most of his time this way. She's convinced that on some dark night he'll strike her family
dead in their sleep.

He distracts her, and tonight, between listening to his
attacks and rushing to feed the crowd of people waiting
on the porch, she's managed to curdle the salad dressing. She looks down at the bowl with blank dismay. Is
this possible? That she can ruin even salad? She admits
that she's a terrible cook, prone to the quick-and-easy—
pea soup, canned chicken fricassee, boxed spaghetti dinners. But when Ben gently reproaches her she says it's
because she has no time. Her roast beef wouldn't over-
cook if she had time to watch it; her potatoes wouldn't

be lumpy if she had time to mash them all the way. She finds housekeeping difficult in this ark. Now she tosses the salad absently, trying to undo the damage. Ben will swear that she's done this on purpose, but she knows in her heart that she's struggled to do things well. She wonders if she can convince her guests that these curdy white lumps are cottage cheese. She was on the right track—she threw oil and garlic, salt and lemon juice over the lettuce—when she remembered reading about a creamy tart dressing in last month's *Family Circle*. She dumped in a quarter of a cup of milk, pleased at her creativity, but her only reward is these cheesy clots. Crumbled mild cheddar, she thinks. That's what I'll say if anyone asks.

Through the screen door she can hear the men talking seriously about money. Ben's father, for once, is actually saying something of his own. In the four years she's known him she can remember him doing this exactly twice—on the November day when Cass was born and on the April day, sixteen months later, when Webb popped out two weeks late. Both times, while Ben and Vivian paced the halls, Bryant came in, laid his fleshy palm on her head, and whispered, "You did good." Except for those times, he endlessly echoes Vivian. What she hears him saying now is, "Don't interfere with Ben, dear. It's his choice."

Penny opens the door to the porch with her hip, sets the salad bowl on the white metal table, and says, "Interfere with what?"

They all turn to stare at her. Vivian glares, her twiggy arms folded over her crisp shirtwaist. Bryant, leaning against the porch railing, forces a dry chuckle. Otis and Cindy exchange glances, Ben frowns, Webb cries from the bedroom nearby. And Cass, shrewd Cass, looks around and says, "Mommy, what did you say?"

"Who knows?" Penny says. She hates it when they treat her like a maid. She returns to the kitchen to stir the rice. Cass darts ahead of her, her legs flashing in the late sun.

"Mommy," she says. "Let me help."

Penny smiles, lifts her daughter up on a chair, and hands her a wooden spoon. At three and a half, Cass is almost violently precocious. From the moment she was born, all spider legs and dark hair, she's seemed to Penny to be watching everything. She never felt cuddly, even as an infant—she was always busy staring over Penny's shoulder, craning her heavy head on her thin neck. She walked early, talked early, and listened to everything. Penny taught her the alphabet one lazy June afternoon, and now she suddenly seems to know how to read.

"What's this?" Penny asks, pointing to a carton of milk.

"Milk!" Cass crows happily, smacking the carton with her spoon. "M-I-L-K!" She taps out each letter vigorously.

"That's right," Penny says. "That's good. Stir up from the bottom, okay?"

"Okay," Cass says. She looks like a baby witch, standing on tiptoe and stirring the rice with her big spoon. Her sundress seems to touch her only at the shoulders; her feet are bare and dirty. She peers into the pot as if she could read a message there, and then she says, "Can we go skiing?"

"Sweetie," Penny says. "You have to have snow to ski. Remember?"

Cass eyes her speculatively. "There's *always* snow when we see Uncle Otis and Aunt Cindy," she says. "I thought it might snow tonight."

"I don't think so," Penny laughs. "That's only because we always see them in the winter."

"We could have winter now," Cass announces. She waves her spoon in the air as if it's a magic wand.

"Not in July, honey."

Cass frowns, stirs too hard, and flips a lump of rice onto the floor. Penny picks it up and sees with dismay that it's crusted brown.

"I think we'll turn this off," she says. "Why don't you go tell Daddy to put the fish on the grill?"

Cass skips off, swinging her arms as if she holds imaginary ski poles. She loves skiing more than anything. Ben took her out her second winter, strapped to his back while he flew down Otis's mountain in New Hampshire; last winter he put her on tiny skis. Now he wants her to start real ski lessons, but Penny's not thrilled with the idea. She spends the winter weekends cooped up in the Nelsons' A-frame, smoking cigarettes and drinking coffee with Cindy while Ben and Otis burn up the slopes. The A-frame sits at the base of SnoGoose, the mountain that Otis designed; from the window she can watch the skiers while she changes Webb's diapers. But when she tells Ben that these weekends aren't much fun for her, he tells her it's her own fault. "We *have* free season passes," he says. "It's not *my* fault you don't use yours." Implying, somehow, that it *is* her fault these children of hers keep her busy and off the slopes; as if she has willfully given up her skiing dreams.

"Penny!" Ben calls from the porch. "Where's the fish?"

"I thought you had it out there."

"Well, I don't!"

She sighs and finds the fish in the refrigerator, where she left it in the morning to thaw. Cindy clicks in on spike-heeled sandals and asks if she can help. "You could take the plates out," Penny says. "And the silverware."

Cindy and Otis haven't visited before—this is the first summer Otis has had any time. Despite this, Cindy seems to know where everything is. She takes the plates from the cupboard with an easy grace that Penny envies. Still childless, she looks the way she did four years ago.

"What's all the talk about?" Penny asks.

"The usual," Cindy says. "Money. Otis is bragging about SnoGoose, and Ben's bragging about how he sold more houses last year than anyone else on the Cape. Sometimes I wish they'd both relax."

"I can tell you one thing," Penny says. "Ben's only going to get worse as long as he's working for that shark of a mother. Her best trick is selling houses you wouldn't keep a dog in to kids who don't know any better."

Cindy spreads her fingers and picks thoughtfully at her nail polish. "So I hear," she says. "But then it sounds like he has bigger plans."

"Oh?" Penny says. But before she can ask about the plans, Cindy takes the plates and vanishes. When Penny takes the fish out to Ben, she sees that the sun is already low over the island across the cove from their house.

"Make me a drink?" she asks Ben. She's suddenly aware that everyone else has the glow of having tucked several away.

"Can't," he says. "I've got to get the bluefish going before it's dark." He's wearing the white cookout apron Vivian gave him, over one of the blue shirts he wears to set off his eyes. Across his belly a lobster smiles on a bed of clams, waving a fork in one claw.

Otis says, "I'll make you something. What do you want?" When he bends over the ice bucket, two soft bulges form at his waist. He's broadened some, as if he, like Penny, has borne children. Only Ben and Cindy seem untouched—Ben as pale and blond as ever but freckled now, still slim; Cindy trim and auburn-haired.

"Gin and tonic," she tells Otis. "Heavy on the gin."

Otis gives her a mock bow as he hands her the drink. His back is to Ben, and so he can't see how Ben is staring at Cindy's legs. Penny can't remember the last time

Ben looked at her that way, as if she were prime rib—
lately, he's begun to wear pajamas to bed. She glides her
hand secretly over the bulge at the lip of her panty girdle, remembering when a garter belt was all she needed.
Her legs are still good but her waist is gone, and she had
to cut her thick brown hair when Webb started tearing
at it.

"Thank you, sir," she says to Otis. She smiles at him
flirtatiously, hoping that she doesn't look ridiculous.
"Why don't you come sit here by me?"

Vivian shoots Penny a sharp look, but Penny ignores
her. Cass, who is weaving a yarn bridge between Vivian
and Bryant's knees, has them linked in a way they'd
normally never consider.

"So," she says to Otis, who stretches out beneath her
with his back against her chair, "what big plans have
you been hatching out here?"

"Good big ones," he says. "Ben's been telling me
about that parcel of land near the golf course. He says
he's only missing a two-acre wedge."

Vivian is still eavesdropping. She leans toward Otis
and Penny as far as her bound knees permit and says,
"Don't let them talk you into it, Penny. It's a stupid
idea."

"Grandma!" Cass says sharply. "Hold still!"

Vivian flips herself back. Talk her into what? Penny
wonders. What crazy idea? She doesn't want Otis to
know that Ben hasn't said a word about this land.
"What do you think?" she asks Otis. "Is it a good idea?"
She's hoping Otis will fill her in while Ben checks the
bluefish and nibbles Cindy with his eyes.

"It's real smart," Otis says. "Wing's Neck Golf course
is bound to grow over the next few years, and if Ben can
lock up the stretch to the north he's sure to make
money. Clusters of houses nestled in the trees, a big
wooded tract set aside as a park—I think summer people will pay a premium price for the right design."

"You're going to design it?"

"Me?" Otis says. "I don't do developments. But we went to school with a guy who's great with these things. Sewage and water will be a problem, of course . . ."

"Of course," Penny says.

"But it's still feasible. I was just telling Ben that I'd like to get in on the deal. I've got some free cash from SnoGoose and with that and another investor or two and maybe a mortgage on the house, he'd have enough to convince the bank. After that, you can just sit back and watch the money roll in."

Penny thinks this over for a minute and then calls to Ben, who looks up guiltily from Cindy's legs and then flakes the grilling fish with the tip of his fork. "So," Penny says, "that golf course deal all set?"

"Near enough," he says, as if he'd told her all about it. "It's looking good."

"Don't be an idiot," Vivian snorts. "You're better off working for us."

Ben frowns. Four years of working for Vivian have made him harder, colder; Penny could swear that this job, more than marriage or fatherhood, is what's dimmed his glow. But he says calmly, "I'll be with you for a while yet—this won't bring any money for a year or two, at best. And then I'll have to start paying off the investors and the bank as soon as we start to sell."

"Work yourself to death," Vivian says. "See if I care."

"Dinner's ready," Ben says.

Penny lights three citronella candles and sets them along the railing, thankful that the sun has set while they've been talking. She doesn't put a candle on the table, in the faint hope that, between the darkness and all they've drunk, the lumps in the salad and the crusts in the rice will be invisible.

"What's with the dark?" Ben asks.

"Romantic," Penny tells him. She notices that he takes particular care to sit next to Cindy. She'd love to

know what games he'll play with his feet during dinner
—he drinks like his parents now and he's had, by her
count, four stiff gins. While she eyes his flushed face,
Cass plunges her hands into her plate and breaks her
bluefish fillet into four large triangles. She props them
up in her sticky rice to form a tetrahedron.

"Egypt!" she crows.

Penny needs a minute to realize what Cass is talking
about—this week, they've been looking at a picture
book about the pyramids. Ben reaches across the table
and knocks the fish down gently. "Don't play with your
food," he says. "Eat up like a good girl."

Cass frowns but eats her fish.

Penny means to ask him if he has to be so strict, but
he looks at her and shakes his head. He says they
shouldn't encourage Cass to think she's different, even
though she clearly is, and so they're careful not to over-
praise her when she turns her Lego blocks into huge
dragons. She's always building something, but although
Ben lets her build with odds and ends he refuses to let
her build with food.

"Don't you feed her?" Vivian asks nastily. "She eats
like a wolf."

"Mom," Ben says. "Let her be."

Penny's sure that he's resting his hand on Cindy's leg.
She imagines it sneaking over slowly like some underwater shark, coming to rest with a light touch that will
grow heavier as the night wears on. Cindy acts as if
nothing's wrong and chatters with Bryant and Vivian
about Otis's plans for a new ski resort in Utah.

"I need another drink," Penny announces abruptly.
"Anyone else want anything?"

They all do. They'll drink, she knows, until they
grow sodden and sloppy and start exchanging old stories. Ben, who can be astonishingly sentimental, will
get all choked up over some remembered happiness.
They'll drink until Pegasus has risen and Virgo has set,

until Cassiopeia spins around Polaris. Penny sighs and fills the glasses, remembering Gram. If she were alone she'd go down to the beach right now, with her field glasses and her dog-eared star book. She'd stretch out with her neck on a pillow of sand and watch the sky until she fell asleep.

Just as she turns back to the table, Bryant whips up his Polaroid and blinds her with the flashbulb. "There!" he says triumphantly. "It's always so hard to get a picture of you."

She staggers to her seat with the tray in her hands. Bryant flips the print on the table and counts off the seconds until he can peel away the backing and expose her face.

When the moon rises, it waxes gibbous and very bright. A cloud drifts by and hides it for a while so that the only light comes from the candles sputtering on the rail. Then the cloud breaks up and leaves the moon to illuminate the dirty plates, now pushed aside, the sweating glasses, and the ashtray that Penny and Cindy have somehow filled. It's past eleven before anyone remembers that Cass should be in bed. And even then, she's withdrawn to the shadow of the porch railing so casually, so completely, that she might have stayed and listened all night if Paine hadn't drifted by in his kayak. It's Cass who points him out, interrupting their lackadaisical discussion of zoning laws.

"Mommy!" she says. "I see a whale!"

Penny starts guiltily and turns to look at the water. Although Cass often exaggerates what she sees, she never makes something from nothing. Sure enough, an enormous pale shape glides through the water just off their beach. In the moonlight, Penny can just make out that this is Paine, too big to fit properly inside his boat. He trails his huge white legs and arms over the sides and paddles languidly with his hands, humming some-

thing from one of the operas he plays eternally. Penny
doesn't know the name of the tune, but she recognizes
every note. The sight of him infuriates her.

"Would you look at that?" she says to Ben, to Vivian,
to anyone who is listening. Her voice is shaking—it's
their fault she has to put up with this; their fault, or at
least Vivian's fault, that her life has gone astray. "No
privacy."

Ben waves his hand in the air, dismissing her complaint. "Come on," he says. "It's no big deal. He's entitled to go out in his boat at night."

"Sure he is," Penny says. "Half drunk, naked—what
do you want to bet?—just close enough to overhear us.
Like he's entitled to shoot birds from his porch and
stare at me through the kitchen window."

"He really does that?" Cindy says. "I'd call the police."

"He *owns* the police," Penny says. "Or at least he
knows all of them. He cruises down Shore Road at sixty
and never even gets a ticket."

"You're making a fuss over nothing," Ben says. "He's
a little peculiar, is all."

"Right," Penny says. "Sure." She wishes that Otis
and Cindy would go to bed and that Ben's parents
would go home. She gets up, stretches, and tries to put
Paine from her mind. There's nothing she can do about
him—he never does more than hover. And hovering is
not against the law. She waits for the day when he dares
to touch Cass or Webb, the day she goes after him with a
kitchen knife. Cass is still peering through the railing at
him.

"Sweetie," Penny says. "It's way past time for bed."

"It's *early*," Cass says stubbornly. "I want to stay."

"Sweetie . . ." Penny sighs, too tired to relish the
struggle that's bound to come. If Cass had her way,
she'd stay up all night. Penny uncrosses her legs, but

before she can get up Cass giggles and runs past her, finally coming to rest halfway down the flight of stairs that leads from the porch to the beach.

"Ha!" she calls. "Come get me!"

Penny puts her chin in her hand and looks helplessly at Ben. "Would you go?" she says. "I'm beat."

"Sure," he says, and then he growls, "Cassie!" in the rumbling dog voice that Cass loves. "I'm coming to get you, Cassie!"

Cass shrieks with delight as Ben lumbers across the porch on all fours. "Grrr!" he rumbles. "Fee, fi, fo, fum —I smell Cassie blood!"

She squeals as he approaches her. She inches up the stairs toward him and then darts back when he closes in, taunting and teasing him until Penny has to laugh. Ben plays along with Cass—after he's had a few drinks he's wonderful with her, full of invention and games. Now he leaps forward and locks his teeth on Cass's sleeve, shaking it until she surrenders reluctantly.

"Get her!" Bryant calls. He has his Polaroid out again, but he's laughing so hard that he can't focus.

Ben growls one more time and then reaches down to scoop up Cass. As he does, Penny sees a pen prod a folded index card from Ben's shirt pocket. Ben reaches quickly for it, but Cass is quicker—she closes her skinny hand on the card, springs from his arms, and darts up the stairs.

Penny laughs at this new twist, sure that Ben will laugh too. But all of a sudden he's stopped smiling.

"Cass!" he demands. "You give me that back right now."

She laughs and flies past the table, past Penny, past Bryant's weak grasp, past Cindy's gentle murmur. Ben follows, chasing her. "I mean it!" he shouts. "No more fooling around! It's time for bed!" He looks so ridiculous that Penny half-suspects him of still playing.

"No!" Cass giggles. "I want to stay up." And then, before anyone can stop her, she scampers up the trellis where the wisteria grows. She still has the card clutched in her hand.

Penny catches her breath. The trellis is old and rotten in places, just barely attached to the stucco wall. As she watches, the whole thing seems to sway slightly. The porch light mounted above the door makes a fuzzy halo of her daughter's hair. "Cass?" she says very quietly. "Can you climb down from there real slow, like a good girl? Or can Mommy come and take you down?"

"Soon," Cass says calmly, looking down at Ben. "But first I read."

The adults laugh uneasily at this, driving Penny into some still, quiet space inside her head. That card, she thinks. They know what's on there as well as I do. There's only one thing Ben would bother to hide from them, the thing he no longer bothers to hide from her and yet won't admit outright. The way they talk about his escapades is for him to pretend they don't happen and for her to pretend she believes him. This time Ben keeps a silly smile on his face, as if he thinks he can fool them by pretending this is still a game. He thinks he's safe, sure that Cass is too young to read. Cassie, she thinks. Just come down from there and bring me the note and I'll buy you a rocking horse. I'll buy you the moon. She can't stand for everyone to hear this. Cass clears her throat and holds the note up to the light.

"You can stay up another half hour if you come down now," Ben pleads.

"Good!" Cass says. "Now I read."

Slowly, sounding out each letter, Cass reads:

> Friday
> Call bank
> Car—fan belt
> Karen, 8

There's a terrible queasy silence when she's done, broken only when Otis clears his throat and says, "Well, you certainly can read. How about coming down now?"

Penny closes her eyes and concentrates on keeping her dinner down. Too much to drink, she thinks. Crusty rice, curdled salad. She forces her eyes open and turns to Otis's steadying gaze, but Otis won't look at her. He stares at Cindy; Cindy fiddles with her stocking; Bryant sucks an ice cube with his cheeks caved in. They're so polite that she could kill them.

Cass clambers down, all proud of herself. Ben snatches the note from her as soon as her feet touch the ground. Now that she's read it, she gives it up easily.

Ben draws back from Cass as if she might bite. "I didn't know you could do that," he says. "Can you read everything?"

"Only little words," Cass says modestly.

"She just started," Penny mumbles. No one is listening to her—they turn their faces away as if she'd just broken out in boils. Is this good manners? she wonders. Is this what they're supposed to do? She looks at Ben, searching for some sign of apology, but he ignores her. She rises from her chair and balances as unsteadily as if she were back on skis. "Come on," she says to Cass. "Time for bed."

"Okay," Cass sighs. She lets Penny pick her up. She's tall for her age but very skinny; she weighs no more than a small dog. She reaches out to open the door, and Penny whispers, "Honey? You sure you read that right?"

"Karen!" Cass crows, so loudly that Penny winces. "New word!"

Penny tilts her head away from Cass's triumphant face. Above her twinkles the slightly bent W of her daughter's constellation. Cassiopeia. It might as well be Cassandra.

"Off you go," Ben says sharply. He doesn't look at

Penny; he turns to Otis instead. Otis plucks at his collar as if it's suddenly grown too tight.

Penny bears her daughter away. She knows the others understood the message, but they're chattering behind her as if nothing's wrong. Friday, the note said. Karen, 8. Karen is the receptionist at the real estate office, and Friday was the day Ben called to say he had to work late. Friday was the night he didn't come home until three o'clock.

Ben stays out on the porch with the others until long after Penny has gone to bed. When he comes in, she pretends that she's asleep. She keeps her back to him and lies very still, but her breathing gives her away.

"I know you're awake," he says. "Did you have to walk out on everyone like that?"

She doesn't answer.

"Hey!" he hisses. "I'm talking to you."

"I'm too tired to argue," she mutters. "And I don't want to wake up the kids." Cass and Webb have the flanking bedrooms; they sleep with the doors open because they're afraid to be alone at night. It's not unusual for Penny to wake and find either or both of them curled at her feet like puppies.

"They're asleep," Ben says. "I checked on them when I came in." He pauses for a minute, and Penny wonders if he's going to try and explain about the note. All he says is, "What did you think you were doing, teaching her to read like that? She'll stick out like a sore thumb when she goes to school."

"It just happened," Penny says. "You know how she looks at the pages when I read to her? I taught her letters from her alphabet blocks, and one day she just started sounding out words." She sounds apologetic even to herself—how did he do that? How did he put her on the defensive so fast?

"Great," Ben says. "Now we'll have to hide everything. When she goes to school they'll think she's a freak." He sounds as disgusted as if she'd taught Cass to spit.

"It's no big deal," Penny says. "She's just smart."

"Hmmph," he grunts. "Guess she didn't get that from you."

Penny doesn't respond to this, although it infuriates her. These days, he often makes her feel stupid as well as ugly. He used to tell her about his work until she got pregnant with Webb, but then he stopped telling her anything. He talks to his mother now, and to Otis and his other friends. When she asks him about work or about their mounting loans, all he ever says is, "Don't worry—we'll be just fine. It takes money to make money." He manages the finances and gives her a household allowance each month. She squirrels away whatever she can in the folds of an extra girdle.

"You alive?" Ben says now. He paws under her night-gown halfheartedly, but gives up and rolls away when she doesn't respond. She isn't drunk enough to want to fuck; he isn't sober enough to pester her. He falls asleep, snoring lightly. For a few hours she puts the note from her mind and sleeps too.

When she wakes it's three o'clock. Cass? she wonders. Webb? She props herself up on her elbows but sees that the bottom of the bed is empty. There is only Ben here, sprawled on his back and sleeping with the same concentration that he brings to his work. With his eyes closed he looks as pale and innocent as Webb. There's something remarkable in the way his face relaxes in his sleep; although this used to touch Penny, it infuriates her tonight. Asleep, he shows the face of the man she married. Awake, he's someone else, the man she's come to know these past four years. This man prefers short women, after all, and fusses over his clothes. His feet are small, his complexion delicate, his digestion sturdy; he's fond of marigolds and other weedy flowers. He believes women like gifts of red underwear and heavy perfume. He loves to fish; he loves to make toys for his kids. He thinks he and Penny would be happy together if Penny would only do what he asks, and, when he wants to, he can be more interesting than anyone Penny has ever met. His mind acts in quick jolts and bursts, leaping from one enthusiasm to the next. He's good at making money, better than his mother, but although he'll probably be rich it's not enough and he has, so far, filled the gap with tennis, golf, light construction, stock-market gambles, gardening, beer-making, women, and cars. He can still produce that sunny, charming glow that once drew Penny to him, but now that glow only makes his infidelities inevitable. He loves his house and, probably, his family, and yet when he spends a weekend at home instead of at work, or wherever he goes, he begins to sip gin and tonics before lunch as he moodily cruises the grounds on his power mower.

This is Ben. Beside him, Penny stirs and thinks about creeping next door and curling up on the flowered sheets next to Cass's warm, bony body. She could lie there with her feet hanging over the edge and dream that she and Cass were somewhere else. In a rocket, perhaps, flying high above the earth like the rocket that left Florida last month carrying two girl monkeys, Able and Baker, inside its tiny nose cone. Smaller than Cass when she was born, the monkeys soared through space in the company of fruit fly larvae, sea urchin eggs, mold spores, yeast cells, onion skins, mustard seeds, and corn. Penny showed Cass the pictures in the magazines— Able strapped to her curved seat, Baker with her gold medal—and now she wonders what that trip would be like.

She sighs and swings her feet over the bed. Cass went to sleep so late that it wouldn't be fair to wake her. Where else can she go? She could hop into the Buick convertible, Ben's pride and joy, and drive off into the night, except that she has no place to hide. She sits and thinks for a minute more, and then she slips jeans and a sweatshirt on, takes a flashlight from her underwear drawer, and tiptoes away, slipping down to the basement. Quietly, she gathers her life jacket, the boat hook, the sailbag, and the little illustrated sailing manual Otis brought as a house gift. She glides out the basement door and down to the beach, where a dinghy lies upside down over its oars. She can just make out their small wooden sailboat, spinning gently around its mooring fifty feet out. Ben hasn't had time to teach Penny how to use it yet, but Penny is teaching herself.

She rows out and clips the dinghy's painter to the mooring. After she loads everything into the sailboat, she climbs in and hanks the sails on. For a minute, then, she's confused—she can't remember whether she's supposed to raise the sail before she casts off. She thinks she's supposed to cast off first, but she doesn't like the idea of drifting while she fumbles with the halyard. She raises the sail, uncleats the sheet, and darts forward to cast off the mooring line.

In an instant she glides away. She heads for the mouth of the cove, where the island that shelters their house from the bay tapers off, leaving a passage. For all the times she's watched Ben sail she still can't get things straight—the wind always feels like it's coming directly from behind her. She lets the sail out cautiously; it fills and stops fluttering. She cleats the sheet and turns her flashlight on, flipping quickly through the sailing manual.

"Points of sail," she reads, by the light of the yellow beam. She's got the basic idea of sailing down and knows what lines do what and how to steer. What she can't figure out is how to get to where she wants to go. The book talks about runs, reaches, sailing close-hauled, tacking into the wind. In the diagrams, little stick figures sit on wedges with arrows of wind pointing at them. She decides that if the wind's behind her she must be on a run. "When you're running," the book says, "be careful not to jibe." This, she knows from watching Ben, is when the boom sweeps over the deck and pulls the sail out the other way. But the boom moves when the boat comes about as well, so how is she supposed to know? The book says, "Always turn *into* the wind—that way you'll come about instead of jibing." But which way is into the wind? At the mouth of the cove she needs to turn right, to clear the sandspit.

She pushes the tiller gently away from her. The sail begins to flutter and so she hauls in on the sheet. The more the boat turns, the more the sail loosens—perhaps this means that she's coming about. The boom swings over with a sudden crack, tearing the sheet from her hand and just missing her head. Apparently she's going to learn the hard way. Now, at least, she knows where the wind is. She resets everything, sets a course down the bay side of the island, and sails that leg easily enough, reading with her flashlight all the way. At the far end of the island, she comes about with a smooth, controlled sweep.

Not bad, she thinks. The water is black and nearly flat and the stars are amazing, even if some of them aren't really stars. Somewhere up there the two Sputniks play tag, circling the earth more quickly than she can imagine. Somewhere up there the debris from all the rockets drifts through space like a cloud of asteroids. The stars are amazing and so is she—she has taught herself to sail, as she has managed a second child to console her first, a house, a garden, Ben. Sometimes she feels that only the strength of her wishes holds her life together.

She returns to the cove easily, and only when she comes to the mooring buoy does she realizes she doesn't know how to pick up the line. She needs another hand, maybe two. She lets the sail out as far as she can and grasps the boat hook clumsily in one arm. Once, twice, she misses the mooring. She's moving too fast. She should drop the sail and paddle with one of the oars, but she's left the oars in the dinghy. She heads the boat up into the wind—she knows now where it's from—and misses the mooring a third time and then a fourth. Jibe, come about, jibe. She's losing track again of which is which. The moon has set, and a pale streak along the horizon hints at dawn. The wind seems to follow her like a shadow.

She jumps when a mocking voice calls her name. "Mrs. Day," she hears, "could I perhaps be of some help?"

That's Paine's voice calling, although she can't tell from where. From his porch, from his beach, from his kayak? Quickly she turns her flashlight off so her sails won't shine. She shivers to think of him drifting near her in the water. He never sleeps. He is always watching.

"No, thank you," she calls steadily. "I'll figure it out." And she knows she will. Sooner or later she'll get it, bring the boat gently to rest and then row away.

Paine leaves. Cassiopeia spins above her, growing paler each minute. She spins about the mooring, coming closer each time.

Fomalhaut
(September 1963)

★　　　★　　　★　　　★　　　★　　　★

It could be summer, Penny thinks. The sky is so bright, the water so blue, the children so brown and loud that fall seems far away despite the shrinking days. She'd never believe it was mid-September if Cass and Webb hadn't been in school for two weeks already. She can hear them outside, shrieking with laughter as they clatter sticks down the slat fence that Paine erected in the middle of their walkway. They couldn't stop him from building this—their property line runs smack down the center—and now the six-foot space between Penny's kitchen and the wall of Paine's bedroom is bisected by ten feet of painted wood. Only Paine would do such a thing; only Cass would torment him for it so constantly. She slips down the sliver left to them, wedges her pointed face in the cracks between the slats, and catches Paine squeezed tight against his house and peering at them. He jumps each time and mutters at her. She falls into the fence accidentally, so that it's bowed at the top;

she burrows little holes underneath and sends ants marching through. And on quiet Saturdays like today, when Paine's settled comfortably into his room with *The Magic Flute* turned up loud, she prods Webb into playing a game where they grate two sturdy sticks against the slats as they chase each other up and down.

Secretly, Penny is proud of Cass for thinking of this. She'd never bother Paine herself, although he bothers her. But she can't seem to make herself stop Cass. She smiles to think of Paine grinding his teeth at Cass's noise.

"Cass!" she finally calls, reluctant to interrupt their game. "Webb! It's time to go!"

They dart into the kitchen so quickly that they skid on the linoleum. Cass's hair sticks up in spikes—the pixie haircut Ben inflicted on her doesn't suit her bony eight-year-old face. Her hair juts over the earpieces of the glasses she had to get two years ago, when they caught her squinting at the board. Webb is filthy, as always—all over and everywhere. His natural color is brown, from his crew cut to his tan belly to his callused feet. A film of dirt coats every inch of him, except for the lighter streaks where his sweat has trickled down.

"Are you going to let us shop?" Cass asks.

"You can help," Penny says. "But wash up first."

Her children disappear into the bathroom, run water, put on their sandals, and pile into the car. As Penny drives them into the village, she sees that Webb has washed only the center of his face. A dark rim extends from his hairline and frames his sturdy features. At the stoplight, she grabs his chin and scrubs at him with a tissue moistened on her tongue.

Webb squirms under her unwanted attention. "Mom!" he says. "Come on!" When she lets him go he paws at the scrap of paper sticking from her purse. "Is this the list?" he asks, squinting at the scribbled words.

"Mm-hmm," Penny says. "And we're only getting

what's on it—we're going to have enough to feed an army." She takes the list from Webb and scans it again while she's looking for a parking place. She's sure she's written down everything she needs for the trip tomorrow. Ben's taking them all on a party boat that leaves from Hyannis—her and Cass and Webb and three of his business friends. Webb and Cass are so excited that they've been screaming all day. When Penny parks they tumble out of the car, nearly flattening old Ellie Wylie.

"Goodness!" Ellie gasps, clutching her bag to her chest.

"You'll have to excuse them," Penny says. "We're all going fishing tomorrow, and it's their first real trip."

"Oh, well," Ellie says. "I know how that is." She looks down at Webb's scruffy head. "Pretty exciting for a six-year-old, hmm?"

"I'm six and a half," Webb says stoutly. When Ellie smiles at him condescendingly, he tugs Cass's arm and they vanish inside the store.

"The kids are hoping for stripers," Penny says. "But we'll be lucky if we catch scup. We're going on the early morning boat from Hyannis."

"A party boat?" Ellie says. "Really? I'd have thought that by now, after Putter's Way, you'd be buying a boat of your own."

"Hardly," Penny says. She doesn't know what else to say. Putter's Way, Ben's first development, went up so fast and sold so well that everyone thinks they've struck it rich. They don't know that Ben's plowed all the profits into a new development in Cotuit. Two-acre lots on the rim of a cranberry bog, tasteful gray saltboxes three times normal size, zoning restrictions as tight as a girdle —this time he's going for big money. But when Penny listens to him planning with his partners, all she thinks about is the money they owe, more money than she can understand. Ben tells her not to worry but then complains about the grocery bills. Penny can't believe a few dollars matter in the face of these huge debts.

Ellie smiles smugly and walks away, leaving Penny to chase after her children. Inside the store, she finds Cass pushing a shopping cart while Webb loads it with whatever looks good—Twinkies, peanut butter, Devil Dogs, Spam. "Webb!" she says sharply. "You can put that all back right now!"

Webb hangs his round head but does as he's told. He's different from Cass, so sweet-tempered that Penny hates to scold him. If Webb had his way, he'd gather up everything good in the world and give it to his friends. He has no enemies.

"Honey," she says. "You can get things from the list, okay?" Cass rolls her eyes, but Webb brightens. Penny hands the list to him and watches while he struggles with the first word.

"Ap—" he says. "Ap-ap-ap-*ples*!"

"*Apples!*" Cass says with disgust. "Aren't you ever going to learn how to read?"

"Don't pick on him," Penny says. "He's got plenty of time."

"Apples, apples, apples," Webb sings. "I knew—I was just testing you." He runs off to the produce counter, and Penny sighs and asks Cass to get a package of Oreos. She won't let anyone push Webb, but she does wonder when things will straighten out for him. Here he is, starting second grade, and still he has trouble with two-syllable words. When the eclipse came a few months ago, Cass watched intently through the smoked glasses they gave her in school, but Webb stood transfixed, staring at the pattern of tiny crescents the leaves from their tulip tree cast on his chest.

When Webb returns with two sacks of apples she decides not to tell him to put one back. "Thanks," she says instead. She sends him off again for paper plates and cups. She picks up bread and chips and cold cuts and asks Cass to get lemons and sugar. Along the way she talks to Bud Nickerson, to Joan Twitchell, to Sarah and Emily Chase. Eight years here in town, and she sees her neighbors only when she's shopping. She tells them she's fine, the children are fine; yes, Ben seems to be doing well; no, she hasn't taken up golf. And then she pays for everything and is back in the sun again. A huge flock of gulls wheels over the bay and heads for the Canal.

"Four sandwiches apiece," Webb says firmly as they drive away. "We'll need at least that many. What if the boat gets lost and we're out all night and a huge shark comes after us . . . ?" He falls silent, dreaming of sea adventures. Penny would give all her fingers and toes to make his first fishing trip everything he wants. He's prone to clumsiness, which makes Ben yell; he's prone to tears when he is yelled at. Silently, she prays for a smooth tomorrow.

"Daddy's friends will just eat them," Cass predicts darkly. "After they drink all their beer."

"Cass!" Penny says. "That's not very nice."

"Well, it's true. They always eat everything."

By now, Penny has learned that there's not much that Cass doesn't see. And she judges what she sees—she has firm opinions on every person Ben's ever brought to the house. Mostly, she doesn't like anyone.

"I'll hide mine," Webb says. "For an emergency. Then, after we've been adrift for maybe a week and the pirates are coming, I'll pull out my food and rescue you all."

"I'll make us a separate cooler," Penny says. "Separate from the men. We'll leave them the beer and some sandwiches, and we'll take all the rest and our own Thermos of lemonade. And the Oreos."

"Can I have an Oreo now?" Webb asks wistfully.

"No. But tomorrow they'll be just for us." Penny stops at the package store for a couple of cases of beer and then at the cleaners for Ben's shirts. One by one, she checks off all the errands on the list. Cass and Webb argue the merits of tautog versus scup. Webb says scup are better, but that it doesn't matter because they're only going to catch stripers.

"You wait and see," he tells Cass. "Tomorrow I'm going to catch the biggest fish on the boat."

"Tomorrow," Cass says, "it will probably rain."

Webb's face darkens and he scrunches up in the corner of the seat. Penny would like to smack Cass for that, but she knows it wouldn't do any good. When Ben spanks her she stares him down until he stops. She cries when she's angry but never when she's hit.

When they get home, Penny cheers up Webb by sneaking him an Oreo. "Go out and play until supper," she tells him. She feels forgiven when he smiles at her.

Ben calls at six to say he won't be home for supper. Webb and Cass, who haven't done their chores, cheer loudly.

"Ha!" Cass says. "No clipping today." She's supposed to clip around the bases of the trees each week, after Ben mows their huge lawn. Each night, she's supposed to sweep the kitchen floor. Webb has to take the garbage out and help Ben wash the car. For this, and for keeping their rooms neat, they get a quarter a week. Webb spends his on penny candy; Cass squirrels hers away. Sometimes Penny slips them a little extra and swears them to secrecy.

"Can we have Chef Boyardee tonight?" asks Webb.

"Sure," Penny says. She doesn't fuss much over dinner on the nights Ben doesn't come home. When he's there she tries her best to get meat, potato, and vegetable on the table in some form or another. But when he's gone, which is more and more often these days, she and the children live from cans. The women's magazines she reads swear that canned foods are vitamin-enriched.

And while she admits that Chef Boyardee doesn't taste like anything homemade, she and the children like the sweet orange sauce and the slippery noodles. She opens and heats two cans of ravioli and makes a little salad to ease her conscience. They eat from bowls.

After supper, Penny sends Cass and Webb off to get their clothes ready for the trip. When they're gone she collapses at the table by the window and chain-smokes cigarettes with her elbows splayed between the dirty bowls. Ben yells at her when she smokes too much, so she abstains when he's around. But on these long empty nights when he's somewhere else, she saturates herself with smoke as if she could store it. She inhales noisily now, trying to imagine where Ben is.

She knows what he's doing: not exactly where, perhaps, and not exactly with whom, but she knows. She no longer keeps track of whom he's seeing, although it would be easy enough for her to find out. These days, she and Ben have begun to fight over what he does, as if they both recognize that they have little left to lose. She asks why and he comes up with excuses: there's too much of him for any one person, too little of her spread between him and the kids, she lets herself go, she ignores him. She thinks of the parts of her he's never found, the questions he never asks, and knows he's telling lies. More and more she blames Vivian for making Ben this way, so hollow that no quantity or quality of Penny's love can fill him. If I even love him anymore, she thinks.

Cass brings out a load of clothes for her inspection. "Should I bring a sweater *and* a sweatshirt?" she asks.

"Better," Penny says, falling down to earth. "Might be cold."

"When's Daddy coming home? I want to show him something."

"I don't know, sweetie."

Webb joins them, wanting to know where the

handlines are and why Ben's not home to help them pack. "He's working," Penny says. She's told worse lies. "The handlines are in the cardboard box downstairs in the little bedroom—you can bring them up yourself if you're real careful."

"How many?" he asks.

"Bring four—one for each of us." She doesn't want to give away Ben's surprise—he's planning to rent deep-sea rods for them tomorrow. Until now they've used rods only on their own beach. Ben taught them how to cast, but he doesn't let them brings rods away from home for fear they'll drop them. When they fish from the railroad bridge, he has them use handlines.

"I'll help," Cass says.

"No," Webb says. "I'll do it myself."

Cass makes a little face at Penny, as if she were infinitely grown up and above these petty things. She stalks back to her bedroom and Webb scampers off alone. It's dark now, and Penny realizes she'll have to get them to bed soon if she wants them up at five-thirty. She promises herself she'll stop staring out the window after one more cigarette. The stars are bright above the water, promising fair weather despite Cass's dire prediction. Low in the southern sky she spots lonely Fomalhaut, her grandmother's favorite star. She can remember asking Gram why that one was so special.

Gram had stared at the star thoughtfully. "Because it's all alone," she said. "There isn't another bright star near it, and so it seems more beautiful. It's called the Solitary One."

Penny wasn't impressed by that then—who wants a lost star? Now she can understand Gram's affection for it. Fomalhaut is visible only from September until late December, and when it arrives it's the only bright star in the southern sky. It comes so seldom and passes so quickly through its low arc that it seems like a gift.

When Webb comes in with the tangle of handlines, she decides to show it to him.

"Come here," she says to her son. "I want to show you something."

"What?" Webb says. He lays the heap of coarse brown twine on the table. "Will you help me untangle these?"

"In a minute. I want to show you the star in the fish's mouth."

"There's a fish star?" Webb says. "Where?"

Penny points to the horizon. "See the real bright star there, way down by itself?"

Webb follows her finger and says, "I think so."

"That's Fomalhaut," Penny says. "It marks the mouth of a big fish."

"Fo-mal-ho," Webb repeats slowly. "I don't see any fish."

"Look to the left of the bright star," she says. "There are some faint stars in a long triangle there—those are the fish. The bright star is in the fish's mouth."

"I see it!" Webb squeals. "I see it! It looks like a huge striper!"

"That's right," Penny says, and hugs him. "That means you'll catch lots of fish tomorrow."

"I'll call them all Fo-mal-ho. But it has to be a secret. You won't tell Cass?"

"Not a word." Her small sweet son lives in a land of dreams and promises; she knows that when she breaks one she breaks his heart.

Webb rests his head on her shoulder while she untangles the lines and wraps them neatly around the frames. "Will Daddy be home soon?" he asks. "It's getting late."

"Any minute," Penny says. "But I want you to go to bed now. You've got to get lots of sleep, so you'll be strong enough to catch all those fish tomorrow. And I've still got to make all our lunches." She holds out the handlines. "There," she says.

Webb hurries off to bed. She tucks him in, checks the

clothes he's laid out, and quietly adds all the things he's forgotten. Long-sleeved shirt, shoes, warm socks—she can read his optimism in what he's omitted. When she's done she walks down the hall and knocks on Cass's door.

"Don't come in!" Cass cries.

"I won't look," Penny says. "I just want to check out your clothes for tomorrow." She waits in the hall for a minute and then opens the door. Cass's room, as always, looks like the wreckage of a sailing ship. In the corner some huge construction of hers hides under an old sheet.

"What are you building this week?" Penny asks.

"Don't look! It's not ready yet." Cass pulls her over to the bed. The room smells strongly of glue and burnt wood.

"Are you using the wood-burning set again? I thought we agreed you'd only do that outside."

"I just did it for a minute," Cass says. "To finish off the towers."

Penny sighs. There's no explaining Cass's mania for building—when Penny wrecked their sailboat last year, Cass built a model of it from crumpled tinfoil and Popsicle sticks. Penny's afraid she'll end up building houses or running a bulldozer somewhere. Even Ben has mixed feelings about Cass's talent: he's sure she inherits it from him, and yet he regards it with suspicion.

"I think I've got everything," Cass says.

She does, even to extra pants and socks in case she gets wet. "That's great," Penny says. "Daddy would be proud of you."

"When's he going to look at my project?"

"Tomorrow, I guess."

"You two have another fight?"

"Of course not," Penny says. "And those aren't fights. They're disagreements."

"Sure," Cass says, sniffing as if she knows better.

"Go to sleep, okay?" Penny closes Cass's door behind her and goes back to the kitchen, where she makes sandwiches and loads the coolers. It's midnight before she goes to bed, and still no sign of Ben.

She sleeps restlessly, dreaming of pelicans. Last winter, when Ben was between girlfriends and trying to win Penny back, the two of them drove to Florida with Otis and Cindy to fish. Penny, perhaps for the last time, was willing to be won; Ben set after her with all the concentration of his younger self. They stayed up late and drank fruited drinks and danced on the balcony. Mornings they fished for sailfish and shark and barracuda; afternoons they slept on the beach and watched the pelicans fish from the piers. A month later, after they came back, Ben had someone else. And now, in Penny's dream, the birds fly heavily behind her as she soars up a mountain in a chair lift. Cass and Webb crouch at the base, somehow left behind. When Penny reaches the summit, the two pelicans settle on her empty chair and crane their necks around, staring suspiciously at the snow. She skis off on a trail that's headed toward a cliff, knowing that when she reaches the edge she'll be able to fly. The birds look as if they'd like to come. "Fly!" she whispers to them. But their feet are stuck in the slats of the chair. The chair lift creaks; the chair with the pelicans whirls slowly around the giant gear; the birds head downhill without her, their mouths open hungrily.

The next morning, the water gleams pink in the sun. On the roof of the loading shed, four long lines of gulls squat sullenly, squabbling at the fishermen. Webb's brown face pales as the party boat pulls away from the dock. The boat is enormous, dirty and loud where they're crammed in the back with the engine.

"Are you okay?" Penny asks him. He didn't eat much breakfast and she wonders if he's seasick already. She feels a little queasy herself—bad coffee, fifty or sixty raucous men on the boat who are joking and tripping over their coolers, fish scales stuck here and there on the woodwork like tiny mirrors. Evil fumes from the inboard hang in the still morning air. Cass and Webb are the only children on board; Penny is one of only four women. The men, strangers except for Ben and his three business friends, are already drinking beer and telling the captain they want to go way out into Nantucket Sound. Penny imagines mountainous waves and wonders how angry Ben will be when she and the children throw up.

"I'm fine!" Webb says.

It seems he's only pale from the excitement. He clutches the rod that Ben rented for him as if he'll never let go, and he fingers the well-oiled gears of the reel with reverence. Cass is much more casual—she's let Ben carry her rod and has asked him to tie on the plug. Penny didn't take a rod, but she has two big coolers to guard and no one to help her with them. The men have already gone forward to jostle for prime territory along the bow rail. "You wait here," Ben said to her and the kids. "We'll be right back." He isn't looking at Penny this morning—he came home at three last night and showered before he came to bed. When Ben stalked off toward the front of the boat, Quincy ruffled Webb's hair and said they'd find him a great spot. Ben's other friends, Don and Matt, only laughed when Cass said, "And me too?"

"Sure, honey," the men said. "And you too."

Penny doesn't like them calling her daughter "honey." From the minute they arrived at the house at dawn, loud and pink and freshly shaved, they've managed to make it clear that this is a male expedition. They have money, connections, things to do. Penny is there to take care of the food and clothes; Cass is there to get in the way. The men kidded Ben for taking Cass along, ignoring Cass's angry flush. Now Cass isn't talking to anyone, and Penny suspects her of plotting dark plots.

Matt comes back to them, inching his way down the row of men and tackle that already lines the side of the boat. "We've got a great place!" he calls. "Why don't you bring the kids up?" He heaves one cooler onto his shoulder and leaves Penny and Cass and Webb to struggle with the other. It's much too heavy for them to lift. They push the cooler toward the bow bit by bit, following Matt and banging the backs of strangers' knees. By the time they get forward Penny feels conspicuous. She's panting slightly, already tired; the three other women on the boat cling to their husbands' sides and eye her suspiciously. Ben and Don take the cooler and push it up to the wooden rail.

"Here," Ben says to Webb. "You can stand on this. And Cass, you stand on the other one."

Penny's stomach somersaults as her children climb up on the coolers. They're wearing life jackets at her insistence, but it troubles her to see the railing only up to their waists. A sudden wave, a quick stop, and they'd be over the side and into the foam below. For a minute she sees their limp bodies streaming through the air like gulls. She catches herself before she says anything. This is their day, their trip; she's promised herself not to spoil it by fussing over them. She's been afraid of the water since she tore the bottom of their sailboat out on the flat rock hidden near the tip of the island. She swims, of course. But floating and floating as she did that day, hanging onto the mast until the current carried her over to the island—then waiting there all alone until dusk fell and Ben thought to row out and look for her—it's changed the way she feels about the water. She's come to love the Cape and the ocean but wonders if she'll ever go out on a boat again, except to protect her children. Now she contents herself by holding her hands just at the edge of their life jackets, unseen and unfelt but ready to grab.

Next to her, the men are checking over the tackle and plotting their strategy. Ben whispers to them, "Lean the rods against the railing. Spread out, spread out! And get Penny up here." He tugs Penny unceremoniously to a spot at the railing. "Matt, you take this front corner. Don, you hold the end of the line next to Webb. Quincy and I will hold the middle."

His eyes are sparkling, his freckled hands directing them as if they are troops. He approaches this trip as if he's a general in a war, scheming for the best position and the most space. It doesn't seem fair to Penny. The herd of other men on the boat have all paid the same five bucks for standing room and the chance to catch a fish. She can overhear their conversations; some of them have driven here from Boston. This is poor folks' entertainment, and she and Ben and his friends aren't poor folks anymore. When she looks around she's embarrassed to see that their group has effectively taken over the bow. Ben shoos away the men who try to squeeze in. He points to Penny, to Cass, to Webb. Women and children first, is what he says without a word—would you crowd happy children and their mother? The men fall back, abashed, and move to the sides. Cass and Webb delight in the space and the open view of the crashing waves. They're unaware of Ben's maneuverings.

They cruise calmly for an hour or so. Ben and Matt and Quincy and Don make a serious dent in the beer— they squat around their cooler drinking and talking about the new development they're planning in Cotuit. Penny eavesdrops occasionally but isn't really interested. The way Ben's described it, he's putting up the brains and the others are putting up the money. From the little she overhears she can't be sure. Quincy in particular is full of ideas and wants to bring in a new architect. Ben agrees with this but twists the conversation until it sounds like his own suggestion.

"Mommy," Cass says. "Can we have a sandwich now?"

It's the first thing she's said all morning. While the men talk and Webb gasps over each new wave and gull and vision, she's been sitting on her cooler with her deep eyes hooded.

"Sure," Penny says. When Cass gets up Penny opens the cooler and digs out sandwiches for all of them. She laughed at Webb yesterday, but she has in fact made them all four sandwiches apiece. Even without pirates and sea adventures, this promises to be a long day. The men take their sandwiches without a word, deep in business discussions. Webb says, "Daddy, when are we going to be there?"

Ben breaks off in the middle of a sentence, scans the water, and says, "Real soon, I bet. The captain will want to get us out to where there's a good rip."

"Right," Webb says. Penny tugs Webb to her and sits him down on his cooler. He's frozen with attention, hoping to be the first to spot fish. Penny eats her sandwich and wonders if this day will ever end. Another hour passes before the boat stops, and by then everyone but Webb is cranky. Penny's tired and sunburned and the men have had too much beer. Cass has fallen asleep. She jumps when the captain's voice booms over the loudspeaker.

"Okay, everyone!" he shouts. "We'll start here. Don't crowd each other, and don't tangle your lines. If anyone hasn't rented equipment yet, please step to the rear and we'll take care of you."

As Penny watches, the whole boat stirs like a hill of ants. The men rush to the rails, check the knots on their plugs, and add pork rind to triple-barbed hooks. Hats fall overboard. Coolers are kicked aside. Webb says, "Daddy? Now, now?" His whole body quivers. Penny

stands behind Cass, trying to stay out of the way. Matt
and Don and Quincy cast their plugs overboard and
then turn to help the kids, but Webb wants to do his
himself. With Ben standing next to him he readies his
plug, flips the bail on the reel, and lets the line go. He's
holding the rod so tightly that his knuckles are white.

Ben's friends help Cass instead. She doesn't complain,
although she rolls her eyes at Penny when Quincy says,
"Let me help you with that, little lady." She lets him
take care of the plug, lets Matt set the reel and Don
show her how to hold the rod. Ben stands behind her,
checking everything from time to time as he gets his
own line in. Only when Cass says to Don, "Are you
sure you wouldn't rather hold this yourself?" does
Penny realize how angry she is. Cass hates to be told
how to do anything.

"Isn't this great?" Ben says, grinning. "Isn't this
great?" He isn't speaking directly to anyone but to all of
them—all except Penny, who isn't fishing. She sighs
and makes up her mind to enjoy the sun. It was her
decision not to rent a rod.

Behind her she hears a huge shout of glee as a bald
man in plaid Bermudas hauls up a small striped bass.
It's two pounds, maybe, certainly no more than three.
Webb turns around and nearly faints when he sees it.
"Striper!" he whispers. "We must be over a school!"

"Go to it, kid!" Quincy laughs. He ruffles Webb's
hair.

Soon the air is thick with cries and exclamations.
"I've got one!" Penny hears again and again. "I've got a
bite!" "It's huge!" "Move over!" Most of the cries seem
to come from the left side of the boat; Penny senses this
along with everyone else and watches the crowd of men
pour over there. The boat tips slightly but is too big to
move much, even though the right rail is almost empty.

"Slide down," Ben whispers. "Fill up some of that
space!" He thrusts his rod into Penny's hands and

makes a quick march down their company. He offers respectful tips to his three wealthy friends—set that drag a little tighter, perhaps? Consider another plug? He's more blunt with Cass and Webb. "Hold your tip up," he tells Cass, reaching around her with both his arms and angling the rod. "You want to be able to set the hook when you get a strike."

Cass nods, her teeth set into her lower lip. She's standing right next to Webb and keeps sneaking looks at him to see if she's doing things right. Webb looks as if he's been fishing for years. His feet are wide apart and his knees are braced; his thumb lies gently on the line to feel the least vibration. Ben pats him on the shoulder and says, "That's great, that's great. Don't forget to jerk hard when you get a nibble. You want to get him right *here!*" He hardly looks at Cass. He reaches around, crooks his finger under Webb's upper lip, and pulls hard against it.

"Okay, Daddy," Webb says. "Okay." He looks startled, but he laughs when Ben stretches his mouth out.

"All right, then," Ben says. "Let's catch some fish."

If Penny didn't know better, she'd swear he had been a Marine. He's on his way back to reclaim his rod when she feels the first little thump. Thump, bump—as if someone is nudging the tip of her rod. She looks at Ben, but before she can ask him what to do she feels a sudden solid jerk and then a burn on her thumb as the line rips off the reel.

"Jesus!" Ben shouts. "Would you look at that!"

"You take it!" Penny screams. "I don't know what to do!"

"Keep the tip up—get your hand off the line. Loosen the drag!"

She doesn't know what the drag is. Something huge is pulling on her line, pulling down on the rod—she feels as if she's hooked a boat. She struggles with the rod, no longer hearing anything but noise. Everyone, it seems, is shouting at her. Ben is right next to her now—she's just about to hand him the rod when she sees Webb's rod bend nearly double.

"Look!" she cries. Ben spins away from her and is at Webb's side in a flash. Quincy reels in his own line and comes to stand next to her.

"You want to take it?" she gasps.

"No," he says soothingly. "You're doing fine. Just keep the tip up while he's tugging, and reel in the minute you feel any slack."

Gradually the feel of the fish becomes familiar. Quincy is a good coach, not as hysterical as Ben; with his help she starts to bring the fish in. As she gets more confident, she's able to sneak glances at Webb. The others have cleared a space around him so he can stand back and brace his feet—only Cass is still jammed next to him. Her own rod lies forgotten on the deck, and she clenches her fists as she hisses encouragement to him.

"Come on, come *on*!" Penny can hear her say. Cass looks as if she'd like to do it herself.

"What a fighter!" Matt yells. "You're doing great!"

Muscles Penny's never seen before are standing out on Webb's soft arms. His eyes are huge, and his face tenses with concentration as he starts to reel in. Penny brings her own fish in almost absentmindedly. She keeps dropping her tip as she watches Webb and brings it up only when Quincy reminds her. A silver fish leaps suddenly from the water near the boat. Hers? Webb's? She's not sure until she hears Ben holler.

"Reel in, Webb!" he shouts. "Keep some tension on the line or he'll shake the hook loose!"

Webb's hands blur beside the reel.

"You're doing fine," she hears Quincy say to her. "I'll get the net."

She wrenches her eyes away from Webb's struggle and sees that her own line points almost straight down. Her fish, directly below them, seems to have given up.

Webb's fish leaps again, closer this time. Once, twice, three times it tosses itself into the air and slams down sideways against the waves. Penny can feel the hook in her own mouth, the struggle to spit it out, shake it free. Almost, she wishes the fish would win.

"Reel in gently," Quincy says beside her. "It's going to feel heavy as soon as it clears the water. I'll slip the net down when it does, and then you swing the tip of the rod over the rail toward the cabin. It looks like a beauty."

Compared to Webb's her own fish seems irrelevant. It's decent-sized, striped black and silver, but very quiet. A lady fish, she thinks. A mother fish, too distracted to fight back. She's sorry she hooked it and wonders if she should set it free.

She turns her head away from Webb for just a minute, just long enough to swing her line over the bow and see her fish lying sleepily in Quincy's net. And then there's a sudden loud splash, a scream, and the sound of Ben swearing.

Penny drops her rod into Quincy's hands, leaving him to cope with the snarled tackle. Webb? Cass? But both her children are standing there, neither of them tossed overboard. Webb is standing there, but his hands are empty.

"I can't believe it!" Ben shrieks. "I told you to hang on!"

The fish is gone; the rod is gone. A little stream of bubbles marks the place where it sinks.

Ben's friends step away, embarrassed. They move to Penny's side and busy themselves with her fish. Penny is frozen. Webb hangs his head and begins to cry. "I couldn't help it," he gasps, as Ben yells at him. "She bumped into me." He points to Cass.

"I did not," Cass says. Penny watches her turn away as if this isn't her brother, isn't her problem. Cass picks up her own rod and reels in a little line.

"Did so!" Webb shouts. "You made me lose my fish!"

Ben cuffs him. "Don't act like a girl," he snaps. "You're just making it worse."

Webb sinks down to the deck in a ball of misery. He's waiting, Penny knows, for one kind touch from Ben, one forgiving word. Ben shrugs and walks away.

When Penny picks Webb up he turns his face from her. "It wasn't my fault," he sobs over and over, as she leads him to the bathroom.

"I know, sweetie. I know."

She washes his face. If Webb says Cass bumped him, Cass did. On purpose? Maybe—after a long day of being alternately ignored and teased and bossed around, Cass might be capable of that. Webb is the only person smaller than her, and she has no one else to pick on. Penny tries to imagine Cass's rage simmering until it popped out in a half-accidental nudge of Webb. She'd like to feed her husband and his friends to the sharks. They might as well have pushed Webb themselves— they've tormented Cass and fussed over Webb until something was bound to happen, and she supposes she's lucky that only Webb's rod landed in the water. This isn't the way she imagined her children growing, pitted against each other in unnatural wars, and she can't stand what's happening to them.

She feels something almost physical shift inside her head, feels herself entering that same circular room she was in when she met Ben. The room is studded with dusty dark doors and, although she has no idea which one she'll open, she knows she's about to open one. Already, she's licking her thumb and scrubbing away at the grimy nameplates, looking for clues beneath the dirt. Before long she'll open one and then follow some long corridor of possibility to its unknown end. As will Ben: The doors aren't there only for her. She can see, as clearly as she sees Webb's hurt face, that sooner or later Ben will fall in love, or in what he thinks of as love, and then he'll divorce her so quickly her head will spin. He resists the idea now, when they discuss it; he says they should stick it out until the kids are grown. But he won't. She can feel his defection coming, knows she ought to bring it about herself while she's prepared for it. She could go up onto the deck right now, shoulder his friends aside, and say: "Listen. I want a divorce." But she won't. She can't imagine where she'd go or what Cass and Webb would do.

She doesn't say anything when they go back up. She settles Webb on his cooler, calmly takes Cass's rod away, and gives the rod to Webb: simple justice. When Ben starts to object, she stares at him until he drops his eyes and backs away. Her own fish, her lady fish, lies disemboweled on the cleaning board. One dull eye stares up at the clouds, already filming over.

PART TWO
Cass

*We had the sky up there, all speckled with
stars, and we used to lay on our backs and
look up at them, and discuss about whether
they was made, or only just happened.*

—Mark Twain, *Huckleberry Finn*

The Region of Perpetual Occultation
(August 1966)

★   ★   ★   ★   ★   ★

Cass and Webb, armed with plastic buckets and slender, sharp-bladed tools, are digging dandelions in the backyard. Ben has promised them a penny for each weed.

"But only if you get the roots," he said. "I'm not counting any where you just get the leaves."

Which figures, Cass thinks. He's never given them anything for nothing. She jabs the blade into the heart of a big weed, severs the root, and splits the crown, knowing that this one won't count. She imagines sticking the weeder into her father's arm. He has freckles all over from fishing so much; she could prick each freckle with the weeder's points. Behind her, she hears Webb working patiently. Thunk, thunk. He throws two weeds into his bucket.

"How many you got?" Cass asks.

"A hundred and thirty-two."

Cass frowns and digs faster. She has only one hundred and five. From the corner of her eye she spies on

Webb. He lacks her speed and dexterity but makes up for it with patience. While she daydreams, pulls, complains to herself, stabs and pulls again, Webb just weeds. She can't beat up on him anymore. At nine, he's suddenly caught up to her in height and outweighs her by ten pounds. When she tickles him now, she has to be careful.

Before them the whole yard stretches, dotted with nodding yellow heads that freckle the grass like stars. She could weed for hours every day and never get them all. She supposes she ought to be grateful for this—even at a penny each the lawn is spread with money.

"When do you want to stop?" she asks Webb. It's almost six and the gnats are coming in. She swats at her face and neck.

"When we get to two fifty?" Webb says. "That ought to hold us a couple of days."

She agrees. Another hour and they'll be done. By then Ben will be home for supper, bringing with him the bovine Diane. She always thinks of Diane this way —in April, when they were first introduced, she'd learned the word "bovine" just in time to fit it to this short, blond woman whose chest juts out like a jiggling shelf. "I'd like you to meet my friend," Ben said. Some friend. Diane has a sweet smile and round blue eyes. She's twenty-three, too young, in Cass's opinion, to be hanging around with a man as old as her father. Too old to act like a little girl, although that's what she does when she visits.

"Shall we play a game?" she's apt to ask Cass and Webb, smiling as if they're still babies and not nine and almost eleven. "Or shall I read you a story?"

Cass would like to fling her books in Diane's face when she says that. She's been reading for seven years now; each summer she wins the local library's reading contest. She takes homes an armful of books, swallows them, and sits down with the librarian later to spit out the plots. And the bovine Diane moos, "Shall I read you a story?" She peers into Cass's room, studies the model ships and cities that Cass has built so carefully from cardboard and balsa wood, and says to Ben, "It's so sweet of you to help Cass like this."

The only time Ben helps her is when he drives her to the hardware store, and lately he hasn't been doing even that. Cass rides her bike down now and loads her basket with glue and wood and X-Acto blades, but she never contradicts Diane. It's no business of hers, she figures, if her father wants to waste his time. He brings home worse friends many weekends, paunchy men with pinkie rings and flamboyant wives. "The money men," Cass calls them. The men who act as Ben's business partners. Sometimes she wishes he had better taste. She understands that Ben needs these people for his business; she writes off Diane, his assistant at work, in the same way. Ben's explained that Diane researches titles for him, scouting out tracts of land he may want to buy. Cass has trouble believing that Diane is smart enough to do this.

She sighs, gives her bucket a vicious little kick, and knocks it over. She's lost track of her dandelion count. Her hands fly over the plants. "One forty-six," she mutters. "One forty-seven, one forty-eight, one forty-nine . . ."

"Hey," she calls to Webb. "How many you got now?"

"A hundred and eighty-four," Webb says serenely. He's wearing a cowboy hat that Ben brought home from some trip. It's too big and rests on his ears, bending them out a little and hiding most of his face. Beneath the brim she can see the dirt that streaks his jaw and neck. She digs faster, realizing that they'll have to stop in time to wash up before Ben gets home. This is Ben's rule, one of the millions he's invented since their mother went away.

"We have to be like soldiers," Ben says, in that self-

pitying voice Cass hates. "We have to take care of ourselves, now that your mother's gone." He posts lists on
their bedroom doors, menus on the refrigerator. They
keep themselves clean, wash up for company, vacuum
and dust and make their own beds. Cass helps Ben cook
each night. "Teamwork," he says. "That's what we need
around here—a little teamwork."

Cass slips her blade under a group of serrated leaves,
feels for the base, and plunges her weeder in thoughtfully. She wouldn't mind Ben's attitude so much if he
didn't pretend it was all her mother's fault. "Your
mother felt she had to leave," he says. "We had too
many disagreements."

Sure, Cass thinks. She knows about these disagreements. She'd seen her mother hurl the coffee pot across
the kitchen at her father, the hot liquid streaming behind the pot like a comet's tail. She'd sat frozen at dinner, holding Webb's hand while her parents hissed and
spat at one another. She knows all about these disagreements, and she knows one thing more, the thing that
makes a liar of her father. She knows what happened
the night before her mother went away.

It was early April when Penny burst into tears over a
plate of franks and beans. Webb's eye was swollen
where Cass had punched him; Cass's beautiful new doll
with the golden hair was full of arrows shot from
Webb's bow. Cass and Webb were still arguing—"He
started it," "She started it"—when Ben called to say he
wouldn't be home for supper. They stopped when
Penny started to cry.

"I'm sorry, Mommy," Cass said. She slapped Webb's
hand down and shot him a threatening glance, knowing
they'd gone too far.

But Penny didn't smile and tell them to make up, the
way she usually did. "It's not your fault," she snuffled.
And then she lit a cigarette and stared out the window
and wouldn't say anything else. Cass tried her hardest

not to fight with Webb anymore; she went into her
room and left him the TV. She propped herself up in
bed with a flashlight and a volume of Poe, so she'd be
sure to be awake when Ben got home.

It was past eleven when he came in. Cass had discovered some time ago that she could hear her parents
quite distinctly when she sat with her ear to the wall in
the closet that faced their room. When she heard Ben's
footsteps she crept into the closet and pushed her shoes
aside. Ben emptied his pockets with a sound of rolling
change, closed the window, and asked, "Did you think
about what I said?"

"No," Cass heard Penny say bitterly. "I did laundry
all day. What do you think I thought about?"

Penny's voice was as clear as ice, and Cass drew back
from the wall a little and made herself breathe quietly.
On her parents' side were glass shelves full of the ceramic elephants that Vivian had given Penny each
birthday, each Christmas, despite the fact that Penny
hated them and that Vivian knew she did. A little ritual
Cass had watched for years: Vivian hands over an elegant box, Penny unwraps it carefully, acts surprised,
draws out another fat pachyderm. Vivian smiles with
her lips, Penny smiles back. Ben adds the new creature
to the shelves he bought at his mother's suggestion. Cass
understood how her mother felt about this because her
own closet was full of Vivian's pink-cheeked china
dolls.

"So?" Ben said. "Let's get this over with."

Penny snorted unpleasantly. "All this time I've been
asking you, and now you're in this big hurry . . ."

Cass heard her father tapping something. His foot,
against the bed? His fingers, against the wall? His voice
was low and reasonable. "The sooner I move out," he
said, "the sooner we'll be divorced."

Cass caught her breath and moved away from the
wall. She knew about divorce—she'd heard Penny men-

tion it before and she knew a girl at school whose parents were separated. No more fishing trips, she thought. No more picnics. No more skiing. But also no more flying coffee pots, no more scenes at dinner. No more of Ben's piggy friends. We'll get used to it, she thought.

She glued her ear to the wall again when Penny laughed bitterly. "I've got news for you," Penny said. "You're not going anywhere. I rented a house in Grey Gables today."

"What?"

"I rented a house. I had a little money stashed away."

For a minute Cass couldn't hear anything, and then there was a sudden loud thump, as if Ben had punched something hard. "You bitch!" he said. "I told you you could have the house!"

"Fuck the house." Cass jumped at her mother's surprising word. "I don't want it. You want to be free, want to marry that bimbo—you take it. You clean it. You deal with Paine."

"You can't just up and move the kids like that."

"I'm not," Penny said quietly. "I'm leaving them with you."

Cass heard Ben sputter, that wet-lipped smacking sound he makes when he's too mad to talk. "You can't do that!" he said. "You wouldn't leave the kids."

"I'm not leaving them," Penny said. "I'll see them every weekend, the same as you would if you left. But I'm getting out."

"What kind of a mother are you?"

Penny didn't answer. The first small crash caught Cass by surprise—just a light, breaking sound muffled by the carpet. The next crash was louder. And then she heard a pop and a tinkle, a crash and another and then another, louder, faster, more deliberate, until she heard one sweeping explosion. The elephants! she thought, wincing at the last sound, which could only be the giant gray one from the top shelf. Sixteen or eighteen ele-

phants, their smooth colored ceramic sides grinding
into each other, their tusks snapping off, their hollow
heads crushed. She heard a firm pop from the floor, as if
someone had stepped quite slowly on one of the elephants' heads.

"Stop that!" Ben roared. "My mother gave you
those!"

A little pop and a tinkle—perhaps the last, smallest
elephant joining the pile.

"Stop me," Penny taunted. "Just try."

Cass tucked her head between her knees. It hadn't
occurred to her that Penny might leave. Always, when
Cass had imagined divorce, she'd imagined Ben gone.
It's true that she and Webb are obnoxious, fighting all
the time and destroying each other's toys. But she didn't
think they'd been that bad. She listened with half an ear
while her parents fought on. She heard crunching
noises, someone pacing back and forth through the elephant rubble.

"You won't get a cent," Ben said.

"Take your money and stuff it. I've got a job."

The noises stopped, and Cass sensed that Ben had
given in. "What am I supposed to do with them?" he
said. "I can't take care of them all week."

"Figure it out," Penny told him.

Ben was quiet for a minute. "Fine," he finally said.
"Fine. I wouldn't let them live with you *anyway*,
you . . ."

Cass couldn't listen to the rest. She crept into her bed
and pulled the covers over her head, pulling her pillow
with her until she came to rest with her head at the foot
of the bed and her feet sticking out in the cold. Was it
the black eye that did it? The arrows in the doll, the
stuffed sailfish they broke last month? The time she set
her pillow on fire with her lamp? The hole in the dinghy, perhaps, where she and Webb dropped the rock.
Or the way she'd picked on Paine. I can fix this, she

thought, as she tumbled into sleep. I'll apologize for everything in the morning and straighten this out.

But Penny came into her room at dawn, carrying Webb in her arms. She slid Webb under the blankets and hauled Cass's head into the light, and then she sat on the edge of the bed. Very softly, she said, "Listen, you two." They were hardly awake. "Mommy's going away now. Daddy and I aren't going to live together anymore, but we still love you and we're still both your parents."

Webb, understanding no more than her tone, started to cry. Cass just stared, wondering why her mother would make such a mistake. "Take us with you," she said. It was so obvious.

"I'll be right down the road," Penny said. "Just a couple of miles away. You'll come see me every weekend, and you'll stay with Daddy during the week."

"Would you stay if we promised not to fight anymore?" Cass asked. "If we're always good?" She nudged Webb and said, "We'll be good, won't we?"

"Perfect," Webb hiccupped.

Penny smiled and hugged them both, but she was crying too. "It's not you," she said. "Sillies. It's just that Daddy and I can't get along, and we decided we'd be better off in two separate houses. You'll have two houses now, instead of one. Twice as nice."

Cass began to cry. Penny wiped their faces with a corner of the sheet and said, "I want you to hang on to these for me." She pressed something small and cold into each of their hands, and then she left.

Ben came in later, while they were still huddled close to each other and clutching the smooth coral earrings that Penny had left them. They were her favorite pair. "Mommy's gone," Ben said. "She hasn't been feeling well, and she needs to be by herself for a while."

Since then, Cass has had little patience with Ben's sighs and put-upon looks. She knows, even if he doesn't, that the change in their lives is his doing. She suspects, now, that he is capable of anything, including forcing the bovine Diane upon them.

"Two fifty," Webb says smugly, tearing her from her thoughts. He tosses his weeder into the air and watches, smiling, as it lands point first in the flower bed.

"Cheater," Cass mutters. She has twenty-five to go, and she'd bet his pail is full of leaves. "Go wash up before the cow comes."

Webb makes a face. "Her again?"

"She's coming for supper."

Webb jams his cowboy hat further down on his head, curls his hands in front of him, and canters off on an imaginary horse. "Queen of the Cows!" he shouts, as he vanishes into the basement. "The bovine Diane!"

He leaves Cass alone with the gnats. "Don't forget to wash behind your ears!" she calls after him. "You know he'll look!"

When Diane arrives, she seems more cowlike than usual. She's wearing a sundress, cut low over her huge breasts and tied at the back with a bow. Her pale, smooth legs are bare. "Look," Cass whispers to Webb, who's watching from the window with her. "She looks like that doll you murdered."

Diane's blond hair curves neatly at her chin; her pink shoes match her dress and pocketbook. She's completely gross, Cass thinks. She really does look like a doll. She promises herself she'll never look like this. I'll wear shorts and T-shirts, she thinks. Even when I'm old. I'll never grow a chest like that. I'll build bridges and houses and airplanes and rockets. I'll go up on a Gemini spaceship and walk in a vacuum. She tugs at her bangs and straightens to her maximum height, an inch taller than Diane. Ha! she thinks. And I'm still growing.

"I brought you a present," Diane says, slinking through the open door. She holds out a large, flat box.

"Thank you," Cass says politely. She nudges Webb, who drops his eyes and mutters, "Thanks." When they unwrap the package, they find a set of Chinese checkers —a thin, curved, metal square with holes punched in the shape of a six-pointed star and marbles in six different colors. They have three sets already, one from each grandmother and one from a partner of Ben's. They never play. They use the marbles as ammunition for the slingshot Cass made, a copy of Paine's—forked stick, thick knotted elastic, leather pocket. When Paine sits on his porch firing pebbles at the gulls, they fire marbles over the fence and hope to strike him unseen. When they hear a muffled curse they know they've scored.

Cass hefts the marbles, noting with pleasure that they're bigger than usual. They'll be good to use against Paine. At night, when Ben works late and leaves them alone, Paine has taken to creeping up to the front door with plates of brownies and oatmeal cookies. "Cass!" he calls. "Webb! I brought you some dessert. May I come in?" Webb is all for letting him in—he says Paine is just lonely and, besides, he wants some dessert. Cass believes that Paine is bad. She pulls Webb into the huge hall closet when he comes, clears a space among the boots, and waits there with her slingshot until Ben comes home. She tries not to hear Paine's plaintive calls. She decides she'll hide these hefty marbles in a shoebox against the night she forgets to lock the door.

"Thank you," she says again. "The marbles are nice."

"I thought we could all play together," Diane says. "After supper."

"Sounds great!" Ben says heartily. "A real family get-together!"

For a minute, then, they are all embarrassed. This is no family, Cass wants to say. Not even close. What she says instead is, "What about the lawn?"

"What about it?" Ben asks.

"Remember? You promised to show me how to use

the mower." She's trying to convince him that she's old enough to do the lawn. She's going to ask him for five bucks a whack—she needs money for her projects and thinks mowing will be faster than dandelions.

"We'll see," Ben says. "Let's eat."

Diane flutters about the kitchen, trying to help Cass and Webb but only getting in the way. Cass has fixed salmon salad and biscuits and Webb has cut up some melon. There's nothing to do but put the food on the table.

"This is so *nice*!" Diane coos. "You're a real help around the house."

"Somebody has to do it," Cass says. When Diane moves near Ben she brushes against him, touches his shoulder, finds reasons to drop her fingers lightly on his arm. Cass slides between them whenever she can, re-coiling at the touch of Diane's soft flesh. She can't imag-ine that Ben likes the feel of that dough.

"Would you take that off while we eat?" Ben says. Webb is still wearing his cowboy hat, hiding his eyes beneath the lowered brim.

"But *Dad* . . ."

"Off. Now."

Cass watches in disgust as Diane lays a soothing hand on Ben's shoulders. She knows Webb would rather burn his hat than owe it to Diane. They've made a deal, a promise to each other, that they'll resist the cow's bribes and blandishments. She does not mean well. Quite deliberately, Cass knocks her salad into Diane's lap. "Oh!" she says. "I'm sorry."

"Goddamnit!" Ben shouts.

Diane jumps up and flushes. "That's all right," she says with a pained smile. "It was an accident." She gath-ers the salmon into her napkin and scrubs at the oily mayonnaise stain with a paper towel. "She didn't mean it, did she?"

Cass shakes her head but tries to say with her eyes

that she did. Go away! she shouts inside her head. Read my mind! I hate you! She smiles, baring her teeth. Diane smiles back, all forgiving sweetness. She's either stupider than Cass thinks, or much smarter. Something is happening here that Cass doesn't understand.

"I'm sorry," she says again. She clears the plates and brings out a bowl of instant chocolate pudding and a can of whipped cream. "Can I help?" Webb asks. She lets him scoop the pudding into small glass bowls. Carefully, she sprays a circle of whipped cream around each perimeter, a smaller circle within, a mound in the center. Bull's-eyes. She studies these, wondering if she can add small rectangles within the concentric circles. If she pushes the dispenser button very quickly, very gently, she could make small puffs, like clouds.

"Cass," Ben says warningly. "Let's not get carried away, okay? We're just going to eat it."

Diane looks down at her bowl, poising her spoon above the edge. "It's almost too pretty to eat," she says. As if to disprove her, Cass stirs her own bowl violently and reduces her design to mush. She and Webb eat silently while Ben tells Diane about some piece of land he's chasing.

"Check the deeds Monday," he says. "See who owns that wedge near the bridge."

"Let's do the lawn," Cass interrupts.

"Why not tomorrow?" Diane says. "You'll have lots of sun then, plenty of time. It'll be dark in an hour or so."

"Tomorrow," Webb announces, "we're going to see our mother. She has a dog and cats and fish."

Ben makes a little face at Diane that Cass knows she's not supposed to see, and for a minute she wishes her mother hadn't suddenly become so purposefully eccentric. Each new thing she does only gives Ben more ammunition, allows him to argue that Penny's not fit to have them. Already he grips Cass and Webb as self-righteously as if he had taken them on purpose. And in fact, if Cass hadn't had her closet she'd never have known he hadn't.

Diane shrugs her plump shoulders. "All right," Ben says and slaps the table lightly. "Let's do the lawn."

The riding mower rests beneath the tulip tree. Ben checks the oil, starts it up, and signals for Cass to hop on behind him. Webb watches jealously—he's stuck with Diane near the door. "Show me how!" Cass shouts over the roaring engine. She's been watching Ben do this for years. She knows where the throttle is, the brake and the clutch and the lever that engages the blades. She knows that she can do it.

"Watch!" Ben shouts. She cranes her head over his shoulder and watches as he puts it into gear, lowers the blade, and steers in gentle circles. Together they mow the small oval of lawn enclosed by their horseshoe-shaped driveway. "Where there's a rise," Ben yells, "mow across it, not up and down. You ready to try?"

When she says she is, he drives the mower over to the side lawn and shuts it off. Diane trails them anxiously. "Ben!" she calls. "Are you sure this is a good idea? She's awful young."

"You promised!" Cass hisses at Ben.

"It's okay," Ben calls. Step by step he explains the mower. Cass nods and nods again—she's seen him do this a hundred times. She understands. Webb scampers away from Diane and runs to the tire hanging from the oak. He stands in the hollow circle, swaying back and forth while Cass mounts the machine alone. "If anything happens," Ben calls, "just turn it off, okay?"

"Okay." She's not nervous—this is simple. Anyone could do it. She starts the engine, surprised at the way the steering wheel vibrates in her hands. Slowly, she lets out the clutch and gives it the gas. The mower bucks, stutters, and stops. Ben makes a motion with his hands, pressing the right one smoothly down while the left rises smoothly up. "Gently!" he calls. "Feather it!"

Cass nods. She knows, she knows. She starts it up again, willing her feet to work together in one smooth motion. The mower glides across the lawn.

"Yay!" Webb calls from his tree. "Yay!"

Cass drops the mower blade and sails across the yard. She looks behind her and sees the clean-mown strip she's made. She turns at the driveway and sails back, setting her right wheel in the track she's just made. The grass falls in perfect bands.

"You're doing great!" Ben calls. "Just keep going!"

"I'm doing great," she whispers happily. She cruises out to the edge of the lawn and decides she'll mow in a spiral, working in toward the center. She looks over at Ben to see if he still approves, but he's not watching. He's standing next to Diane with his hand on her waist; Diane's head is tilted up to his, as if she wants to lick him. As if, Cass thinks, he is a giant ice cream cone. Diane pivots around Ben's hand, coming closer to him. They will kiss, Cass sees. If not now, soon. Alone, if not in front of her. She can't keep her eyes from Diane's feet, which are inching across the grass toward Ben like stealthy snakes. "Watch out!" she wants to call to Ben. "Keep an eye on those feet!" But Ben isn't paying attention.

"Cass!" Webb shouts. "Can I come up?" He's left his tree and is running beside her now, somehow aware that Ben isn't watching them.

"Sure," Cass says. She slows the mower and hauls Webb up behind her. He wraps his arms around her waist and yells, "Giddyap!"

It's not Cass's fault that she mows down a mole the next morning. She's sulky and dirty and hot, her legs itching from the cut grass; she has the whole back yard to do yet and it's much less fun that she'd imagined. She

steers blindly, angrily. Worse than the mowing is the
dark suspicion bubbling in back of her eyes. She heard a
car slip into the driveway last night, an hour after Diane left. She heard Ben tiptoe down the hall and open
the door, although no one knocked or rang the bell. She
thinks she heard Diane's voice toward morning; she
knows she heard a car drive off near sunrise. And yet
Ben was there for breakfast, smiling dreamily and playing with his cereal. She is mulling over these odd bits of
information, thinking how much she hates this feeling
that things are happening behind her back, when she
sees the mole just in front of her. Crouched in the grass,
his long nose lowered and his plump feet splayed, he
huddles as if he could flatten himself out of danger. She
wrenches the wheel, but she's on top of him before the
mower responds. With a shudder she looks over her
shoulder, expecting blood and dismembered limbs and
perhaps, worst of all, a head—but there is nothing. No
sign that the mole was ever there. Maybe he got away,
she thinks. More likely she has vaporized him. There
may be small moles underground, fatherless now; she
may have erased a whole family without seeing them.
She parks the mower at the edge of the lawn and stalks
inside, leaving a great wedge of uncut grass waving in
the breeze.

She's still sulking when Penny comes to pick them
up. The mole's fate, still unknown, merges in her mind
with the late-night car sounds, the secret looks, the
snakelike feet in the grass. When the horn honks for her
she's lying frozen on her bed, trying to stop the world
from spinning so quickly about her. She doesn't want to
stay here; she doesn't want to go to Penny's, where even
after four months she still feels like she's visiting. It's
not home there, no matter what Penny does; their own
home isn't home without her. I hate this, she thinks
wildly. She grabs her bag and checks the lawn again for

the mole's remains, for his orphaned offspring, before she joins her family in the driveway. The lawn is clean.

Penny kisses her and tosses their bags in the car. "Webb," she says, "did you bring your homework?"

"Yup," he says. "And coloring books."

Cass snorts. Webb reads poorly, does math on his fingers, and colors outside the lines. Their teachers can't believe that he and Cass are related. They think she's so smart, but she can't see what good that does when all these things are happening behind her back.

Chuck, Penny's Chihuahua, greets them at the other house. His head bobs up, disappears, and bobs up again as he leaps between the aquariums that line the porch walls. "Mom!" Webb squeals. "Look at Chuck!"

"You ought to put that thing out of his misery," Cass grumbles. She hates Chuck, hates his smooth shining body and the way his skin shows through his hair. Mizar and Alcor, Penny's twin cats, are chasing Chuck mercilessly. He bounds from the chair to the table to the tanks, in peril of falling through each hinged lid. Cass hopes he'll drown. She hates him and she hates this small, cramped house, where she has to share a bedroom with Webb and shower in a narrow metal stall. Webb runs in before her and throws himself on Penny's bed, which takes up half her room.

"Mom," Cass says. "Will you help me with my project?"

"I had to bring a pile of stuff home from the office," Penny says. "But I'll try and help you later, after I finish and after I help Webb with his homework."

"Thanks," Cass mutters. Penny has a job at Canal Hardware now, and it drives Cass crazy that she brings work home. That stupid adding machine and its rolls of tape, big ruled ledgers, special pens—all in a house where old magazines already silt up the corners. There are no elephants here, but there are aquariums green with algae and huge sprays of reeds and rushes and cat-tails already losing their fluff.

"Where's my stuff ?" Cass calls from the kitchen.

"Under your bed," Penny says.

"Wonderful," Cass says. Last week she left her X-Acto knife, heavy cardboard, masking tape, black construction paper, Elmer's glue, and a can of lumines-cent paint on the kitchen table—everything she needs for the celestial sphere she's making. *Build a Star Dome!* read the caption in the astronomy magazine. The pic-ture showed a boy with a goofy grin holding a big card-board hemisphere over his head and pointing out the constellations. *Your Own Miniature Planetarium!* It looked easy. Last Sunday she made patterns from newspaper, cut the cardboard and the construction paper to shape, and numbered the pieces. Using the map in the maga-zine as a guide, she drew the constellations on the black paper and marked each star with a dot of luminescent paint. Now she's going to glue it together, if she can manage to find anything. Penny's clothes and books and dishes are strewn throughout the house, but each week, between their visits, she tucks away the few things that Cass and Webb have left behind. Like she's hiding us, Cass thinks. Like we don't exist.

She roots under her bed and finds her tools and frag-ile pieces of cardboard in a box. In the other bedroom, she can hear Penny murmuring with Webb over his spelling list. "Complete," Penny says. "Spell 'com-plete.' " Webb stumbles over even this.

"Complete," Cass mutters. "Completely dumb." The kitchen table, where she always works, is piled with Penny's junk. She stacks the bills and papers on the floor, spreads out the pieces of her project, and settles in to work. She has twelve pieces of cardboard in front of her, each one shaped like an elongated, slightly rounded wedge of pie. She has twelve pieces of black construc-tion paper cut to the same shape and dotted with pale green stars. She glues each black sheet over its cardboard mate and lets the pairs sit. No problem, she thinks. This is the easy part.

"Now," the instructions say, "lay the pieces on your work surface, black side down, and join the tips together. Make sure the pieces are evenly spaced, and then tack them in place with masking tape. Cut a circle of cardboard one and a half inches in diameter, and glue this over the tips to anchor them in place."

She clenches her tongue between her teeth and forms a twelve-petaled daisy. "Let dry," the instructions read. "Meanwhile, cut twelve narrow cardboard strips the length of the sections, and set them aside. These will be your reinforcing strips."

She reads ahead, trying to get the final steps clear in her mind. Somehow, she has to bend the petals of this daisy into a hemisphere. She plays with her newspaper patterns, tacking them with masking tape as she bends the edges down and in. Miraculously, they meet and, until the tape pops off, she holds half a fragile globe. This is going to be one of those theory things, she sees. In theory it works—the twelve sections should form a perfect hemisphere when she anchors them to the rim. But in practice they're going to fly apart. "Overlap the edges slightly, and glue the reinforcing strips over the joints." The instructions don't tell her how to hold the stiff cardboard sections in place, or how to keep them from springing out like rubber bands. "Bend each section gently," they say. They don't say how.

All afternoon she struggles with this. She tries paper clips, bobby pins, masking tape—the sections fight back as if they're alive. The hemisphere is like a bridge, each piece under tension until the whole thing is done. She uses too much glue. Her hands get sticky. Her hair jabs in her eyes. Penny comes in, takes a look at her, and leaves quietly. Webb wanders by to grab some cookies but goes away when she won't talk. She can't talk.

"Cass," Penny says gently, hours later. "It's time to eat. You want to stop for a while?"

When Cass looks up, a just-glued section pops from its place. She bursts into tears. Nothing, she thinks, is ever going to work again. She can almost hear what her mother is thinking: that she made the right decision, that Cass and Webb don't belong in this small, dark house with the birds and the cats and the dopey dog, especially not while Penny is figuring out what she's doing, what she wants. Some part of Penny's mind (or so Cass thinks) envisions Cass and Webb better off just because they live in a clean house with a man and a visiting cow willing to act as parents. Remember Vivian? Cass wants to ask. The elephant woman, Miss Priss? Think she was fun to live with? Cass never visits Bryant and Vivian if she can help it, and she can't understand how Penny would want her to live like that. As if it makes a difference that they're fed well, dressed well. As if they would die if they were left alone. So you made a stupid decision, she wants to tell her mother. Undo it. Take us back.

She continues to cry. Penny looks at her helplessly and says, "Don't take it so hard—I'll help you after supper, if you want. But come eat, okay?"

Cass sniffs and wipes her face, wishing she could put her head in Penny's lap. But she's no baby—she's almost as tall as Penny. Webb lays his soft cheek on her head and says, "I'll help you later." They eat canned chicken fricassee in bed and watch the news while Chuck curls in Penny's lap. After supper they feed the angelfish. Webb holds the lid open while Cass sprinkles in the flakes, and this gives her an idea.

"Can I borrow your hands?" she asks Webb. "And yours too, Mom?" She leads them to the table and has them anchor the sections as she bends them down. "That's great!" she says. "Don't move."

"But honey . . ." Penny says.

"Just for a minute." Quickly, Cass spreads glue on a reinforcing strip, bends it to shape, and presses it over the joint made by two sections. She moves one of Penny's hands over the joint. "Press," she says. "But not too hard." She glues another section, another and another, using the hands of her mother and brother as clamps. When the glue sets she anchors four more sections, and finally the last four. She has a hemisphere as fragile as their lives.

"No one move," she says.

"I want a Coke," Webb says.

"In a minute."

Webb sighs patiently. The three of them stand with their hands spread in a circle at the base of the dome. Cass forms the rim and tapes it into place, gluing it down with more reinforcing strips. "That's it," she says. "Let go."

They pull their hands away one at a time and step back slowly. Cass waits for the dome to fly apart, but nothing happens. It's done. Penny fluffs Cass's hair and says, "It's beautiful. Really. Why don't you come watch TV with us now?"

"In a minute," Cass says—she has a surprise for them yet. She takes the dome into the bathroom and holds it to the light for five minutes, and then she brings it into Penny's room and turns off the TV and the lamp.

"Hey!" Webb protests. "We were watching."

"Watch this," Cass says. She stretches out on the bed between them and holds the dome over their heads. In the dark room, the special paint that marks the stars glows furiously. The stars stretch above them in a twinkling curve that echoes the night sky.

"I'll be damned," Penny says. She draws her head closer to Cass, so that they're all crowded under the dome. "Looks almost real."

"That's the idea," Cass says. She turns the dome so that the Big Dipper is right side up, and she names the constellations as Penny taught her. "Big Dipper, Little Dipper, Cassiopeia, Cepheus, Hercules—"

"Draco," Penny points out. "Corona Borealis."

"Where?" Webb says. "All I see are dots."

Penny traces the constellations for him. "Wow!" he says. "This is great!"

"You did a good job," Penny tells Cass.

Cass is so proud she could fly. She didn't build the dome for Webb, but she's glad he likes it. They can use it to show him everything—he gets lost when they take him up to the roof at night. The sky doesn't make sense to him; the dots are just dots.

"If you rotate this," Cass tells him, "you can see how the stars rise and set at night." She spins the dome and shows him Andromeda rising. Penny's arm is warm about her shoulders. For a minute they're silent, and Cass imagines them lying in a dark field with the sky spread out above them. No Ben, no Diane, no confusion of houses and schedules. Just the three of them, watching the stars at night.

"Mom," she whispers. One last try. "Can we come live here?"

Penny doesn't answer. She never does.

"Mom," Webb says. "Where's the other half?"

"The other half of what?"

"The other half of the star dome—the part that isn't here. Isn't this only half the sky?"

"You built it," Penny says to Cass. "See if you can explain."

"We can only see half the sky from where we live," Cass says hesitantly. She knows this isn't much of an answer.

"Why can't we see the rest?"

Cass shrugs. Why can't we live here? she wants to say. Why did Penny leave them? Why is the sky blue? "I don't know," she says.

"It's complicated," Penny says gently. "It has to do

with latitude and horizons and the local celestial meridian. But you're right—there's a whole other dome of stars that we can't see from here, from the south celestial pole to a certain place below the celestial equator."

Cass is listening with great concentration. She knows the stars a little but not the way that Penny does; she built the star dome without thinking about the missing half.

"It's called the region of perpetual occultation," Penny says. "The place where we can never see the stars rise. When something's occulted, it's hidden from view."

"The region where the stars hide," Cass murmurs.

"They're lost?" Webb asks.

"Not lost—just invisible to us. People who live in other places can see them, but then they can't see the ones we can."

Like everything, Cass thinks. Everything important in her life seems to be hiding in that region, lost from sight, lost to her. No matter how hard she works to understand the things she can see, she'll never get the parts, just as important, that are hidden from her. She shivers and wonders where Ben is this night, remembering Diane's feet snaking through the grass.

Webb sighs happily. "This is great," he says. "Will you let me use it sometimes, if I'm good?"

"Whenever you want," Cass says with sudden decision. "I made it for you."

He flips on the light and hugs her. "Thanks," he says. "You can show me all the stars."

"I can show you what's here," Cass says.

Webb cuddles up to Penny and leaves the star dome to Cass. In the light it's just a cardboard ball spotted with glue and tape.

By Gemini
(April 1967)

★　　　★　　　★　　　★　　　★　　　★

The TV flickers like a spirit in the darkened room. Against a backdrop splashed with a Gemini spaceship lifting off in a cloud of flame, two newscasters sit with their heads inclined to each other. From the way they gesture at the scene behind them, which shows now an astronaut floating in space, tethered by a silver umbilical cord, now the nose of a capsule nudging into alignment with a docking station, they might be reviewing the entire space program. Cass can't be sure of this, because she can't hear their words; the TV is silent because, over the past half hour, she's reached up secretly several times and lowered the volume until it's off. The room is perfectly quiet now, so still she can hear the waves gnawing at their beach.

"Cass?" Webb whispers. "Are you awake?"

"Shh," she says. "Yes." She rolls across the floor to him, over the nest of pillows and quilts that Ben spread out for them earlier. They're at the foot of the big bed, where Ben and Diane are finally asleep. Her secretive arm reaching up for the knob was a test they both failed.

Webb nudges her knees with his scratchy soles and opens his mouth. "Quiet," she says. "Don't wake them up."

His face is blue in the light of the TV. "I won't," he whispers, with the corners of his mouth turned down. He leans his head against her shoulder and mutters, "What a birthday."

For a minute she's afraid that he'll cry. This tenth birthday of his has been a disaster, and although Penny tried to cheer him this morning with pancakes and a new tackle box, even her efforts couldn't take the sting from the minute when they climbed from her car to face Ben and Diane beaming in the doorway. "Happy Birthday!" Ben called. "How about giving your new stepmother a big hug!"

The day has only gotten worse since then. Cass and Webb hugged when they were told to, smiled when they thought they should, and nodded politely when Ben and Diane told them about their honeymoon in Vermont. They struggled through an awkward dinner, unable to watch Diane cook on Penny's stove and handle Penny's plates, unwilling to admit how good the lobster really was. Cass made her face a perfect blank, imagining how she'd flee to her room the minute dinner was done. Webb's foot tapped the floor next to her, twitching with the same desire—a need to be alone so fierce that it rushed them through the homemade chocolate cake and ice cream. They put down their spoons and stood when they were done, but Ben shepherded them into his bedroom before they could get away. He moved Diane's half-unpacked boxes back against the wall, spread quilts and pillows on the floor, and said, "Let's all watch TV in here tonight. It'll help us get comfortable."

Cass and Webb looked at each other and rolled their eyes. Ben ignored the display. "Go put your pajamas on," he said. "And then come back in here." They dawdled for as long as they could. When they returned, embarrassed to be wearing pajamas in front of a stranger, they found Ben and Diane propped up in bed in their nightclothes. Webb's mouth opened so wide that Cass had to kick him. He closed his lips with a swift pop.

"You can sit up here with us," Ben said easily. "Or you can sit down there on the floor."

Without a word they lay on the floor, not protesting even when Ben changed the channel to one of the old war movies he loves and they hate. They stared at the flickering screen, watching tanks crunch over stone walls, bazookas expel big clouds of smoke with a hollow crack. An American ducked into an alley and successfully hid from a Nazi platoon, despite the fact that his coattail was visible. Diane yawned, and Cass turned and caught her. A man with a mustache lobbed a grenade into a dilapidated barn. Cass wondered if she might die of boredom. Ben said, "Look at that," and "Watch this guy," but Cass and Webb refused to respond. Gradually Ben grew quiet until, by the time the movie was over, he was slumped against the wall and Diane was slumped against his shoulder.

Now Webb eyes their fallen shapes and says, "How long do you think they'll make us hang out with them at night?"

Forever, Cass thinks. They'll lock us in a room and make us sit with them forever. No reading, never any time alone. No playing. Just the four of them, some strange illusion of a family. "I don't know," she says. "Maybe it's just for tonight."

Webb sighs. "It smells in here," he says. "It's hot. You want to sneak outside for a couple of minutes?"

"I don't know—we should probably go to bed if we're going anywhere. They're liable to hear us."

They're quiet for a minute, evaluating the sounds from the bed. Ben snuffles with a sound somewhere between a breath and a sneeze. Diane makes no noise at all. On the TV screen, the scene changes to show a crowd of people writhing under the flashing lights of a discotheque. Cass flicks the set off and decides that what Webb smells is only Diane, some mixture of soap and perfume and shampoo that rises from her crisp flowered nightgown and freshly washed hair. She smells like a department store, like a dressing room. Already, she has wrinkled her nose at Cass's rumpled clothes and ragged hair.

"We could try," Cass says. She has a sudden fierce urge to breathe clean air. "But be real quiet."

They creep across the floor as if they're mice. Cass creeps into the hall and Webb follows her, dragging a blanket. They pad down the hall, through the living room, and out onto the balcony. It's cool out here, and very clear. They huddle under the blanket with their backs to the wall.

"That's better," Webb says. He juts his lower lip out and blows so that the hair on his forehead rises. "Do you believe the way Dad looks at her?"

"Or the way she waited on him at supper?"

Webb holds his nose and singsongs: "I hope you'll give me a chance. I want to be a real mother to you."

"Ha," Cass says bitterly. "Like we don't have one already."

"Like she'd even know how." Webb picks up a stone and tosses it over the railing and into the sea. "I *hate* her," he says vehemently. "Big cow."

Cass doesn't know what to say to make him feel better. She'll be twelve this fall, and so she feels that she ought to know, but she's afraid that whatever she says will be a lie. It won't get better. It will never be all right. They'll never learn to like Diane. This is war they've entered, and their father is on the wrong side.

"Shit," she mutters. She draws her knees up to her chin and tilts her head back. The stars drip a smooth, fat light that seems to coat the silvery trunks of the trees, the cool coarseness of the concrete railing, the foam tipping the waves.

Webb looks up too and says, "Show me something." He's been studying the star dome Cass made last summer, but he still can't find things unless she orients him.

"Look along my arm," she says, pointing to the North Star. "There's the Little Dipper, and Draco, and Leo. And just below Leo, down near the water—that's Gemini. You know Gemini."

"Castor and Pollux," Webb says.

"Like us—Cass and Webb."

The heads of the twin brothers are so close that they seem to touch, their single eyes shining down on the water. Webb tucks his head in closer to Cass's. "Will we have to call her Mom?" he asks.

"I don't think so."

"Will we have to kiss her good night when we go to bed?"

"I don't know." She can't predict how their lives will go or how this war will end.

"We could run away," he says thoughtfully.

"We can't. We're too young." She's just come to understand that they can't survive alone yet. We need food, she thinks bitterly. Money. Clothes. A place to sleep. All the things that come as a matter of course to adults but that come to them only as gifts. Penny says this part of their lives won't last forever, but Cass can't see how it will change until they grow up. They're trapped in these small bodies, stuck in a land where the natives treat them as if they're deaf, blind, and crippled. They can't work until they're sixteen. They can't live alone until they're eighteen. And how are they to survive until then? She ducks her cheek until it touches Webb's hair. Her only refuge is that place inside her head where she retreats with her books and her projects. She can go there more and more; she can go there as much as she wants. But she doesn't know how to bring Webb with her.

"Suppose we lived on a boat," Webb says dreamily. "Just you and me. We'd go to islands, catch fish, tie knots with our teeth . . ."

She lets him dream. Suppose we lived on a star, she thinks. About as likely. She doesn't want to tell him that they're stuck where they are. They drift into a half-sleep, huddled close while Cass dreams of living underground like some small mole. They wake to Ben's voice.

"What are you doing out here?" he says.

Cass jumps and puts her arm around Webb. Ben is standing in the doorway in his pajamas and his robe; his hair is sticking up. His voice is low but not natural—the kind of low it gets when he's trying not to shout.

"You fell asleep," Cass says firmly. "You were snoring. So we left." She's determined not to grovel.

"Come back inside," he says. "I'll make some popcorn, and maybe we can talk about what's bothering you."

Webb groans quietly and Cass pinches him silent. Talk—more talk. They've been talking all day and most of the night, so earnestly, so solemnly. As if talking could make things better. This is something new for Ben, which Cass blames on Diane. Always, before, he's just ordered them around, but although Cass hates being told what to do she finds this new approach worse.

They follow Ben back inside. Diane has turned on the light in the bedroom and she sits bolt upright, looking rumpled and scared. "You found them!" she says to Ben.

"On the balcony. I'm going to make us all some popcorn." From the look Ben and Diane exchange, Cass guesses that they thought she and Webb had run away. Ben leaves, shutting the door behind him. Cass and Webb crouch on the floor, waiting to be punished.

"Come up here," Diane says, patting the bed. "Come get warm. It must have been cold out there."

Cass can see her loose breasts jiggling under her nightgown like cats.

"We're okay here," says Webb.

"I know. But come up anyway."

They sit on the bed stiffly, as far away from Diane as possible. She holds out the covers invitingly, but they remain outside. "Can't we talk?" she says. "Can't we try?"

Sure, Cass thinks. I'll say we hate you and you'll say you'll go away and leave us alone. I'll say you shouldn't have made my parents get divorced. You'll apologize. Sure. No problem.

"Webb?" Diane says.

Webb hangs his head and says nothing.

"Cass? What about you? You've been so quiet all day."

"I don't even *know* you," Cass blurts. "And you don't know us." She bites her lips to keep from saying more. She has sworn herself to silence, the only way she knows how to fight. And now she's made a mistake.

"Well," Diane says gently. "That's what we need to do, then—get to know each other. What would you like to know?"

Nothing, Cass thinks. Except why you're here. She wills Webb to be silent and stays silent herself. Like a captured soldier, she'll reveal nothing. They can pull out her fingernails, rip out her hair—she'll never talk. Webb picks at a scab on his chin and peers at Diane through his lashes. He's promised Cass he won't talk either, but Cass suddenly understands that he's going to give in. He's just a little kid. It won't be his fault.

He traces the outline of a flower on the bedspread. "Where did you grow up?" he asks Diane shyly.

She smiles. "Buzzards Bay—across the bridge. Do you know where that is?"

Cass smirks to herself. The question is so stupid that

Webb scowls and pulls back—he hates being treated like a little boy. Give up, she thinks. Don't say anything else.

But Webb says, "Of course I know where it is. Do your parents live there?"

"My father died when I was about your age. But my mother runs a little take-out restaurant there—subs, sandwiches, stuff like that."

Webb ponders this for a minute. "Is she nice?"

"Pretty nice. She's sort of unusual—she reads horoscopes."

He stares at Diane as if she's turned into a snake charmer. "She's a *fortune*-teller?" he breathes.

"Not exactly. She's what they call an astrologer—she makes up horoscopes from knowing when and where people were born and what the stars were like then. Like the ones you see in the paper. They don't really tell your future, but sometimes they help you decide what to do."

"My mother looks at stars," Webb says. "Cass too."

Cass snorts. "We look at *real* stars," she says. "That's astronomy. Astrology is just superstition. Only stupid people believe in it."

Webb slides her a look from the corner of his eye, clearly amazed at her boldness. Diane shrugs and looks annoyed. "I grew up around it," she says. "And I think some of it makes sense. But I didn't say *you* had to believe it."

"Good!" Cass huffs. "I don't."

They glare at each other across the bed. Cass, who has never lost a staring contest at school, decides to try this out on Diane. She locks eyes and refuses to blink. Diane stares back for a minute and then flushes and looks away. She turns to Webb and says, "Maybe we'll take a drive to my mother's place some afternoon. It's called Sal's Subs."

Webb smiles. He's just like a cat, Cass thinks tiredly.

He's like Mizar and Alcor, loving whoever feeds him and whoever scratches his ears. He'll make friends—she can see this coming. It'll be easy enough for him. Diane seems to like little boys, and she won't pick on him. She won't try to make him into a little lady, won't razor-cut his bangs and buy him plaid skirts and a training bra.

Ben pushes the door open with his hip and enters bearing a big bowl of popcorn. "Here we are," he says. He plops down on the bed with them and passes the bowl around.

"No thanks," Cass says. She locks her hands behind her back and shakes her head, even though she's hungry. She's a prisoner of war, alone in a strange land. Prisoners refuse all bribes.

"Sit here by me," Ben says.

"No."

Ben frowns. "Look," he says. "None of your mouthing off, understand? Sulk all you want, but it won't change anything."

"I'm not sulking," she says. "I'm tired. I want to go to sleep." She wraps a blanket around herself and stalks away.

"Young lady . . ." Ben calls after her warningly. But Diane says, "Let her be."

Cass marches into her room, hurls herself down on her bed, and pulls the blanket over her head. I could suffocate, she thinks. Seal off all the air until I turn blue, and then I'd have to go to the hospital and I wouldn't leave until they let me go live with Mom. She pulls the blanket closer to her ears, trying to shut out the murmur of voices from the other room. She can hear Diane being sweet, Ben being hearty. She hates it when he's hearty. She hates them all.

Because their house is tucked into the side of a hill, their basement is only a basement on one side. The two rooms opposite the driveway look out on the lawn and the ocean through pairs of long windows that open like doors; the walls are painted white and glimmer with cool shadows from the balcony above. These rooms have been empty ever since Cass can remember, but she hardly complains when Ben moves her and Webb into them.

"You're growing up," he says that Saturday. "You should have some independence. This way, you'll have the whole basement to yourselves. You can have your friends over, and we'll bring the old TV down. You can have a whole room just for your projects."

Webb takes the east room and she takes the west; they set aside the rooms with no windows for projects and the Ping-Pong table and Webb's archery set. Cass makes a token protest at the move only because it's against her rules to show any enthusiasm, only because she's afraid Ben would take their new kingdom away if he knew how much she and Webb liked it. From their first day down there they knew they'd been lucky, and now they excuse themselves early each night and plead homework so they can slip into their basement world. They shoot arrows and wrestle and draw pictures of Diane, which they burn in a wastebasket set on Webb's windowsill. They turn out the lights and make shadow puppets with a flashlight and their fingers; they turn off the flashlight and tell scary stories. It's a mistake, Cass thinks. A simple mistake. Ben, wanting privacy for himself and his new wife, has inadvertently given Cass and Webb their only refuge.

Cass gathers her strength down there and plots her plots, delighted that she's won something without a fight. She and Webb launch a campaign of small irritations, unpunishable clumsinesses, innocent slips of the tongue; at night they compare notes and keep score. They lose consistently—the things Diane does to them always seem to outweigh their petty victories. But Cass keeps her eyes open for anything she can use to her advantage, and sometimes she gets lucky. The next thing she plots comes from nowhere, like a gift from the stars.

The thought springs into her head when Penny picks them up the next weekend. Penny looks pale and tired and nervous, full of problems of her own. Too much work, Cass would guess. Not enough money, squabbles with Ben, gray hair sprouting along her part. Cass knows she ought to give her mother a break, but she can't make herself do it after a week that's included new glasses (blue, with tip-tilted corners), a new haircut (longer at the chin than at the neck), and orders that she change her underwear every day. She's broken three plates in retaliation, let them slip through her soapy fingers as she washes up, but even so she's way behind and needs to do something. So she lets her face droop and hides her eyes behind her lashes, and when Penny says, "How was your week?" she answers, "Awful. Like being in jail." She sees with some satisfaction that this makes Penny quiver with guilt. Webb, in the back seat, taps her head and says, "It's not so bad. It's okay."

"Is it?" Penny asks. She touches Cass's new hair and frowns.

"Sure," Cass says mournfully.

Penny waves her free hand in the air and says, half to herself, "I thought it would be the best thing for you. If I'd taken you, your father would have regretted it as soon as he got married and got someone else to do the dirty work. And then he would have tried to get you back, and would have pulled all kinds of dirty stuff to do that, and there you'd be, stuck right in the middle . . ."

Cass, who was hardly paying attention when Penny began, listens closely now. Penny continues, "And he would have won. He's got the money and the connections and the house and the new wife. I thought if I just left alone now, and got my own life in shape, we could have each other weekends without a big fuss and everything would be better."

"So you *gave up*?" Cass says in disbelief. "You just gave up, without even a fight? Without asking us?" This is the first explanation Penny's offered them, and it's nowhere near good enough.

"I didn't give up," Penny snaps. "I made the best compromise I could. You're not old enough to know what you need, and I'm not strong enough to fight him and win . . ."

"I have always known what I needed," Cass says haughtily.

"Cass," Penny says. "Please. I'm doing the best I can. And we shouldn't even be talking about this."

Cass shrugs and leans against the car seat, closing her eyes as if she hasn't the strength to lift her lids. When Penny sighs and says, "So what would you like to do today? What would make you feel better?" Cass moves cautiously.

"We could go to Buzzards Bay," she murmurs. "If you want."

Webb bounces behind her. "Let's go to the tackle store! I need some new plugs."

Penny smiles. "Would you like that? Maybe lunch in town?"

This is what Cass has been hoping for. "Sure," she says. "Better than sitting at home." She doesn't suggest a place for lunch; she wants things to unfold naturally. And so she drifts listlessly through Ryder's Bait Shop, sitting on a pile of orange life jackets while Webb dickers with the owner over some spinning plugs. Penny sits down next to Cass and wraps an arm about her shoulders.

"You're awful quiet," she says. "Want to tell me what's going on?"

Cass does. She'd like to lay her head on Penny's shoulder and pour out the indignities she's suffered this past week. She'd like to weep, to yell, to fall into a dramatic swoon, but she knows she'll do better if she keeps quiet. "No," she says. "There's nothing to talk about. You know they moved us downstairs?" She means this to sound bad, and it does.

Penny sucks in her breath. "In the *basement?*"

"The two small rooms facing the water. But it's okay."

Penny picks at her nails and says, "Maybe it's for the best. At least you'll have some space of your own."

"I guess. How's work?" She asks as politely as if Penny is a stranger.

"Oh," Penny says impatiently. "Work. Same old stuff —numbers and numbers and numbers. I'm going to start taking some courses this summer, see if I can do something better. Where'd you like to go for lunch?"

"Anywhere," Cass says. "A sub might be good."

She has looked up the address for Sal's Subs and knows it's down the main drag, not far from the bait shop at all. And so when Penny says, "Fine," Cass says, quite naturally, "Why don't we head down Main Street and see what's around?" She is able, when they come up on Sal's Subs, to say, "This looks good—why don't we stop here?"

When Webb opens his mouth in surprise she scowls him quiet. This will be like a raid, she thinks—a foray into enemy country. She'll gather secret information, as if she's a foreign spy. She'll know something about Diane that Diane doesn't know she knows. She's not sure why this seems useful, but she's convinced that it is.

"Okay," Penny says. "You want Italian with everything?" She gets out of the car and slams the door, prepared to fetch the sandwiches herself.

"I don't know," Cass says. "I need to look at the menu."

They pile out of the car and follow Penny inside. The sub shop is smelly and dark—an old counter stained with coffee and grease, torn posters tacked to the wall, a cash register with grimy keys. When they open the door a small bell tinkles. An enormous woman, sprawled in a corner chair with one leg up on a pillow and a cat in her lap, looks up at them over half-rimmed glasses.

"Can I help you?" she asks. Her voice is husky and low. When she rises she anchors the messy papers before her with a coffee cup and lifts her leg from the pillows as if it's dead meat. Penny wrinkles her nose and says to Cass, "Are you sure this is what you want?"

Webb's mouth pops open. "You think that's Sal?" he whispers.

"What?" Penny says. "You want salad?"

"Salami," Cass says. "Salami, capicolla, ham, provolone . . ."

"Italian," the woman says, and limps behind the counter. Her left leg seems stiff at the knee.

"Three," Penny says. "Hot peppers, onions, oil, no mayo."

Cass needs to make sure. She points to the sign on the wall and says, "Are you Sal?"

"Sure am," Sal says, and turns her broad back to slice the rolls with a knife so big that it looks to Cass like a sword. Her housedress is some pale mushroom color, sleeveless and shapeless; her upper arms are bigger than Cass's legs and she doesn't seem to be wearing any underwear. Or not enough, at any rate. She has a soft roll of flesh that starts under her arms and flows into the pillowlike mass of her breasts, a roll beneath that circles her back and her belly, and another that blooms over her kidneys and then hangs low in front. When she moves, some parts need extra time to catch up.

Cass can't tear her eyes away, and Webb stares so hard that Penny tugs his sleeve. He slides away from her grip and inches down the counter to the cash register, where a small business card is taped. Cass slides over to join him.

"What's that?" she asks.

He taps the card and grins. The card reads:

Sal's Star Charts
○ *Individual charts & analysis*
○ *Mini-readings*
○ *Compatibilities*
○ *Business astrology*

It's true, then. She feels as if she's been handed a box of rifle shells, ammunition for the war. Surely Diane wouldn't have brought them here herself, despite her offer. Surely this is useful information. Penny frowns and signals for her to leave the card alone, but Cass can't pass up this opportunity. "Sal," she says. "Do you do horoscopes?"

"That's what the card says." Sal wraps their subs in waxed paper, tucks the ends in swiftly, and takes the money Penny holds out. "Do you know your signs?" she asks.

Penny frowns. "I don't believe in astrology," she says. "And I don't like to encourage the kids."

Sal shrugs. "Suit yourself. When's your birthday?"

Penny doesn't answer.

"June 12," Webb says helpfully. "And mine was last week."

"Gemini," Sal nods at Penny. "Figures. And you," she points at Webb, "Taurus. As loyal as they come."

"Thanks for the subs," Penny says. "We have to run."

She turns and signals them to come, but Cass can't seem to follow her quite yet. Sal is staring at her, pinning her feet to the floor with her narrow eyes. "Do I know you?" she asks.

"No," Cass says, shuffling her feet. She's nervous, suddenly—this is a bad idea, a terrible idea. They'll meet as family, sooner or later, and this woman isn't the type to forget a face. What will she say then? That this meeting was a coincidence? She ducks her head and starts to back away, but Webb points at her and says, "What about Cass? Her birthday's November 8."

"Of course it is," Sal says. "Scorpio. Smart, creative, vindictive as all get out. Am I right or am I right?"

"Don't be silly," Cass sniffs, but she grabs Penny's hand and almost runs from the shop. She's related to this mind-reading mountain now, and she's done something bad, for which she knows she's going to pay. Tea leaves, horoscopes, crystal balls, palms—it's just superstition, she knows. She's scared just the same.

"Hey!" Sal calls after them. "Want me to cast your charts? Half an hour, no more. Half price for the kids."

"No thanks," Penny mutters. She pulls them out of the shop and into the car.

"Mom," Webb says, unwrapping his sub. "You know what?"

"What?" Penny asks absently.

Before he can answer Cass kicks his foot and snaps, "Eat your sandwich." Her own smells wonderful, but she's afraid to eat it.

That night, before they fall asleep, Cass swears him to secrecy. "Don't tell Mom about Sal," she whispers. "And don't, don't, *don't* tell Dad or Diane."

"They wouldn't care," Webb mumbles. He is almost asleep.

"They would," Cass says. "Trust me. Just don't say anything."

"Whatever you want," he whispers, and then falls silent.

His gentle breathing is so calm, so soothing, that Cass almost believes their visit wasn't important. She closes her eyes and times her breathing to Webb's, and at first she dreams of soaring over the ocean on huge, skin-covered wings. She smiles in her sleep and rolls gently from side to side, wrapping her blankets about her like a cocoon. She wakes for a minute when Mizar and Alcor streak through the room on some late-night cat mission, rumbling and scrabbling around in the clothes on the floor. When she falls asleep again, she dreams that Sal is her mother. She dreams that the sub shop is home, that her clothes smell of olive oil and onion. That she and Sal sleep in a nest of blankets on the floor, kept warm by billowing folds of fat. She dreams that she's as big as Sal, with matching chipmunk cheeks and huge thighs that rub together. Her throat clamps shut when she tries to call for help; her hands are bound to her sides.

She wakes to find Penny bending over her and untangling the blankets. "Shh," Penny says, and strokes her sweaty head. "It's all right. You were just dreaming."

Cass pulls her hands from the blankets and runs them along Penny's back. No fat, just Penny's strong shape. No smells except for the slight whiff of the bubble bath that Penny always uses. She's safe, at least for now. "Mom," she whispers. "Can I stay over one more night?"

Penny slips under the blankets and holds her tightly. "I'd let you if I could," she says. "But it would make your father angry, and that'd only make things worse for you at home."

Mizar and Alcor pad into the room to investigate the voices. Alcor jumps up and sticks her cool nose against Cass's neck, kneading the soft skin there with her toes. Her claws prick, and Cass tosses her away. "Why do we have to live like this?" she says. "I hate it."

"I know," Penny says. "It's not fair, but it's just for a while. I couldn't have lived with your father another day. And anyway, he wouldn't have let me, once he made up his mind about Diane."

"I hate her," Cass snarls. "It's all her fault."

"It's not," Penny says mildly. "She just brought things to a head. It's our fault, your father's and mine. I thought he was someone he wasn't, and I don't know who he thought I was, but it wasn't me. We never should have gotten married."

Cass thinks about this for a minute and then says, "Don't say that—that means I wouldn't be here." Mizar pounces on her toes, which she taps rhythmically under the blanket. She kicks the cat away.

Penny laughs softly. "Sure you would. I was pregnant with you before we got married."

"You were?" She has only a hazy picture of how babies get made—something to do with a seed that goes from father to mother when they kiss. But she has always believed that the seed couldn't grow until the parents were married. Webb pointed out two dogs last fall, one climbing the other and poking away with some wet, red thing. "People do that too," he told her. But Cass took one look and knew it was impossible.

"How could you be?" Cass asks her mother.

"It just happens sometimes—an accident. But if we hadn't gotten married we wouldn't have Webb, and that would have been terrible."

Webb rolls over in his sleep and curls his hand around his pillow. Mizar spots the movement and leaps from Cass's feet to Webb's hand. He's a pain sometimes, but Cass wouldn't want to be without him. "Then I'm glad you did," she says. "You sure I can't stay over?"

"I'm sure. And besides—I have a date tomorrow night." Penny plucks at the blanket and smoothes Cass's hair.

"You do?"

"Mmm-hm."

"With a man?"

"Mmm-hm. It's a blind date—some people at work set it up. He's divorced too. I'm not real thrilled with the idea, but everyone's bugging me to get out."

Cass looks up at her mother's tired face. "You should wear your coral earrings," she says. "And put your hair up. The gray doesn't show as much that way. What time are you going?"

"Around five. I thought I'd bring you home a little early so I'd have time to get ready. If you don't mind."

"It's okay," Cass says. "I'll take Webb fishing or something."

Penny kisses her on the ear. "You'll be okay?"

"Sure," Cass says. Her dream is already fading. Alcor crawls under the blankets and curls into the curve of Cass's arm as Penny slips away. Cass bends her head against the soft, dark fur and falls asleep again.

When Cass awakes, she believes she's put Sal's piercing eyes behind her. The smells and sights of the sub shop fade during the day she spends with Penny and Webb, only returning to haunt her while she's out on the Boston whaler later that afternoon. This isn't where she'd meant to be—she'd thought that she and Webb would slip out the basement door with their rods in their hands and walk down to the old railroad bridge, but Ben found them just as they got their tackle together and decided that they ought to come out in the boat with them.

"That's all right," Cass said. "I'll stay here."

"Fine," Ben said. "You can help Diane with dinner, then."

"I'll come," Cass said.

Now they drift through the rip at the mouth of the Canal, fishing for pollock while Ben complains about the old Evinrude. The motor is slow to start, easy to stall, and as temperamental as an old fiddler crab, but Ben hangs on to it, or says he does, because it was his as a boy. Webb tries to enjoy himself despite the constant flow of words. He hums as he ties on one of his new plugs, and he casts with a practiced flick of his wrist. Cass watches tiredly as Ben criticizes Webb's technique. Webb's smile changes to a taut nervousness.

Cass reels in her own line before Ben can tell her what she's doing wrong, and then she sits quietly and watches the rolling waves. Right now, she thinks, Penny is putting on lipstick and getting ready to greet her date. Perhaps she's cleaned up the house a little, hidden the magazines in the attic and stuffed the dirty pots in the oven. Perhaps she is wearing a dress. In another house, Diane is baking bread. Twin houses, twin lives—it makes her brain rumble to think of these women whose only similarity is in the man they married. Her head has that cottony feeling it gets just before her stomach acts up. Ben's voice, louder and louder, seems to come at her from some point high in the sky. The boat lurches, settles, and lurches again. Just a little twist of fate, she thinks, just a little turn, and Penny could be home baking bread while Diane dressed somewhere for a date with a man they'd never meet.

"Cass," Ben says. "Why don't you put your line in? You're looking a little green."

"I'm fine," she says.

Webb hooks something and hauls it in—a small cod. "Good for you!" Ben shouts. "That's the way!"

Webb glows in the light of this sudden rare praise. A Taurus, Cass thinks. As loyal as they come. He's loyal to anyone who treats him well, even to Ben. Even after they've sworn not to be nice to him.

The waves spread out in the gentle rolls of late afternoon. No chop, no foam—just long, undulant swells, almost oily, sliding under the boat. Like olive oil, Cass thinks, and gets a sudden strong whiff of Sal and her shop. Vinegar. Sliced meat, smelly cheese, pickled peppers, dirty napkins. Rolls and rolls of fat spilling like waves under Sal's dress, hiding dark creases that maybe she can never reach to wash—she leans over the side of the boat and throws up breakfast and lunch. "Ugh," she shudders, and rests her head on the gunwale.

Ben groans. "I *told* you to keep fishing!" he says. "You

always get sick if you don't keep busy when we're drift-ing. I swear you do it on purpose."

Webb touches her arm. "Are you okay?"

She nods. She smells capicolla and onions on his breath, lingering from yesterday. She knows the smell can't be there but she smells it anyway. She leans over and heaves again.

"Daddy," Webb says. "Let's go home. She's really sick."

Cass can barely hear him through the roaring in her ears. "Lie down," Ben says. "You'll feel better." He splashes some water on her face and mutters, "There's a good hour left until twilight, and the fish are feed-ing . . ."

"It's okay," Webb says. "I was getting cold anyway."

Cass squints up and sees the April sun low in the gray sky. Ben steps over her and goes back to the motor. He gives the starter a single sharp pull, but nothing hap-pens. He pulls again and again until the smell of gas hangs heavy over the boat and sets her stomach trem-bling.

"Shit," he says in disgust. "The damn thing's flooded."

He throws the cover up and fiddles inside. Cass closes her eyes and tries to still her surging stomach. Far away, she hears the boom of a ship's horn, some freighter readying itself to enter the mouth of the Ca-nal.

"Webb," Ben says. "Hand me the pliers."

She can hear him banging on something. The horn booms again, closer this time, and she sits up enough to scan the water. Against the horizon she sees the dark hull of an approaching ship. "Dad," she says. "There's a boat coming."

"No problem," he says. "I'll have this fixed in a sec-ond."

They drift gently with the waves, closing in on the

buoy that marks the shipping lane. Cass rolls onto her side and shuts her eyes, oppressed by the smell of gas and the sudden strong memory of Sal's parting comments. She hears that husky voice as if it's come to live between her ears. "Do I know you?" Someday she'll have to share Christmas dinner with that woman. She'll have to smile politely while Sal discusses stars as if they're people or gods.

"Hold that little valve open," Ben says to Webb. She hears them only faintly above the echo of Sal's voice. "Gemini, Taurus, Scorpio." Labels—as if that could explain them. The waves slapping against the hull lull her half asleep for a while. It's almost twilight when she wakes.

"Goddamnit!" Ben shouts. "Stupid piece of shit!" The motor is closed and he tugs at the starter cord.

"Daddy?" Webb says. He sounds frightened. Cass sits up and looks around. They've drifted right into the center of the shipping lane, and the freighter, once so far away, rises huge out of the water now and towers over them. When the horn blows it almost knocks her over.

"Dad!" she shrieks.

The horn sounds over and over again, warning them out of the way. She knows the ship is too big to turn in time.

"I see it," he says. "Don't get hysterical on me." His voice is very steady, as if he's willing it calm, but his face is covered with sweat.

"Put on your life jackets," he says. "Right now. And grab those paddles under the seat. Webb, you help Cass paddle."

"Which way?" Cass asks. The shipping lane suddenly seems as wide as a lake, the two sides equally far away. It's my fault, she thinks. That woman put a curse on me. She wonders if she was born under an evil star, if her horoscope for today would have read, Stay inside. Stay away from water. It crosses her mind that they may drown, but she pushes the thought away and paddles. "Harder!" she says to Webb. She doesn't want to scare him, but the freighter is so close now that its bow blocks out the sky. Somewhere up there, hidden by both the sun and the ship, are the constellations she showed Webb just a week ago, before Sal smeared them with her greasy words. Somewhere up there is Gemini, which Penny said was the guardian constellation of sailors threatened by the sea. She doubts that even Gemini can save her from this ship.

Webb starts to cry. "Stop that," she says. "Paddle." Ben struggles frantically with the motor. She pushes her seasickness out of her mind, sends her thoughts of Sal away. Tries to forget everything but the feel of her blade in the water and the picture of the twins in the sky, their arms around each other's waists as they smooth her way across the water. She hears a sputter and a grumble, smells gas, and hears her father's voice.

"Please, please," he begs. "Come on!"

The motor catches, and they roar away so quickly that the water tears the paddles from their hands. Cass grips the gunwales and looks over her shoulder, where the bow wave from the freighter arches after them in hot pursuit, breaking and dissolving just before it arrives. The horn blows angrily.

Deep-Sky Objects
(January 1968)

★　　　★　　　★　　　★　　　★　　　★

In the darkness, the car roof arches over Cass as tight
and smooth as the shell of a clam. She might be a mol-
lusk trapped inside, for all the room she has—her head
lies on the edge of a suitcase, padded with her parka,
while her feet search for space between the bags and
boots and poles that cram the station wagon. Webb,
stretched beside her with his foot on her knee, breathes
wetly on her neck. He's been asleep since they crossed
the Canal; she's only pretended to be. When the passing
headlights illuminate the car she counts the tiny holes
in the vinyl above her and shapes them into patterns,
eavesdropping all the while on Ben and Diane.

"You'll like it," Ben says in the front seat. "I know
you will." His voice is soft and low, gentle and persua-
sive. He's trying to convince Diane to rent a pair of skis
and take her first skiing lesson tomorrow.

"I don't think so," Diane says. "Certainly not now.
I'd be just as happy staying inside with a book."

Ben snorts, abandoning the quiet approach. "You can't *read*," he says derisively. "We'll all be skiing!"

Diane sighs, apparently unable to think of a response. Behind her, Cass smiles to herself. It's typical of Diane to simply collapse in the midst of a conversation—she has no fight to her at all. Probably, Cass thinks, this is why Ben married her. Webb starts to smack his lips in his sleep, and Cass turns her chin away from him. At home, Diane slinks around with a dog's timid smile as she cooks and cleans and fusses, driving Cass crazy with her constant apologies. Why? Cass wonders. Why does she do that? Why does she give in to Ben so easily? Cass thinks that maybe it has to do with Sal, or with Diane's being so much younger than Ben, but she can't be sure and so she tumbles her theories around in her mind as if they're stones in a polisher. These days, trying to pry her way into Diane's head is her favorite occupation.

Suppose, she thinks, using the silence from the front seat as a clue to start her wonderings. Suppose Diane was real fat when she was little, a regular butterball, and suppose she's afraid she'll look like Sal someday and she hates cooking for us because she's afraid she'll eat what she makes, but she doesn't want us to know because we'd make fun of her—Cass's thoughts flare out into a coral reef of suppositions, branches of possibility she could explore all night if she weren't interrupted by the sudden blare of a horn as Ben, who can't stand having anyone in front of him, pulls around to pass a truck and narrowly misses an oncoming car.

"Would you take it easy?" Diane asks softly. "I don't feel so great."

She gets carsick! This is a new fact. Carsickness has been Cass's trick, up until now. During all the years they made this trip as a family, she could always be counted on to throw up somewhere between Methuen and Manchester. Penny took care of her then, back in the days when they visited Otis and Cindy every other winter weekend. Cass knows this route the way she knows her own hands. Always the same roads, always the same excitement—lessons and lunches and lift lines and races, first up the hill, last off. She and Webb learned to ski so early that it came to them like breathing, and as she tucks her chin into her shoulder, away from Webb's restless head, she tries to imagine skiing without Penny. They have always skied better than her —because Penny never found another teacher she liked, and because Ben never had time to teach her, Penny's skiing never progressed beyond a sloppy, crashingly fast, intermediate stage. Cass and Webb always left her on the easier slopes while they raced off with Otis and Ben, but still, Cass can't imagine the mountain without her mother somewhere on it. Even worse than Penny's absence is Diane's presence—Diane hates the cold and can't ski, and she's bound to be a drag on everything. That's what happens, Cass thinks, when you grow up pale as a mushroom in the corner of a sub shop. She knows Diane didn't really grow up in the shop, but it pleases her to think of Diane there. She shifts under her blanket and considers spraining her ankle on purpose, so they can all go home and stop pretending this is fun.

Diane interrupts her thoughts again. "Ben," she says. "What's that light?"

Cass cranes her head enough to peep over the seat. A red light glows on the dash, and a glance out the window tells her they're in Manchester. If they're in Manchester, the fan belt is probably broken.

"Shit," Ben says. He pulls over and looks under the hood. The fan belt has broken three times in Manchester that Cass can remember, three different winters in three different cars. She lies still, curious to see what will happen next. Back in the old days, Ben used to storm at Penny and grind his teeth, blaming her for every mechanical failure. She wonders if he'll find a way to blame this on Diane.

He slams the door when he gets back in the car. "If you'd brought this in for a checkup," he snaps, "like I *asked* you to . . . The fan belt's busted. Anyone could have seen it was worn and replaced it."

Cass nearly giggles.

"Really?" Diane says meekly. "I'm sorry. Can we make it to a gas station?"

"If we're lucky. I think there's one about a quarter of a mile from here." He turns his blinkers on and begins limping down the highway.

Cass sits up and stretches, trying to look as if she's been asleep. "Where are we?" she yawns. "What's happening?"

"Manchester," Ben growls. "Where else? The fan belt snapped."

Diane turns awkwardly to face Cass. "Shh," she whispers. "Is your brother still asleep?"

"I think so."

"Let's be quiet, then. Maybe he can sleep through. Can you go back to sleep?"

"No. Is there anything to eat?"

"In the cooler. You'll have to get it yourself."

"No fooling," Cass says, biting back a snicker only when Ben turns to glare at her. Diane can hardly move —she's not quite six months pregnant and she's as big as a ship. Her feet and wrists and ankles have swollen until she seems to be made of cylinders joined awkwardly together. When Cass finds the chips she rustles the bag more than she has to, crunches a little louder than is really necessary. Diane, who loves salty things, can't have any until the baby is born.

"There's an Esso," Diane says.

"I see it," Ben snaps. "I'm not blind." He pulls in, stops in front of the first bay, and stomps inside. When he returns he's followed by an old man in a greasy green cap.

"What seems to be the trouble?" the mechanic asks.

He has a lopsided smile and two missing teeth, but Cass likes the way he stands with his thumbs outside his pockets.

"Fan belt's busted," Ben says.

The mechanic sighs. "Don't know that I can help—depends on the size and what we've got here."

Ben waves his hand impatiently. "Just do what you can—improvise something. I've got two kids and a pregnant wife here."

"That so?" The man peers into the car and smiles at Cass. "They could wait inside if they wanted."

When Ben waves at her, Cass wakes Webb and pulls him into the grimy office. Still asleep, he trips on the sill —he's always lost for half an hour or so after he's woken up. There are two orange plastic chairs inside, next to a soda machine, and with a sigh Cass props Webb up in one and waves Diane to the other. Diane sits heavily, one straight line from chin to knees like a pyramid wrapped in white wool. Cass shakes off a shiver of sympathy. No one, now, would mistake her and Diane for sisters the way they sometimes have over the past nine months. Diane looks thirty now, although she only admits to twenty-four. The skin across the bridge of her nose is puffed and red in the fluorescent glare. Her finger is swollen around the sapphire ring Ben gave her as a wedding band.

Cass scrunches down on the floor and listens to Ben and the mechanic in the shop next door. "Can you hurry it up?" she hears Ben say. "We don't have all night."

"Doing the best I can," the mechanic drawls. Cass hates the way Ben's acting, this snotty manner he's adopted with almost everyone. Nothing anyone does is ever good enough, fast enough. Since he sold out Cranberry Acres and Bayview so quickly and started on his new place near Nauset, he's become as obnoxious as the rest of his rich friends. Impatient, she thinks, listening to the snap in his voice. Not mean, exactly—just sharp, as if no one's time is worth shit but his.

Webb has fallen asleep in his chair, his mouth open wide enough to swallow bugs. Cass considers dropping something in but decides against it—with Ben this cranky anything could start a fight. "I'm going outside," she tells Diane. "It smells in here."

"Don't go far," Diane says. "They'll be done in a minute."

Cass steps outside and pants like a dog, blowing off the stale fumes. The gas station sits on a hill overlooking some small, dark river; she gauges the distance against her memory of fan-belt repairs and darts down the hill to the frozen water. The winter stars are out, sparkling brighter than they ever do at home. She spots her namesake constellation near Cepheus and Andromeda. Queen, king, princess; Cetus the sea monster threatening the princess; Perseus to the rescue with a Gorgon's head in his hand. She feels more like Andromeda than Cassiopeia. She squats down on a snowy rock, imagining it as a rock in the sky and herself as a princess chained to it. Glub, glub—the sea monster snakes through the water, ready to swallow her. She tilts her head, awaiting the hero or winged horse who'll steal her away. Which was it? The man or the horse? She seems to remember Penny saying that the rescuer was Perseus, but in the sky the princess seems to be riding away on the horse.

In the old days, she could have run back to the gas station and asked Penny how that story went. Now, everything has to wait for the weekends. Without Penny, Cass feels like she's forgetting everything important. And she knows that Penny, without them to anchor her, without Ben to pit herself against, is finally floating free. During the week she eats cold ravioli from cans and then climbs onto the roof with her new telescope and stares at deep-sky objects. Clusters and nebulae, double and triple stars. The great spiral galaxy in Andromeda. Penny signed up for astronomy instead of accounting when she went back to night school, and now her house is littered with star charts and atlases that contrast oddly with the ledgers from her job. Cass knows now why Penny keeps that dumb job—she can do it even half asleep. And since she spends her nights crouched in a beach chair, sighting by declination and right ascension, her days often pass like dreams. Cass shakes her head and smiles. Not your typical mother, but Cass would a million times rather have her and her stars than Diane. As far as Cass can tell, Diane's brain is just a pool of ads and recipes.

She tosses a pebble onto the ice and listens to the echo. She's just about to inch out there when she hears Ben's angry voice. "Cass!" he calls. "Goddamnit! You want us to leave without you?"

"Coming!" she yells. She'd love for them to leave without her, but she doesn't know where she'd sleep if they did.

While they sleep, an icy front pours silently down from Canada, rushing through the valleys to settle, at last, around the high peaks. By Saturday afternoon it's so cold that the hairs in Cass's nostrils freeze as she rides the lift. She doesn't care. She hasn't felt her toes since noon and she doesn't mind that either, not so long as the snowbunnies stay inside, huddled around the fire in their sky-blue stretchpants. The cold has stripped the slopes of all the uncommitted, and Diane hides in the base lodge with Cindy, Cindy's two-year-old Roger, the picnic basket, the Thermos, the boot racks, and the shoes. She's right where she belongs, Cass thinks. With the other mothers, the other babies, the New Yorkers drinking at the bar. And meanwhile, Cass is free.

Only she and Ben and Otis and Webb are out, skiing

the backside of SnoGoose where Otis cut the expert trails. The narrow, twisted runs keep most of the skiers away even when the weather's good—today, they have the area to themselves. The trees are bent with snow; the sky is blue. The wind howls up the runs and tears the top dusting of powder off the ice. Cass perches at the top of "Kiss It Good-bye," with her ski tips hanging over the drop. Webb's behind her, followed by Ben and then Otis, who likes to ski sweep in case anyone racks up. She takes a deep breath and jumps over the tip, her skis pointed down the fall line. No room for hesitation here, no place to check or stem or stop—the trail is no more than fifteen feet wide, rutted and moguled and icy down the center. The edges are banked and drop sharply off into the trees. Only a crazy person would ski like this. It's her favorite trail.

"Yaah!" she shrieks, plunging down the left side in a snakelike series of turns. Hands up, she thinks. Shoulders forward. Hips loose. Plant those poles! She's skiing like an angel, like a bird, and all the fears she's had about her new body drop behind her. So what if she's growing a chest after all? So what if she's getting an ass? She can still ski the way she could when she was light and hollow-boned. She hears the hiss of skis behind her, hears Otis shout, "All right, Cassie!" She hears someone pull out beside her and then catches a glimpse of Webb from the corner of her eye. His nose looks like a cherry and he's grinning fit to break his face. He matches his turns to hers, mirroring her down a thin rim of softer snow along the right edge. There's just enough room for both of them to tear along together.

Her edges bite like razors, with the same crisp finality she feels mitering two pieces of wood into a perfect joint. Her tails flick over the rim of the trail and hang in air, and yet she feels herself to be on solid ground. If she could spend her life just skiing she'd be fine. She races past the bend where they usually stop, deciding to do the run in one fast pass. Her nose feels frozen solid. Near the bottom, where the trails feed into the wider slope under the lift, she looks quickly uphill. When she sees no one coming she keeps flying right to the base of the lift, stopping at the hut in a flurry of snow. The others snap into place beside her—crunch, crunch, crunch. Webb laughs and punches her in the arm. "The Olympics in '72!" he shouts.

"Sure," Cass laughs. "You and me, kid." Already, they're too old to train. The racers she knows all started when they were five.

"That was real nice, Cass," Ben says. "You too, Webb." His face is pink from the wind; his blue eyes gleam. Standing there, dressed all in black, he looks like a kid. Cass can't understand how he looks so young when his wives look so old so fast.

Webb says, "Did you see the way I took that jump?"

When Ben laughs and nods, Cass takes the opportunity to slide back a little and align herself with Otis. The lift attendant waves them on, his face hidden deep in the fur-rimmed tunnel of his hood.

She and Otis take a chair three back from Ben and Webb. They're the only people on the lift, and their chair sways eerily in the wind as their weight bows the cable down. Below them, a lone skier picks his way through the moguls between the lift towers. He's working hard—she can hear him panting even this far away. She pulls down the safety bar and settles her skis on the support. When she turns, she finds Otis scanning her face.

"What's the matter?" she asks. She's known him forever, but she isn't used to having him stare at her. Does he know? she wonders. Do I smell? She believes the whole world knows when she has her period, smells the faint taint of blood and sees the outline of the napkin.

"Looks like a little frostnip on your cheek," he says. "You've got a white patch here."

To her surprise, he pulls off his glove and lays his palm along her face. Her skin warms instantly, more from her embarrassed flush than from his hand. If she were twenty-two and not twelve, and if Otis weren't married, she thinks she'd marry him herself. He's short —shorter than her—and has an odd, bullet-shaped head and thick glasses. To her he looks just gorgeous. He never shouts, never orders, never demands, seeming to hold his family and friends around him by good humor and energy.

"There," he says, smiling. "All better."

She drops her eyes and wonders if he still kisses Cindy. They have a baby and so she knows he must, as she knows what Ben must have done to Diane to get her pregnant. She's read books. She's talked to Webb. Still, she can't imagine Ben and Diane actually doing it. She can imagine Otis and Cindy, though—and she can imagine Otis and her. Would he kiss her? His mouth is soft and pink below his bristly moustache. She knows, from seeing him in swimming trunks, that he has hair on his back.

A great gust of wind sways their chair like a yo-yo. "Jesus," she says. "It's freezing."

"I know," Otis says, and grins. "Ain't it great?"

She likes the way he jokes with her as if she's grown up. "It's neat," she says. "It's like when I was little, when Dad used to carry me down the mountain in his backpack."

"You remember that? You were just a baby."

"Maybe I only remember what Mom told me," she says. "But I *feel* like I remember it. Dad had wooden skis then, and a black hat that used to fly in my face. I remember everything rushing by, but there I was, perfectly safe."

"That's right," Otis says. "I remember you grinning behind his head. It used to drive your mother crazy, but you *were* safe all along. Ben never fell when he was carrying you."

Cass looks up in time to see a hawk floating heavily above the trees. Ben's still a good skier, but she's no longer safe with him. She wonders if he'll take the new baby skiing, wonders if the baby will remember if he does. She thinks of the way the trees flashed past her then, the amazing combination of speed and safety she felt on her father's back. Her life now seems completely reversed, slow and threatening.

"We used to ski back here before the lift was even in," says Otis. "Me and your father and a bunch of guys from school."

"How'd you get to the top?"

"A big Cat towed us around to the lift on the other side. We all grabbed onto a rope behind the treads and tried not to run over each other. It was wild." He laughs and waves his hand over the slope. "This one's still my baby," he says. "Even with all the others, I still like this one best. We had good times here."

Cass chips at the snow on her binding with her pole, trying to imagine Otis and Ben as wild young men. She likes Otis so much that she can't understand why he likes Ben. "I wish Dad did this," she says. "Instead of what he does. All he builds are those dumb houses and roads with stupid names. He filled in a whole cranberry bog for a handful of houses."

Otis shrugs. "Nothing wrong with that—he's made a lot of money. I still wish he'd worked with me, but he seems happy enough."

"I wish he'd stayed with you too," she says. Penny's told her the story of how the two men almost worked together, and it still makes her sad. Everything would have been different if they had. Ben could have stayed married to Penny and carved trails through snowy mountains. Instead, he's married to some dumb cow and carving up the Cape.

"Too late now," Otis says.

Cass taps her ski pole against the chair. "Maybe *I'll* do this," she says. "When I grow up."

Otis laughs. "You wouldn't like it."

"Would so. I'm real good at math and science, and I'm good at building things. I made a model of the London Bridge last year, and a castle, and a dinghy, and some planes. I helped my mother make a telescope from a kit."

"No fooling. How's your mother, anyway?"

"Good. She's teaching herself astronomy."

"She always did like stars." He claps his hands and swings them around, trying to warm them up. "What's she doing these days?"

Cass knows he means how does Penny live—does she have a house, a job, a boyfriend? Does she miss Ben? She doesn't think he should find this out from her. Let him call, if he's interested—she's puzzled that he doesn't talk to Penny anymore. "She doing deep-sky objects," she says, picking the one thing from Penny's life that she knows Otis won't understand. "Stuff you can only see with a telescope. It's pretty fun."

Otis shifts uncomfortably. "Pretty strange, if you ask me. She'd be better off taking care of you."

"It's not *her* fault," Cass snaps. "This was all Dad's idea. He's the one who makes us live this way."

"Hey," Otis says. "Didn't mean to pry."

She wants to ask why he never calls Penny, why he lets Diane into their world even though she's an imposter. She knows he'd only laugh if she asked these things. She needs a telescope to train on his heart, something that would resolve the tiny points of light into huge clusters of stars and swirls of gas.

"Do you like me?" she asks. It's not what she meant to say at all. She ought to lick her ski pole, freeze her tongue there where it won't get her in trouble.

Otis laughs. "Of course I do—I'm your godfather.

Anything happens to your folks and—boom!—you're stuck with me."

"Yeah," she says. "Right." She throws back the safety bar and hooks the straps of her poles over her hands. They're almost at the top. "When I grow up," she says, "I'm going to build things. I don't care what anyone says."

Otis taps her ski with his. "Yeah?" he says. "I'm not trying to stop you. You can come work for me when you're ready, if that's what you want. I can always use a smart girl."

"Don't laugh," she says. "I'm not fooling."

"Who's laughing? If you've got half your father's brains, you'll do just fine." He looks at her for a second and then grins. "I don't know," he says. "Maybe you'll be too pretty to spend your time with a slide rule. You got a boyfriend yet?"

She blushes so hard that her ears burn. "No."

"You want to do this run one more time?"

"Sure."

They whiz down the ramp, past Ben and Webb huddled behind the hut. "Come on!" Otis yells to them. "Wake up!" They blow past their startled faces.

Cass sips at the grown-ups' drinks all that night, offering refills with her sweetest smile and then, behind cover of the kitchen door, sucking up what's left beneath the ice. Mixing drinks is a party trick Ben taught her years before, when the house was full of company, and although she hated waiting on his guests, tonight she's glad she learned. Act like a monkey, she tells herself. No one will notice anything if you smile. She could be in bed already, asleep with Roger and Webb. Only her skill and a flair for penny-ante poker have bought her these late-night hours. She has this warm buzz going through her fingers and her toes, this cozy tickle in her breasts. Her whole body tingles.

She adds fresh ice, bourbon, and water to the men's glasses. She mixes screwdrivers for the women. When she closes her eyes for a minute, just to still the hum in her ears, the room swims like a spiral galaxy. She shakes her head, rubs her eyes, and carries the tray daintily into the living room. Careful, she thinks. Be cool. If she trips, someone will wonder why. She lifts her feet high at the edge of the rug.

Otis whistles and says, "Look at those legs!" He's sprawled on the floor in front of the fire, next to Ben. Cindy and Diane are curled at opposite ends of the sofa. A chair for Cass is drawn up near the low coffee table, but she ignores it and stretches out beside Otis. He's been teasing her all day about her legs ("Like a colt," he says. "Like a dancer") and now, when she unfolds them toward the fire, she sees them through his eyes. They're very long, very thin. They don't seem to belong to her at all.

"Five-card draw," announces Ben. "One-eyed jacks wild. Ante up."

Cass stares at his fingers as he deals. She isn't sure, but she suspects he may be cheating. He's been playing for blood, not at all the way he plays when they sit down with Bryant and Vivian at home. There, they play a casual game—lots of joking, weak bluffs on bad hands. No objections when Diane, who can't remember the difference between a straight and a flush, asks to check the list of winning hands in the middle of a game. Tonight Ben's brow has a faint line down the center, over his nose. He keeps checking his pile of pennies against Otis's, to see which one is bigger.

She peers at her own cards. The numbers blur in the firelight, as if she's reading them through the edge of some faint nebulosity. The bright stars of the Pleiades, perhaps, shining through their hazy cloud. Is this being drunk? Everything's a little soft, a little fuzzy. No wonder the grown-ups like drinking so much.

She discards an eight and a three and picks up two low clubs. When she looks through the haze again, she's holding a flush. Ben takes one card; Otis takes three. Diane and Cindy chatter too much to pay attention.

"Ladies," Ben says, "how many?"

"You're carrying low," Cindy says to Diane. "I bet it's a boy."

"Me too," Diane says. "Did your back hurt you all the time?"

"All the time."

"How many?" Ben asks again.

They each take three cards, but they barely look at them.

Ben opens and Otis raises him two cents. Diane and Cindy look up and say. "What? How much to us?" They smile and touch each other's arms confidingly, but Cass isn't sure how they feel. Diane's face resembles a mask sometimes, a smooth, blank surface that Cass hasn't figured out how to read. All politeness, all charm. Cass has found Diane in the kitchen, talking to Paine, with this same perfectly sweet smile that's maybe a little too constant, a little too stiff at the corners. Perhaps Diane is remembering that Cindy was Penny's friend.

The two women pull their cards in and lower their voices, so that Cass knows they're delving into the deep gossip, the dirt that makes then lean back on the sofa pillows and lock their arms protectively over their breasts. She hears her mother's name embedded in a low, nasty buzz, and then she hears Walker's name as well. Walker's name makes her smile. He's six feet tall, red-haired, and meaty bellied; he's also Penny's boyfriend and Cass's and Webb's friend. Ben and Diane can't stand him. He lives in a wooden sailboat— ". . . a boat!" Cass hears Diane say—and she and Webb have been forbidden to visit him at the marina. They sneak there as often as they can.

"You folding?" Otis asks her.

"Not me," she says. She calls—he has a pair of sevens and a pair of fives, about what she figured. Ben has four queens. "Shit," she says, and spits a little when she says it.

Otis laughs; Ben frowns and says, "Don't swear;" and Diane just flicks her eyes over lightly and returns to discussing intimate family secrets as if Cass weren't there. She does this when she's on the phone with Sal and it drives Cass crazy. Jabber, jabber, discussing their private lives and analyzing their problems—there's nothing she won't talk about once she's warmed up. Just now, Cass hears her whisper to Cindy that Webb's been wetting his bed. Cass knows the stories could just as easily be about her. Will be, in fact, as soon as she goes upstairs.

"Anyone want another drink?" she asks abruptly. When the two men nod, she takes their glasses to the kitchen and drains them, taking a hit off the bottle for good measure as she refills the glasses. The walls of the room pulse like a variable star. Her nose feels warm.

"Cass!" Otis yells. "Your deal!"

When she returns to the living room she deals out seven-card stud, her favorite game. The cards cover the table like a constellation—five arrows, faceup, facedown. The women stop gossiping long enough to bet on each card. Ben has three jacks showing, but Cass knows he doesn't have the fourth. With a pair of kings showing and another down, she takes the hand.

"Well?" she asks, waiting for the next hand. Nothing happens. Diane and Cindy have only a few pennies left; Ben and Otis seem to have equal amounts. It's Cindy's turn to deal now, but she and Diane are discussing the baby again and the men are talking about Hawk Commons, Ben's new development in Nauset. Stupid name, Cass thinks. Like all the rest. She gathers the cards and pushes them to Cindy. Ben's already planned to name roads there for her and Webb, as he has in each of his developments. This one will also have a road named for the new baby. It's so gross, she thinks. It's so ridiculous.

She leans back against the legs of the chair and grazes Otis's thigh with her foot. Still talking to Ben, he grasps her foot and says, "You ticklish? You used to be." When she giggles and tries to pull away he moves his fingers from her sole but still hangs on. That's fine with her—his hand is warm and strong and she likes being connected to him by this light touch. The cards lie on the table, waiting for Cindy's shuffle.

She glances around—no one is watching. She pulls the cards to her and starts to build a house. Four rooms on the bottom, a layer of cards as a roof, three rooms on top of that. Ben frowns at her when he glances over and sees what she's doing, but he doesn't say anything and she ignores him. She lays a sheet of paper across the three rooms so she won't run out of cards, and then she builds two more rooms on top of that. A breath, and the house would tumble. A touch on the table and it would fall. But her hands, warm from the bourbon, are as steady as they've ever been. The cards might as well be glued together. She crowns the last story with another sheet of paper and then adds a final A-shaped room, resembling this house in which they sit. She has one card left. She lays it on the fulcrum made by the last two cards and lets it teeter there in gentle balance.

The men are the first to see. Ben frowns again and shakes his head, but Otis says, "Damn! That's great!" and squeezes her foot.

The women turn at the sound of Otis's voice, some tale of blood and babies still caught in their throats. Diane sets her glass on the table. The cardhouse collapses in a flurry of color.

Algol, the Demon Star
(November 1970)

★　　　★　　　★　　　★　　　★　　　★

Outside, a branch beats persistently against the wall, driven by the gusting wind. It's two in the morning and darker than the inside of a drawer; rain plinks irregularly in a puddle. Cass smiles at this harmless noise, not hearing it as anything more than it is. She knows that Ben and Diane, had they stayed up for the news and seen the message flash across their screen—"It's eleven o'clock. Do you know where your children are?"—would have answered, "Yes."

"Asleep," they would have said. "Downstairs." They'd be right about Webb, Cass thinks—Webb is snuggled deep in his bed, dreaming about striped bass. But they'd be wrong about her. The two of them, who haven't stayed up past ten o'clock since the birth of their daughter, Jordan, haven't discovered that Cass isn't nestled downstairs most nights with her lights out and her homework done. They haven't discovered that ever since Labor Day, when Paine Westfall closed up

his house and left for Boston, Cass has been sneaking
out of her double French windows and crawling along
the grass to meet her friends in Paine's rec room. Any
night she and her friends can get free, they slide in
through the basement window that Leo managed to un-
latch. Tonight, with all of them safely inside, the room
feels as warm and cozy as a cave.

"More?" Cass asks Beverly, who's holding out her
glass. "You sure?"

Beverly nods, giggles, and says, "Absolutely." Her
face is red and her eyes are swollen; she's puked twice
already on the rocks that line Paine's beach. This is the
first time they've all managed to get out for the whole
night. Suzanne said she was sleeping at Beverly's, Beverly said she was sleeping at Cass's, Chip said he was
going to Leo's, and Leo just said he was going out. So
Cass figures it's Beverly's business if she wants to get
stinking, and she fills Beverly's glass. They're drinking
a concoction that Cass mixed specially—gin, vermouth,
bourbon, Scotch, rum, and red wine (all skimmed from
Ben's bottles), mixed half and half with Tab. Cass calls
this a "Black Eye."

"Want a hit?" Leo hisses, holding out a joint rolled in
pink paper. Leo gets grass from his older brother's
friend; when he takes a hit the skin beneath his cheekbones hollows. He's part Indian, or so he says, and in
the dim light of their scented candle Cass is inclined to
believe him. His hair, caught in a ponytail, is black and
very straight. His chest is smooth and tan and hairless.

He'd be two years ahead of Cass in school if he hadn't
been held back once, and ever since she met him on the
beach this summer she's seen him whenever she could.
They meet secretly, because Ben's forbidden her to
know him. She's not in love with Leo, but she's in love
with these dark nights, with the trailer he shares with
two dogs and his uncle, with his secret ways and his
Volkswagen van that smells of grass and golden re-

triever. She's in love with the way he saunters up to her
in school, his thumbs hooked in his low-slung jeans and
his hooded eyes daring the hall monitors to interfere.
He's been suspended twice, but he's never been caught
stealing cigarettes from the A&P, liquor from the package store, or albums from the K mart in Buzzards Bay.
Cass is sure that he's charmed, sure that nothing can go
wrong as long as he's around. When Ben drops her off
at school dances, she walks in the front door and
straight out the back door, where Leo picks her up and
then drives her to the railroad bridge. He's the sort of
guy who carries Visine to clear their eyes, and because
of his cleverness they never get caught.

She takes a hit and passes the joint to Chip. He un-
curls his arm from Suzanne's shoulder, pushes his limp
blond curls behind his ears, and pinches the roach between his thumb and a fingernail. "So," he says to Cass.
"You high or what?"

"Or what," she says.

Leo laughs and pulls her closer. They're lying in an
orange lounge chair with a broken leg, in a corner
where the blankets and the empty jars are piled. The
floor is littered with matches and cigarette butts and
paper cups, remnants of all the evenings they've spent
here. Chip makes a face in the dusty mirror over the
built-in bar. Leo says, "Check out March."

He holds a *Playboy* out to Chip, snapping it so the
centerfold flips open and reveals Miss March. Cass
sneaks a glance, wondering where they grow these
women with their perfect round breasts and slender
hairless legs. Paine's collection of magazines—ten years'
worth or more—is stacked on the floor between the
lounge chair and the Naugahyde couch, within easy
reach of Chip and Leo. Within easy reach of the girls,
too—Cass isn't above browsing through these when
she's alone or with her girlfriends. She and Suzanne
and Beverly read the letters and the juicy parts of the

articles out loud to each other when there's nothing better to do. They've learned all sorts of things their mothers never told them, like how many calories are in a
teaspoonful of sperm and what to look for in a rubber.
None of them has gone all the way, but they think
they'll know what to expect when they do. In the mean-
time, they keep their reading secret from the guys and
make fun of them for looking at the pictures.

"Booga-booga," Chip says, rolling his eyes behind his
wire-rimmed glasses. "Nice kazongies."

"Nice kazongies, my ass," snorts Suzanne, who is
Cass's best friend even though she's Beverly's cousin.
"You'd about reach her belly button." She cranes her
neck for a last hit off the roach, inhaling so hard that
Chip's fingers burn.

"Shit!" he yelps. The ember falls to the floor and he
turns to bite Suzanne's neck. Suzanne makes a face at
Cass and Cass pushes the candle farther into the dusky
corner, so that the room dims and is almost dark.

If Beverly had stayed at home, Cass thinks, everything would be perfect. It's only recently that they've
paired off—for most of the summer the five of them
drank Black Eyes and smoked grass and listened to
Leo's Eric Clapton records as a group. It was only when
they started coming here to Paine's that the guys moved
in on Cass and Suzanne as if they'd been waiting all
along, and now Beverly's the odd one out. If she weren't
here, Cass would blow out the candle and let what's
going to happen happen. She's read enough about it.
She feels ready, knows that if she lets Leo in she has to
kick him out in time. Suzanne and Chip are making out
already, breathing as heavily as if they're alone in the
room. Chip's hand is rooting around under Suzanne's
shirt. And, just as Cass notices this, she feels Leo's hand
inch from her stomach down into her pants. She wishes
Beverly would just pass out—she's had enough to drink

to floor a horse. But Beverly's dancing around now with two tennis balls jammed under her sweater.

"Look!" she giggles. "Miss November!"

Chip doesn't even look up. Leo does, but only to mock her. "Bev," he says. "You're wrecked."

"That's true," she says. "Wrecked, wrecked, wrecked." She fills her glass again and gulps it down. Cass feels sorry for her but doesn't know what to do—Bev's narrow face is spotted with zits, and she has skinny legs and no chest and blue glasses. No one is going to ask her out. She's funny and smart, but she doesn't need to count sperm calories. While Cass watches, Beverly collapses at the base of the bar and starts humming to herself. "All you need is love," she burbles. "Doo-de-doo-de-doo-de-doo." She burps and then falls silent.

Leo pulls his hand from Cass's pants and goes over to peer into Beverly's face. "Out cold," he says.

Suzanne lifts her head just enough to look. "Should we try and wake her up?" she asks. "Some coffee, maybe? Or we could take her outside and dunk her in the water."

"She'll be all right," Cass says. "She doesn't have to sober up until tomorrow. Why don't we let her sleep it off?" She's annoyed at Suzanne's concern. Why wake Beverly now? With her asleep, with the candle blown out and another Black Eye, anything could happen. She has the feeling this is the night when she and Suzanne will put their magazine knowledge to use.

"I don't know," Suzanne says hesitantly. "Will she be all right?"

"She'll be fine," Cass says. She blows the candle out.

"Well," Leo says, stretching in the lounge chair and wrapping himself around her. "Well, now."

Cass's head is spinning. She's not ready to puke yet, not even close, but her head has that warm, fuzzy feeling it gets when she's had just exactly enough to drink.

When she closes her eyes the room circles slowly, the way the polar constellations circle the North Star. Leo rolls over, crushing her beneath him, and starts to push against her stomach. She can feel a big lump stretching from the top of his pants pocket to the base of his zipper.

"Touch me," he groans.

He grabs her hand and slides it between them, over the lump. She gives it a gentle, experimental squeeze and then pulls her hand away when he groans again and jams himself into her hipbone. When he starts tugging at her zipper, she doesn't push his hand away as she always has before. She closes her eyes and turns her head so her mouth is on his neck. He hisses softly as her pants open. Before she has time to wonder what will happen next, he slips a finger inside her and unzips his own pants. There's this warm, hard, sticky thing beating on her belly, and she doesn't know quite what she's supposed to do with it. Should she hold it, as if she were shaking hands? Stroke it, as if it were a cat? And then there's his hand on her, his finger wiggling inside. Is she supposed to stay still for this? She wishes he had cut his fingernails.

She hears complicated rustlings from the couch across the room, and then something light and soft lands on her face. It's a shirt, probably Suzanne's. Suzanne whispers, "Hey! I'm cold!" and then giggles. More rustlings. Chip whispers something that Cass can't understand. Beverly makes a small gasping noise like a fish and rolls over, dead to the world. It's a good thing—between Suzanne's giggles and Chip's hoarse pants, Leo's mumbles and groans and her own surprised breaths, anyone, even Beverly, would know what was happening here. Leo inches down on her and takes his hand away, replacing it with this heavy wet thing that jumps like a bluefish on a hook. She touches the top and feels a little bead of something wet. Has he come already? She's not sure—it's nowhere near a teaspoonful. Has she? She's not sure of that either, although she definitely feels something, some warm itchiness. She pushes her pants down over her knees and is just about to let Leo in when she hears something scratching at the basement door.

"Shh," she says, holding Leo's head as if that would stop him now.

"Cass," he mumbles. "Cassie."

"I thought I heard something."

Leo shakes his head no, but the door rattles as if someone's pulling it and then a thin beam of light flashes under the bottom crack.

"Door's locked," Cass hears someone say. Ben? It sounds just like Ben.

"Get up!" she whispers frantically to Leo. "Someone's here!"

Leo groans loudly and comes all over her thigh. It's much more than a teaspoonful. There's a deadly silence from outside, and then Ben (it's definitely Ben) says, "Did you hear that? Someone's in there."

"Maybe we should call the police," a woman says. It sounds like Diane. "There could be burglars."

"Bullshit," Ben says. "You know who it is. Step back from the door."

Cass heaves Leo off her. He rolls to the floor with a heavy thump and says, "What? What?"

"Get *dressed*!" she hisses. She pulls her pants over her hips and struggles with her zipper. Her head is spinning and her ears are roaring as if they're full of water. This can't be happening. "Chip! Suzanne!" she whispers. "Someone's here!" The room is so dark that she can't see her own hands.

Outside, Ben bangs away at the flimsy lock and pulls on the door. He hasn't figured out yet that they came in through the window.

"What's going on?" Suzanne mutters. Cass tosses the

shirt over but knows it's a useless gesture. She can't stop whatever is about to happen. She's too drunk, too high; it's too late. She lights the candle, knowing that Ben will be through the door any second and hoping that the dim light will make things look better. Maybe they can pretend they were just playing cards. A friendly slumber party, a few games of poker—sure. When she sees that Chip and Suzanne are completely undressed, covered only by a blanket; that Leo's pants are around his knees and his eyes are red slits; that Beverly lies in a pool of vomit and spilled Black Eyes; she blows the candle out. She can't imagine what she looks like, but she knows she might as well die right now. There's a big, rasping wrench and then the door swings open, letting in the cool night air.

Inside the other house, the kitchen glows with a harsh light that floods every surface and stain. Ben pushes Cass through the door, slams it behind her, and then tosses Beverly into the car and roars away. Sal waits at the kitchen table, wearing a stained flannel nightgown that sticks to her ripples and bulges and hugs a stomach so big that she might be pregnant. Sal is spending the weekend here to help take care of Jordan, who has another of her famous colds. She doesn't seem surprised to see Cass.

"I thought so," she says. "It figures."

Diane clomps over to the refrigerator and pours herself a glass of milk. "You were right," she says. Her nightgown is cleaner than Sal's but almost as big; she's gotten so heavy that she and Sal look more like sisters than mother and daughter. When Cass looks at their soft hanging bodies her stomach seems to spin around some cold hard center, some walnut of liquor and fear. She stands near the door, not knowing where to look or what to do.

"Where did Ben go?" Sal asks.

"To the hospital, with one of Cass's little friends," Diane sneers. "Too much to drink, and *this* one too busy fooling around to notice." She speaks as if Cass isn't here in the room. "I'm going to bed," she says. "I've had enough of this." She drains the glass and marches away without even looking at Cass, without telling her what happens now.

"Might as well sit down," Sal says, and motions Cass to a chair. She's holding sleepy Jordan in her arms, dabbing at her drippy nose with a tissue and brandishing a jar of Vicks. Jordan sneezes every few minutes and looks sad in between. "Cashie," she murmurs, lifting her head for a minute.

"Hi, bunny," Cass says, perching on a chair at the far end of the table. She stares at Sal. Somehow, she thinks, Sal is responsible for this.

"Pleased with yourself?" Sal says. "Happy now?"

"Fuck off," Cass says tiredly. She and Sal don't bother to be civil when they're alone. "Leave me alone." She gets up and heads for her room.

"Sit," Sal says. "Right here, where I can keep an eye on you. You don't fool *me*, sister. Not for one minute."

"Yeah?" Cass says. "You don't know squat."

She says this the way she might say a charm to ward off an evil spirit, but the truth is that Sal seems to know almost everything. The truth is that Sal, stupid Sal, always knows when Cass is lying. Only last Christmas, Sal caught her out in a complicated scheme designed to spring her for a weekend-long ski trip with her friends. Cass laid the plans out smooth as butter over Christmas dinner, and she had Ben half convinced until Sal said, "So you wouldn't mind if we called your mother to check the arrangements, right?" Sal, gaudy in red silk, laughed when Cass choked on her mashed potatoes. And now Sal says, "Want to know how I knew?"

"Sure," Cass says. "Since you know everything. Did you see me in your Tarot cards?"

Sal laughs. "You're not that tough," she says. "Beverly's mother called here looking for her. I got the phone, since I was up with Jordan, and since Beverly wasn't here I got the bright idea to check your bed. When you weren't here I came up to tell Ben, and that's when I saw the glow from Paine's basement window. All I did was put two and two together." She says this quietly and yet proudly, as if Cass should be impressed.

"So what do you want?" Cass says. "A medal?" It figures that it all came down to Beverly.

"What do *you* want? Just to be the world's biggest pain in the ass?"

Sal never talks to Webb like this—she's kind to him, even fair. It's only Cass she picks on, and Cass knows she's brought this on herself. She hates Sal; she always has. And when she's alone with Sal her hatred shows.

"Know what I want?" Cass snaps. "I want you out of my life. I want you to stop spying on me and stop putting ideas into Dad's head."

"Fat chance, sweetie." Jordan sneezes and bats at Sal's hair, and Sal's face softens instantly. "Shh," she whispers to Jordan. "Go to sleep."

Cass sniffs. She can't stand to watch Sal with Jordan —although Jordan's the reason Ben and Diane stay married, and although Cass thought, at first, that she could reasonably blame this baby for almost anything, she has never managed to hate Jordan the way she hates Sal and Diane. Jordan is sunny and blond and sweet, and when she first crawled after Cass and nodded off in her lap Cass fell in love with her. She admits this only to Webb and Penny, but she's afraid that everyone else knows. She loves Jordan so much that she can't stand to admit that Sal is her grandmother, entitled to touch her whenever she wants.

"Let me hold her," Cass pleads. Only Jordan can settle her spinning stomach and calm the crazy fears sprouting in her head.

Sal shrugs and dumps Jordan into Cass's arms. "I shouldn't," she says. "You'll probably poison her, the way you did your little friend."

"She's not poisoned!" Cass snaps. "She just had too much to drink." She runs her hand over Jordan's soft hair and smooths her lids over her eyes. "I'd never hurt Jordan," she says.

"Sure," Sal says. "Not unless she got in your way. You may fool your parents, but you don't fool me. You've got a black Scorpio heart inside of you."

"Ha," Cass says bitterly. "What do you know? You're not even family."

"Maybe not," Sal says. "But I'm not going to let you make this family miserable."

"Oh, sure," Cass says. "Right. Gonna cast a spell on me and turn me into a toad?"

"Watch me," Sal says, with an odd smile. "Just watch." She waves her hand over Cass's head and says, "Disappear! Get lost!" And then she snatches Jordan from Cass's arms and floats away.

Three nights later, on her fifteenth birthday, Cass sits alone in her dark room, fingering the earrings Webb gave her. They're long and light, shimmery slices of acetate hooked to a central chain, and they're her only consolation. Her friends are gone; Paine's rec room is boarded up. She's been grounded indefinitely, banished to this basement, and Penny hasn't come home. "I'll be back for your birthday," she told Cass last May, just before she cast off the bow line and sailed away with Walker. Cass believed her absolutely. All last winter she and Webb helped Walker and Penny overhaul Walker's old wooden sloop, and so she was hardly surprised when, on what seemed like a moment's notice, Penny closed up her house, sold her fish, and took off for the Caribbean with Mizar and Alcor, her telescope, and her books.

"It's time," Penny told her. "Time for me to go exploring. You'll understand when you're ready to do the same thing. But you stay out of trouble until I get back, okay? I'm counting on you."

Cass knows she could have kept Penny from going: all she had to do was say, "Stay here. I need you" or "Don't go—we can't manage alone." One hint of the trouble to come and she knows her mother would have stayed, and yet what did Cass do? Looked Penny right in the eye and said, "You two have a great time. We'll be fine." Knowing already that she and Webb were heading for deep shit.

Maybe, she thinks now, I did that because I wanted someone to blame. Or maybe I just wanted to make her feel bad for leaving us the first time. Could that be true? She picks at the chipping paint on the windowsill, remembering all her precautions. There was the sewing machine—whenever Leo ripped off liquor for her she hid it carefully under the sewing machine cover until she could sneak it to Paine's. There were the breath mints and the eyedrops and the careful arrangements to get back to dances before Ben came to pick her up. These things seemed very clever all summer, but now they seem completely stupid and apparent to everyone, almost as if she messed up on purpose. She has lost, she thinks, all sense of perspective. And all she wants to do right now is to slip over to Penny's house and talk until she gets it back. That's the advantage, maybe the only one, of living apart: Penny, who doesn't have to discipline Cass, can simply listen, and until now Cass has believed that she could tell Penny anything. If Penny were here, Cass thinks she'd tell her about Leo, although maybe not about the last few minutes of that. She'd tell about the basement and about what Ben said, and she smiles when she imagines how this conversation would go. She can hear how Penny would sigh and groan and click her tongue against her teeth, hear the half-chuckle that would slip out when she described Ben's face. They'd both laugh then, and then Cass would move on to the bad part, the part where she found out that Beverly nearly died of alcohol poisoning but didn't because they got her stomach pumped in time.

It's this she really wants to talk about, the strange, almost sickening coincidence that's been at the base of her brooding for the last three days. Suppose, she imagines saying to Penny. Suppose Beverly had died? She strains her ears against the silent night for the answer Penny might give, but she hears nothing. Suppose, she thinks, growing queasy at the thought of how that might have been. Waking at dawn in a dirty room with Leo near her and Chip and Suzanne on the couch; all of them, working together, unable to wake Bev. That's what would have happened if they hadn't been caught, and this is what she wants to ask Penny. Is it an omen, a sign? This getting caught, the worst thing that's ever happened to her, kept her from something worse. She wants to ease up to Penny with that question, and then slide in the big one, the question hiding behind: How did Sal cause all this? Was it the curse? Sal said "disappear" as if she had the power, as if she'd seen Bev through the walls of both houses and reached out a fat arm to save her. "Disappear," she said, as if she could make it happen.

Cass wedges her fingernail under a big flake of paint and then coaxes it back, back, past the point where it was meant to break off and into some region where it clings to the wood like skin to flesh; back past that point, ripping until she's torn a long strip free and scarred the wood for good. There. If she had an ax she'd chop the walls to rubble. She can't talk to Penny because Penny hasn't come home, and without Penny all she can do is sit and wait until they send her away. Ben's been on the phone these past three days, calling private schools all over Vermont and New Hampshire. He's settled on one near Otis and Cindy that's famous for its strict discipline. "You're going there right after Christmas," he said, although she doesn't think he knows how to pay for it. From the way he talks, she might have planned the night in Paine's basement just to bankrupt him. "I'll sell all of Hawk Commons at a loss," he said. "If I have to. But you're going away to school."

Until then, she's stuck here. She digs with her fingernail again, finding a splinter of wood much deeper than paint and ripping at that too, coaxing the fibers to part. She can't even leave the house to go to school—Diane brings home Cass's books and assignments after working out plans with her teachers. The splinter comes free with a sharp crack that leaves a pale gouge in the sill, much too deep to be filled with paint. They'll have to putty this, Cass sees with satisfaction. She wonders if they'll rent her room out after she's gone or just leave it to grow moldy and dark. It's Sal's doing that she's stuck here—Sal's and Diane's. It's Sal's fault that she's going away. "Disappear," Sal said—and look what's happened. She should have taken Sal seriously. She's been disappeared all right, banished to a school for smart delinquents miles and miles away. She won't be able to cause trouble anymore, won't get in anyone's hair. She won't mess up this family because she won't be part of it. There's a new family now, Ben and Diane and Sal and Jordan and maybe, just maybe, Webb. It seems to her that everything that's happened has been inevitable. She sighs and turns off the small light near her bed, throwing the stars outside her window into focus. Somewhere, she thinks, Penny floats across the water gazing at these same stars. The stars are what Penny used to pry herself free, and Cass sits up straight at this odd thought, which she has never had so clearly. That's it, she thinks. Penny saw the difference between day and night and chose the night, a clear, cold space where she could be alone. I wish . . . Cass thinks, but she doesn't know what she wishes for. She presses her nose to the cold glass and strains to see the stars the way her mother does.

Andromeda, Pegasus, Perseus. She remembers Penny saying how she used to chant the names of the first-magnitude stars to herself, to ward off bad things. Cass chants constellations, but it doesn't seem to help. She casts her eyes along the Great Square of Pegasus, out the long handle of Andromeda and to the western arm of Perseus. A bright star glows there, the severed head of the Medusa that Perseus holds. "Algol," she whispers. The Demon Star. She and Penny used to watch it dim and flare and dim again, and Penny told her its name came from the weird way it winks. Every couple of days, she said, it dims to a third of its normal splendor, as if an eyelid drooped lazily over it. Astrologers call it evil—violent, unfortunate, dangerous. People like Sal, believing the stars rule their destinies, believe this.

Cass knows better: Penny taught her science, not superstition. She has her own eyes with which to read and see, and she knows that Algol's winking occurs because it's an eclipsing binary. Nothing more, nothing less; no dark magic. When it dims, it's not because someone waves an arm and says, "Disappear," but because it and a small, faint companion star revolve around each other. Once each revolution, the companion star partially eclipses Algol. Cass, knowing what it is to be eclipsed, has a clear picture of this. She knows the rational explanation, and yet tonight she wonders if blinking Algol might not be malignant, after all. Disaster, she thinks. Penny told her the word means "evil star."

She gouges a deep trench into the windowsill and then starts a parallel trench nearby. "Mom?" she whispers into the cool dark night. There isn't a chance in hell that Penny will get home in time to rescue her. The pointed tip of the file catches and she hammers it in with the palm of her hand, almost as if it were a chisel. The sill is beginning to look like it's been clawed by a bear, and now Cass remembers the last time she gouged wood like this—the winter when she was eight, when Penny and Ben took off for Florida on a fishing trip with Otis and Cindy. They left Cass and Webb at home with a baby-sitter, a fat woman named Marge with a curiously high voice and a puckered scar over one elbow. Marge moved in with her own three kids, promising to cook and clean for the bunch, and Penny couldn't have known that those three kids would torment Cass and Webb each day. Cass doesn't blame Penny for those two weeks, but she'd bet that Algol blinked balefully down then too. She warded off disaster then by locking herself into the bathroom with Webb and tossing the key out the window into the ocean below. Webb fell asleep in the tub while she used the tweezers to carve deep parallel tunnels into the windowsill. She can't remember what they were meant to be, anymore than she recognizes the tracks she gouges now. There were five of them, like the tracks left by a clawed hand. Marge had to call the fire department to get them out.

She starts another gouge, wishing she could think of something that would save both her and Webb. Nothing comes to mind. Gently, she knocks on the wall between her room and Webb's, in the hope that he's awake. A minute later he opens her door and steps into the dark room.

"Hey," he whispers. "You okay?"

"Yeah," she says. "I was just feeling lonely."

"You're not taking off, are you? Because if you are I want to come."

"What's the point? They'd only catch us."

"I guess," he says, and sits down on the bed next to her. He's taller than her and outweighs her by twenty pounds. Despite Ben's protests he's let his hair grow below his ears. It's very curly and sticks out in stiff clumps. "You won't go?" he says again. "Not without telling me?" He's unhappy that Cass crept out all those nights without him—more than her being caught, this is what's bothering him.

"I won't," she promises. She didn't bring him with her to Paine's at night because she didn't think he was old enough, but now she wishes she had. "Some birthday," she mutters, almost to herself. "Can you believe this?"

"Some life," he says, and stares morosely at his hands. "You think they're really going to send you away?"

"Believe it," she says.

"Assholes," Webb sniffs. "Ever since Jordan came, they've been acting like such assholes. I can't figure it out—we're both good with her."

"I know," Cass says. "It's not her fault. I think it's Sal."

"Will you have a roommate?" Webb asks. "At school?"

"I guess so. Will you be all right here?"

"Sure. But it won't be any fun without you." In the darkness he reaches for her hand, something he hasn't done in years. She can feel his fingers touching the windowsill next to her little finger, his fingertips exploring the tracks carved there even as his palm presses against the back of her hand. She can't find anything to say to him. He's tough and probably old enough to care for himself. He has his trombone for when he feels bad. He'll be fine, but she feels like she's abandoned him to the gypsies. She'd change things if she could, fix things somehow so they'd never be separated. She's going to lose him soon, and Jordan too. She'll never be part of a family again. She's made up her mind not to cry, but despite herself she does.

"Cass," Webb says. "Please don't . . ." She never cries in front of him.

"Shit," she sobs. And she brings up her right hand, still holding the file, and jabs the point so deeply into the windowsill that it stands there quivering. Webb grunts with surprise.

"I'm scared," she says, more quietly. She squeezes her eyes shut, feeling as if she's about to be shipped to some cold planetary moon. The only thing holding her here to the earth is Webb's warm hand, which leapt away when she stabbed the windowsill but has settled back again, lightly, over hers. "Look," she says, and points at the sky. "Look at the stars. I bet that's what Mom is doing right now."

"Maybe," Webb says.

He tilts his head up, and together they watch Algol blink. They're bound as tightly as a binary pair, locked in dependent orbits, and through Cass's mind flashes a muddled picture of a shadow slipped between then like the incoming tide.

PART THREE
Diane

*No man should hold it to be incredible, that
out of the astrologers' foolishnesses and blasphemies
some useful and sacred knowledge may come.
That out of the unclean slime may come
a little snail, or mussel, or oyster, or eel,
all useful nourishments . . .*

—Johannes Kepler, *Tertius interveniens*

The Sea of Tranquillity
(July 1971)

★　　　★　　　★　　　★　　　★　　　★

In the water, Webb sports about as if he's some sort of dolphin. The top of his round head breaks the water like a seaweed-covered boulder, and then his brown eyes show (not a boulder after all), his solid neck, and the smooth humps of his shoulders. He laughs and leaps free of the water and then plunges in again.

"Baby J!" he calls when he surfaces. "Come on in! You can do it!"

"Come on, sweetie," echoes Ben, who stands in the shallows with a white terrycloth hat sheltering his bald spot and his baggy bathing suit just touching the waves. While Webb darts about, Ben mines the soft mud with his toes and flips up quahogs, tossing them into the floating basket that trails behind him from a narrow rope. He moves like the Leo he is, proud ruler of his bay, and when Diane squints at his figure against the sun she imagines him draped in a golden cloak.

"Go on, honey," she says to Jordan. They are perched

on the soft edge of the lawn where it crumbles away to beach. Jordan squirms away from her and runs back toward the house. She stops after twenty feet or so, squeals "Watch me!" and runs for the water.

"Baby J!" Webb shouts. "Come and get me!"

He lowers his head so his chin is in the water and scuffles toward shore making shark noises. Diane wishes he hadn't made up this name—it's stuck since the moment he first used it, and now it springs to everyone's lips but hers. Baby J, indeed. To her it sounds like a candy bar.

Jordan streaks for the water gleefully, her fat tanned legs pumping and the yellow frill at the top of her bathing suit fluttering in the wind. Come on, sweetie, Diane thinks. Put your arms over your head and dive. Break the water, open your eyes, and hold your breath. Jordan peels past and hits the water full tilt—this time she's going to do it. Her body's arched to dive; her hands are clasped over her head.

"That's right!" shouts Webb. "Now dive!"

She runs forward, body still arched, until the water reaches her frill, and then she hops once, twice, and closes her eyes. Diane arches her own body and waits for the final splash. Jordan's white curls stay as dry as wood shavings, and she smiles with her eyes still closed. Perhaps she thinks she's already underwater, as wet as she needs to be. Diane holds her breath and waits for Ben's disparaging comment, but he and Webb both applaud. "That's okay," Ben says mildly to Jordan. "As long as you're having fun." He is often gentle with this daughter.

"That's great!" Webb shouts. "You want to try it again?"

"Yes!" Jordan shrieks.

"Do like me," Webb says. He holds his arms up, closes his eyes, and dives beneath the surface. "See?" he says, when he comes up. "It's easy."

"Okay," Jordan says. She wades out of the water, runs up the lawn, and gets ready again. Ben flips another quahog into his basket. "You're doing great," he calls.

"I love you, sweetie," Diane says. "Be careful."

"I love you too," Jordan says, and then she runs for the water as if she hasn't done this ten times already, as if she hasn't been doing it all summer.

Nothing ever seems to upset her. She's a mystery, still, to Diane—her own flesh and blood and yet, except for her pale eyes and hair, different in every way. Her real name comes from Sal, who moved in that last awful month when Diane could hardly waddle from toilet to bed. Sal started messing with a natal horoscope before the baby was even born, working from Diane's estimated delivery date. "A water baby," Sal predicted then. "Even with a sun in Taurus. Probably a girl." She buried her head in her ephemeris, consulted some books, and muttered something about the four royal stars of astrology guarding the four great districts of the sky.

"What should we name her?" Diane asked Sal then, trusting already that it would be a girl.

"Jordan," Sal said firmly. "Works for a boy or a girl, but I know it's a girl." She hummed a few notes and then broke into this:

> I looked over Jordan, and what did I see,
> Coming for to carry me home;
> A band of angels coming after me,
> Coming for to carry me home.

"Pretty," Diane remembers saying. "But I don't know. It sounds more like a boy's name to me."

"Trust me," Sal said. "I got a feeling. Name the kid Jordan."

And so she had. Ben wouldn't come into the delivery

room because he couldn't stand the blood, but Sal came in with a stopwatch and timed the instant of the baby's first breath. "Jordan!" she called. "Welcome!"

"Girl," the doctor said. "A healthy girl."

Sal finished Jordan's horoscope before she came to visit Diane that night. "Sun, Mercury, Mars in Taurus, with Pisces ascendent," she said. "Moon and Venus in Pisces, Saturn in Aries, Jupiter in Leo, Uranus in Virgo, Neptune in Scorpio."

Ben, holding Diane's tired hand, frowned and said, "What's all this?"

"Mom made the baby a horoscope," Diane said weakly. "No big deal."

And it wasn't, really. Diane doesn't put much faith in horoscopes herself, although she's been watching Sal cast them for years. They're like insurance, she thinks— little harm in them, and possibly some good. She had Sal cast charts for Cass and Webb too, and now she keeps these, along with her own and Jordan's, in a sealed plastic bag in the back of the freezer. Safe from fire, she thinks. Safe from floods. During the months after Jordan's birth she took her daughter's chart from the freezer nearly every night, tracing with her finger the curled symbols clustered at the cusps. She'd stare at her lovely sleeping daughter for a while, at her gentle, eerie, ever-present smile; she'd stare at the chart, trying to fathom the mystery of her happy child. It was the moon, Sal said, when Diane asked her why Jordan never cried and always smiled. Jordan's moon was very strong.

It seems that Sal was right. The moon has never looked the same to Diane since Jordan's birth, any more than it has since the astronauts first orbited it. She remembers how Jordan liked those first pictures beamed back to earth by astronauts halfway to the moon. A toothbrush floating; a gray, grainy lunar landscape that caught her eight-month-old child's attention. "We can see the terminator clearly," said the astronauts, describing the sharp line dividing day and night. She held Jordan in her arms in front of the TV on her first Christmas Eve, and together they looked at the moon pictures and listened to the men describe the view. Vast, one of them said. Lovely and stark and forbidding. Black and white. Jordan fell asleep on her shoulder and she slept too before the broadcast was done, quieted by the smooth surface of the Sea of Tranquillity. "Tranquillity Base here," the astronauts said seven months later, when they touched down on that same dark plain. "The *Eagle* has landed." The astronauts talked to Houston while the whole world listened; Jordan, listening to the crackling exchange, talked to her. "Da," Jordan said, pointing to the screen. A ghostly gray figure stepped backward from a spiderlike machine, groped down a ladder and stood swaying on the surface of the moon. "Look," Diane whispered to Jordan, pointing at that first pale footprint. Jordan smiled broadly.

She still smiles, at everyone and everything. She floats through her life as if the moon's dark seas and their own small bay were all one tranquil pond for her to play in, and although no one knows why she won't put her head underwater they know she has her reasons. "Mommy!" she calls now. "Watch me!"

Diane squints over the water and sees that her daughter, for the tenth or hundredth time, has dashed up to the frill on her bathing suit. Her arms are stretched toward the sky and her eyes are closed. She smiles blissfully at no one, while her frill floats on the water like a leaf.

Hours later, after they've dried themselves and had two small squabbles before retreating to the four corners of the house, after Diane's bathed and Ben's worked outside, after Webb's read his comic book and Jordan's napped in the rope hammock strung between the balcony and the cedar tree, Diane makes chowder from Ben's quahogs. She browns salt pork and onions, steams the shellfish, and adds, at the last minute, hot milk and butter. Jordan sits on the counter, sniffing happily and running a fork through her hair.

"Hungry," she announces.

"Are you, sweetie? Me too."

Jordan knows a lot of words but can't manage sentences yet. She's not like Cass, who (according to Ben) talked and read so young. Neither is she like Webb, who took forever to speak. She's just exactly on schedule, without particular dullness or brilliance except for her unusual disposition. Diane smiles at her and pulls a pan of biscuits from the oven. Ben sits down at the table wearing the half-glasses he's recently acquired, which lie solidly on his high-bridged nose and make him resemble his father. He reads while he eats, flipping through a thick folder of documents related to the Mashpee Shopping Center. He's given up residential developments since the trouble with Hawk Commons; now, with a new set of partners, he's building and leasing commercial space.

Outside the picture window, two gulls dart back and forth, squabbling over a fish. The sun is a huge red disk over the island. Her family is so quiet that she can hear her breath, and Diane's question to Ben—"How's the project going?"—breaks the silence like a siren.

Ben looks up and blinks, a spoonful of chowder halfway to his mouth. "This?" he says, pointing at the folder. "It's fine."

She waits to hear the details but he offers nothing else. This afternoon they argued over the position of three flagstones; now he looks at her as if she's cantaloupe. How did this happen? It's not, she thinks, as if I don't understand his work. It's true that when she first met Ben she was fresh out of secretarial school and stupid as some new fruit, but she hasn't been that way for years. Ben taught her to read titles and maps in land offices and then set out to scout the Cape for likely sites. She turned out to have a knack for this, a nose for aging landowners with money troubles, and Ben said she was the best help he'd ever had. Those first few years they worked together side by side, and she'd thought they'd continue after they got married. Things haven't worked out that way. Ben asked her to quit work and stay home when she got pregnant with Jordan, and now she hears about his deals only from his partners, who feed her ragged scraps of information between mouthfuls of the food she's made for them. She only knows how well Ben's doing when he brings her a check.

"How long does this have to last?" she asks each time. Some of the checks are huge.

"I don't know," Ben says. "Until the next one."

The way he works, the next one may come in a week or a month or a year. When he sells something they live like kings, redecorating and stepping out. When he doesn't, they borrow money from his parents and hole up inside the house. They're in a middle phase now, a few months since the last check but with prospects for a new one soon. Everything they buy, they buy on credit.

Ben crinkles his papers. "Can I type something for you?" Diane asks. She'd love a look at those letters.

He shrugs. "Marlene can handle it." Marlene, with her pale skin that reddens across her nose and her constant blush around Diane, is the college girl Ben hired for the summer to do the work Diane used to do. She's twenty or twenty-one—younger than Diane was when she met Ben but still not safe at all. Diane hates her. Cass was meant to have the job, but Cass turned Ben's offer down cold and went to work for Otis Nelson instead, staying with him and Cindy in New Hampshire. Cass says she's never coming home. She roughs out drawings for Otis, who says she has a real flair for drafting and ought to consider engineering. After all the trouble Cass gave her last fall, Diane never thought she'd want her home, and yet right now she'd be grateful to see her face. Anything would be better than this Marlene.

"Oh, Mar*lene*," Diane says scornfully. "She can hardly type. I could whip the letters off here in half the time . . ."

Ben shrugs again.

Webb, sitting next to the high chair, helps Jordan with her chowder. He ladles a scoop into the Peter Rabbit bowl, blows to cool it, and tests it himself before giving Jordan the spoon. When she dribbles or misses her mouth altogether he wipes her face with the corner of her bib. "Good?" he asks.

"Good!" She waves her spoon in the air, and Ben looks up for a minute and smiles at his children. Webb blushes under this unaccustomed gift. He's not quick enough, smart enough, strong enough for Ben, and it's hard for Ben to do anything but criticize him. It's like the flagstones, Diane thinks—the three stones in one formation were good, they were fine, but shifted just half an inch over and to the right they were a little better, and so it made sense to Ben to dig them all up and tear out the turf, as it made sense, when Webb worked so hard this spring to raise his math grade from a C to a B, for Ben to say, "Maybe next year you'll get an A." Webb has a stammer now, slight except when he talks to Ben. When Ben criticizes him, it's apt to turn into a full-blown, red-faced stop.

Webb pats Jordan's cheek dry and looks up at his father. "Can I go to Tommy Cavallo's?" he blurts. "There's a little party there tonight."

Ben's smile vanishes. "Did you finish the lawn?"

"Yup."

"Clip around all the trees?"

"Yup."

"Will his parents be there?"

"Yup."

Ben pauses to consider for a minute, and then says, "I don't know. I'll think about it. Did you practice your trombone?"

"Yup."

Ben slips back into his papers as Webb answers. The corners of Webb's mouth sink, but he continues to help Jordan eat. He's so sweet and honest and simple and straight that Diane knows, sometimes, that this thing she feels for him is love. When Ben works late, Webb sits beside her and watches TV, telling her about school and band and Susie Cabot, whom he'd like to ask out but can't because he's too afraid. He talks to Diane as if she's a person, something Cass never did. Sal attributes his patience, good humor, and quiet strength to his Sun and Venus in Taurus, with Taurus rising. It's true that, like some lazy warm animal, he can lie in the hammock for hours.

"Let him go," she says to Ben. She knows how hard it was for Webb to ask. "Come on—he's practiced his trombone plenty. It's just for a few kids, and he'll be home by eleven." She turns to Webb. "Won't you?"

Webb lifts his eyes, brightening at this sudden stroke of luck. "Absolutely," he says. "We're just going to play some records and stuff."

"Mommy?" Jordan says, pointing to the biscuits. "Muff?"

Diane breaks one into pieces and lays it in her dish. Ben, without looking up from his letters, says, "Biscuit, honey. It's a biscuit. Not a muff."

Before Ben leaves he suggests to Diane that she spend the night putting pictures in the three thick albums he gave her for her birthday. "Since you'll be alone," he said, not nastily at all but as if it only made sense to keep her busy. Now Diane sits in the living room, with a shoebox of pictures spread before her on the coffee table. She picks up an oblong Polaroid print and squints at the date along the edge—it's her, at twenty-three. The picture is only five years old and yet she can hardly recognize herself. That waist! That even, fine-pored skin! Her hair seems much lighter and her eyes seem big and clear. That's not me, she thinks, feeling her cheek reflexively. That's someone else, a girl who fell in love with someone's husband and said yes when, one night after work, he asked her to walk down the beach with him and look at the stars.

Of course I said yes, she thinks, remembering what seemed to her then like a magic evening. Of course I did, and of course he didn't know anything about the stars and couldn't even find the Big Dipper. They stopped at the Dolphin Bar for margaritas, which always made Diane feel like a meteor. They drove to the beach, hardly talking, Ben's thigh just touching hers and his pale hair glowing. And there, Diane smelled for the first time the smell Ben gets when he is fired up, a warm, blond sharpness suggesting split cedar beneath the sun, and salt hay, and warm rocks. She knows now that this, more an aura than a smell, draws women to him as if they're heat-seeking missiles and he's an open flame. By the time he held out his hand to her, she would have followed him over a cliff. Which he knew: he didn't know his stars, but he knew enough to bring her down to the picnic table at the end of the cove, to stretch out on his back for star-gazing and get her to stretch out too. He knew enough to talk softly to her while he slipped his hand inside her shirt.

"But your wife . . ." she said, just once, when it was already about to be too late.

"It's all right," he said, and it was. The other women she knows would count her lucky—Ben actually left his wife and married her. There was a year of meeting in dark bars and grappling in the office, and then this—all she dreamed of then—a daughter, a house, even money.

She has no explanation for what's gone wrong in the midst of all this plenty. Sal says she's subject, like everyone, to influences; perhaps Sal is right. "The stars," Sal says, "don't predestine your life. But they shape its limits and possibilities."

Diane sorts the pictures into piles. There are pictures of her alone, before she was pregnant—surreptitious Polaroids, showing her breasts to advantage, which Ben hid in his office until he was safely divorced. Wedding pictures—Sal in a huge blue tent, Vivian in mauve slubbed silk, Bryant in a pinstriped gray suit. Ben in charcoal with black shoes, and her, looking faintly silly in shiny pink brocade. Cass and Webb pictures—Webb on a rock, Cass with her ant farm, Webb in a band, Cass in a tree. Jordan pictures—at birth, at bath, awake, asleep, first word, first step, first everything. Teetering in Diane's high heels, wearing a baggy diaper and holding a wedge of watermelon. Drowning her duck in the tub. Pictures of them as a family—the smallest pile—including a Christmas picture where Ben's hand rests tenderly on her thigh and the children crouch before them; a beach picture showing her, Ben, Webb, and a very tiny Jordan near the waves; and a skiing picture with the five of them posed in front of the Nelsons' A-frame. Cass sulks in every one.

The house is absolutely still, the loudest sounds the rasp of her fingernails against the pictures' serrated borders and the occasional crisp snap of bugs fried in the porch light. Two hours until she can pick up Webb, hours more until Ben comes home. She could call the office, just to know that Ben's there. She doesn't, because she's afraid he's not. She finds a picture of their house half buried in a freak snow storm, and this one stills her restlessness.

The house looks like a castle, with a storybook frosting of vanilla snow and a gingerbread cottage just visible next door. This is how she first saw it, the picture

Ben showed her long before the day he drove her into the horseshoe-shaped driveway. This is how it still feels to her. Out there are Penny and Walker and Cass, Sal and her astrological wonders, Ben's partners, business deals, Marlene. Inside are her and Jordan and Ben and Webb, a sea of tranquillity safe in a dark lunar landscape. Four bathrooms in here, a wavy tile roof—she feels safer here, even when things go badly, than she has ever felt in a place before. It takes her all week to clean and she doesn't mind, relishing the feel of smooth porcelain accepting cleanser after the porous surfaces of the dumps she shared with Sal.

She sets the picture aside, thinking that perhaps she'll have it blown up as a Christmas card. On top of it she piles Ben's secret pictures of her, telling herself that she'll hide these somewhere, maybe in the freezer. If no one sees those pictures perhaps no one will notice how big she's gotten. A few years of ice cream, cookies, warm chocolate cake, complicated pastries made late at night when Ben's working and she's bored, missing his sharp tang; a pound here, a pound there, added to the weight she gained with Jordan and has never lost—how did this happen? The last time she weighed herself the scale said one hundred and sixty pounds. Even the scale at the golf club, known to be forgiving, whispered, "One fifty-five."

She files the wedding and family pictures in one album, Jordan's pictures in another, and the odds and ends in a third. Head to toe and side to side, in orders they'd all deny, she juxtaposes Bryant and Vivian, Otis and Cindy, casual acquaintances met in New Hampshire, friends of Webb, Sal. Sal bizarrely coupled with Paine Westfall at the barbecue last July, when he wandered over and stared so wistfully Diane had to ask him to sit down. He picked up Jordan, who now thinks he's wonderful, and he flirted with Sal, admiring her strapless sundress and her onyx sundial medallion. He al-

most fell at Sal's feet when she offered to cast him a
horoscope, and now Diane has to ask him over whenever Sal visits. Cass and Webb swear he's crazy, but
here, bulging from his madras shorts, he only looks
comical. She sets this picture, filled to the edge of the
frame and beyond by these two huge people, next to a
picture of Bryant and Vivian. Bryant and Vivian huddle in the center of their picture like sticks adrift in a
river.

The pictures of Sal depress her—in another ten or
fifteen years she's afraid she'll look like this. She heaves
the filled albums into the bookcase and shuffles together
the orphaned pictures of herself. She'd save them for
Jordan if she weren't afraid that Jordan would look at
them someday and say, "Mom—what *happened* to you?"
Especially when part of what happened to her was
surely Jordan. Hungry all the time, Diane ate half gal-
lons of ice cream during her pregnancy as if they were
cones, and after she had Jordan her belly grew softer
but hardly shrank at all. Her once-smooth thighs resemble cottage cheese and she's lucky, now, if Ben compli-
ments her hair. Despite this she knows he loves her—
how could he not? She's produced his favorite child.

She sticks the pictures in her underwear drawer and
then wanders through the house aimlessly, tidying papers and rearranging knickknacks. She's been cleaning
all week, and there's nothing for her to do. She goes
downstairs to check Webb's room but it's neat already:
shoes lined up, radio off, clothes in the closet, trombone
in its case. His music teeters in a haphazard stack; she
tidies it into a cube and sets it on his desk.

The door to Cass's room, next to Webb's, is closed.
She opens it with a sense of invading something secret,
but finds only a stripped bed and a few dust mice. Cass's
closet is empty except for a pair of shorts and some torn
sneakers; her records and posters have vanished. The
room feels abandoned, so barren that Diane chews her

lower lip and wonders, suddenly, if Cass is gone forever. Until now she's assumed that Cass would come
back sooner or later. She's left nothing behind but her
old cardboard star dome, which hangs on one of the
coat hooks like a hat. On a whim, Diane picks it up and
places it over her head. Nothing happens. The greenish
dots are faded and unrecognizable. She turns to leave
but remembers Webb chattering about this very dome,
how it glowed in the dark after being charged. She
holds the dome up to the light for a minute. When she
hits the switch and sticks the dome back over her head,
the stars leap out at her.

"Jesus!" she gasps. It's as if the whole night sky had
suddenly shrunk to the size of her head. Pricks of light
twinkle everywhere, and not one is known to her. She
stares at the dots for a while, marveling at their patterns. When she leaves she takes the dome with her.

She kills the last bit of time until eleven by sitting on
the porch and trying, without success, to match the
stars in the sky to the dots in the dome. The dome's
center doesn't line up with the sky above her, and she
can't find a way to bring the two together. With a sigh
she sets the dome aside and tiptoes into Jordan's room,
bundling her daughter in an unnecessary blanket. Jordan stirs and droops her head over Diane's shoulder.
"Sail," she mutters, or "snail" or "nail," clues to a
dream that no one will ever know. Diane carries Jordan
out and lays her on the car seat, Jordan's head in her
lap. Jordan sleeps on.

It's one of those clear, cool nights when the stars
twinkle furiously. Above the moon, two larger stars
glow. Planets, perhaps—she doesn't know which ones
but she feels, tonight, as if she could learn. She could
turn her life around, she thinks, if she had something to
do. Ben's laughed at the other ways she's kept busy
since Jordan's birth—decoupage and macramé and fur-

niture refinishing, needlepoint and crewel—but this would be different. She could find Cass's old star books or buy her own. She can hear herself explaining this to Ben, telling him how this would be something for her sleeping brain instead of her hands. *Something different.* She can hear his disbelieving snort.

Jordan's pale head moves on Diane's thigh, and she reminds herself—again, again—that she's vowed to stop these mental arguments. *Yak, yak, yak*, says the Ben-voice in her head. *Blah, blah, blah*, says her own voice back, neither voice real, nothing they say worth anything, less than a dream; and yet she sinks so deep into these fantasy scenes that she sometimes forgets what she's actually said and what she's only meant to say. It gets her nowhere.

She pulls into the Cavallos' driveway and sees that all the lights in the house are on. No one comes to the door when she taps the horn. "Shit," she mutters, lifting Jordan's head gently from her lap and sliding from the car. She trots up to the front door. "Webb?" she calls loudly. Rock music blares from the basement. "Webb?" she calls again. "It's time."

She hears a door slam, and then she sees Webb and Susie giggling their way down the hall to her. Susie's freckled nose is flushed, and Webb grins so hard his face seems about to crack. His hair sticks up behind his ears in kinky tufts. When he reaches the stoop he says, "Hi" and trips, which only makes him laugh. Susie giggles so fiercely that she has to cover her mouth with two hands. "Hello, Mrs. Day," she gasps.

"Hi," Diane says, looking them over. "You two have a good time?"

She slides back into the front seat, where Jordan has curled up like a snail. Webb and Susie clamber into the back. Diane drapes an arm over her daughter and checks out Webb and Susie in the rearview mirror. Webb is sending off a peculiar uneasiness, an unwillingness to meet her eyes, and as she backs out of the drive-way it hits her—the Cavallos' car isn't here. She knows these signs, the bright eyes, the rosy cheeks. She has seen them with Cass. She stares at Webb in disbelief, hardly able to keep her eyes on the road.

"It was okay," Webb mutters, finally answering her question as if he's unaware of the minutes that have passed. Susie breaks into giggles again and Diane feels a plug of panic rising in her throat.

"Have you . . . ?" she says, but doesn't finish her question. She might be wrong, and it isn't fair to accuse him in front of Susie. They drive silently to Susie's house, the engine's hum punctuated only by occasional whispers from the backseat. Susie glides out clumsily, catching her moccasin on the corner of the door. She giggles one last time, shakes her head, straightens her shoulders, and says, "Thank you, Mrs. Day." Then she marches off to her front door, no doubt thinking that she's walking perfectly straight.

"Come sit in front," Diane says to Webb. This is Ben's job, or even Penny's, but when he climbs in next to Jordan she reaches over her daughter's head and sniffs his breath. Beer.

"Webb!" she says despairingly.

He pulls himself to the far side of the seat, no longer laughing. "What?" Jordan makes a peculiar sound and flops her legs twice. Perhaps she's dreaming about the water.

"Tommy's parents weren't home, were they?"

He picks at the door lock, snapping it up and down. "No," he says finally.

She can see his lips trembling—lying comes hard to him. She gambles that he'll tell her the truth. "Did you know they weren't going to be?"

"No!" He turns to face her. "Really, I didn't. There were only five of us there, and so his parents decided to go to the movies. It's not my fault they left."

Diane wills herself to be calm and reasonable. "You were drinking," she says quietly. "Weren't you?"

She can almost hear his brain working, wondering whether to tell her the truth. She'd bet that he has arguments in his head. Tell me, she wishes silently. Tell me and I won't be mad. Just don't lie.

"I had three beers," he admits. "I split the last one with Susie. We just wanted to see what it felt like."

"Where'd you get it?"

"From the refrigerator in the basement."

She's quiet for a minute, and then she reaches out and touches Jordan's hair. If only I could keep him home, she thinks. Safe, like I keep Jordan. "I'm disappointed," she says softly. "Especially after I convinced your father to let you go . . ."

"Are you going to tell Dad?"

She can hear the fear in his voice. Is she? Ben's the disciplinarian and she knows she should tell him, but she also knows that Webb's punishment will be swift and sure if she does. Grounded for the summer, maybe for the year. Webb, like any Taurus, will get stubborn if he's crossed—she foresees a whole series of rebellions and punishments and counterrebellions, culminating in some great disaster. Cass just went her own sneaky way, ignoring Ben's rules as if they didn't exist. Webb's more likely to obey and then do something awful.

"I'll make you a deal," she says. "I won't, if you promise never to do this again. I'll bet you didn't even like it."

"Tasted pretty bad," he admits.

"See? You don't have to do this just because your friends do. Promise me you won't?"

"Okay. Promise you won't tell Dad?"

"Promise," she says.

He inches toward Jordan until he's nearly touching her, and then he reaches over and pats Diane's hand.

She smiles in the dark. "I just don't want things to go bad for you," she says. "Like they did for Cass."

"I'm not Cass!" he flashes. "You and Dad always say shit—stuff—like that. Just because she got in trouble doesn't mean I will." He bangs the door with his fist to emphasize his point, and Jordan's eyes snap open.

"Bebb," she murmurs.

"Baby J," Webb says fondly, his anger quieting as he turns to her. His voice, just beginning to change, cracks on the J. Diane turns away to hide her smile. He has a razor hidden in his room, but he won't need it for a while.

She parks in the driveway and lifts Jordan into her arms. "Look," she says, turning to Webb. "I didn't mean to say that about you and Cass. But I worry about you, just like I do about Jordan."

Webb sighs. "I know," he says. "But how come everything's so crazy around here? Dad's gone all the time and then he's mad when he's home, and he drinks too much, and Cass never visits and acts snotty on the phone, and you're always sitting around the kitchen looking like you're hearing voices from Mars. How come we can't just be normal?"

"I don't know," she says. It upsets her that he should think this already. She tries not to argue with Ben when Webb's around, tries to keep Ben from drinking during the day, tries to keep their weekly phone calls to Cass pleasant and superficial. She thought she'd been doing pretty well. "We love you, you know," she says, cradling Jordan against her neck. "All of us."

"I know," Webb mutters. "But sometimes it doesn't help."

Zodiac Haze
(December 1973)

★　　　★　　　★　　　★　　　★　　　★

All morning the sky has hovered between rain and fog.
Sometimes the fog shrouds the house in a close gray
vest; sometimes it cracks to show monstrous splinters of
water and land. As it presses against the walls, Diane
puffs on a cigarette (a new habit, supposed to make her
thin) and slowly turns the pages of the book her mother
gave her. *New Astrology*, trumpets the cover. *For the Age
of Aquarius!* The pages, littered with fanciful drawings
of constellations and astrological signs, have helped her
dream the day away while Jordan's at school. There are
dragons with wings and fangs here, lions wearing
crowns; lists of Sabian symbols with their cryptic titles
linked to the degrees of the zodiac. "Brightly-clad
Brownie dances in the dying light" reads one descrip-
tion. "Plaid rabbit changes into dancing elf." Who
writes these? she wonders. They sound like tabloid
headlines, and only Sal would read them seriously. On
one page is a multilayered representation of a soul,

quartered and sliced. Her soul? Not likely, but from where she sits, at the window overlooking the bay, the landscape seems to have been replaced by a hazy version of the zodiacal belt. She squints her eyes and sees a centaur bearing arrows, made from Paine's porch light. A stinging scorpion, made from an apple tree.

It's thirty-four degrees outside, and at any minute the fog may fall as snow. Should she walk to the end of their dirt road and meet Jordan at the bus? Jordan's the only child to come down this road and it's possible, although only just, that she'll lose her way in this low-lying cloud. Her bright yellow slicker keeps her safe from cars, but suppose she stops for a handful of leaves and then wanders off in the wrong direction? Still a water baby, she gets lost easily on land. The phone rings just as Diane closes her book and decides that yes, she'll go.

"Mrs. Day?" stammers a strange woman.

"Yes?" Outside, the fog parts to show a mooring buoy.

"I'm the school nurse."

Diane's neck prickles. "Jordan?" she says. "What's happened to Jordan?" Instantly, instinctively, she knows it's Jordan, squished on the road or blue on the cafeteria floor, with a hot dog lodged in her throat. She sucks in a breath that, like a drug, speeds up and blurs the world around her.

"It's Webb," the woman says. "Your son." Her voice is high and fast.

Diane jams the receiver against her ear, but still she can hardly hear the nurse. "Pills," she hears. "Pills . . . in his pocket . . . fell off his stool in shop . . . thought he fainted . . ." The thumping she hears, drowning out the nurse's tinny words, is blood banging inside her head. Webb is on his way to Hyannis, in an ambulance. Unconscious still. A whisper, something she can't understand. "What?" she says. "What?" Politely, the nurse says, "You should go to the hospital immediately." Diane hangs up.

Webb, not Jordan. Webb, who is so sturdy. Her mouth tastes as if she's been sucking on a tarnished spoon. She dials Ben's office and then slams the phone down when the prim receptionist reports him out. She leaves no message. He is always out, thinking he fools her with tales of work and then coming home after the moon sets with the soft smell of peonies in his hair. In her mind she hears herself screaming at him: *Where are you?* She calls Sal, who promises to come right away. She runs over and pounds on Paine's door. Thank God he retired, she thinks. Thank God he's here. He opens the door wearing a smoking jacket that just meets around his enormous middle.

"What a lovely surprise!" he says.

"Webb's in the hospital," she blurts. "I have to go. Sal's on her way over, but Jordan will be here before her—can you come over and watch her for a minute?"

His fat cheeks settle into folds of concern. "Of course," he says. "Anything to help." She watches impatiently while he gathers his pipe, tobacco, a pair of slippers. Everything he does takes so long. "What happened?" he asks.

"I don't know," she says. She opens the kitchen door for him, spins toward the car, and then swears and darts back inside the house, brushing Paine aside. Penny, she thinks. Quickly she dials Penny at work. She'll have to talk quietly, so Paine can't hear.

"Canal Hardware," Penny answers. Her voice, so brisk and efficient, cuts through some of the fog in Diane's head.

"It's me," she says. "Diane. Webb got sick at school— he took some pills or something, I don't know what. They're taking him to the hospital in Hyannis . . ." Before she can finish she bursts into tears. Paine looks up.

"My car's busted," Penny says tensely. "Can you drive?"

"Yes," Diane says. "Damn."

"Meet me at my house, then. I'll have someone run me home—it'll save a few minutes.

Diane hangs up and smears her running mascara with the palm of her hand. "Pills?" Paine says. He's already settled in her chair.

"I . . ." she stutters and flies out the door. She roars down the road to Grey Gables, passing Jordan's school bus before she screeches to a stop in front of Penny's house. "Come on," she mutters, leaning on the horn. A small, ratlike dog hurls himself against the door of the sagging porch, yelping the news of her impatience.

Penny gallops out, her grizzled hair streaming behind her and her purple checked coat open in front. "Let's go," she says, throwing herself into the car. "Want me to drive?"

"I'm okay," Diane says. "You can navigate."

Quickly, Penny gives directions. She wears no makeup and her face is strangely yellow. White, Diane guesses, under her dark tan. Her skin has the texture and sheen of grained leather. "Did you call Ben yet?" Penny asks.

"Tried to—he's not at the office."

"Figures," Penny says. "We'll try from the hospital."

Diane drives as fast as the fog allows. She turns her headlights on, but that only makes the haze worse; she settles for parking lights, to ward off other cars. Along the side of the road, dogs and cats and children seem to leap out at her and then melt back into the fog, so that she starts from time to time and rubs one eye and then the other. She's seeing things, but it's not her fault. She glances at Penny beside her, wondering at Penny's apparent calm. They've gotten together before only to talk about Cass and Webb, all business. I'll do this, one says. I'll do that, says the other—setting up rules for a double household. Diane clears her throat. "Pills," she says quietly. "They didn't say what kind. Do you have any idea?"

Penny lights a cigarette and blows the smoke out through her nostrils. She could be a man, but for her long, dry hair—all muscle and bone, angle and hardness, broad shoulders. She shows none of the signs of the care Diane lavishes on herself. No cosmetics, no creams. Her eyes are sunk in a web of creases and two long lines groove her face from nose to chin, giving her the look of a wise bird. "No," she says. Her voice is calm. Her fingernails are clipped short and tobacco-stained. "He hasn't seemed happy for a while, but he doesn't talk to me much anymore so I never know. He misses Cass—sometimes he talks to Walker about her when they're working together. And Walker lets him have a beer at the end of the day, but we've never seen him drunk."

"I wish—" Diane starts. Penny waves her hand in the air, dismissing the complaint like smoke.

"I know," Penny says. "You wish I wouldn't let him drink, you wish I wouldn't let him stay up so late, you wish I made him do his homework. But he's sixteen—he can make up his own mind sometimes. It's not like Ben ever lets him."

Diane's in no mood to stick up for Ben. "Maybe you're right," she says. She looks at Penny's cigarette. "Can I have one of those?"

Penny lights a cigarette and passes it over. "I didn't know you smoked—Ben always used to hate it."

Diane shrugs and passes her hand vaguely over her alarming bulk. She takes the cigarette, acutely aware that it's passed to her from Penny's mouth. But then so did Ben, once, and when she thinks about the ways she and Penny have been connected, the flesh and spit and pain they've shared, a wet-lipped cigarette doesn't seem like much. Her mind leaps forward to Webb and crashes there. She can't talk about him. She can't even stand to think about him until she sees him. She looks at the harsh lines of Penny's profile and finds herself thinking, instead, about all the things she's never asked Penny. What did Penny do when Ben stopped coming home at night? Was she jealous? Did she hate Diane then? Did she leave her children behind just out of spite? She knows almost nothing about Penny's real life, only the odd facts Webb chooses to tell her. She doesn't want to think about Webb.

"Have you heard from Cass?" she asks, trying to find something neutral to talk about.

Penny eyes her curiously but plays along, as if they're laying out the first cards of double solitaire. "She's fine," Penny says mildly. "We talk a lot. She's having trouble with freshman physics but she's doing great with math and her surveying field work. And she's got a boyfriend. You probably know that."

Diane remembers the boys in Paine's basement and smiles wryly. "I didn't," she says. "But it's no surprise."

Penny smiles. "I suppose not," she agrees. "He's a second-year grad student. I called Cindy and made her promise she'd take Cass to her gynecologist."

"For an exam?"

Penny stares at her. "For birth control pills, of course. You think I want her to go through what I did?"

"I guess not," Diane says. The thought makes her queasy—Ben would have a fit if he knew. She wishes Penny hadn't told her that.

"She's old enough," Penny says. "Almost as old as I was when I met Ben."

Diane peers through the fog and drives silently. She doesn't want to think about when Penny met Ben, doesn't want to imagine her young and vulnerable. It isn't safe to talk like this. She turns when Penny tells her to, slows down when she can't see. She doesn't want to think about Cass and her boyfriend either—it's not just what Cass is doing but that she tells Penny about it. Cass and Penny, Webb and Walker, seem united in some quiet conspiracy that she can't understand and Ben will never see. If Cass had come home that first summer, Ben might not have met Marlene. If she'd come home the next two, he might not have had the chain of young women who followed.

They pull into the parking lot of the hospital and leap out into the lamp-lit mist. At the desk, the nurse asks their names and they say together, "Mrs. Day." The nurse looks annoyed. Quickly, Penny says, "This is Webb Day's stepmother—I'm his mother. Can we see him?"

The nurse's face softens and she looks down at her files. "They're just bringing him to intensive care."

As she speaks, Diane hears the rattle of gurney wheels along the cold linoleum floor. She turns to see four people, wrapped in crocus green, wheeling Webb past. "Penny!" she whispers, pulling at the purple coat.

Webb looks like the husk left behind by a new-hatched moth. Tubes run from both arms and down his nose; a rubber bag lies on his chest, attached to a cold, curved pipe jammed down his throat. Part of his head is shaved and his skin is dusky blue. "Webb!" she calls. Penny is frozen beside her. The walls and ceiling suck the light from Webb and hold him in their dim gray mesh. The people push past them so quickly that she can't be sure what she's seen. If it wasn't for Penny calling "Webb! Webb!" in a voice as faint as the fog, she'd know this was a dream.

Hours later, the only news they have of Webb is that he's still alive. The doctor lets them peek in once after he pumps Webb's stomach, so they can see the slight flush of color that's crept into his gray cheeks. "That's from the oxygen," the doctor says. "We checked out the pills left in his pocket—it looks like he took a little of everything. Has he had a drug problem for long?"

"No!" Diane says.

"Not that we know of," says Penny.

The doctor frowns. "We can't rule out a suicide attempt. But my guess is that he was just horsing around. He was in over his head before he knew what hit him."

"That would be Webb," Penny says calmly. "He'd take whatever anyone offered him and ask questions later."

The doctor shrugs. "I wish he'd asked questions first. All we can do now is hope for the best."

His words linger in the air like smoke, like soot, long after he slides his green-wrapped body behind a green door. Diane collapses under the weight of them, so that it's Penny who does the comforting. "Shh," Penny says, stroking Diane's hair. "He doesn't know Webb. Webb will be fine." Diane, exhausted, props her legs on the coffee table, her fat knees nearly touching Penny's bony ones. They reassure each other endlessly and smoke cigarettes until Diane's lungs feel fused together. This is how Webb's brain feels, she imagines—harsh, burned, crisp.

"What a mess," Penny sighs. "Why don't you try Ben again?"

Diane, who has called Ben's office five times, nods and tries again. "Shit," she mutters, when she gets his answering machine. *Where are you?* He could be in Boston, at a meeting. He could be here in town. She calls home and tells Sal, again, that nothing's changed. When she returns to her chair, it seems to her that Penny stares. "I know what you're thinking," Diane says bitterly.

Penny picks at a loose knot on her sweater. "I'm not thinking anything."

"Sure you are—you're thinking it serves me right to have Ben like this, after what I did to you." All of a sudden this thought seems very important to her, as important as Webb. She doesn't want to think about Webb.

Penny rolls her eyes comically and manages a tired smile. "I'm really not," she says. "I was glad to get out."

"You weren't mad?"

Penny shrugs. "Sure I was, but not at you. And anyway, that was then. Now I've got my house and my animals and Cass and Webb and Walker—I can't complain." She pulls a fresh pack of cigarettes from her purse and offers them to Diane.

"Why don't you marry him?" Diane says. She takes another cigarette, knowing it will only make her mouth taste worse. What she really wants is a half gallon of fudge ripple and a spoon. Or, better yet, something strong and fragrant and savory. Curry. Bouillabaisse.

"Walker?" Penny pulls a hank of graying hair behind her ear. "Because I don't want to be married. I like having him around and I love traveling with him, but when we're here on the Cape I'd rather be alone at night. I like having the stars to myself."

"You and your telescope?"

"Something like that."

Diane tries to picture Penny alone on her roof at night. She can't imagine this as fun. Shyly, she says, "You know, I tried to teach myself the stars once. I found this old star dome Cass made—"

"I remember that!"

"And I tried to use that to figure out the sky. But it seemed like each night everything was in a different place." On the dome, she remembers, the constellations of the zodiac stretched in a narrow, unmistakable belt. In the sky, she couldn't find any of them.

"They move," Penny says. "That's why. They move around the pole. Didn't your mother teach you that? Cass told me she's interested in astrology."

"She never looks outside," Diane says. "She does it from books."

"I could teach you," Penny says. "Come over some-time—I could show you in a night."

The idea's attractive. Instead of trying to imagine the significance of planets she can't see passing by constellations she can't find, she could actually look at stars. "Maybe I'll do that sometime," she says.

"Whenever," says Penny. "I'm going to go call Cass at school—let her know what's going on. Yell if the doctor shows up."

"Sure," Diane says. Her skin feels coated with a light, greasy film. She takes off her shoes, curls up on the couch, and drops into an uneasy, overheated sleep. The blips and bleeps and coded announcements of the hospital fade. She dreams she's lying in the rushes by a lake. It's misty, near dawn; slowly some huge animal rises into the sky before her. "A heron," Ben's voice says. "A great blue heron." But she can see quite clearly that this is no bird. It's a centaur bearing a quiver and a bow. He rises weightlessly into the sky, Peter Pan lifted by invisible strings, and is followed by a goat with a fish's tail, a bearded man bearing a water jar, two fish side by side, a bull snorting fire, a pair of boys, a blue crab, a tan lion, a pale woman, a brass scale, and a scorpion with tail upraised and quivering. They arc across the sky like a rainbow and seem to be waiting for her to speak. "Herons," Ben's voice says solemnly. "All birds." She's just about to tell him how wrong he is when she hears a rustling and then feels a hand on her shoulders. "You okay?" a voice says. "You okay?"

It's Penny.

"You fell asleep for a minute. You all right?"

"Dreaming," Diane mumbles.

"I'll say. I couldn't reach Cass, but I called Otis and Cindy and asked them to get in touch with her."

"I was dreaming about the zodiac," Diane says. For just a minute, she's forgotten what's wrong. "I think.

All the signs my mother taught me. How come I can't find them in the sky?"

"They're there," Penny says. "I'll show you sometime."

"Could you see them when you were sailing?" Diane tries to conceal her envy of Penny's travels through the Caribbean.

"The sky's different down there," Penny says. "I had to learn all over again."

"I wish . . ." Diane says. She doesn't know what she wishes for—maybe everything. She wishes she were smart, pretty, thin again; that she and Jordan could travel around the world. She wishes Webb would get better.

"You wish," Penny says and sighs. She looks at Diane seriously. "You could leave him, you know."

"How?" Diane laughs bitterly. "I haven't worked for six years. I've got a little kid and no skills and I've gotten so fat—I'd never get a job. And Ben would cut me off without a cent."

"He wouldn't get away with that—you might even get the house. And even if you didn't you could always find work. I did."

Sure, Diane thinks. You did. You left your kids behind. You live in a moldy house with a bunch of fish. What she says is, "Maybe so. But I'm not ready yet."

Penny shrugs. "I left a message for Cass to come home if she can—will you try to stay cool if she does?"

"Sure," Diane says. "I promise."

"You're not bad," Penny says with a smile. "For a homewrecker."

Diane stares at her for a minute and then begins to laugh, all the strain of this long wait pouring from her until Penny laughs too and pats her arm helplessly. The doctor finds them gasping for breath.

"Ladies," he says softly.

They sit back and wipe their eyes quickly, trying to

read the doctor's face. They stop laughing. The doctor smiles. "He seems to be coming out of it," he says. "That's one lucky young man. You can go in for a minute, if you'd like."

They enter the ICU together, following the doctor to Webb's bed. Diane narrows her eyes against the tubes and drains and flashing monitors, weapons against the death that is, apparently, going to pass Webb by. Webb lies alone at the end of the row. They've pulled the pipe from his mouth but left tubes in his arms and down his nose. He is breathing on his own. Diane takes one of his hands; Penny takes the other. Webb's eyelids flutter open for a minute.

When they leave, it's with the promise that they can return tomorrow. "He's out of the woods," the doctor says. "At least for the short term. Tonight, what he needs is rest." His face, clean-shaven, shines open and fresh. They believe him. They need rest themselves. They gather their coats and purses, too tired to pick up the litter of cellophane and cigarette butts and cups and crumbs they've strewn around the waiting room.

Diane lets Penny drive them home. "Why don't you just drop me off?" she says. "And take the car—you can pick me up tomorrow on your way back here."

"Great," Penny says. "Then I could run over to the office in the morning before visiting hours."

"Whatever." She's tired all the way down to her toes, too tired to talk or drive or think. She has to think. She has to decide what she's going to tell Ben. *While you were out*, she thinks, remembering those small, pink message forms she filled in so neatly when she worked for Ben. Time, date, caller, message. *While you were out, Webb got sick. Took some pills by mistake. Some pills on purpose.* She doubts that Ben will check her story—she could even say Webb just fainted. But eventually Ben will run into the doctor and then he'll find out. No—better tell the truth. But Ben, lacking that first awful sight of Webb as gray as mist, won't be able to temper his anger with relief. No—better lie. Get the doctor to say it was an accident. It *was* an accident. No one is sure what happened. She closes her eyes and lets the road slip past. Counseling for Webb, the doctor suggested. Maybe family therapy for all of them. *Sure,* she thinks. *As if you'd go.*

She doesn't open her eyes until Penny stops the car. They are at her house; the driveway is empty; the road is dark. *Still out?* she thinks. *Having fun?* To Penny she says, "Ben doesn't seem to be back yet. Want to come in for a drink?"

"I could use one," Penny says.

Diane flicks on the kitchen light, and Penny gasps as if she's startled.

"You don't like it?" asks Diane. Soon after Jordan was born, she stripped off the yellow wallpaper and painted the walls a matte tan, replaced the linoleum with terra cotta tiles and changed the porcelain sink to stainless steel. The new refrigerator, enormous and almond-colored, hums.

"It looks great," Penny says. "I never got around to decorating."

"Nothing else to do," Diane says, and shrugs. "You want some Scotch?" When Penny nods she fills two glasses with ice and sets them on the table with a bottle. She is looking forward to a long talk, eased by the Scotch and this night they've shared. "I'll be right back," she says. "I have to look in on Jordan."

Penny settles into the chair facing the kitchen window, where Diane dreams away her days. Diane walks down the hall to her bedroom, toward the low purr of the television. It is almost one o'clock. Her door is ajar; the light is out. She opens the door gently, expecting to find Sal and Jordan asleep in front of the late movie. What she finds instead is Paine and Sal stretched side by

side on top of the quilt, like two great whales. Paine's
massive body just touches the ocean of Sal's flesh. On
top of them Jordan curls like a small, pink crustacean,
clutching the sash of Paine's smoking jacket in her fist.

All the anger Diane has been saving for Ben spurts
out. "Wake up!" she hisses. Sal is often inappropriate,
but this is outrageous even for her. Is this what her
astrology book hinted at this morning—plaid rabbit
changes into dancing elf? Paine, on her bed, wrapped in
his tan plaid jacket. He and Sal touching, even fully
clothed, with Jordan here. She could scream at them
both. Jordan wakes first.

"Mommy?" she says sleepily, lifting her sleek head.
"Where's Webb?"

Diane plucks her from the mound of Sal's stomach.
"Still in the hospital," she says. "But he's going to be
home in a couple of days. Before Christmas, for sure."
She disentangles the sash from Jordan's hand. "What
were you all doing here?" Sal grunts and stirs, and
Paine begins to roll over.

"Three little bears," Jordan says. "Paine was Papa
Bear, and Gram was Momma Bear, and I was Goldi-
locks. Paine let me hold his pocket watch."

"Wonderful," Diane says. She'll deal with Paine later.
"Now, how about we put you to bed?" Sal opens one
eye and squints at them.

"Carry me?" Jordan pleads.

She carries Jordan to bed and tucks her between her
favorite shell-printed sheets. Her head lies like a fluted
scallop between a conch and a whelk. Along her window seat, angel's toenails and limpets and snails and
clams spill their grit each time they're touched. Diane
has to vacuum in here twice a week; it's like vacuuming
the beach. "Night-night," she whispers.

She ought to get back to Penny, but she returns to her
room and switches on the overhead light. Sal and Paine
stretch themselves awake without the least embarrass-

ment. "So?" Sal says. Her flowered housedress gapes at the waist. "How's Webb really?"

"He'll be fine—they got him pumped out in time." She sucks in a deep breath, so angry that she can't even look at Paine. He was supposed to stay for an hour, not move in. "What the hell has been going on here?"

"Here?" Sal says innocently. "Nothing. We got to talking, so I made us supper and then we watched a movie and Johnny Carson together."

Paine adjusts his smoking jacket. "A lovely evening," he says, and smiles. "We had a most interesting talk— synchronicity, you know."

Diane stares at him as if he's turned into a toad before her eyes. "Come again?" This man is a lawyer.

"Synchronicity," Paine says. "The great acausal connective principle." He waves his arms with enthusiasm. "Astrology. Alchemy. Jung. You know—everything that happens here and now shares the qualities of this moment. Your mother—Sal—is *most* interesting."

Sal smiles shyly down at her feathered slippers. Diane can't quite envision what's been happening here, but whatever it is she wishes Jordan hadn't been present.

"Great," Diane says to Paine. "Glad you enjoyed yourself. It's time to go."

"Zenith and nadir," Paine says, adjusting his jacket. "Meridian and horizon. Equator and ecliptic. Ascendent, descendent, vertex, and antivertex. Declination and right ascension. The great dichotomies of life!"

"Have you been drinking?"

Sal looks hurt. "Of course not. I was just teaching Paine a few things."

"We're drunk on life," Paine says. "On the communion of like souls." His eyes have a glitter that unnerves Diane. Ever since Cass trashed his basement, Diane has been waiting for him to take revenge. She cleaned up the mess herself, replaced the broken chair with a better one and explained as best as she could, but although Paine smiled at her then she's not sure they're in the clear.

"Good night," she says, almost pushing him from the room. He backs out, his huge bulk filling the doorway.

"Good night," he says, lifting his pale fat hand in a benedictory pose. "Mrs. Day. The light, day; the darkness, night; the light divided from the dark . . ." Still mumbling, he vanishes.

"I have to go," Diane says sternly to her mother. "Penny's here. But you can count on discussing this in the morning."

Sal wraps the quilt around her shoulders like a robe. "Don't get all bent out of shape," she says airily. "I'm entitled to talk to whoever, whenever." She slips away.

Diane's hands shake. The three of them, curled there on her bed, looked like a family. Perhaps it is really this that's upset her. Below her, down in the basement where Sal sleeps when she stays over, she hears heavy footsteps, a toilet flush, a thump that might be an elbow against a door or a window opening. Do they kiss? Diane wonders. Is this romance? She understands, from the stab in her ribs, that she is jealous. The enthusiasm in Paine's voice, Sal's shy smile—they could be Ben and herself, a few years ago, before everything flipped into another orbit. I'm entitled to talk, Sal said, and of course she is. Unmarried, she can do anything, change her life around completely. "Lucky," Diane mutters, as she enters the kitchen.

Penny still waits in the chair by the window, her legs crossed and her face still. Only her drained glass suggests the minutes Diane has been gone. "Lucky?" she says. "Who?"

Diane had almost forgotten she was here. She shakes her head. "No one," she says. "My mother."

Penny holds out a full glass. "You probably need this," she says. "I almost spilled mine on the floor a minute ago, when Paine came up behind me. I heard footsteps, but I thought they were yours until he said, 'The other Mrs. Day! How delightful!' "

Despite herself, Diane laughs as Penny imitates Paine's booming tones.

"I'll bet it's five years since I last saw him," Penny says. "Some things never change."

Diane shrugs. "What's changed is that he's retired and lives next door full-time now. I asked him over this afternoon to watch Jordan for a few minutes, and it turns out he stayed all night."

"You're friends?"

"Not really," Diane says. "But he's close to Jordan and my mother."

"No fooling." Penny sucks an ice cube thoughtfully. "Well, he's okay."

"I guess," Diane says. "Jordan and my mother sure think so." She sips at her Scotch, trying to clear her head of Sal and Paine and Ben and an unpleasant, bubbling feeling that's come to rest behind her ears. We were going to talk, she remembers. Me and Penny, Penny and me. About Webb and Cass and Walker and Ben and anything, everything. Stars. Boats. Love and marriage and kids. "I . . ." she says shyly, not sure what's supposed to come next. It's been years since she had a friend.

Penny taps the last ice cube into her mouth and sets her glass down. "I'd better hit the road," she says. "Ben's bound to be home soon."

"Sure he is," Diane says faintly. Her talk vanishes into the haze. Maybe tomorrow, in the car. She looks down at the floor and then, as Penny rises, reaches up and touches her hand. "You'll pick me up tomorrow?" she asks.

"Of course," Penny says. "I'll call in the morning." The grooves between her nose and mouth seem deeper now. She pulls on her purple coat and steps into the foggy night, her gray hair sticking out in spikes.

The First Point of Libra
(September 1974)

★   ★   ★   ★   ★   ★

During the week, day breaks for Diane before the sun is fully up. Into her sleep-stunned brain seeps the bustle of Ben rising at quarter past six and grunting through his sit-ups, then showering, singing, shaving, muttering as he loads his suit pockets with memos and papers and lists. She knows she has to move before the mutter. She wraps a robe around herself and bumbles into the kitchen, clattering dishes as, still half asleep, she fixes breakfast. She yawns. She watches the pale light spread from the edge of the island over the sky. She listens to Ben chew and swallow and gulp. And then, just as Ben leaves and she sinks into a chair with her first cup of coffee, Jordan bounds in with her questions and chatter and a low rumble from the basement says Webb's awake and late again.

This morning Jordan, who's been taking ballet lessons, greets her with an unsteady arabesque. "How do I look?" she asks, teetering on one foot. With her outstretched arms and upthrust chin she resembles a sand-piper. She's wearing a new pair of jeans, a purple sweater, and a crisp white shirt printed with pastel moths. Her books are tucked into a small blue knapsack shaped like a teardrop; her pale hair, carefully combed, is long but for the bangs in front. She looks like any other second-grade girl except for her eyes, which are large and green and so beautiful that they're out of place in her puckish face.

Diane focuses and says, "You look wonderful." She reaches out to adjust Jordan's collar. "Better hurry up and eat."

Jordan swoops toward the table and snatches a bowl of cereal from her place mat. She eats standing up, rocking gently from heel to toe and back again. "Will you make my lunch today?" she asks. "The school lunch is gross fish sticks. Yuck."

"Yuck is right," Diane says, wrinkling her nose in sympathy. She pushes herself up from the chair and fixes a sandwich for Jordan's Wonder Woman lunchbox. She adds fruit, cookies, and a Thermos of juice; then she takes the cookies out. No sense encouraging a sweet tooth.

"Can I bring Iris home after school?" Jordan asks. She tips the bowl to her chin and drains the last drops of milk.

Diane checks her watch—still no sign of Webb. "Not today, sweetie. I have to go out for a while this afternoon, and Gram's going to come take care of you until I get back. Promise you'll be good?"

"Promise," Jordan says. She flexes her knees, splays her feet until her heels touch, and does a few clumsy pliés. Diane turns away to hide her smile—Jordan doesn't seem to be cut out to dance.

"Is Paine coming over?" Jordan asks breathlessly.

"I don't know. It's up to Gram."

Jordan sweeps an arm low across her knees and

promptly falls. "Where are you going?" she asks from the floor.

"Just out," Diane says vaguely. She reaches over and helps Jordan up. "I have a few errands, but I should be back by four."

A car pulls into their driveway and beeps its horn. "Webb!" Diane calls. "Lenny's here!" Through the screen door she can just see Lenny's curly blond head bobbing up and down to something blaring from his radio. His long, spatulate fingers, which Webb says can coax everything but conversation from his electric keyboard, drum against the steering wheel. While Diane watches, he throws back his head and shouts some words to his song, words that seep through the door only as, "Uh, Uh, Uh." Diane smiles but thanks her stars that Ben's not here to watch. She's not sure if she approves of Lenny or not. Webb met him in summer school while he was making up the classes he missed last winter and Lenny was retaking the math he failed. He and Webb have a band now, with a drummer and a bass player, and he seems to be good for Webb. Ben's quite sure how he feels about Lenny. He calls Lenny hippie slime.

"Webb!" she calls again.

"Coming!" A minute later he sticks his head around the door and says, "Is Dad gone yet?" When Diane nods he slinks into the room. His shirt is untucked and his hair sticks up in spikes. One eyelid droops slightly, as it has since his hospital stay last winter. He has his trombone case in one hand and a pair of flute cases tucked under his arm. Jordan dances up to him, kisses his cheek, and stuffs a piece of cold toast into his mouth.

"Sleepy head," she says. "You're a mess."

"Grr," he growls and swats at her. She dances away, giggling—this is just a game. "Watch out—I'm still asleep."

Lenny honks again, beating out a syncopation on his horn.

"Gotta run," Webb says. "We're practicing at Lenny's after school—I'll be home around five."

He gathers up his belongings and vanishes before Diane can ask him anything. Just as well, she thinks. Ben asks Webb enough questions for both of them, grilling him about every detail of his life until Webb, white with anger, retreats to his room and refuses to come out. Only Jordan and Lenny can pry him free. She looks out the door and sighs as Lenny's Plymouth backfires and roars away. Webb is fine now, his eyelid the only trace of the week he spent in the hospital. In many ways he got off easy. But against Penny's advice, and against her own intuition, Diane told Ben the truth about Webb's accident. I had to, she thinks. He would have found out somehow. Her honesty or fear—whatever it was— worked against all of them. Ben blew up worse than he had with Cass and blamed all of them—Diane and Penny and Walker and Webb's school—for being too permissive. And although she tried to stand up to him— *he's a kid,* she remembers saying. *Kids experiment. He made a mistake*—Ben restricted Webb to the house for the whole winter and spring. Even now he keeps close tabs on Webb. The only thing that saves them is that he's hardly ever home. When Ben and Webb are both home, she feels like she's juggling eggs and wants Ben away. When he's away, late at night, she wants desperately to have him home. *He's just a kid,* she tells him silently. *You could give him a break.* She taps her finger on the table, imagining Ben, long gone now and roaring down Route 3 in his new Oldsmobile, snorting with disgust. He'll never relax his hold on Webb. If Penny hadn't put her foot down last winter, screaming at Ben and threatening to sue him, even this late, for anything and everything, Ben would have sent Webb away to school, to someplace gray and military. Diane thinks often of

Penny, who is sailing with Walker somewhere around the Windward Islands. They might have been friends.

"Hello?" Jordan says. "Earth calling Mommy—come in, come in." She kisses the air near Diane's cheek as Diane turns to smile at her. "I have to go or I'll miss my bus."

Diane nods and hands her the lunchbox, then takes it back and drops in the cookies. What the hell, she thinks. Jordan is still thin. "You be good this afternoon with Gram," she says. "And have fun in gym."

Jordan nods and runs away, banging the screen door behind her. The sound echoes in the empty house, newly silent after a summer of having Jordan and Webb home. *Tok*, says the clock in the dining room. All summer she organized her days around the places she had to drive Jordan and Webb—Jordan to the beach, ballet lessons, the store; Webb to summer school and music lessons, and, when they could manage it, to his friends. He has his license, but Ben won't let him drive now until he graduates. Idly, she rinses the breakfast dishes and sponges down the table. Nothing to do, with the kids back in school; this is the price she pays for running her life around them. At least she has something for this afternoon. She picks up the phone and calls her mother, who answers on the seventh ring.

"Hello?" Sal says sleepily.

"It's me," Diane says. "I just wanted to make sure you could still come this afternoon."

"Two," Sal says through a big yawn. "Right? What time is it?"

"Past eight. Did I wake you?"

"Of course you did. I'll be there at two. Now let me sleep for a while." She yawns in Diane's ear again and hangs up.

There's nothing to do now but wait. Her children are gone; her mother is asleep; Ben won't be back until late. The house is as clean as it needs to be, and so, after a last look at the floor, which she could wash but chooses not to, she goes into her bedroom and unearths her job folder from its secret spot behind the shoes. The folder is thick with want ads clipped from the newspaper, copies of her resumé, and carbons of the letters she's sent off, mingled with a few terse rejections. Most of the people she's written haven't bothered to respond. She clutches the folder to her chest. *What do you want to do this for?* she can hear Ben say. *Hell, what little you'd make would just bump us into a higher tax bracket.*

She has kept this secret from everyone, from him, because she knows she'll lose her courage if he starts in. I'll get the job lined up, she thinks. And then just announce it when it's too late for anyone to stop me. She's combed the papers since Labor Day, looking for anything even remotely possible. The one job she really wants is the only one for which she's gotten an interview. Perhaps they made a mistake when they called her. Perhaps they meant to call someone else. She looks again at the magic ad.

Needed: Talented, versatile person with excellent secretarial and administrative skills, to serve as Assistant to the Director of Development. Liberal tuition benefits, health insurance, and pension plan.

Below it is the address of the local community college. And carefully paperclipped to the ad is a carbon of the cover letter she labored over for days, trying to make herself sound interesting. On paper, she knows she doesn't look like much—a year of secretarial school, a few years working for Ben in his real estate office, and then a big, blank stretch of nothing. In her letter she puffed up her old job a bit and tried to sound as if she had a lot of responsibility. She didn't mention her marriage or Jordan, figuring she could best deal with those blank years by not dealing with them. Somehow, the letter worked.

Her appointment isn't until two-thirty, but she sits down at her dressing table, plugs in her hot rollers, and spends the rest of the morning fussing with her face and hair. She sets her hair, decides it's too curly, wets it down, dries it, and sets it again, so that the ends curve firmly but casually under her chin. She puts on more makeup than she has in years, trying to recreate the face she wore when she worked with Ben. An even layer of foundation smoothed with a slick sponge, concealing cream under her eyes for the circles, blusher, lipstick, dark blue shadow in the hollows above her lids. Two coats of navy mascara. When she's done she stares at herself in the softly lit mirror. Her face looks good— nearly perfect, in fact. She might be twenty-three again. She angles her face to one side, and sucks in her cheeks until her bones stand out. Good, but perhaps a bit much. Her neighbors in the village wear hardly any makeup at all—but then, they don't work. And she needs a little extra help to distract attention from her figure.

From the closet she takes the simple, expensive navy suit she bought in Hyannis last week. There's no concealing all of her, but it helps hide the worst of her bulges. She lays the suit on the bed and then gathers dark panty hose (to make her legs look slimmer), navy pumps, and a frilly white blouse. There. She adds a simple strand of coral bead and matching button earrings, remembering the voice of Mrs. Gibbs, her teacher at school. "Always look professional. Even if everyone else is dressed casually, make an impression by looking businesslike." She's not sure this is still good advice, but it's all she has.

For lunch she has a cup of hot bouillon—the fit of her new skirt doesn't allow for even a sandwich. And then she sits at the kitchen table and waits until it's time to dress.

Sal bounds in at quarter of two, carrying a plastic bag stuffed with books and papers and bottles of diet soda. "Yoo-hoo!" she calls. "I'm here!"

"In the bedroom!" Diane shouts. She's struggling with a row of tiny buttons and beginning to breathe hard. She can't decide which blouse to wear, after all. The frilly white one, the tailored cream one, on and off and on again until now, for the fourth or fifth time, she's wrapped in frilly white. When Sal comes in Diane fastens the last two buttons and says, "How do I look?" Her stomach is sucked in so far that it feels like it's touching her spine.

Sal eyes her cautiously. "Whose funeral?"

"Mom," Diane says impatiently, "there's no funeral —I just have a business appointment."

"Oh?" She looks at Diane again. "Well, I guess you look all right."

Faint praise, Diane thinks uneasily. Perhaps she should have picked other clothes? But then she looks at her mother's baggy saffron shift and stretched-out sandals and thinks, Hey—this is only Sal. I look fine. She clips her coral earrings on and tries for a deep breath, but the waistband of her skirt binds like a hot wire when she exhales. She sucks in her stomach again, watching as Sal sprawls on the bed and spreads her books and papers in a half-circle around her. Against her legs she props an enormous bottle of diet orange soda.

"What are you going to do this afternoon?" Diane asks. She takes a few short steps in front of the mirror, checking her posture and angling this way and that. In certain positions her hips look much smaller. Perhaps she can enter her interviewer's office this way. Sidelong, like a crab.

"Cast some charts," Sal says. "Play around. You know what today is?"

Diane sighs. "Surprise me. No, let me guess—Madame Blavatsky's birthday?"

Sal sniffs and then smiles knowingly. "Autumnal equinox," she says. "Silly. Where the sun crosses the celestial equator at the First Point of Libra." She smiles and waves her pudgy hands in the air, as if this would explain things more clearly. "The day is *charged* with potential," she says. "Can't you feel it? Everywhere on earth day and night are of equal length, poised in perfect balance—you should be celebrating this, you know. Everyone should. You should pay attention."

"Mom," Diane says wearily. "I'm too busy for this."

"Busy? You're so busy with nothing that you can't take a little time for yourself? This is a critical day—the First Point of Libra marks the balance between day and night. The underworld and the visible world, things potential and things actual . . ." She holds her hands out, palms up, and slowly lowers one while she raises the other. "Libra," she repeats. "The scales of justice, the balance of power . . ."

Is this how she talks to Paine? Is this what they both find so fascinating? "I have to go," Diane says. "I'll be late."

"You want me to do a quick chart and see if today's lucky for you? It'll just take a minute."

"No," Diane says firmly. She wants to get out of the house before Sal asks her where she's going.

Sal shrugs. "Suit yourself," she says. "Now, Paine—he wants to invest some money today, and I told him I'd examine his aspects and see if they're favorable. Paine has his moon in Libra, and of course that makes things interesting . . ."

Diane leaves Sal muttering to herself, knowing from her hints that Paine will be visiting this afternoon. She can't forbid it—Jordan likes him and he's a model guest, picking up after Sal like a faithful maid. He and Sal will sit in the kitchen all afternoon, sipping tea from absurdly small cups and exchanging occultist gossip. Whose disciple left for another leader, who's using the radical new system that takes the precession of the equinoxes into account, whether those cattle out west were really killed by UFOs. Whether their fates are written in the stars. In another chair, or hanging over Sal's shoulder, or perhaps perched on the counter like an elf, Jordan will listen quietly, her head turning from Sal to Paine and back again as if she's watching a tennis match. Sal says there's no harm in her listening. Diane is not so sure.

She shakes her head and eases into the car, smoothing her dark skirt carefully. She pats her purse, neat and perfectly organized. She pats her hair, already smooth, and then she drives out their dirt road and heads for Mashpee, following the directions given to her over the phone by that man with the lovely voice. "I'd take Route 28, if I were you," he said, after he arranged all the details of the interview. His voice sounded warm, welcoming. When she said she'd never been to the college, he told her exactly where to turn and where to park. "Don't worry," he said. "You'll figure it out in no time." As if she already had the job and had all the time in the world.

She's nervous, of course. She tells herself it's only natural, only anticipation—she wants to meet the face attached to that voice. That's the point of this, isn't it? To get out, meet some new people. She'll meet this man and he'll introduce her to others. She turns at the sign, where the man told her to. The college is only a few years old, and she's surprised to find it tucked into a barren meadow near a marsh. The buildings are low concrete and glass, with occasional splashes of color in odd places. Red exposed stairways. Narrow stripes below windows. Small junipers and creeping shrubs hug the foundations. Along the walks are trees so young and frail that they're anchored to the ground by paired wires. She follows the signs to the personnel office and parks in the visitors' lot.

As soon as she cuts the engine she breaks into a sweat. Breathe, she thinks. Breathe deeply. Her waistband slices her—worse than a girdle, more like a leash. She gets out of the car, trembling so hard that she has to sit down again. She has ten minutes, no more, in which to calm down. Students pass her car in clumps of three or four, looking brisk, lively, smart—all the things she fears she no longer is. They remind her of Cass. The girls wear tight jeans and flannel shirts, old sweaters or sweatshirts. There isn't a skirt in sight. Their faces are scrubbed clean and their hair hangs innocently down to their shoulders. They look serious, determined. When did this happen? She's been away from this world for seven years, and somehow everything has changed.

The more she looks at these girls the more ridiculous she feels. She pulls down the sun visor and stares into the mirror. Her face is wrong—all wrong. Her makeup, which looked fine in the soft glow of her mirror at home, looks garish out here. "Shit," she mutters. "They won't want me like this." She takes a tissue from her purse and scrubs at her eyelids, trying to soften the harsh blue streaks. She runs her fingers through her hair, trying to make it look as if it were never set, and then she moistens a fresh tissue and scrubs at her cheeks. All she can seem to do is move the colors around. She smudges eye shadow on her cheekbones, blusher onto her nose. The more she fusses with herself the worse she looks, until finally she utters a squeak of despair and flips the visor up. In a minute she'll cry.

It's two-thirty and she's supposed to be inside. She swallows hard and unties the ribbon at the neck of her blouse, tucking the collar under and undoing the first two buttons in the hope that this will make her look more casual. And then she teeters up the walk to the main door, gives the receptionist her name, and follows her down the long, cool hall to the glassed-in office that looms at the end. Her stomach gives a warning chirp.

She waits for ten minutes, during which she has nothing to do but worry and finger the bright orange wool of the chair. When a slim woman finally emerges from one of the cubicles and calls her name, she is sure that this is another secretary.

She is wrong. "Miriam Weiss," the woman says. "Personnel Representative. Would you follow me?"

Diane's heart sinks. The man who called her, who brought her here, had a lovely, low, dark voice, and it was him she had in mind when she dressed today. At night, while she lay in bed waiting for Ben, she'd attached that voice to a gray-haired, distinguished man just old enough to appreciate her but still young enough to be attractive. If he were here, she knows he'd sit across from her smoking his pipe while she looked up at him through darkened lashes and laughed appreciatively at his jokes. Her suit would blend in with the furniture and camouflage her size, and all would go smoothly, just as it went years ago when Ben interviewed her. But the man is nowhere to be seen.

She follows Miriam numbly into her neat cubicle. No frills and flowers here—just a matched leather desk set, a framed print on the wall, and a calendar hanging above a beige file cabinet. Miriam wears tailored pants instead of jeans, a quiet sweater instead of a flamboyant sweatshirt. Despite this, she resembles the girls crossing the lawn outside. Her graying hair is layered and has never seen a roller. Her dry cheeks are innocent of makeup. She clears her throat and flips through her file thoughtfully. "May I call you Diane?" she asks.

"Of course," Diane murmurs, in her best phone-answering voice. It's wasted, she knows—there's no gray-haired man here to appreciate her throaty tones. The harsh fluorescent light makes her hands look raw, and she's sure she has lipstick on her teeth. She can just imagine what her face looks like. She fights a fierce urge to excuse herself and flee for the nearest bathroom, where she can scrub her face and start all over again. Miriam turns a page. Diane tries to breathe quietly through her nostrils and lets out a little snuffle. Sweat springs out on her forehead and trickles down her sides, dooming her to keep her jacket on. She wonders why she didn't think to wear dress shields, why she didn't wear a plain shirt and pants. Her jacket pulls across her back like a sausage skin ready to pop. When she crosses her legs, preparing to return Miriam's level gaze, her stocking catches on a corner of the desk. She watches in disbelief as a fine line races down the dark nylon to her ankle.

"Well," Miriam says. Her eyes seem to catch each bead of sweat as it emerges. "Why don't you tell me why you're interested in this job?"

Diane looks down at her clamped hands. Because I have to get out of the house! she wants to scream. Because I'm turning into an acorn squash! She clears her throat and says, "I've always wanted to work at a small college, and of course the tuition benefits here are attractive. I'd like to finish my education." She doesn't say that she never started it.

"Have you ever done fund-raising work before?"

"No."

"Have you ever coordinated bulk mailings?"

"No."

"Do you have any writing experience?"

"No—not really. I used to draft letters for my boss at my old job." She doesn't mention that her former boss is her current husband.

"Hm," Miriam says. She is silent for a minute, and Diane can see her wondering how she got this interview. Diane can't tell her—she doesn't know herself. She picked up the phone one afternoon, and there was this man with the warm voice. Why did he call her and then abandon her? She looks wildly around the office, as if he might materialize from the walls.

"Your skills may be a little rusty," Miriam says gently. "After all this time. You've had no employment since the real estate office?"

"I was raising a family," Diane says faintly, forgetting that she wasn't going to mention this.

"Ah," Miriam says. "A homemaker. How many children?"

"One. Well, three, really . . ."

When Miriam looks up in surprise, she quickly corrects herself. "One of my own," she says. "Two stepchildren from my husband's first marriage. One's a senior in high school and one's a sophomore in college." This is more than she meant to say, but Miriam's eyes seem to be fishing information from her with long, barbed jigs.

"Really?" Miriam says. "You don't look old enough." She drops her eyes to Diane's resumé, looking for a birthdate. Diane left it off on purpose.

"My husband's quite a bit older than me," Diane murmurs.

Miriam runs her hand through her close-fitting hair. "Ah," she says again. In Miriam's mouth the soft sound is perfectly noncommittal. "Let me tell you something about the job. Unless John described it over the phone already?"

"No," Diane whispers. "He didn't say much at all." His name is John, then. All she recalls is that resonant voice saying how interesting she seemed. If he was here she could make him hire her.

Miriam launches into her speech. Phrases like "aggressive, self-motivated, organized individual" keep cropping up, and although Diane knows that she should be nodding in response to them, indicating that, yes, this is her, this describes her exactly, all she can do is stare blankly at the calendar pinned to the wall. The days are marked off in big squares, with today's square shaded light red. Not an official holiday, then—these are screened a darker red—but one of those days, like Groundhog Day, that merits a little splash of color and a few italicized words. Reminders, for the curious, of the rhythm of the seasons. Cues for people like Sal. As she stares at the calendar, Miriam's words roll by like water. This isn't Diane she's describing. This is someone else, perhaps one of those slim girls walking outside among the infant trees. A woman with no children, no husband, no responsibilities; a woman who can sit through an interview without sending rivers of sweat coursing through the creases on her back.

Miriam, finished, looks at her inquisitively.

"Well," Diane says. "I type very quickly."

Miriam raises an eyebrow. "The job doesn't involve all that much typing—just letters and whatnot. Still, that could be an asset. Do you mind taking a typing test?"

"Not at all."

Miriam leads her into another cubicle and seats her in front of a fancy electric typewriter. Next to the typewriter sit a timer, a stack of paper, and some exercises clipped to a stand. Miriam explains the test and Diane nods—she did this a million times in school. She rolls a sheet of paper in, rests her hands on the keys, and signals that she's ready. Miriam sets the timer and says, "Now." But when Diane reaches under the typewriter she can't find the switch that turns it on. It's not at the back, it's not underneath, it's not on the keyboard. By the time she finds it, hidden in a recess along the left edge, her fingers have stiffened in panic. The typewriter has a spinning ball instead of keys and she can't see how to set the margins. She can't see how to set the tabs either, and the first exercise is a table with four columns.

Next door is a cubicle in which some other woman is being interviewed for some other job. Or maybe for the same job—the two women, interviewer and applicant, seem to be having the same conversation that Diane and Miriam had minutes ago, except that the applicant's strong, self-confident voice answers the questions promptly, picking up on all the phrases that Diane let fall. Diane's fingers fumble with the unfamiliar keys and finally stop altogether as she listens to these women. The interviewer tells a joke, the applicant chuckles, and then they laugh together with a sound like nesting doves. The joke has something to do with Nixon, and they move easily from there into talk of politics.

Politics? Here? Diane listens with rapt attention to the women's irreverent, opinionated discussion. It's been years since she heard talk like this. In her house they go to bed before the news comes on, and Watergate might never have happened. Ben, who thinks Nixon shouldn't have resigned, refused to discuss the hearings with her, and so she sat alone near the TV for months, watching with dark fascination as the endless stream of witnesses ducked beneath the rain of questions. The men, tall or short, bearded or clean-shaven, pudgy or thin as rails, all alike reminded her of Ben's friends. Although, if pressed, she could not have said why. She had no one to discuss this with, to explain how this small, secret happening blossomed so huge. Some sort of justice was happening here, she thought then. But how? As she listens to these women now, she knows she was right to think she was missing something. She has missed everything all along, but not these women: they've cut their hair; they've shed their bras; they've paid attention to war and demonstrations and shouting crowds, to students throwing vegetables at effigies, to the odd telling phrase dropped during a routine speech. Their lives have changed while she was sitting in her house, and now she can't follow their easy asides and insiders' jokes. She will never know the things that, here, everyone knows as intuitively as weather. Her hands fall into her lap.

Ten minutes pass while she eavesdrops on this other world, and then Miriam comes in, clears her throat, and says, "Not typing?"

"I can't," Diane says. "I'm sorry." Her fingers feel like wood and her stomach shrieks. "I'm not feeling too well," she says. "I ought to go home."

Miriam tilts her head to one side, resembling Sal for just that minute. "This isn't going to work out," she says, almost sympathetically. "Is it?"

"No," Diane agrees. She has a sudden, sharp craving for a sundae—a hot fudge sundae with double whipped cream. She may want two. The office seems oddly suffocating and she removes her jacket and rolls up her sleeves as she follows Miriam back to her cubicle. Why did she think she wanted to work here? The people are strange, their politics alien. She'd miss seeing Jordan after school. She plucks at her blouse, which clings damply to her back.

In Miriam's office she picks up her purse. The calendar catches her eye again as she nods good-bye to Miriam; quite casually, she reaches over Miriam's head and taps the light red square that marks this day. "You know," she says, "today's the autumnal equinox. The First Point of Libra, the beginning of fall . . ." Horrified, she claps her hand to her mouth. Where did that come from? The words sprang out like toads and weren't what she meant to say, not at all. The First Point of Libra has nothing to do with this dreadful day, when everything is off balance and when the scales of justice have been tipped against her as firmly as her own bathroom scale tips each day toward new, impossible weights. If only the low-voiced man were here, to climb up into the other brass pan and balance her despair. There is no man. In the whole office, in the hum that rises from the rows of cubicles, she can't hear a single male voice.

Miriam fidgets with her papers. "Yes," she says. "I suppose it is."

Diane tries to say something gracious, but the words that press against her lips are Sal's and not hers—First Point of Libra leads to First Point of Aries, to celestial equator, ecliptic, the length of days and the darkness of nights . . . If she stays another minute there's no telling what she'll spew. She bolts from the cubicle and down the endless hall, through the campus swarming with slim students, into her car, down the road through the dry meadow, past the marsh and the great blue heron who, unaccountably startled by her, flaps clumsily from tree to tree, until, at last, she comes to herself in the orange vinyl booth of a Howard Johnson's, her long-handled, small-bowled spoon poised daintily above the remains of a triple banana split. She has always loved bananas. From somewhere above her head and just to the right she hears Ben's voice—*Look at you!* he hisses. *What do you think you're doing?* She ignores him. *Nothing, nothing, nothing,* she answers. *Leave me alone.*

Black Holes and Heavenly Bodies
(April 1976)

★　　　★　　　★　　　★　　　★　　　★

For six months, Diane's pen, like the planchette on some Ouija board, has run completely out of control. Whenever she picks it up she starts writing—on napkins, place mats, cereal boxes; on matchbooks, envelopes, Jordan's drawings, Ben's business mail. She scribbles letters on these odds and ends of paper and then, when she's done, files them in the dark space between her mattress and her boxspring. At night the papers rustle as she shifts her weight in search of Ben. Ben, who sleeps in the guest room these days, makes no complaint; she can hardly remember his feel or his sweet, sharp tang.

She's in bed this Saturday morning, although she has no business here. Jordan's eighth birthday party is this afternoon, and Diane knows she should be fussing in the kitchen, putting the final touches on the coconut cake she made in the shape of a giant starfish. Instead, she's huddled under the covers, while Jordan watches

TV in the den and plays Monopoly with Sal. She has her pen, her checkbook, a box of doughnuts, a stack of index cards, and heaps of Sal's old magazines—back issues of *American Astrology*, an assortment of occultist publications, pamphlets purporting to hold the secret of life. The sheets are powdered with cinnamon sugar.

She is organized. She is systematic. She tears out whatever looks interesting and marks the scraps with her own codes. She reads four articles with great attention: "Create the Life You *Want*," "This is Your Lucky Month!," "Cattle-killing UFOs," "Moon Cycles—Know the Power of Luna." None spells out the answer she seeks. She reads ads for books explaining salt power, Edgar Cayce, the Lost Continent of Lemuria, the Hidden Bible, the Master Key, Prosperity Power, the Truth of Life, the Means, the Way, theosophy, Nostradamus, numerology, reincarnation ("You Need Never Die!"). She studies other, smaller ads hawking crystal balls, yin and yang earrings, free Rosicrucian booklets, astrological calendars, pyramid jewelry, magic squares, psychic gems, Tarot cards, miracle crosses, mystic candles, aura goggles, wishing dolls, talismans, incense, love magnets. She consults the April timetables, which list the best days for her to bake or can, have a permanent or a haircut, buy clothes, paint her nails, plant, graft, or pollinate, mix concrete, cut timber, catch fish, start a diet. Her pen follows behind her eyes, checking this, underlining that, filling in order blanks. She sends away for everything free and for most things that cost less than five dollars. She drafts letters to the astrologers, mediums, psychics, spiritualists, and numerologists who advertise in the classified section. She would like some answers. The claims all look like lies but they may be truth disguised that way.

"Dear Madame Clair," she writes.

"Dear Saul. . . ."

"Dear Jeane Dixon. . . ."

She does not confine her letters to the famous, but writes her family as well.

"Dear Ben—If you think I am upset by this, you are wrong."

"Dear Sal—What are you doing with Paine?"

"Dear Webb—Where have you gone?"

She knows that she won't mail these—she has just enough balance left to recognize that her pen, if not her mind, is out of control. If Ben saw these scribblings he'd use them against her, as he uses her still-increasing weight, her fading hair, her inability to entertain his friends. And so she writes but hides what she's written, waiting for the day when she'll either mail these all at once or burn them and hope for answers from the smoke.

She inhales another doughnut and washes it down with cold coffee, aware that she ought to get up. When her hand tires, when her concentration flags so that she can't scribble on her magazines, she props books on her belly and reads these instead. They are Sal's, like the magazines—Sal let her take everything when she gave up the shop and moved in next door with Paine. Sal said, "What do you want with this old stuff? You never used to be interested. And besides, I could teach you anything you'd want."

Diane couldn't explain why she wanted it. She doesn't want to follow her mother's teachings, her footsteps—not now, when Sal blooms like some fat desert flower and drifts between Diane's house and Paine's in the hand-woven shifts that Paine buys her. Not now, when opera music floats from Paine's house at night, as Paine teaches Sal harmony and Sal teaches him astrology. Diane wishes them every happiness, but this isn't the way she wants to go. She has not, like Paine, succumbed to the charms of the occult. Not her—all she wants is some answers. She'd like to know which evil aspects of the stars have brought her here. This isn't

like her childhood, when one of fortune's blows—her
father's death, their lost house, her mother's strange
preoccupations—might strike her flat for a few months.
This is serious. She's been lost for six months now—
more, really, if she counts back to the job she didn't get
—and she wants to know what's happened to her.

A hard square, perhaps? A difficult opposition? She
skims the books, struggling to decipher the ominous
charts of the rich and famous. Freud had a stellium in
Taurus, with a Gemini moon on the vertex. Van Gogh
had his moon and Jupiter trine to Mercury, with heavy
Pisces involvement. Baudelaire had a single huge stellium spreading from Pisces through Aries, with a cardi-
nal square from Capricorn to Cancer. They all survived.
As for her, her own chart is difficult but not impossible,
and when she looks at this evidence it's clear that the
fault must lie with Ben. Ben, who alone of all her family
has no horoscope. He won't reveal his time of birth; Sal
can't cast a chart without it. Which reminds her: "Dear
Penny—Do you happen to know the exact moment of
Ben's birth?" She ought to give Penny a call. Penny has
been in Nantucket but has recently come home.

She delves into her books again, reading about the
angular distances between the planets which are known
as aspects. "Saturn," she reads, "has a completely different geomagnetic field when it transits the vernal equinox than when it transits the winter solstice. The *angles*
formed among the planets at the moment of your birth
create the conditions of your life."

Sure, she thinks. Right. The angles formed among
her family—her dead father, her feckless mother—are
more likely causes for her past, just as the angles form-
ing now among her mother and Paine, Cass and Webb,
Ben and Jill and Jordan and her seem more likely causes
for her present. "There are laws of nature," she reads,
"that are independent of causal laws. The patterns the

planets present at your birth are meaningfully coincident with your nature."

This sounds more reasonable to her. Not that the stars and planets determine her life, but that some other force, still unexplained, affects both her fate and the position of the heavenly bodies. She can almost believe this. She could call Penny to talk about this, and Penny might listen without laughing. She scribbles a quick note: "Dear Penny—Could there be forces related to the stars' positions that affect both the planets and us?" She slips this under her mattress to join the others.

She reads an article called "Black Holes—Mysteries of Space?" with some attention, and from this she forms a hazy picture of a gravitational field so strong that it swallows everything, even light. A collapsed star, the author claims. A bend in the field. She writes: "Dear Dr. Fielding—A picture would have been helpful here. What does a black hole look like?" Sweating, covered with crumbs, she draws a large circle on a green envelope and blackens it completely with her pen. A black hole—it doesn't look like much. A black hole, like Ben. Once he looked to her like a star, all light and fire. Now she can see that he's only a star imploded, a gateway to nothingness. What goes into him goes in and is lost forever. He lies in wait until love touches the edge of his gravitational field, and then—*swoop!* Love falls in. It and the person doing the loving, vanished forever.

He's threatening to leave her—in love, he says, with his red-haired typist, Jill. No more taste than that, no more finesse than to repeat with Jill what he did with her, another wife discarded for another, younger girl. How smart can he be? She would bet, now, that he took Jill to the same beach where he first took her, that he tried to show her the same stars and still didn't know a single one. For all she knows, he tried that trick with Penny too. Which reminds her: "Dear Jill—Beware black holes." She crumples this and throws it away—

she owes nothing to Jill. A black hole has no light of its own and can't, like a dark nebula, be lit from within by the stars it swallows.

She isn't getting anywhere. Her pen is running dry. She needs a bath before the birthday guests arrive—a bath now, another after the party, another late tonight. She can't get by, the way she sweats, on fewer than three a day. It's all this reading, writing, thinking that makes her so nervous. It's all this fat that makes her sweat. As she wipes her face, Sal pokes her head around the door.

"Honey?" she says. "Are you all right?" Sal, even Sal, is concerned for her. Sal says she should take better care of herself.

"Just a little cold," Diane says. "I'll be up soon."

"We're going next door for a bit," Sal says. She is radiant, flushed with contentment; she has a new love, Jordan nearby, and money for the first time in her life. Her chart shows a grand trine, most harmonious of aspects. "I'll bring Jordan back in time to get dressed," she says. "Want some aspirin?"

"Maybe later," Diane says. For the past six months, ever since Ben told her about Jill, she's been fighting off one cold after another. She sees the cause now—Ben has eaten her light.

Sal leaves. Diane finishes the last of the doughnuts and dashes off a quick response to the ad of one Professor Allemande. "I will reveal your secret personality," the professor's ad says. "With my help, you will receive at last and instantly all the things you have longed for in vain. Free! Just answer the questions below and mail."

"Diane Day," she scratches. "Born January 6, 6:30 P.M., 1943, Buzzards Bay, Massachusetts. Please send me my free horoscope."

Perhaps it will contradict the natal horoscope Sal cast for her. She has hopes, still, that one of these tricks will save her, but some small voice in her, fed by Sal's worried looks and Jordan's questions, knows the answers aren't likely to come from this fortress of paper she's built. She should get up, get dressed, lose eighty pounds, and cut her hair. She should take a bath and polish her nails, do something—as the *Ladies' Home Journal* advises—to put the zip back into her marriage. But she has given up reading women's magazines—all lies, disguised as sweet truth. She could have her breasts lifted, dye her hair, become young and beautiful again. It wouldn't matter. Ben would still be busy licking the edges of a fresh new star.

She rises just after one, when Sal returns and when Jordan, looking worried, climbs on her bed and shoves her books and papers to the floor. "Get up!" she says, in her clear, sweet voice. "And put a dress on, okay?"

Diane sends Sal to dress her daughter and then bathes herself, trying to sponge away the grayness that has settled on her skin. She pulls her fading hair into a twist and dabs the wisps down with a cotton ball soaked in hairspray. She puts on coral drop earrings and a flowered peach dress that skims the massive shelf of her hips and makes them look less broad. This is a party, after all; she doesn't want to embarrass Jordan. And although she can't let Jordan ride a bike or go out on a boat or visit her friends—anything might happen if she did— she makes up for this, or tries to, by welcoming Jordan's friends here. On weekday afternoons the house is full of little girls playing in the basement and shrieking through the halls. On summer days they play—never over their heads, of course; never unsupervised—in the water near the porch. She still feels, despite her days in bed, that she's more watchful than the other mothers. They don't understand what lurks out there the way she does. She's tested the cold, black waters with her own two feet, and she's not about to let Jordan fall in.

Still, this is a party. It's important that she look civilized. To her face she adds two wedges of pink blush, two streaks of blue shadow, two dark coral lips. She finishes just as Jordan bounds in.

"How do I look?" Jordan asks. She twirls on her toes so that her new dress flares out. It's fluffy tangerine with a shiny sash and a frill along the bust that makes her look grownup; with it, she wears black patent-leather flats and white socks with a ruffle.

"You look beautiful," Diane says, kissing the white line of her part.

"You look nice too," says Jordan.

Together they stand in front of the mirror, Diane a faded version of her daughter. She is peach where Jordan is tangerine, sallow where Jordan is glowing cream, faded ash where Jordan is gold—as if, as on a balloon expanding, her colors have faded and thinned where they stretched around her enlarging bulk. Sal joins them as they gaze into the glass, and Diane sees that her mother, who has been shrinking since she moved in with Paine, is now no bigger than her.

"Hey!" Sal says. "We look great! Paine wants to take a picture of us."

Diane makes a face. "He's coming?"

Sal drops her eyes. "He's in the kitchen hanging streamers."

Diane sighs. This is already an old discussion. Somewhere along the line, perhaps while her back was turned, Paine has become part of the family. He takes Jordan for walks, bakes her treats, brings her little presents. He has, along with Sal, taught her to waltz. There is no way that Diane can send him home.

He waits for them in the kitchen, wearing a buff-colored suit that makes him look royal, two-toned cream and buff shoes, and Jordan's Christmas gift to him—a brown tie flecked with beige shells. He stands on a chair, tying green paper streamers to the light and balancing, all two hundred and forty pounds of him, on the ball of one foot. When the three of them walk in, he lets himself down gently and then grins at them.

"Looking good!" he says. "All of you. How about a picture?"

He poses them in front of the refrigerator. Diane stretches her lips to match Sal's and Jordan's smiles, but even as the flash explodes she's plotting to seize and burn the print. The doorbell rings before she can grab the camera, and the first carload of little girls pours into the kitchen. Ellen, Sarah, Heather, and Renée bear neatly wrapped gifts, which they pile along the counter. Iris, Jordan's best friend, carries a large box into the dining room with a secretive smile. Donna, Jenny, and Marisa arrive next, followed by Robin, Brooke, and Stacy. Paine, drawing on some secret pool of courtliness and charm that Diane doesn't recognize, greets each girl and sets a paper party hat upon each head. Sal lays out paper plates, napkins, party favors, and the giant cake, missing the fine, dark lines of icing Diane meant to draw along the edges. Even without these it looks great.

"Look!" Robin squeals. "A starfish! Jordan's favorite!"

The girls stare greedily at the cake. And Diane, who means to thank each girl for coming and compliment each pretty dress, is so busy trying to remember when she cut those layers into wedges and welded them into a starfish cake that she can't make a sound. Someone, somewhere, pressed coconut into the soft frosting on the side. It must have been her. She must have done it in a dream. Her mouth freezes in a smile and her arms hang uselessly at her sides.

Sal gives her a sharp look and lights the birthday candles. Paine leads the birthday song. Jordan, somehow sensing her mother's absence, sets about making each of her friends feel welcome. She beams at the singing, unwraps each gift slowly, and exclaims with delight. She coos over the charm bracelet, laughs at the Day-Glo

Frisbee (although she already has two), tucks the new Barbie doll into the chair beside her. She might be some politician at a dinner, some gracious lady holding court. She hasn't a trace of Diane's stiffness—when she turns to thank each girl she knows just what to say. This is Jordan's talent, Diane can see. She hasn't Cass's brains or Webb's musical way, but she has something else, an easy charm that comes, perhaps, from always having been so beautiful. She is beautiful still, even in the Groucho Marx glasses-and-nose that Heather gives her as a joke.

Iris saves her present for last. When all the other gifts are opened and admired, all the wrappings neatly folded and the ribbons tucked away, Iris hops up in her raspberry dress and darts into the dining room. She returns with a box that has holes punched along the sides. "Here," she says, holding it out to Jordan. The box gives a little leap of its own and falls into Jordan's lap.

"What is it?" Jordan squeals. "It's moving!"

"Open it," Iris says.

Jordan tears off the wrapping, pries open the lid, and lifts out a squirming black and white puppy, so small and nearly hairless that it might be a baby pig.

"Oh!" Jordan gasps. "It's the twin—the other puppy!"

"Nashoba's brother," Iris says modestly, fully aware that her gift has completely eclipsed the others. "I'm keeping Nashoba—I thought we could train them together."

"He's so cute," Jordan says. She brings the squirming ball up to her face and then lowers it to the table, where it buries its fat snout in the remains of her cake. The girls laugh and clap their hands, and Jordan passes him around the table.

"So soft," Heather murmurs.

"So little," Sarah says.

Their eyes turn inward as they hold the puppy, each girl in turn crooning to it as if it were a favored doll.

"Um?" Diane says. She's about to find some way to say the puppy has to go when Sal grabs her forearm and tugs her into the dining room.

"Don't you say a word," Sal whispers. "You have to let her keep it."

"Mom," Diane says impatiently. "I can't take care of a *dog* right now—I can hardly take care of myself."

Sal looks her up and down. "Maybe so," she says. "But that's not Jordan's problem. She *deserves* a dog—it's not like you ever let her *go* anywhere. If you don't take the puppy, Paine and I will." She sets her jaw stubbornly.

"No!" Diane says quickly, afraid that, with the puppy next door, Jordan will never come home. She spends too much time there already.

Sal lays her small dimpled hand on Diane's arm. "If you would stop acting so crazy," she says quietly. "If you would just wake up and look around . . ."

"I'm trying," Diane whispers. "I am." She flinches as her mother touches each of her earrings.

"Try harder," Sal says. "Wear earrings more often. Stop reading those old books and magazines, and get outside in the sun."

Diane pulls her head away. "They're *your* magazines —who do you think made me this way?"

"You made yourself," Sal says sharply. "And I never used that stuff the way you do. The stars are just a guide, you know—it's all in how you read them."

Diane snorts. "You're the one who runs around casting horoscopes."

Sal shakes her head impatiently. "Fishing lines," she says. "A chart's just a tangle of fishing lines cast into the ocean—your intuition tells you what fish you've landed. Common sense, girl. Intuition. Seeing what's already there."

"Yeah?" Diane says. "Well, my intuition says I'm fucked."

"Smarty," Sal snaps. "Your intuition—your chart, for that matter—says what you think it says. Now stop being so crazy and go tell Jordan she can keep the puppy. She needs a friend in this house."

Diane bows under her mother's sharp words. Sal could be right—since Ben ripped this hole in her life, Diane hasn't been the kind of mother she means to be. Less attentive, less kind, less sympathetic—she could break her own legs for this, and yet she can't seem to clean up her act. She bites her ring finger just below the nail, swearing to herself that she'll do better. Then she slips back into the kitchen and says, "What are you going to name him?"

Jordan's face relaxes. "Willie," she says. "Willie and his sister, Nashoba." She hugs Iris and then, so the others won't feel jealous, touches each of her gifts again. Paine makes a nest for the puppy in an empty box.

They're so busy that no one notices at first when Webb walks in. His nineteenth birthday was yesterday, but he spent the night at Penny's and so it passed with hardly a ripple. Now he sets down two black cases—his trombone and his saxophone, which he brings with him everywhere—and murmurs "Hello" to no one in particular. Jordan, who has radar for Webb, hears him instantly and rushes over to hug his long legs. He smiles, looking thirteen again for just a minute. "How's the birthday girl?" he asks.

"Great! Look what I got!" She shows him all her other gifts and only then leads him to the sleeping puppy.

"Cute," he says, tickling the black-spotted chin.

"I knew you'd like him," Jordan says. "Will you help me train him?"

"Sure. Want to see what I brought you?"

Jordan's friends hang back, shy in the presence of this

tall, broad-shouldered stranger. Webb opens his trombone case and pulls out a narrow bundle wrapped in a square of faded silk. "I made it," he says, almost shyly. "I hope you like it."

Jordan unfolds the silk, revealing two long cylinders punctuated by holes, and a third part with a short, curved mouthpiece. The wood is as smooth and fine as ivory.

"It's a recorder," he says. "Lessons included." He slips the parts together and plays a few notes that hang in the air like bells. The girls tilt their heads up. "See?" he says. "Easy."

"It's *beautiful*," Jordan breathes.

Webb holds the recorder to her mouth and folds her slim fingers over the holes. "Blow," he says. A sweet note drifts out. He moves her fingers over the high holes, the low holes; she blows a note each time, with her wide eyes shining. Together they shape the tune to "Twinkle, Twinkle, Little Star."

"Like it?" When he smiles at her, his whole face softens so that his eyelid hardly droops.

"I *love* it!" She kisses his thin tan cheek. Her friends, charmed by the new toy, crowd in around her. As they do, Webb backs away.

"Catch you later," he says, shutting the case and gliding toward the door.

Even Jordan can't hold him here, but Diane rests her hand on his arm anyway. "Stay a little?" she pleads. It's his birthday too, or near enough, and she'd like for him to join the party.

He shrugs. "Naah," he says. "You know . . ."

They exchange a long glance. She knows. In his eyes she can read everything that's passed between them and, although they've never discussed it directly, she knows that this house, so full of odd vibrations, works on him like poison. Webb has a new house now, which he rents from Walker: a small, gray shack in the heart of a cranberry bog. He has a new job too. Despite Ben's protests, or maybe because of them, he turned down college last spring and went to work for Walker instead. Now, although he visits Jordan often, he won't set foot in the house when Ben's around and he shies away from Diane when they're alone together. She knows what that's from, too—he's afraid she'll confide in him, explain the separate bedrooms and Ben's frequent absences. She rubs a small patch of skin on his forearm with her thumb.

"Webb?" she says.

He shakes his head, taps her shoulder lightly, and slips away.

Banished to the basement, the puppy sleeps in a box with a towel and a clock for company. He pees on the floor when he's let out, unerringly finding the cracks and corners where Jordan hasn't laid newspaper. This gets Diane up, if only occasionally, to help Jordan clean the floor and mix Willie's food. Willie—what a name. And yet it's Willie who brings her back to earth a few times each day, interrupting the chain of letters she is drafting to Cass.

The horoscope she requested from Professor Allemande hasn't arrived; the three questions she asked of Madame Clair haven't been answered. It's only been a week since she wrote and she knows these things take time, but time is what she doesn't have. *Tok, tok, tok* she hears from the clock in the dining room. *Tok.* She lets the clock wind down but still hears its insistent beat. In one of Sal's books she reads how a series of divisions created the universe: heaven from earth, darkness from light, the waters from the waters. Space from time, she thinks. The time before Ben fell in love with Jill from now. She has no time. What she has is a sense that she's about to fall into a dark and nasty place, and an even stronger sense that only Cass can save her. She can't explain this, even to herself, but it has something to do with Cass's voice—strong, happy, aloof—over the phone. During school vacations Cass camps and skis and walks the mountains out west, planning trails and buildings for Otis's new ski resorts, and when she's not working or not in school she lives in a room over Otis's garage. Next year, she says, when she graduates, she'll work for Otis full-time. Diane thinks that perhaps Cass's energy and determination could be catching, like mumps. She's sure she hasn't been vaccinated. But it is more than this—it's that when she calls to mind Cass's face, what she sees are green eyes narrowed and pointed chin upthrust in defiance of Ben. Doors slammed. Blows shrugged off. Thin lips shaping the word *No.*

Diane bends her head over an index card and tries the straightforward approach. "Dear Cass," she writes. "Jordan asks about you all the time. How would you like to come home and work with your father this summer?"

No—not flashy enough. Diane has a hope, half dream, that Ben will get rid of Jill if Cass comes home. She tries again. "Dear Cass—How would you like an exciting summer job drafting plans for a new office complex?"

That'll never work. If she had money of her own she'd offer a bribe, but all her money is Ben's. She has nothing else to give. On a soiled sheet of newspaper she tries another approach. "Dear Cass—Your father and I are both well, and Jordan has a new puppy. We'd love to have you home for the summer." She imagines Cass striding into the house with her low, knowing laugh, hissing in Ben's face until Jill has vanished and Ben is sorry and Diane's life fits together again. But Cass has no reason to come back.

Diane throws the letters away and starts another batch, and then another. When Saturday rolls around again she still hasn't found the right words, and so she's tempted when Ben asks, for the tenth time that week,

"Are you sure you wouldn't rather stay home tonight? It's just another boring political dinner—me and the rest of the committee and Allen and a bunch of people you don't know . . ."

Diane considers his offer for a minute and then says, "I'd better come. They'll be expecting you to show up with your wife." She'll dress up, she decides. Act nicely. Just to show him that she still can, that he can't dismiss her just by wishing.

She puts her letters away and tries to pull herself together. It's not until later, as she enters the Cummaquid Hotel on Ben's arm, that she knows she has made a mistake. Beneath the huge banner—*Reelect Allen Bell!*—mill guests wearing strapless gowns, dark suits, discreet jewels, narrow shoes. The women, who clearly never sweat, have the well-preserved chic of the rich. The men all look important. Only she lacks a taut, carefully exercised waist; only she has ripples over her kidneys and a beaded forehead. She nods, smiles, nods again and again at the people who greet Ben, until finally they reach a round table near the front. *Benjamin Day, Chairman*, she reads on one cream place card. *Paine Westfall*— on the committee, she knows, because of his political ties in Boston. She makes a face when she reads *Mark Reilly, Treasurer.* She sees a card with her own name, and then one more card. *Jill Roarke.* Jill, here with them? She stumbles into her seat between Paine and Ben.

"Mrs. Day," Jill says, as she sits down. "So nice to see you again." Her red hair springs from her temples in licks of flame, tamed behind by a shiny clip. Her eyes are long and narrow and cool, and she adjusts the low neckline of her black dress with a pale, fine hand.

Diane nods to her, some small organ deep in her belly —kidney? liver? bladder?—leaping about like a fish. Jill is as beautiful as Jordan, with the same open eyes and velvet skin. Mark Reilly, whom Diane has disliked ever since he became one of Ben's partners, lays his thick hand on Jill's bare back and says, "This little girl here organized the whole dinner. Isn't she something?"

Jill smiles modestly and lowers her eyes. "It was nothing," she says. "I was just helping." Tall and proud, she stares at Ben. Ben stares back at her.

Diane slides her napkin into her lap and begins shredding the hem in the heavy linen. *Why did you let me come?* she hisses silently to Ben. *What do you think you're doing?* Ben smiles. *What I want,* she imagines him saying. She breaks her nail on a coarse thread. *Make her go.* Ben, as if he's heard her, turns away. *No.* The room fills; the waitresses bring drinks. Paine, sitting quietly near Diane, touches her thigh with his gentle fat fingers and whispers, "Relax. It doesn't mean anything."

Sal must have told Paine; Ben may have told everyone. How could he resist bragging about this lovely girl? She taps Ben's arm and tries to relax her jaw. "I'd like to talk to you," she says quietly. "Outside."

Ben blinks at her and then shakes his head, annoyed. He turns to Mark, whispers something, and then rises and walks to the front of the room, where a podium stands.

"Ladies and gentlemen," he begins. "As Chairman of the Committee to Reelect Allen Bell, State Representative, I'd like to welcome you here. You've all been most generous, and . . ."

Diane loses his words in the train of her own thoughts. *You shit,* she beams at the podium, smiling all the while. *I hope that podium collapses.* For a minute she has a vision of chipboard draped in bunting, crumbling to the floor with a great crash just as Ben leans on it. *Let your tongue dry in your mouth,* she thinks. *Let your legs turn to water.* Here Sal spent all those years teaching her astrology when she could have taught her something really useful, like old curses. Diane can only make them up. *Let your hair turn to lice,* she thinks. Ben is half bald already.

Paine leans back in his chair, staring at the ceiling as if there were stars painted there. Jill stares at Ben, leaning forward on her smooth elbows to catch each word. Ben might be flinging out poetry from the way she listens; he might be speaking only to her. Diane tunes into his speech again but hears nothing new—incentives for business, broad-based tax reform, blah, blah, blah. From this distance the fine lines on his face are invisible. He is cordial, smooth, affable; funny and witty and strong. The women in the room light up as he looks at them, and he is careful to look at each one. Diane can remember when she lit up too, when a touch from him was like a solar flare. But she can't remember the last time he touched her. Christmas, perhaps? A dry peck on the cheek in exchange for a cashmere robe. A comment of Ben's touches off a spatter of applause. He smiles and launches into a joke, which Diane ignores. It's an old joke she's heard a hundred times before. Ben always tells it at business meetings. Jill laughs as if he's just invented it.

"Of course," Ben winds up, "it's just a joke. But there's a lesson we can learn from it—it's all too easy to fall for the first candidate who seems to have a reasonable answer. The trick lies in waiting for the man with the *whole* answer. Ladies and gentlemen, I give you Allen Bell."

A smooth speech, Diane thinks. A gracious speech. The podium continues to stand. He could be a politician if he wasn't so smart, if he didn't know that his interest lay in doing what he did and then buying the right help. *Trip*, Diane thinks, as Ben heads back to the table. He doesn't. Mark slaps him on the back and says, "Well done." Paine smiles. Jill glows as though she'd like to stretch out under the table for him right here, right now. Why can't she see through him? Diane wonders. He's just a hole, a tunnel in the sky.

Diane is sweating now, sudden big drops. It's the

food—the heavily sauced chicken stuffed with ham, the undercooked asparagus. It's the company. She feels a foot bump into hers, and then another. As if she could see through the table, she pictures Jill's dainty, high-arched sandal seeking Ben's sturdy wing tip; toes slithering up calves like snakes; the slick, smooth feel of a nylon stocking; a touch of hairy shin. She has played these games herself. She remembers what they were like.

The tip of Jill's nose turns pink and her eyes half close. Ben's teeth show. A sun-warmed eucalyptus smell cuts through the fog of food and coffee like a San Diego wind, but only the women seem to catch it. Mark and Paine talk about the coming election, seemingly unaware of the drama beneath the table. The hum of the room grows to a roar in Diane's ears and she excuses herself unsteadily, past caring if anyone's watching her. Halfway across the carpeted room she trips and then kicks her offending shoe aside. A few heads turn. Poor Ben—that's what they're thinking. Poor guy, with this fat slob for a wife. She looked like Jill once, or near enough, but these people don't know that. They see her separate chins and wince.

She makes it to the bathroom but not to the toilet; she vomits on the clean tile floor. And then, after she wipes up the mess and washes her face, she takes a pen from her purse and scribbles a note on a brown paper towel.

"Dear Cass," she writes. "Come home. I need you."

PART FOUR
Two Mothers, Two Daughters

We know a few things which once were hidden, and being known they seem easy; but there are the flashings of the Northern lights. . . . there is the conical zodiacal beam seen so beautifully in the early evenings of spring and the early mornings of autumn; there are the startling comets, whose use is all unknown; there are the brightening and flickering variable stars, whose cause is all unknown; and the meteoric showers—and for all these the reasons are as clear as for the succession of the day and night; they lie just beyond the daily mist of our minds, but our eyes have not pierced through it.

—Maria Mitchell, from her *Diary*

The Lesser Light to Rule the Night
(July 1976)

★　　　★　　　★　　　★　　　★　　　★

Morning. The rest of the world is recovering from the Bicentennial celebrations, but Cass, who has missed all the fireworks and all the parties, is awake after a night spent tossing on the narrow bed downstairs. Tired, bewildered, she stands in the room that was once her parents', in the house that was once hers. She is twenty, but she feels fifteen, fourteen, twelve—as confused as she felt when she last lived here, when everything important seemed to be happening behind her back. The room is empty now. The sheer white curtains that Penny had have long since vanished; the shutters Diane installed before Jordan's birth are gone as well. Over the windows hang dank, dark drapes splashed with maroon flowers and oversized olive-green leaves. The smell seems to be coming from these, a smell of cooking and smoke and mildew that stamps the drapes as Sal's, probably bequeathed from her old apartment over the sub shop. But why would Diane hang them in here?

Why, then, any of this? When Cass was fifteen, fourteen, twelve, making up names for Diane and waging the small wars that were all she could manage then, she could never have predicted this. Nor wished it, even— such total defeat, such embarrassment, for the woman who once marched triumphant through the house. It's a joke, she thinks. The room is disgusting, past disgusting, past anything she can believe. A parody of deterioration, designed to strike those who enter it dead with guilt. How long has it been this way? How long since anyone but Diane set foot in here? Because she has to do something, anything, Cass breathes shallowly through her mouth and sets to work.

Under her inquisitive hands, overflowing ashtrays appear from behind the dressers, under the bed, in the closets, on the windowsills. Empty diet-soda bottles roll out from under chairs. Half-open bottles of nailpolish, dusted with a fine powder that could be talcum or ash, lean against broken lipsticks, smeared tubes, greasy jars. There are small, sharp smells overlaid on the background smell, making Cass's nostrils quiver. Queen of the Cows, she thinks, remembering the names she and Webb once made up. The bovine Diane. Porcine is more like it. A pig, a family of pigs, would not leave a room this way. She recoils as her hand touches something foul and soft and rubbishy beneath the bed. It might be alive. It *is* partly alive, a doughnut overgrown with parti-colored mold. Shuddering, she wipes her hand on a rag. I could just walk out, she thinks. Get the hell out of here. It's revolting, this obvious plea for sympathy. As desperate and sloppy and crude as the letter that brought her home. There they were—her and Cindy and Otis and Roger—celebrating the Nelsons' twentieth anniversary and cutting cake. A normal night, everything cool, when Otis said, "Oh, you got a letter today." A plain white envelope, as normal as could be. She opened it right there in front of them and found a single faint line, her name and the message scrawled in fuzzy letters on a scrap of paper towel. Come home, it said. I need you. No explanation, no apology, no nothing. No signature, but the vowels fat and round, the *A* in her name the same plump, pumpkin shape as on the tuition checks.

As if she had a claim, Cass thinks furiously. She works in from the dark corners of her stepmother's den, methodically heaping the trash in the center. As if we were friends. She would not have come back, she would never have come back, if it hadn't been for Jordan. She has a job this summer in Idaho. She read the letter, looked at Otis, and stomped out to the room above the Nelsons' garage where she'd spent five years of school vacations. One room, very large; peaked ceilings, slanted walls, windows set in dormers. Hers. Home since Diane and Sal booted her out. Her narrow bed covered with a bright red quilt, her drafting table, her stool, her desk stacked with paper and Mylar and triangles and scales, plastic-lead pencils and technical pens— her room. Her walls hung with blueprints and drawings. She sat on her bed and stared at this strange note —a joke? It couldn't be a joke. The curled spot where something had evaporated, the jagged edge, the fuzzy letters—all sent messages different and worse than the simple words. Come home, it said. A joke? Diane never wanted her home.

Cass remembers crumpling the note, tossing it down, almost returning to the cool house where Roger, the Nelsons' son, was cutting the cake that he and Cass had baked. She had her foot on the top step, her head bowed beneath the doorframe, when Jordan's face caught her eye. Webb had sent this photograph just a month ago, with his letter—Jordan, in a pale blue bathing suit, perched on a rock with a puppy Cass had never seen, identified by Webb only as Willie. Jordan's hair was pulled back into a braid and her face was still and beautiful. What's it like for her? Cass wondered. Eight years old and stuck there with crazy parents? Webb, in his laconic way, had mentioned that things at home were worse than ever. A shiver crept down Cass's spine as she stared at her sister's face. Unable to call Webb at his shack in the bog, unwilling to call Ben, Cass finally went home on the basis of that shiver. I'll make sure Jordan's all right, she told herself. Spend some time with my mother and Webb, find out what's up with Diane, stay out of Ben's way, and be back up here in a week at most, ready to head for Otis's new mountain in Idaho.

She sighs and rubs her nose. She has saved the worst for last and now she has to face it—the bed. It's the bed of an invalid, filthy and rank, sheets unchanged for months, old socks and underwear caught in the folds, crusts and stains on the pillowcases. A gumdrop, flattened and glued to the spread. Even at my worst, she thinks, even when I was a grubby kid, I never lived like this. She's afraid to look in Jordan's room, afraid to look in the bathroom. The kitchen is bad enough, bearable only because Paine has been over a few times to clean up after Sal's cooking experiments. Paine and Sal—but that's a whole other problem which she'll deal with later.

The mattress crinkles when she pulls out the bottom sheet. She presses it hard with her hand and it crinkles again. Newspapers? Old potato chip bags? It could be anything. She slips her hand warily under the mattress and feels paper everywhere. What now? What else? With one hand she lifts the edge of the mattress; with the other she sweeps the mass of papers toward her, spilling them onto the floor. When she bends down to look at them she sees crooked line after crooked line, spattered with fat round vowels. "Christ," she whispers. These are letters, piles of letters scratched in Diane's sprawling hand. That panicked scribble . . . Cass sits back on her heels and fingers the letters cautiously. Has it been only a week since her first hint of this? A week since she got that note, two days since she finished setting up for her trip out west and left New Hampshire for here? She shudders, remembering that first sight of Diane beached like a lost whale on this smelly bed, staring at her as if she'd dropped from Mars. When Diane finally spoke, her first words were "Ben's gone."

"Gone?" Cass remembers saying. The one thing she'd never have guessed.

"Gone. Took off, split, moved in with that nasty, red-haired Jill—vanished. Left me Jordan and the house."

"What a guy," Cass sneered, before she could stop herself.

"What a guy," Diane echoed hollowly.

Cass knew it was bad then; now she knows it's worse. Some of these letters are written on napkins. "Much worse," Cass mutters to herself. Diane hasn't explained anything, but these letters . . . Cass touches them again. They're addressed to psychics, senators, astronauts; to strangers and friends; to her and Penny and Ben and Webb, full of hate, full of confusion. They lay blame in strange places, make wild accusations, cry for help, and promise retribution. Was mine the only one she mailed? Cass wonders. Did I just get lucky? Or am I the only one dumb enough to answer? The letters are strange enough to burn her hands and, despite herself, she feels a great stab of sympathy. That's just what she wants me to feel, Cass thinks, dropping the letters to the floor. She did this just to get me—but no, that can't be right. No one could write these letters just to get sympathy.

She shakes her head impatiently. Impossible to sort through all this shit, the years of grief and anger and disgust and sorrow and irritation that lie between her and her stepmother. She should have stayed up north. Diane's beyond help, Cass thinks. Beyond mine, anyway. Still she continues to clean. A bad smell rises from this room, a hopeless smell that emanates from the curtains. I can't do much, Cass thinks. But I can clean up this room and get rid of the stink, get this weirdness away from Jordan. She rips the curtains down quickly and stuffs them in the garbage bag, past caring what Diane will say. It's Jordan she came home to help.

Outside, she can hear Jordan playing with Willie, her fat, rambunctious puppy. "Come," Jordan calls in her clear, high voice. "Come. Sit. Stay. Good dog!" Over and over she repeats her commands, very patient. She seems to know intuitively how to train him, just as she knows to stick close to Sal and Paine right now and leave her mother alone. Has she seen these letters? Cass wonders. Has she smelled this room? Cass scowls and jams the letters into the bag, on top of the foul curtains. Jordan shouldn't be exposed to this. She shouldn't even know about it. "A week," Cass mutters to herself. "Maybe two. No more." She'll clean this up, arrange for some help—housekeeper, baby-sitter, doctors, whatever—and then she'll get out of here. She closes her eyes and imagines the cool pine woods around the Nelsons' house, around her room; the chortle of hidden nighthawks. My place, she thinks. Where I belong.

Diane lies where Cass deposited her, deep in the musty cushions of the old chaise on the porch. From here, she listens to Cass crashing and banging through her room. Like a tornado, Diane thinks. Like a hurricane, like the storm that sent seawater sweeping the streets of Buzzards Bay all those years ago, when she was as young as Jordan is now, before her father died. She closes her ears, shutting out the sound; her eyes, shutting out the sun. Her body is as heavy and still as clay. She is a nose, smelling the thick, sweet scent of the roses that blanket the porch wall. She has about that much common sense, about that much energy.

The rumble of Cass tossing open another window pierces her lethargy. "Christ!" Diane mutters. Is Cass going to tear down the room? So clumsy, so abrupt. Diane hardly recognized Cass when she strode in last night. She was thin still, as thin as a child, with her hair newly cropped and curly, glasses shed somewhere, faint pencil around her eyes. Pretty, after that awkward childhood—an elf, only tall. With an elf's cool distance, an elf's quick gaze taking in the mess around here and judging instantly. *Tik, tik,* went her neat, crisp steps, like hooves on pavement. "I got your note," Cass said. No hug, no smile, no expression of concern; a disapproving set to her lips. I'd have stabbed her if I had a knife, Diane thinks. It's not like I meant her to come.

She sighs, remembering her note. Ben was still here the night she scrawled those unthinking words; she'd imagined Cass striding home, hissing at Ben, forcing him, magically, to behave. And then she hadn't sent the note after all, any more than she'd sent any of those letters. And then Ben left. "Call me if there's an emergency," he said, pressing Jill's number into her hand. What's an emergency? Jordan picking listlessly at her food and staring at the phone? Webb in a shack in a cranberry bog, unwilling to come home? Paine managed the bills for her, and he and Sal cooked meals; the house was in no danger of collapsing. Inside it Diane lay, growing stiller, heavier—not an emergency. She forced herself to call Penny, hoping to resurrect that moment years ago when they'd almost made friends. Penny had gone to Nantucket. She cornered Webb one day when he came to visit Jordan, and begged him to come home for a while. "I can't," he said then, averting his drooping eye. "I just can't." Who was left, then? She has no friends; her mother and Paine are locked within some happy astrological game. There was only Cass.

Dash, smash—has she taken an ax to the room? There are thuds, clanks, crushing papery sounds. Diane hears

a screech of curtain hooks on rods and frowns, knowing
that Cass is fooling with Sal's curtains. She has no right,
Diane thinks. No right at all. Those curtains are old, a
little heavy perhaps, but full of memories. So odd to
have Cass here. For years, maybe all the way back to
when Webb was sick, or before, back to Marlene—for
years, Diane has wished Cass home just long enough to
chase Ben's women away. Saint Cass in armor, riding a
horse, her sword pruning away all of them, from Marlene to Jill, and then vanishing as soon as the work was
done. Riding off to the mountains with a last flourish of
her lance. Odd powers, Diane recognizes, for an adoles-
cent girl. If her head weren't so heavy and dull, she'd
shake it in impatience at her own stupidity. Where is
that slender, bright girl who once put together real estate deals for Ben? Where is that Diane? I was dreaming
the whole time, Diane thinks now.

She concentrates on the rose smell, trying to remember how she finally came to send the note. It sat limp
and soiled in her purse for weeks, almost forgotten in
all the excitement. And then one morning, two weeks
after Ben took off, Diane dreamed that she flew off this
porch, right here, and smashed on the rocks below. She
woke up with the dream still blazed on her brain, and
she said to herself, I'll drive to New Hampshire and see
Otis and Cindy and Cass, get out of here, pull myself
together . . . the idea came from nowhere, maybe de-
livered by the dream. She left Jordan with Sal and Paine
and drove down Route 3, over the Canal, through Wey-
mouth and Braintree to Route 93; through Milton and
Brookline, a dart through Boston; Somerville, Medford,
Andover, Methuen—by then she was in New Hampshire, but by then the energy propelling her had vanished, leaving only a terrible, weary woodenness.

She blamed this on the setting sun, on the rising
moon hanging full and low in the sky. In her natal chart
her own moon dominates her sun, and that's what took

over as the sky grew dark. Faster and faster she drove,
moonstruck, a lunatic. Past Manchester, past Concord,
where she felt the moon's pull for real. Was it the moon?
Something evil and dark, a distant planet, a cold rock
empowering each overpass to call to her. I could close
my eyes, she remembers thinking. Just let go . . . the
car flying effortlessly, out and over the moonbeams like
a bird. She'd be asleep when she hit the road below.

The road poured past her. Villages with white
churches, backyards sprouting rusty cars, dogs chained
to porches, furiously barking. Her car inched, crept,
drifted closer to the rails. The road was empty. As it
arched up over the river she took her hands from the
steering wheel and closed her eyes; only the screech of
her hubcaps on the railing saved her. The noise, harsh
and low and cruel, jolted her awake and reminded her
of Ben's metallic words, the swordlike flicker of his
mind. She saw herself broken on the roads below and
she thought, *This is just what you want*, the words re-
sounding inside her head. *Well, fuck you.* If she roared
out into the night he'd get Jordan; the rest of Jordan's
life would sound like clashing metal. She wrenched the
wheel hard, and then turned and drove to the nearest
motel, where she slept in a cold bed and dreamed about
the moon. The lesser light, Sal called it. The lesser light
to rule the night. Had the moon pushed her near the
railing, or pulled her back? She couldn't tell, but by
morning her new-found defiance had vanished, along
with the voice that chased Ben away. Confused, thinking of Jordan and of what might happen if the railing
called again, Diane bought an envelope and a stamp
from a machine in the stairwell, dug the crumpled note
from her purse, and mailed it to Cass. Better her than
Ben, Diane remembers thinking. If worse comes to
worst.

Now all she can see is what a fool she's been. Cass's
idea of help is a child's fantasy—fresh air and cleanli-

ness, as if closed rooms and germs bred despair. And
Cass's face is a shadow of Ben's. Hard to see, with the
strong nose softened, the cheekbones brought out, hair
darker—in fact, an outsider might say that Cass looks
like Penny, although all Diane can see is Ben. His face
hangs in her mind like the man in the moon, vague and
yet solid. It used to hang over her at night. "A divorce,"
he said. "I want a divorce." He left her the house and
money enough, but she has nothing. "Look how you've
let yourself go," he said. "You're such a mess."

She *is* a mess. She runs a hand down the billowing
slope of her chest and stomach, thinking *I owe it to you*,
tracing each bulge to a harsh word of Ben's. The bigger
she got the less he took her out, and the more she stayed
at home the more she ate. That's what Cass is smashing
and crashing through in there—the evidence, the remnants of treats. Crisp-crusted doughnuts, melting ice
cream, the tender resistance of caramel. She used to be
so hungry. Now, she wonders if she'll ever eat again.

She hears a door slam and then there's silence for a
while, the only sound Jordan's soft commands to Willie.
Quiet, darkness—this is what she needs. She shuts her
eyes and draws the silence in gratefully, faintly curious
as to what's left of her room but not curious enough to
move. It's probably cold and bare in there, sterilized,
clean. It doesn't matter. "Come!" she hears, in Jordan's
faint voice. "Stay!" Diane imagines Willie, his fat body
twisted happily, trying to follow Jordan's commands.
"Come!" Jordan calls again, just as Diane sinks into
sleep, just before a new voice interrupts.

"Jordan!" Cass calls. "How about a swimming lesson?"

Diane's mouth goes dry. She struggles up onto her
elbows and sees Cass, in a black bikini, bending over
Willie. The bathing suit is tiny; the bottom might fit
around Diane's upper arm. Diane swallows hard. No
reason to panic, she thinks—Cass is an excellent swim-

mer, and Jordan already knows how to float and paddle around. And she could be there in a flash if anything happened—except she couldn't. She knows she couldn't. Her limbs are as cool and heavy as stones; her feet feel waxen. The only one who can rescue Jordan is Cass. Diane watches jealously, fearfully, as Jordan giggles at something Cass has said, something she can't hear. Together the girls splash into the water, while Diane's heart beats bump, thump, thumpety-thump— what is this? She sees a flash of yellow, a frill in her mind, and then Ben, trailing a basket behind him while Jordan splashes into the water behind Webb. She hears a shriek, a splash, "Come on!" someone says—was that then or now? Did they ever, any of them, notice her? She concentrates on her arm, tenses it, wills it to rise. The girls pay no attention whatsoever.

Near the porch the water is cold. Willie sits among the pebbles and weeds, wagging his skinny tail; Jordan and Cass stand shivering as the waves lick their knees.

"Let's do it," Cass says. "It won't be so bad once we're wet all over."

She dives and comes up gasping. The water's cold, cold enough to strip away the clinging smells of Diane's room, the film of dirt and smoke. Cold enough to dispel the cloud in her brain. "Freezing," she tells her sister. "But it feels good. Come on in."

Jordan slips easily into the water and wiggles below the surface, her braid streaming out behind her. Webb must have taught her this—Cass can see a translation of his quiet kick in Jordan's feet. Three gulls stand at the tip of the jetty, their beaks open in raucous laughter. Cass chucks a pebble at them and they squawk away. Willie barks.

"That's good," Cass says. "You swim great underwater."

"Webb taught me," Jordan says. She adjusts the top of

her blue bathing suit, which has slipped down on her narrow chest. I could have taught her, Cass thinks. If I'd been here.

"Can you teach me the crawl?" Jordan asks. "I can only dog-paddle."

"We can do that," Cass says. "It's easy." She has Jordan hold out her arms, roll her head, stroke and breathe while she stands in water up to her waist.

"How's this?" Jordan asks.

Her voice is very soft, barely more than a whisper even when she's excited. I know how she got that voice, Cass thinks—it's what Jordan evolved after years of listening to her parents bark at each other. It's a tiny voice, a light voice that doesn't get in anyone's way and that wouldn't aggravate the grumpiest man. It's a tentative voice, suggesting but never demanding. Charming, but Cass wishes it were a little louder, even a little shrill. She doesn't want Jordan fading away.

"That's great!" Cass calls, making her own voice strong and loud as she lowers herself into the water. "Let's try it here—I'll hold you at first so you won't sink." She wraps her arms around Jordan's narrow waist as Jordan lays herself down in the water. Jordan inhales and seems, for a minute, to flinch at Cass's touch. She relaxes into a dead man's float and then, to Cass's delight, she plunges her face into the water and begins to practice her stroke. The only thing she forgets to do is breathe.

She stands up after a minute. "How did I do?" she gasps.

"You were great!" Cass laughs. "Except you forgot to roll your face up and catch some air."

"Oh," Jordan sighs. "I guess I did." She folds Cass's hands around her waist, ready to try again. Willie barks at her and splashes in a few inches, but then darts back in alarm as the water hits his chin. "This is fun," Jordan says softly. "I'm glad you're here. Can you stay for a while?"

Cass's tongue sticks in her mouth. Stay? Here? She has a job this summer, another year of school, and then her life waiting for her. But this is her life too, even if she's been away from it for five years. "What do you want?" she remembers Sal asking, just before they sent her north. "Just to be the world's biggest pain in the ass?" And yet last night, when Sal first saw Cass, she had smiled, nodded calmly, and said, "Welcome back" almost as if they'd been expecting her. Almost, Cass thinks, as if they wanted me here. But probably only Jordan does. As she searches for an answer, Jordan peers over her shoulder at something on the porch. Maybe *Sal* sent that note, Cass thinks suddenly. But no, that wouldn't explain the letters hidden in Diane's bed. She turns and sees a waving arm, ticking slowly back and forth. Diane, waving at them. "There's your mother," she says to Jordan. "Wave hello."

Jordan smiles and waves and then throws herself into the water again, apparently forgetting her question. Cass holds Jordan's belly and watches that waving arm. The motion is broad and fast, less a greeting than a summons: Diane is signaling them. Cass sighs. She knows, or thinks she knows, what's in Diane's mind— Diane's afraid to see Jordan in the water and she wants Cass to bring her out. The water is calm, the sky is blue, there's no reason to be afraid; Jordan, submerged now, isn't even cold. It's ridiculous, Cass thinks. All this worrying—it's part of that musty room, part of being locked up in this house. The only cure is to ignore it. Cass turns her back on the waving arm, which is ticking more and more frantically. "Stroke, stroke, breathe!" she calls to Jordan, hoping her words penetrate the water.

This time Jordan's mouth opens when she rolls her face up. Her eyes are still squeezed shut, but she takes a huge gulp of air and kicks herself free of Cass's arms, swimming off alone.

Because Jordan, glowing and damp, cuddles up to Diane and praises both her newly clean room and Cass's skill as a swimming teacher; because Sal, last night, made Diane promise not to fight with Cass in front of Jordan; because Cass has two beers while she's getting changed—only because of these small facts and because Sal and Paine appear for lunch are Cass and Diane able to avoid a huge, catastrophic fight. They come to the table ready, bristling: You ignored me, Diane means to scream at Cass. Tore up my room, took Jordan swimming without permission . . . You're being stupid, Cass means to say. Even stupider than you always were, always . . . They are like cats, claws bared, and yet Sal and Paine, chattering calmly, and Jordan, wedged between them and smiling for the first time in months, somehow avert the storm. Declawed, defused, Cass and Diane look at each other across the table only when their attention isn't held by Jordan or Paine or Sal. Which is hardly ever—it is almost as if these distractions have been planned. And having smiled, passed salad, talked inconsequentially through those first few minutes when they should have been fighting, Cass and Diane can't very well start up when Paine and Sal retire. They slip uneasily but quietly through the long afternoon, through the excellent dinner that Paine returns to cook. And now, with Jordan tucked away for the night and Sal and Paine next door engrossed in *The Marriage of Figaro*, Diane and Cass have settled on the porch with a bottle of wine and two glasses.

The night air is soft and balmy. They are feeling oddly calm, oddly purged, almost as if they'd had the fight that they've avoided, almost as if they'd punched each other and, like men, settled things that easily. Like adults, Diane thinks. Like civilized people. Her anger has leaked away and now she's only tired. She stares down at Cass's feet, which are large and bony and a strange blue-violet color, darker at the nails. "Not such a bad day," she muses out loud.

"Not so bad," Cass echoes. "At least your room's clean . . ."

Diane gives her a tight-lipped smile, determined not to fuss about the curtains, her mother's curtains. Sal said she didn't care—the curtains were old. And while Diane misses them, she has to admit that her room is cool and clean and comfortable now, and it *does* make her feel better. Perhaps she should accept what looks like help. "I appreciate that," she says. And then, with her eyes still fixed on Cass's curious toes, she says, "God, your feet are *awful*." She means the color— they're almost gray and they look terribly cold despite the warm night. She wonders if she should offer a blanket.

But Cass flushes, shrugs, and tucks her feet beneath her. "I guess they are pretty ugly," she says. "You always used to say I had the biggest feet in the world."

Diane frowns, cursing her awkwardness. "I just meant they looked cold," she says. "That's all—they're such an odd color . . ."

"Bad circulation," Cass says. She shrugs again and then sits silently, trying to read her stepmother's mind. The air about them is dark blue, not quite black yet; at the mouth of their cove are the last pink traces of the sun. All the birds have gone to sleep. In the distance, two tree frogs send up a thin duet, an exchange of trills that might mean love or warning, food or war. That's how we talk, she thinks. A trill across space, a faint answer, signals easily misunderstood. Croak, creak. What did she say? What did she mean? Should I answer? Fireflies flicker over the railing, warning the others of danger or calling them to come. Cass clears her throat, trying to forget her insulted feet and to think of the message she's meant to send. She thinks of what Penny would do if she were here; she thinks of the times Penny has sat with her and transmitted something that made her comfortable enough to talk. I'm grown up, she thinks. I should be able to do this. We have to do it sooner or later. She ducks her head and looks out over the cove. "So," she says quietly, pitching her voice soft and low. "Want to tell me what's been going on?"

Diane sighs. "I don't know," she says, picking at a loose piece of webbing from her chair. "So much stuff . . ." She sighs again, the words pressing at her lips like a bubble. Ben's face halts her for a minute as she imagines his fury. And then she thinks, *Well, someone was bound to hear—it serves you right.* She can hear Ben, *Don't you dare.* But she pushes his face and his words away and she tells Cass everything, the words like bile, like bitter stones. Ben this, Ben that, Ben everything and nothing. The darkness covers the waves of blood that flood her face; the trilling frogs help conceal the quiver in her voice. She is determined not to cry, but when she is done her life seems to lie on the grass below her, spread out ugly, and she is suddenly terrified. If you say the wrong word, she thinks. If you laugh . . .

"I'm sorry," Cass says quietly, still sitting on her feet. "I saw the letters, you know."

"The letters?"

"Under the mattress . . ."

"Ugh," Diane says, and shudders. This is worse than anything she said. She can't remember all those letters, but she knows they're full of poison. She hopes Cass didn't read them.

The moon rises over Cass's shoulder like a huge, shining egg. Cass wants to say something wise and smart and old, something that reflects none of their past but which will fix their future. She doesn't know enough. For a minute she longs desperately for her quiet room in New Hampshire, where there was only her and where her worries were her own. "Why didn't you call me before?" she asks. "Maybe I could have helped."

Diane shrugs. "You wouldn't have come."

This is true, Cass knows—she wouldn't have come. If it was just Diane in trouble, Cass would have stayed in her room. "I'm sorry," she says again.

"Stop apologizing," Diane says irritably. "It's not your fault."

"Sorry," Cass starts to say again. She stops before the word is fully out, struggling to distance herself and forget what's passed between them over the years. She'd like to listen to Diane as if Diane were just another woman, telling another tale of woe—the way she'd listen, say, to one of her friends at school. Her hands twist in her lap, longing for a pencil. She always scribbles when she listens to her friends.

"My weight," Diane muses. "If you want to blame yourself for something, blame yourself for that."

Cass stiffens. "Your *weight*?" she says. "What did I have to do with that?" Her good intentions roll away.

"I started getting this way when you and Webb started giving me so much shit."

Cass stares at her. "You started when you got pregnant with Jordan," she says. "Or at least that's how I remember it."

"No," Diane says firmly. "It started with you and your brother."

The phone rings, a distant trill in the kitchen that saves Cass from saying anything. "I'll get it," she says, and runs from the porch. Could that be true? she wonders. We were kids. We had problems of our own . . . What she remembers is Diane crouched over the table, eating and eating and eating. Why do I still care what she says? she thinks. She picks up the phone and, before she can answer, a man's voice says, "Hello? Hello?"

It's Ben. She nearly drops the phone.

"Hello?" he says impatiently.

"Yes," she says.

For a minute everything is quiet. Click, click, click, she hears—June bugs, banging into the picture window. "Cass?" Ben says. "What are you doing there?"

She doesn't know. "Visiting," she says sourly. "What do you think? Picking up after your mess."

"Cass," he says warningly.

She waits, but he says no more. "What do you want?"

"I want to talk to Jordan."

"She's asleep."

He sighs. "Would you wake her up? I want to say hello."

The soft blur in his voice tells her he's been drinking: still, again. "Try during the day," she snaps. She slams down the receiver and stalks away, grabbing a pencil and a pad of paper as she goes.

Diane still lies in her chair. "Who was that?" she asks.

"Wrong number." Cass throws herself into the other chair. She scratches a forest of dark lines across a sheet of paper and then hatches a careful series over those. The paper is too slick, the pencil not soft enough. She scribbles anyway, in a dark flurry of anger. Ben calling here. Diane hating her feet, hating her help, blaming her for bizarre things; Sal and Paine, so smug next door, listening to their Mozart—everyone sucks, and if it weren't for Jordan . . .

Diane stares at Cass's hands, scratching the paper as if she means to tear it. She has lost the thread of their conversation. So much energy, she thinks. Scratch, scratch, scrawl. She half expects Cass to leap up and build a bridge or a spaceship. Already, she regrets what she has said. Too much ammunition—Cass is smart, she'll use it. Maybe not, though. Maybe she only means to help. The face engraved in the moon seems to be tilted away from Diane, the eyes unwilling to meet hers. Like the eyes at the store, the post office, the eyes of everyone. No one wants to see what's bubbling in

her head. She gulps at her wine. I shouldn't have criti-
cized her feet, she thinks. Or said that about my weight.
She can feel Cass brooding, turning the words over in
her mind and worrying them into something bigger
than they were ever meant to be, the way she always did
when she was little.

"Look at the man in the moon," Diane says, pointing
to the pocked orb. She knows that Cass still studies the
sky, and she thinks that maybe here they can find some
common ground. "See the way it's tilted? I never noticed that before."

"The lady in the luna," Cass says grudgingly. "My
mother taught me to see that as the face of a woman."

"That's interesting," Diane says. "The moon is always female in astrology."

Cass snorts. "Still reading that junk?"

"Sometimes . . ."

"You ought to stop."

"I know," Diane says simply. "Even my mother says
that."

Cass smiles uneasily. She can feel Diane reaching out
for her, trying to frame a space where they can talk
without stepping on each other's toes. Scratch, scratch.
She sketches a box and then darkens the top. I can be
civilized too, she thinks. She says, "Craters, rays, maria,
rills—and we see it as a face. A woman's face, because
women are lunatics."

A distant plop and splash in the water startles them
both. "A fish," Cass says. "Just a fish."

"Mm," Diane says. "At least it's not Paine. You know
they're getting married this winter?"

"He and Sal?" She might have seen this coming—
they deserve each other.

"It's true," Diane says. "Jordan's real excited. She
wants to be able to say that Paine's her grandfather."

"What an idea," Cass says.

Diane squints over Cass's shoulder at the lunar face.

She lends hair to it, softens the nose, and sees a mysterious female. "I can see it as a woman," she says. "With a little work."

"What? Oh, the moon."

"But what about the tilt?"

"Librations," Cass says.

"Li-what?"

"Librations—the way the moon seems to turn different faces to us. Sometimes the lady looks to the left of us and sometimes to the right, and some nights we see her chin and some nights her forehead." Quickly, Cass sketches four fat moon faces, each face angled differently. "See? We see different faces because the moon's inclined on its axis relative to its orbit." She draws an impish smile, a Jordan smile, on each moon face. She smiles herself.

Diane looks at the drawings and shakes her head. It isn't clear to her at all. "Where'd you learn all this?" she asks.

"Some from Mom, some from books. And I'm outside a lot at night. When I'm camping, there's nothing much to do after dark but stare at the sky."

"When you're camping?" Diane says incredulously. "You camp?" She has almost no idea of what Cass does when she's working for Otis; to her, camping means axes and big bugs.

"Of course," Cass says. "When I'm surveying or checking out new mountains—haven't you ever slept outdoors? Even here?"

"Never," Diane says. Never. She has never slept outdoors, traveled outside New England; never flown in a plane, worn a backless dress, danced on a table, smoked dope. She has never done any of the things that Cass has done so casually, so young. Her jealousy crimps like a hand around her heart. She stares up at the sky again, breathing slowly through her mouth, and she says, "I've always been curious about the sky. I used to watch the moon landings on TV with Jordan and wonder how all those craters got made. And once I tried to teach myself the constellations from your old star dome, but I never got that figured out."

Cass grunts. "You never seemed all that curious to me."

"We weren't exactly talking," Diane says. "How would you have known?"

"That's true," Cass admits. "Well—what you need to do is spend some time outside, with someone who can show you what's what. That's the easiest way. You should learn and then you should teach Jordan."

Diane waits, but Cass says no more and Diane's bladder insists that she get up. Would you teach me? she thinks. Would you do even that, stick around long enough for that? She can't make herself ask these questions out loud. She looks up at the moon again, where footprints that will last forever march pale and ghostlike across the vast seas. Jordan, just a baby, saw the first footprint set in the Sea of Tranquillity. The moon, now, seems to have Jordan's pale hair. The moon, the moon, the moon, she thinks wildly. The moon and the stars— is this the best we can talk about? Cass unfolds her feet, as long and jointed as spiders. They look stranger than ever and, somehow, in Diane's tired, half-drunken brain, the image of them merges with a memory of ridged footprints set in the grainy lunar dust, tracks going here, going there, going nowhere, leading off into the distance to nothing and then returning only to end, lifted off the moon by a buglike machine. Armies of strong, blue feet, women dancing across the moon while birds fly above them—birds? She shuts her eyes and breathes deeply, slowly. When she opens them she sees only Cass, a slim young woman with curly brown hair and a mild, narrow-nosed face that regards her quizzically. I'm sick, Diane thinks. I've got to get better.

She reaches down and touches Cass's cheek. "You'll

give Jordan a hand," she says. It is not a question; she knows Cass will say yes. Cass nods slightly and Diane lumbers away, acutely aware of her own tiny feet struggling to uphold her huge bulk. In the distance, one last tree frog shrills a questioning note.

Gravity Extends from Pluto
(September 1977)

★　　　★　　　★　　　★　　　★　　　★

There is no particular significance to this Sunday night. It is no one's birthday, no one's anniversary, no one's graduation or first day back in school, not even the point that marks the end of a long illness or the completion of a thankless task. It is simply a cool, clear, late-September evening during which six people gather to eat the meal that Diane has prepared. The house is sparkling; the windows smell of vinegar. Cass watches as Diane, Webb, Jordan, Paine, and Sal unfold their napkins into their laps and toy with their silver as if they were a family, any family, sitting down to any meal. At the head of the table Diane sits, her spoon poised over a steaming dish.

"Pass me your plate," Diane says to Cass.

And Cass does, holding her breath as Diane dishes out the homemade ravioli. Let it be perfect, Cass thinks. As perfect as the starched place mats, the clear-burning candles, the neatly arranged plates; as perfect as Diane wants it to be. A family dinner, said Diane, who is sixty pounds lighter than she was a year ago. She wanted to do it; she said she was ready. Cass, looking at the flowers and the spotless glasses, thinks Diane may have been right. This is good for her, she thinks. Maybe even good for us.

Cass runs her eyes around the table, admiring her family's fancy dress. Here is Paine, in a buff suit and a matching tie dotted with shells; Sal in blue silk with an emerald butterfly buried in her upswept hair. Jordan wears crisp slacks and a white shirt with a bow at the neck, while Webb has borrowed a tie and an elbow-worn jacket from Walker. Even Diane looks pretty. She's had her hair cut in a thick shag that frames her face, and she's put on careful makeup and an old but handsome dress. Cass tastes her ravioli, which is wonderful, and thinks of the moment hours ago when the whole evening rode on that short-sleeved, size-fourteen dress. She'd walked into the kitchen, her arms full of groceries, to find Diane sniffling at the window. "What is it?" she'd asked gently, aware, as she has been for more than a year, of the things that can set Diane off; hoping, as she has hoped all this summer, that the flare-ups will continue to diminish in size and intensity. "I don't have a thing to wear," Diane sobbed.

Almost, Cass smiled. Everyone's complaint, not necessarily a tragedy. If Diane weren't still afraid of department stores they could have solved the problem easily. Instead, Cass thought for a minute and then led her stepmother upstairs into the attic, where Diane's old clothes were stored in all their different sizes. Marked off by cardboard tags, separate sizes, separate lives—twelve, fourteen, sixteen, eighteen, even larger. Cass riffled through them and pulled out a yellow dress with a full bodice and a forgiving waist. The sundress that Diane wore years ago, when she came for dinner and Cass slid salmon salad into her lap? Probably not—

she thinks that dress had no sleeves. "Here," she said. "Try this." It just fit.

She is just about to compliment Diane's cooking when Paine, who brought the wine from his cellar next door, lifts his glass with a great flourish and proposes a toast. "To our hostess," he says. "And our chef and daughter and friend."

A streak of pink flares across Diane's cheeks and Cass smiles at her. Webb reaches over and lays his thick brown hand on Diane's wrist. "This is great," he says. "Really. I haven't had it in years."

Diane blushes again and Cass winks across the table at Webb. There he sits, so grown up in his tie and so well mannered, after all his grumbling when she picked him up this afternoon. "Why the big fuss?" he said then. He'd changed from his work clothes into clean but ragged shorts and an old T-shirt, and he didn't see why he should dress up. "What's the big deal?"

"It's her first big dinner," Cass said gently, wondering why he couldn't see what was obvious.

"So?"

"So it means a lot to her."

Now Webb lifts his hand to smooth back a wisp of Diane's hair. What had he said then? Shrugging, eyes down, "It's not *our* fault she's been so weird . . ." So bitterly, so guiltily, that Cass understood why he hadn't been able to move back during the tough times.

"We didn't help any," she said softly.

He threw a rock through a spider's web and said angrily, "We were kids. We had troubles of our own."

"No one's blaming us," she said. "But we're not kids anymore." The obvious, again: it still surprises her how often Webb needs her to state the obvious. He's so smart in other ways. How does he miss so much?

Cass drains her glass and refills it with Paine's soft old wine. Paine, whose hair has thinned to a monkish silver fringe, leans forward and rests his hand on Sal's neck.

Sal bends her cheek to his hand and says, "I was reading in a magazine about the influence of Pluto—all those horoscopes everyone cast before the planet was discovered? There were disturbances no one could account for, little perturbations in the orbit of Uranus . . ." She licks her fork clean, arranges the salt and pepper shakers in front of her, and draws orbits on the cloth around them with her fork. "There was something *here,*" she says, jabbing the cloth near the salad bowl. "Something they could feel but couldn't see." She points her fork at Cass. "*You* should know about this," she says. "The Scorpio baby, the Pluto kid."

Diane hisses, "Mom!" but Cass makes a face at Sal and then laughs. I was so scared of her once, she thinks. Scared of what? Scared of her the way I used to be scared of Paine, all that weight, all that power—and yet both of them seem harmless now, often funny, sometimes charming. Maybe because Sal is half her former size, and Sal has tamed Paine. She says easily, a little mockingly, "Sure I feel it. At night, when I'm half asleep, I feel something small and distant and very heavy, pulling at me."

"That's it!" Paine says. He brandishes his butter knife like a sword. "You see, my dear—it's *gravity.* Gravity provides the scientific underpinnings for astrology, only no one understood this until recently. When the planets align in certain ways, it has nothing to do with mysticism and everything to do with gravity. Curved space. Bent time. The planets pull on you, like the moon pulls the water into tides. I mean, here's this Pluto, cold and dark and a zillion miles away, with this huge moon that never sets and a year that lasts two and a half centuries, so small we can hardly see it, and yet its presence affects all of us. It's *gravity,* extending all the way to here . . ." He lifts his hands in wonder, or maybe in mock wonder. With him, Cass can never be sure.

Webb snorts into his ravioli. "Come on," he says.

"No, really," Paine says. "It's an important concept. It's like, it's like . . ." His eyes roam from face to face while he searches for the right comparison. "It is like your father," he says finally. "Action at a distance."

Cass looks up in time to see Webb's face freeze. She stretches her leg out under the table and taps her toe comfortingly on his instep. *It's all right, it's all right*, she tries to tell him with her foot. He looks at her and, finally, rolls his eyes and smiles weakly. Sal taps her fork against Paine's balding head. "Dolt," she says affectionately. "You can't say things like that here."

"No?" Paine says. "But still—everyone should know about Pluto. Don't you think? It could be an escaped moon, or a planetisimal, so interesting . . ."

"Enough, already," Webb says. "All this astrology makes me crazy."

"That's your stubbornness talking," Sal says serenely. "Your Taurus practicality."

"That's my *brain*," Webb says. "This thing in my head. And it tells me your astrology doesn't work if I don't believe in it."

Jordan, who has been quiet until now, turns to Webb and says, "In school, Mrs. Brown told us a story about some Indians who picked two wise men to stay up every night and pray that the sun would rise and the world would be there in the morning. Because they thought the world would go away if they stopped praying."

"But it wouldn't," Webb says impatiently. "The praying had nothing to do with it."

"I guess that's the point," Jordan says. "That morning comes anyway."

Sal smiles at her. "Smart cookie," she says approvingly. "That's the point exactly. Webb can sniff all he wants, but the stars still influence him."

"Mom," Diane says helplessly. "Paine . . ."

Cass shakes her head in amazement. Is anyone listening to anyone else? Paine and Sal believe in astrology, Diane has sworn off it, Webb thinks it's crazy, Jordan pays no attention. They're all talking around each other and, besides, they were talking about Pluto—astronomy, not astrology. Did I miss something? she thinks. The link?

Paine says, "It changes everything if you accept it. The influences are still there, whether or not you believe in them. But if you accept them, if you pay attention, you can work *with* them."

"I work with my hands," says Webb. "That's what *I* believe in."

"Say what you will," Paine says. "All my life, until I met Sal, I was always butting and crashing against everything, arguing like a lawyer. Like your father, fighting everything. Anyway, Sal made me see how I could live like I was in a kayak all the time. In a kayak, when you come to a wave, you can fight it or you can listen to it until it tells you how to go. If you fight it, you'll tip over."

Cass smiles, remembering how Paine used to drift across their cove, with his huge white body overflowing his kayak in all directions. Maybe he didn't mean to be scary, she thinks. It was us, the way we saw him. Maybe he was listening to the water?

"Let's turn off the lights," Jordan says. "And just have candles."

"Good idea," says Sal. She reaches behind her for the switch, and the room darkens and then seems to lighten again as their eyes adjust. The sky, shut out by the overhead light, springs to life in the picture window.

"There are your stars," Cass says quietly.

The sky is perfectly clear, perfectly still, punctuated by a crescent moon that hangs over the island. "Can we see Pluto?" Jordan asks.

"No," Cass says. "Even with a big telescope it's hard

to see. But you can see Virgo, who's connected to Pluto
—there, way low in the west."

"Where?" Diane asks.

"There," Cass says, pointing. "That star and that one
and that one—see? I like to imagine Pluto behind Virgo,
in the background there. My mother tells this story,
which she says her own grandmother told her, about
how Virgo represents a young girl, the daughter of a
goddess named Ceres. This girl was walking along one
day when Pluto burst up through the ground and captured her and dragged her back to the underworld with
him."

"Some story," Diane says, hugging herself as if she's
cold.

"Pretty bad," Cass agrees. "But it gets better—eventually the girl's mother rescues her and then she has to
go back for only a few months each year, because she
ate some seeds." Is that right? she wonders. A girl with
a sheaf of wheat and a hairy god in a chariot? There was
another story Penny told her, about a girl and a horse or
a girl and a bull or a girl and a huge white swan, and she
thinks she may have gotten these confused. No—she's
sure it was Virgo and Pluto who were linked together.

"If you ask me," Sal says, "it's just as silly to believe
in those stories as it is to believe in astrology. Sillier."

"I didn't say I *believed* them," Cass says. "They're just
a way to remember things."

Webb smacks his hand against the table, startling
them all. "You're all star-struck," he says, his nostrils
pinched with annoyance. "Always looking at the sky.
Why don't you pay some attention to what goes on
down here? Here's where we live."

"Webbie," Jordan says soothingly. "Come on. They're
just playing."

Sal laughs. "That's right," she says. She peers into her
coffee cup as if she could read the grounds, looking just

for that minute like the witch Cass remembers from the sub shop. She has hardly eaten anything.

"Let's go for a row," Webb says suddenly, turning toward Jordan. "Enough of this Pluto talk. Come on. Let's you and me and Cass take the dinghy out to the island. I'll bet you five bucks you can't row the whole way."

Diane laughs nervously. "Webb," she says. "Don't be silly. It's dark out." She reaches for his plate and piles on more ravioli. "Eat your dinner," she says. "You like it, right?" Her smile is very tense.

Webb turns to Cass. "How about it?" he asks.

She'd love to—it's a perfect night and she's tired of sitting. "Well," she says. "Maybe, when we're all done here . . ."

"Eat your dinner," Diane says again. She snaps the prongs of a fork against the table, her face pale.

"Never mind," Cass says to Webb. She signals him to stop pushing, but it's too late. Webb, who can't read the currents floating in the air any better than he could when he was small, stands and sweeps giggling Jordan onto his shoulders. "Off we go!" he says, whirling her around.

"Come on, Cass!" Jordan calls.

"Not me," Cass mutters, waiting for what's bound to happen. Every time, she thinks. Every single time Jordan wants to do something the least bit unusual. Unless it's planned and signed and sealed, perfectly safe, Diane goes out of her mind.

"Well," Webb says. "I guess it's just us chickens." He carries Jordan halfway across the room before Diane explodes in tears. "What is it?" he says, freezing on the tiles. "What is it? What's wrong?"

"Don't you dare take her out there!" Diane sobs. "It's *dark*!"

"So?" Webb says, bewildered. "It's dark, so what? It's real calm and we'll be extra careful . . ." He doesn't mean to argue. His voice is reasonable. Cass shakes her head helplessly, and Sal and Paine exchange a glance and begin to clear the dishes.

"Go ahead," Diane says bitterly. "Make me look bad for saying no. Make it all *my* fault."

Webb scowls and lets Jordan down.

"Come sit," Cass says. She'll have to talk to Webb later; she knows what he'll say. He'll say that Diane babies Jordan and that they all baby Diane, and then he'll slink back to his bog house and swear he's never coming out.

Webb throws himself into a chair and mashes a ravioli. "We're just going out in a *dinghy*," he mutters. "Big fucking deal."

"Another time," Cass says.

Paine and Sal start discussing Mozart while they rinse the dishes. Jordan inches up to Diane and nuzzles her cheek in a way that Cass can hardly stand. Where did she learn that? she wonders. How does she know that already?

Diane pulls Jordan close to her. "Tomorrow," she says. "Or next weekend—you could go with me, during the day."

"Sure," Jordan says easily. "Another time."

For a minute, Cass wishes that Jordan would scream or throw something. She would have, at Jordan's age. She wouldn't have let herself be pushed around like that. But she had Penny, not a mother as fragile as mended glass. She sighs and then smiles at Jordan. "We'll all go," she says. "Another day." The list of things they'll do another day would stretch to Pluto.

There are apologies, later—Cass to Webb, Webb to Diane, Diane to Jordan and Webb—but despite these, the dinner leaves an uneasy residue that persists for days. Cass hides in the basement, drawing; Diane hangs out in the attic, bagging up her old clothes; Webb returns to his bog house; and Jordan goes directly to Sal and Paine's after school each day for a week, wondering if things will always be so difficult. Was it just the trip in the dinghy? Jordan wonders. Or was it all that talk about Pluto and astrology and gravity and Ben? Probably all these things, along with things she can't begin to guess at, things she'll never understand. If I was older, she thinks, I wouldn't miss so much. Meanwhile, she sees her mother briefly, in the evenings, and she tries not to mention things that might upset her. She carefully avoids talking about the new girl at the bus stop, who has a jackknife and a fearsome scowl and an older brother. She doesn't mention falling off the trampoline in gym and lying there with the wind knocked out of her, and she doesn't talk about the car that almost hit her in the parking lot. As the weekend approaches no one says anything about the promised boat trip, and she doesn't dare bring it up. "I'll be eighty," she grumbles to Sal one afternoon, "before they let me do anything."

Sal winks and says, "Forty, no more," but when Jordan doesn't laugh she draws her into her lap and says, "How about doing a dog show for me and Uncle Paine? We'd like that a lot." And that's how it happens that Saturday morning finds Jordan standing in front of a row of dogs who sit, heads high and backs to the water, along the edge of the lawn. Sal calls "Now!" and Jordan runs to the far side of the hedge.

"Willie!" she calls. "Come!"

Willie, who has grown from a round ball to a lean, muscular dog, tucks his legs up like a horse and clears the hedge easily. "Nine point five!" Sal calls from the judging stand—two lawnchairs and a little table. "At least!" Paine lowers his camera and calls, "I got him in the air!"

"Good dog," Jordan whispers to Willie. She and Iris have trained Willie and his sister, Nashoba, to sit, stay, come, retrieve, and jump almost anything; Iris helped her organize the show. They have Randall with Ginger, his golden retriever; Holly and Irene, from their fourth-grade class, with Holly's beagle, Trixie, and Irene's setter, Sneakers; and Iris's older sister, Sue, with Muffin, who is Willie and Nashoba's mother. And Willie and Nashoba, of course. Jordan couldn't ask for anything more except, perhaps, her mother and Cass in the audience. But today, Saturday, is the only day all her friends could come—and on Saturdays, no matter how nice it is, Cass drives Diane to the doctor's, where they spend the morning. Which is important, Jordan thinks loyally. The doctor makes her mother better. Tucked away in the back of her mind is a fainter, further hope: That as her mother gets better she'll let Jordan do a few more things.

They have finished Beauty, Charm, and Obedience, and now they are doing Tricks. Willie wins the high jump easily but fails at the water jump, and Paine snaps a picture of him dripping water and shaking his puzzled head. "Uncle Paine!" Jordan calls. "Take another one!" He leans over, a beaked cap shading his puffy eyes and his plaid Bermudas bulging. My grandfather, Jordan thinks. Or almost, since he and Sal got married. Step-grandfather? Is that the right word? Iris asked her once to explain how all these people were related to her, and although she started glibly enough—mother, father, half sister, half brother, two grandmothers, grandfather —she slowed down a little when she got to the difficult ones. Stepgrandfather, for Uncle Paine? Step-half-mother, for Aunt Penny? For Walker, who sometimes lives with Aunt Penny, and for Jill, whom she never sees, she could find no names at all.

Nashoba jumps over the puddle with Trixie and Sneakers at her heels. After Paine takes a few more pictures, Jordan lines them up for Playing Dead. Willie is particularly good at this, although he's good at everything. Because I worked so hard with him, Jordan thinks proudly, noting his regal stance. All last summer, during that hushed, weird time when her father first took off and her mother stayed in bed and Cass came home to help. It was worth it, the work last summer and then every day after school once Cass went back to New Hampshire to finish college.

The dogs lie on their backs with their paws in the air, their eyes rolling as Sal passes by to judge. Sal, who pretends this is a dog Olympics, never gives less than a nine. "Nine point five!" she calls six times. "They all win." She adds to the colored ribbons she's tied onto their collars for each event, so that the dogs look like Christmas presents.

"So," Paine calls. "Are we done?"

"Not yet!" Jordan cries. There is still the grand finale. "Get ready," she whispers to each of her friends, as they walk the dogs out the low, stone jetty. "On three," she whispers to Iris.

"On three," Iris says to the others.

"One, two, *three!*" The dogs, as well trained as a circus act, leap into the water with a great splash. If it was just a little warmer, Jordan thinks, I'd jump in too. The dogs look so happy paddling, like spotted fish except for their heads, which are held high above the water. She can just remember when she held her head like that, years ago when Webb first tried to teach her to swim. He is working today, like everyone else, but back then he used to call, "Come on in, Baby J! Dive!" No one has called her Baby J for years. When he called she ran down the sand with her arms stretched over her head while her mother watched carefully, nervous even then. Was her mother always afraid? "Come on!" her father called, trailing a quahog bucket behind him. She ran in right up to the top of her chest, but she never dove and all of them thought that was odd. Because of the sun on my head, she thinks now. So simple—that lovely feel of cool water up to her neck and hot sun on her head, crabs bumping at her ankles and seaweed on her legs. "Baby J!" they called again and again, thinking she was scared, when she was only enjoying everything. She swam for them one cloudy day.

The sun is hot on her back when the breeze dies down. She looks at the leaping dogs and with a shout dives in to join them, holding her breath and moving her legs as one in a curving mermaid's kick. She imagines her legs as a thick tail with a dainty fin at the end, and she snakes through the water until she surfaces in front of Willie. He barks happily and throws his paws up on her shoulders.

"You crazy!" Sal calls. She is laughing.

"Come on in!" Jordan cries. Iris, always a good sport, splashes in; the others roll up their pants and wade in gingerly. A wave soaks the edges of Paine's shorts, but Paine doesn't seem to mind. For a minute they all wrestle with the wet dogs and toss water at each other. Randall falls in, shrieking with laughter, and Jordan thinks, Would Daddy yell if he was here? Would they yell at him? Everyone's mad at him. When he comes every few weeks or so, to take her out for the day, her mother and Cass won't talk to him and Webb won't come near the house. And yet he is not so bad. When she looks at him, she sees a man whose blond hair is thinning, especially at the back; a man whose small belly and quiet clothes make him seem much older than other fathers, harmless, almost an uncle. If they'd just *talk* to him, she thinks. He's awkward sometimes, during their trips to New Bedford and Provincetown, but he's never mean and always asks about school and her friends and Willie. He fumbles with his hands and, when he drops her off, kisses her hair and says, "I love you, sweets."

"I love you too, Daddy," she says, but he is coming to seem more and more like some kind visitor. She would like him to be around more, so Cass and Webb could get over being mad at him and they could all do things together.

"Come on out!" Paine calls. He snaps one last picture before they wade out and head for the refreshments. Jordan rolls on the grass, drying herself like one of the dogs, and then she walks over to the table and looks at the Polaroids. In one, she and Willie leap from the water at the same time, as if they've been caught in a ballet. She picks this out and says to Sal, "I'll give this one to Daddy."

"That would be nice," Sal says, brushing the wet hair from Jordan's forehead. "I'll hang on to it for you until he visits. Okay?"

"Okay." She gives the picture to Sal and joins her friends, who are handing out dog biscuits. "Ginger!" she calls. "Catch!" She tosses a biscuit high in the air and watches it fall toward Ginger's head. Ginger leaps up and snaps it between her teeth. "Trixie!" she calls. "Sneakers! Nashoba!" She aims more biscuits at them.

"That was great," Holly says.

"Great," Iris echoes. "We ought to do it every weekend."

"We should do it after school," Jordan says. "So the rest of my family could come."

Jordan saves a pile of photos for her mother, but her mother gets home late and then heads straight for bed. "Just for a little while," she promises, brushing Jordan's hair with her lips. "I'll get up before supper. How did your hair get so wet?"

"Grammy washed it," Jordan says smoothly, careful not to say anything about her swim. On these Saturdays her mother's face often looks as though it might crack; today it looks as if it has cracked already. As her mother closes the bedroom door, Jordan finishes her juice and silently dumps the pictures into a basket. *Tok*, whispers the clock in the dining room. *Tok, tok.*

Outside there must be noise, but in here the air has turned to cotton. Her friends have gone. Sal and Paine are napping next door, and Cass has slipped into the basement to work on the sharp-lined drawings she mails to New Hampshire each week. *Tok*, says the clock. *Tok*. If she stays here much longer the air will liquefy and her eyelids will slowly, slowly, sink like her heavy head. She jerks her chin upright. Everyone is busy or sleeping and so, with a little sigh, she pulls out her shell book and walks down to the beach.

The fresh air slaps her awake. She settles into a corner between the stone jetty and the lip of their yard and begins to sift the sand, hardly needing the book. She knows all the common shells by now, quahogs and clams, limpets, periwinkles, snails and whelks, mussels and scallops and angel's toenails, sea urchins, sand dollars, starfish, barnacles. Nothing uncommon ever washes up in this little cove. She thinks about living in Florida, where she could find cones and conches and bright corals like the ones Aunt Penny sent her from her sailing trip. She thinks about living in a normal family that might vacation together, somewhere—Cass and Webb and Dad and Mom and me, she thinks, closing her eyes and imagining them stretched out in a neat row on identical beach chairs, someplace where palms wave overhead and the shore is dotted with extraordinary shells. Maybe Sal and Paine in a separate cabin, nearby. But they have told her over and over that none of this will happen. They're divorced now, she thinks. Permanently. As separate as Aunt Penny and her father, whom she can't picture ever married. She squats near the highwater mark, sifting dried seaweed and popping the blisters and remembering picnics with her whole family together, long ago. Her blond head sticks up over the edge of the lawn, just high enough so that Cass can see it from her bedroom.

Cass's drawing board is set before her double window, in the clear light that streams over her bed. A sheet of tissue is taped to the board, overlapping a sheet of Mylar. Cass sits on her stool and draws lines with a sliding ruler and a Rapidograph. She's finishing a drawing for Otis but she works absentmindedly, her attention focused on Jordan's head. Shells, she thinks. Shells and shells and more shells, in boxes and jars and along the windowsills, filling Jordan's room—is it healthy? Is it smart? When that room was hers it was filled with balsa wood and glue and papers and knives, half-built projects, strange books. She tries to remember how she felt when her own parents split, and all she can see is a black wave, sharp-edged as a razor. Angry, she thinks. Angry all the time, at everyone, for everything. Jordan's head rises above the lip of the lawn like a huge yellow dandelion, and Cass remembers being angry, once, even at yellow weeds. She and Webb out there on the lawn, stabbing and stabbing at the cold white roots—we needed money for something, she remembers. Some project of ours. Penny was gone or about to go, and Diane had arrived or was about to, and we were angry, stabbing at weeds.

Impatiently she draws three sharp, parallel lines. The lawn is dotted with weeds now and her anger is over, far away. She could never explain to Jordan what she felt like then. She scores two lines perpendicular to the first three—there. Enough for today. On the bottom corner of the tissue, which she knows she'll trim away, she sketches a tiny thumbnail of Jordan's clean profile. Someday, when she has more time—this winter, perhaps—she'd like to draw this house. The porch, where she and Webb huddled one cold, dark night. Were they running away? Hiding, she thinks. From someone, something. She'd draw the kitchen table where Penny used to sit and smoke and where the three of them, she and Jordan and Diane, sit now on certain calm evenings; the living room, where the Christmas tree stood year after year; this room, this cubicle, and the matching cell next door where Webb once slept.

She sits back, still staring at her sister's head. Here I am, she thinks. And for what? Her room, her work, her friends, Otis—all left behind, all gone. Even her lover, Carl, with his two blond sons—but she had to leave that, it was good to leave that. All left behind, so she could sit and listen to her family discussing Pluto over dinner. Last summer she drove here just to check on things, not counting on Jordan needing her so much, not even thinking that she'd return this summer, once school was over, to stay until—when? For what? She can still hear Paine's excited voice: "Gravity," he said. "Action at a distance, extending all the way to here . . ." That's the way we talk about Ben, she thinks. Or don't talk. That's the way we talk about everything. Hints, cues, misdirections, and all the while waiting for things to get better. The surprising thing, the thing she can't understand, is that they do. Day by day nothing changes, but at the end of a month, a summer, a year, things are better. I sit here, she thinks, and Diane sits upstairs and Jordan sits out there and Paine and Sal wander back and forth, and sometimes we meet and say nothing, or what feels like nothing, and things get better. And so how can I leave? Perhaps this is what it means to be home.

Cass lays her pen down and stretches her arms above her. As she does, Jordan's hand reaches above the lip of the lawn and deposits a line of shells on the grass. More shells. Cass walks out to join her. Jordan's hair, wet this morning, has dried into loose curls, and when she smiles at Cass her nose wrinkles, peeling at the tip. "You want to help me with my shells?" she asks.

"Sure," Cass says. Jordan's smile is dazzling, even with two missing teeth. She smiles all the time and seems to trust everyone, even Ben; she smiles like a child should smile. Cass, grinning back at her, can't remember ever smiling like that. In the pictures Ben took of her and Webb she was always scowling, sulking. An awful child, she thinks. Awful to dump in a young woman's lap.

Jordan holds out a pink-tinged scallop shell and a white periwinkle. "Look what I found," she says.

"Pretty." Cass runs her fingers through the sand, sifting until her fingernails scrape something chalky. She flips up a sand dollar.

"Perfect," Jordan says, holding it up to the sun so that light streams through the fine slits.

"All yours."

Jordan lays it on the grass above their shoulders and then searches for something to say. "We had a dog show this morning," she finally blurts. Why did she say that? It's not what she wants to talk about, not at all.

"I heard. Was it fun?"

"Great. Everyone liked it." She keeps her head lowered while she tells Cass about the tricks and the dog biscuits and the pictures and Paine. Will she understand about jumping in? she wonders. She'll think I'm stupid. Often, she wishes she could do something extraordinary to impress her tall sister—dive from a cliff, speak perfect French, dance like a ballerina. I can't even dance, she thinks. Can't do anything. "I went swimming with the dogs," she says shyly. "At the end of the show."

Cass laughs. "Is that how your hair got wet?"

"Don't tell Mom, okay?" She picks up a pair of limpets glued belly to back and tries to separate them with her teeth.

"She wouldn't mind," Cass says gently. "Not about that."

"She minded last week about me rowing with you and Webb."

Cass shrugs. "That was different—it was dark, and it was just me and Webb, and she doesn't always believe we'd take good care of you . . ."

"I could take care of *myself* some, you know," Jordan sniffs. "I'm not a baby."

Cass touches Jordan's arm and says, "I know, sweetie. I know. Anyway, you shouldn't worry so much what your mother thinks. She's getting better."

"Really? She always looks awful when she gets back from the doctor. What does he do to her?"

Cass untangles the clear shell of a tiny horseshoe crab from a knot of dried seaweed. "They talk. That's all."

"She goes to the doctor to talk?"

"He's a special doctor. He gets her to talk about things that bother her, things that maybe happened a long time ago and that she can't tell us. The idea is that if you talk about these things, they don't make you so unhappy. But it makes her tired."

Jordan tries to imagine a kind of talk that would make her tired. Paine and Sal talk to each other all the time and never get sleepy; when she talks to Cass she feels more awake then ever. "Do you talk to the doctor too?" she asks.

Cass shakes her head. "I just wait. Sometimes I read the old magazines." These visits exhaust her in a way she can't explain to Jordan. It's the dim bluish light in the waiting room, the soft chairs, the framed pictures hung so low that they're at eye level when she sits down and give her the feeling she's entered a kingdom of dwarfs. The dull hum of the air conditioner hypnotizes her; her head grows heavy while she waits and tries to imagine what Diane is spilling behind that heavy door. Secrets, she knows—the kind of dark, humiliating tales that Diane used to tell Cindy and Sal years ago, always as if Cass weren't right there listening. Except that these secrets will be worse. Does she say how hard it was to raise Cass and Webb, how awful they were to her? They called her names, smashed her favorite dishes, bent her spoons in the garbage disposal and pre-tended these were accidents. They waged war against her until, when it was too late and they'd have taken it back if they could, they won. Now it seems to Cass that the doctor eyes her strangely when he leads Diane out. Perhaps this is only her imagination.

Jordan lifts her head at a sound across the yard. "Willie!" she calls. He gallops across a sea of yellow weeds, skidding to a stop near her even lines of shells. "Sit!" she commands. He thumps his rear end to the ground and pants, his pink tongue hanging. Jordan scratches behind his ears and asks Cass the question that's been troubling her all week. "Is it because of Daddy?" she says. "That Mommy feels so bad?" Everyone seems to blame everything on him—even Paine, who likened him to some nasty planet.

Cass is silent. The dog, sitting just above her, gives off a smell of fish and salt grass. She pulls away from his tangled coat and dirty ears, knowing she's not seeing him with Jordan's eyes. She can't see anything that way. When she looks at her own life, at Diane's and Jordan's and Webb's and Penny's, all she can see is the ways they've bent to avoid Ben. Penny off in the islands. Webb in his cranberry bog. Her in New Hampshire all those years, Diane lost in her bed. They've survived, all of them, but the sharp black wave lies just below the surface, ready to slice at them again. "Yes," she could say to Jordan. "It's because of him." She bites her lips and says, "Not exactly—your mother's lonely without him, but it's no one's fault. She's just sad right now— sick in her heart, like you get sick with a cold. The doctor makes her feel less sad, and so do you. She loves you a lot, you know."

"I know," Jordan says quietly. "But that's not really what I asked." She leans against Cass's shoulder, thinking, Do they love me? All of them? Alone or with any of them—Sal or Paine or Cass or Webb, her mother or her father—she can feel that they do. But when they're all together the air sparks and she's not sure who loves who. "I was wondering . . ." she says hesitantly.

"What?"

"There's a big soccer game at school in a couple of weeks and I was wondering—all my friends are going, you know, and . . . do you think you could come? You and Webb?"

"I don't know," Cass says absently. "Maybe."

"If you could . . ." Jordan says, twisting a bit of Willie's neck hair around and around, "if you could—some of my friends don't believe you're really here, you know? Or even that I really *have* a brother and sister." Or a father, she adds silently. "Because you guys are away so much. I thought I could sort of show you off . . ." Her voice trails away in an embarrassed whisper.

Cass tilts Jordan's head up so she can look at her. "Sweetie," she says, "why didn't you tell me that before? Do they think you invented me?"

Jordan squirms away. "I don't know," she sighs. "They just think my family's weird."

"I suppose we are," Cass says as lightly as she can. "Anyway, I'll come for sure, and we'll try and get Webb to come too."

"Yeah? He never goes anywhere with us."

"He'll come," Cass says, hoping she's right. She'll talk to Webb tonight, tomorrow, as soon as she can; he'll come if he understands. "Of course we'll come." We'll come, she thinks, if nothing goes wrong, if Diane's all right, if Jordan can even get permission to go, if Sal doesn't announce a star-crossed day when it's unsafe to leave the house, if Webb stops sulking and I don't leave, if we don't all succumb to the planet's gravity . . . "We'll come," she repeats.

Pegasus Transformed
(October 1977)

★   ★   ★   ★   ★   ★

In a corner of the house, where the wall outside
Jordan's bedroom joins the outswelling curve of the
porch, two pigeons crouch each morning exchanging
news. Most mornings their conversation is what wakes
Jordan up, but this particular Saturday she wakes to the
sound of her own heartbeat dancing a polka inside her
ear, which she has clumsily folded partway over. More a
swish than a beat, a liquid rush that sounds like a wave.
She wakes with a start, her mouth dry and her toes
tense before she even remembers that this is the day
she's been waiting for, planning for. She has talked to
Cass and made her promise to come; she has talked to
Diane and gotten permission to go; she has even asked
Paine to drive Diane to her doctor's appointment. Now,
as she remembers all her plans, she wraps her pink robe
around herself and slides quietly past her mother's
closed door, through the dining room and out the

kitchen, over the damp, cold grass to her grandparents' house. She has one thing left to do.

The door swings open, unlocked for her. So what if I'm not good at much, she thinks, as she pads down the ivory-colored hall. So I can't dance. I'm good at this, good at all this planning . . . She shivers a little as she passes the old Flemish print Paine hung for her right at her eye level, so she could stare as long as she wanted at the swollen river vanishing into the plain. Everything will be settled before her mother returns from the doctor's. I'll walk right into Mom's bedroom, she thinks, with all of them around me, and I'll say Mom—look what I brought you! And she'll smile at me, and we'll be a family again . . .

Sal and Paine are up already as they always are, no matter how early she arrives. Up late, listening to records; up early almost every morning—when do they sleep? They are in their bedroom now, eating breakfast in their huge bed strewn with books and magazines and petals from the vase of chrysanthemums that sits on a shelf over their heads. Sal, wrapped in her magenta silk kimono, has the bamboo tray on her lap and the corduroy bedrest behind her. Paine, in his green-striped pajamas, nestles in the midst of a mountain of pillows and pours tea from a yellow pot as he reads to Sal from a small book bound in pale leather. As happy as clams, Jordan thinks. They don't need me—and yet they seem even happier when she slides between them, into her accustomed place, and kisses their plump, dry cheeks.

"Morning, chickadee," Paine says happily. "Couldn't sleep?"

"Of course not," Sal answers for her. "Today's the big game, isn't it?"

"Uh-huh." Jordan helps herself to a piece of raisin toast and snuggles closer into Sal's shoulder, not wanting to look into her face. "All my friends will be there,

and Cass and Webb both promised to come. Cass is driving us."

Paine and Sal exchange a look above Jordan's head, a
look she's not supposed to see but which she intercepts
anyway. Once again she thinks, Should I invite them
too? She knows they'd like to come, but her friends all
know them already and then there are other problems
as well. She opens her mouth and then closes it again.
No. Things are too complicated already. As innocently
as she can she asks Sal, "Do you still have that picture of
Willie and me from the dog show?"

Sal crunches down on a piece of toast and gazes at
Jordan steadily while she chews. "The one you were
saving for your father?"

"Mm-hmm."

Paine looks up from his tea. "Is your father coming
over?"

"No," Jordan says coolly. "I just wanted the picture. I
thought I might keep it."

"Sure," Sal says. "You just want it."

"That's right," Jordan says, and now she is actually
sweating, as if she had done something wrong or has
something to feel guilty about. It's her picture, after all,
her business how she uses it. "Forget it," she says, pout-
ing a little. This always works. "It's no big deal."

"No, no . . ." Sal fishes in the drawer of her bedside
table, flipping through a stack of photographs until she
finally finds the one that Jordan wants. "Here," she
says, but she keeps her hand on it even as Jordan grasps
the other edge. "By the way, what time is your game?"

"Around noon," Jordan says vaguely.

"Right," Sal says. "Well, then, you've got plenty of
time to eat some of these eggs here, before you have to
go home and get clean and dressed. You know what
they say about a good breakfast."

Jordan, anxious to move on but even more anxious
not to do anything to arouse Sal's suspicions, flips her

blond pigtail forward and settles in for breakfast, forcing the scrambled eggs past the knot in her stomach. She can feel something cold and probing reaching out from Sal, something pricking at the small corner she's closed off inside herself. She shifts uncomfortably, as if Sal's intelligence were an elbow in her side, and she thinks, I wish I could tell her. I wish I could ask her if it's going to work. Sal could cast a chart, although Sal hardly ever does this anymore. Sal could tell her if the stars were auspicious. She has not knowingly lied to her grandmother before, and now she feels, just for a minute, as if this alone may doom her plans. And then she thinks, No—I can make this work.

She stubbornly chews her way through a piece of bacon, listening to Paine chatter on about the skylight he's installing. All the while she holds in her mind's eye this picture that keeps coming back to her like a memory, like a dream, this vision of her family magically reunited on some tropical shore. Her and Diane and Cass and Webb, crouched in front of a palm tree with Ben behind them, smiling. No Jill—that marriage, only a few weeks old, means nothing. Any lawyer could undo it as fast as he undid her family to begin with. She has begun to dream this family scene at night and daydream it when she's awake, and she believes that she dreams it only because it is meant to be. Would I see it otherwise? she thinks. If it wasn't already there, just waiting to happen?

Meanwhile Cass, trying her best to work up some enthusiasm for the game, dresses carefully in the blue and white that are Jordan's school colors. She tries, but her heart's not in it and her fingers move as slowly as sheep. She is tired today, and worried about all sorts of things, and so homesick that she's not even sure which home she's sick for. She misses everyone today—Otis and Cindy, her roommate, Penny, even Webb. She

misses Jordan the way Jordan used to be, before she got
so nervous. Today Jordan seems more flighty than
usual, almost irritating, and during the drive to Webb's
place Cass can hardly follow her rambling, excited chatter. Cass knows this is just Jordan's way of worrying,
trying to guess the shape into which their lives will gel,
but for these few minutes she's unable to stand it. So
unable that when they reach Webb's gray, weathered
bog house and Webb introduces Jordan to Marmalade,
his new kitten, Cass signals to him that she wants to go
inside and talk to him alone. This isn't hard for Webb to
arrange—Jordan's more than happy to stay outside
when Webb says, "You watch Marmalade, okay? We'll
be out in a minute."

"I won't move," Jordan promises.

Webb pushes open the silvery door and Cass follows
him inside, smiling despite herself at the way he has
made this one-room tool shack into a home. "Want to
get high before we go?" she asks. "I'm beat, and Jordan's
making me nuts."

Webb smiles. "Little sister wired again?" An old rag
rug hangs on one of his walls; another covers the floor
near his narrow bed. His cast-iron cooking pots hang
neatly on a pegboard behind the woodburning stove he
salvaged from a friend. Dried herbs and flowers hang in
bunches from the ceiling. A low shelf houses his music
and his instruments, his woodworking tools and some
aging wood. Drawings—some of them Cass's—dot the
walls. His bed is topped with an old quilt, and in the
corner are two small bowls holding cat food and water,
and a box lined with a blanket.

"She is," Cass says. "I don't know what gets into her
sometimes." Although she does know, perfectly well—
this has all happened since Ben remarried. She collapses
on the bed with a sigh and says, "Anyway. I always
forget how nice it is in here. Reminds me of my room at
Otis's."

"Sorry you left?" Webb asks. He sprawls down beside her, plucks a cannister from the shelf on the wall, and pulls out a plastic bag full of dope and some rolling papers. He rolls perfect joints, his thick spatulate fingers delicate as some fine machine.

"Not really," she says, an answer that's true enough most days but not true at all today, when she is missing everything. "I mean, I do and I don't, you know?"

Webb grunts, tapping an even brown line onto the folded paper. Was he always so quiet? It seems to Cass that he talked more when they were young, when he scampered around the yard in a cowboy hat and shot arrows at her dolls.

She reaches into her purse and pulls out an envelope, balancing it in her hand for a minute. In here are the negatives that put her in such a bad mood this morning, foggy pieces of film that shouldn't mean anything. She'd been going through the old leatherette album she'd found buried in the attic, taking out some pictures of herself. The album opened like a book, a vertical row of plastic leaves lining each cover; inside each leaf was a pair of pictures sandwiched back to back. The pictures hadn't surprised her, although some of them made her wistful. She'd seen them all before, pictures of her with a stuffed elephant, Webb with his hat, the childhood pictures of everyone, common as worms. She knows Webb's seen the pictures too, and these are not what she's brought for him.

"Can I show you something?" she asks. When he nods, what she holds out to him is this handful of negatives she found sandwiched between some of the pairs of prints. Not the negatives *for* each print, as she had at first supposed—these are negatives for which there are no prints, or at least no prints that she has ever seen. They are old, square, larger than modern negatives; ghostly gray with everything reversed. Right is left, left right; black white and white black. Ben holds a giant flounder with its eyes facing the wrong way. Many of them are from a time before she remembers anything. They are negatives for pictures that someone has thrown away, and she wants to know if Webb has ever seen them.

Webb shakes his head and then thumbs through them slowly, holding each one up before his window. Here is Penny in a dark sweater, with a leaf in one hand and a cigarette in the other; her hair parted way to one side and her ankles shrouded in wrinkly socks. Behind her is a little girl in a white blouse with puffed sleeves, and this girl, this Cass, sits next to a playpen in which an infant Webb lies. In the background stands a Christmas tree hung with silver balls, and in front of the tree, bending protectively over his family, stands Ben. The picture makes Cass's throat swell, and she feels her glands as if she had mumps or as if her throat belonged to someone else. Webb moves on to the other negatives, which Cass has left in their original sequence. These are Christmas pictures too, several Christmases set in the same living room while she and Webb grow older and bigger and Penny's face grows bleaker, her eyes more veiled each year, almost opaque, her face more turned away.

Cass clears her throat. "Ever see these before?"

"Don't think so," Webb says. "Where'd you find them?"

Cass tells him how she found them almost by accident. They sit quietly for a minute, listening to the wind, and then Cass says, "Didn't Mom look awful then?" although what she really means is, How did we manage not to notice? She would like to ask Webb this and a thousand other things, if he remembers those times and who took those pictures, if they make him feel as strange as they do her. But she can't because Webb's face has closed down the way it always does now, whenever she tries to get him to remember anything. He doesn't want to talk about the day he lost the fish. He doesn't want to remember holidays.

Webb shrugs and says, "She looks like Mom, only younger and a little sad, I guess. You going to give her those?"

"I don't know," Cass says, surprised. She hadn't thought of this. "You think she'd want them?"

"Nope," Webb says. "Not any more than I do. I don't even think she'd want to know you had them." He lights the joint and passes it to Cass, and then he holds his lighter suggestively near the film. "Want to get rid of them now? We can pop them in the woodstove."

Cass snatches them back. "I want to keep them," she says. "For a while, anyway."

"Suit yourself. You keep picking around in old things though, and you're bound to make yourself miserable. You ought to go with the flow a little more, stick with the times." He flicks the negatives with his middle finger, so that they rustle like leaves. "Look at us—some family. We're better off the way we are now."

Cass nods ruefully, staring again at the first Christmas picture. He's right, she thinks. She's gotten herself all worked up over nothing. What she's wistful for is the way her family looked in that picture, not the way they were. She drags on the joint and passes it back to Webb, thinking how much she likes getting high with him. They never did this together before she went away, but they do it often now that she's home. Webb gets even quieter when he's high, but it's a different quiet, more relaxed, and somehow Cass doesn't mind this. She looks around his shack, at its neat secret charm and its view of the bogs, and she thinks she understands why Webb lives here. Not because he's crazy or because he's hiding from anything, but because at night he watches the hawks settle in and the bats dart among the trees. She feels closer to him here than anywhere else.

They smoke the rest of the joint in silence, finally

stubbing it out in an old dish. "There," Webb says. His face is very peaceful. "That ought to hold us for a while."

"Fortified," Cass says. "Always a good idea. You're coming, aren't you? Jordan really wants you to."

"Sure," he says. "As long as you'll handle the small talk with her friends. You go ahead and get Jordan—I gotta get organized here. And lose those pictures, okay?"

She nods and then opens the door and slips onto the stoop, where Jordan is horsing around with Marmalade. As Cass bends down to tickle Marmalade's ears and scratch Jordan's back apologetically, she hears the harsh sweet sound of Webb's saxophone. He's playing "Amazing Grace" slowly and sweetly, keeping time with his footsteps as he walks around the shack.

"My song!" Jordan says happily. "Webb taught me to play that on my recorder."

"That's nice," Cass says quietly, wishing Webb would stop. She knows this song—once, on a geology field trip, she sang it along with her classmates while they rode home on a bus. The man who taught the course led them with his clear baritone; later, he became her lover. He had a wife and two sons and chose to stay with them, and he is one of the reasons Cass doesn't go back to New Hampshire. She would not, not for anything, play Diane's part.

"Sing," Jordan says. "I don't know the words."

"I forgot them," Cass lies, remembering the two blond heads of Carl's sons peering out at her from their father's car. Webb plays the tune again. When he walks out the door he still wears the saxophone strap around his neck.

"Come on," he says, tossing Marmalade inside and tapping Cass lightly on the head as if to dispel her mood. "Let's get this circus on the road."

The game has already started by the time they reach Jordan's school—the same low, brick building that Cass remembers wandering through with Webb. She hasn't been back here in years, and now she studies the building as she parks. It's cleaner than she remembered and seems to have grown new windows and wings.

"Want to go in?" Jordan asks. "You can see my homeroom."

"No," Cass says firmly. Even from here she can smell the thick, sweet dust from the boards and see the row of miniature desks where she once sat so impatiently. She heads out back, where the ragged patch of dirt and grass she remembered has been transformed into a neat, green playing field lined with crisp stripes and studded with fancy nets. The school is bigger now, and must have more money as well—when she was here they played, if they played at all, without equipment or uniforms or rules. A herd of stick-legged boys scurries across the field in pursuit of a black and white ball.

"That's our team," Jordan says proudly, pointing at a group of boys dressed in navy-blue jerseys, blue shorts piped with gold, and high socks.

"Fancy uniforms," Cass says, the pictures in her purse fading from her thoughts already. Her head buzzes pleasantly, and she leans on Webb's arm as they follow Jordan to the bleachers. Webb looks like a giant here; she feels like a giantess. In their disguise as adults they sail past Mr. Reardon, who taught them both in sixth grade. His crew cut is gray now, and he doesn't even blink at them. Cass relaxes. Of course they don't recognize me, she thinks. Thirty kids a year, every year, all the years since I was here—she can stare at the teachers unseen, as if she's a fly on the field. "Look," she whispers to Webb, as she recognizes another face. "Mrs. Jaspers."

The heavy woman flicks at her iron-colored curls just as Webb turns to watch her. "Shit," he says, laughing softly. "Remember when she used to do that in class? She hasn't changed a bit."

Cass can tell by the lift of his lips that he feels this invisibility too. It's remarkable how no one can see them. They might be ghosts.

"Want to meet my teacher?" Jordan asks. "She's over by the railing."

"No," Cass says kindly. She doesn't want to disappoint Jordan, but there's a limit to what she'll do. "But we'd be glad to meet your friends."

Cass focuses on the blue team out there on the field. The boys are slight, the size of Carl's sons, too small to be screaming and running around like this. A thin boy with a shock of black hair takes a tumble and she winces, wondering if he'll cry. He bounces up like a yo-yo and flies down the field. A golden figure she can't make out is splashed across the back of his shirt.

Jordan stands and waves at a girl in a blue sweatshirt. "Amy!" she shrieks. "Over here!"

Amy smiles coolly and begins to walk toward them. "Sit up!" Jordan whispers to Webb, who is slumped against the seat behind him. Amy beams at them. "Hi," she says easily, swinging her legs over the bleachers. "Who are your friends?"

"My brother and sister," Jordan says proudly. "Cass and Webb." Say something smart, she wills them fiercely. Say something wonderful.

Cass holds out her hand and says, "Amy. What a pleasure—I've heard so much about you. Pep squad and band, right?" Jordan nearly laughs with relief at Cass's smooth words. Webb nods and says, "Glad to meet you, Amy. I didn't expect Jordan's friends to be as pretty as her."

Amy flushes and simpers. "Oh well . . ." She pivots and points to a chunky boy driving the ball toward the goal. "You meet Frank?" she asks. "Jordan's got a crush on him."

"Do not!" Jordan squeals. She can feel her face redden as she taps Amy's arm. She does have a crush on Frank, but he's two grades ahead of her and doesn't know she's alive.

Amy smiles knowingly. "Sure," she says. "Right."

Her back is to Cass, and now Cass sees that the same golden figure she saw on the boys' uniforms is splashed across the back of Amy's sweatshirt. It's a horse—a winged horse on his hind legs, with his front hooves flashing in the air.

"There's Iris," Amy says. "And Irene and Holly and Sue. I'll go get them." She bounds down the bleachers and vanishes into the crowd.

Jordan leans against Cass's knee. "You were great," she says. "Do you mind meeting the rest?"

"Whoever you want," Cass says, smiling over Jordan's head at Webb. Webb winks slowly and comically, and then hunches down into his coat. A cold wind blows off the Canal. The blue team scores a goal, and Cass taps Jordan's arm and says, "What's with the horse uniforms?"

"It's from their name—they're the Flying Feet. See the wings?"

"Pegasus," Cass says. "Like the one in the sky."

"Right," Jordan says, embarrassed that she hasn't made this connection before. Cass smiles approvingly and Jordan thinks back to the night, more than a year ago now, when Cass gave her that fragile, cracking, cardboard star dome. Cass turned off the bedroom lights, lay down on Jordan's bed, and held the dome above their heads while she slowly pointed out the constellations. The Big Dipper first, and then the pointer stars tracing a path to the Little Dipper; Draco, with Hercules on his head; tiny Lyra off Hercules' knee; Cygnus and then, low in the sky, Pegasus and Andromeda. It was like learning the alphabet, almost that easy, and before winter Jordan knew them all. She matched the stars on the dome to the stars outside during the months while Cass was finishing school, and when she asked Cass questions over the phone Cass answered them all and then said, "Now that you know how to use that dome, why don't you try teaching your mother?" Jordan managed to teach Diane all the major groups before Cass came home again.

Pegasus, low in the sky, and this horse on the boys' backs—she has never connected them before, but it makes sense. She turns to the field just in time to see Frank kick in a goal. Everything is going well, so well, even if the picnic's not here yet. She is hardly hungry, and now Amy makes her way back to them, trailing a crowd of girls who have never seen Cass and who have only glimpsed Webb from a distance. Jordan introduces them with a little hum of pride—the girls are clearly impressed with these tall strangers. A whistle blows.

"About time," Cass says. She rises, tugging Webb's hand; the girls scatter before her and run out onto the field to the blue-dressed boys. The boy that Jordan has a crush on tosses the soccer ball into the air, where it hovers like a gull. Is his name Frank? Cass wonders. The low sun shines in her eyes and makes her squirm; her head is beginning to ache and she's tired of this. She wants to go home, wherever that is. "Let's go," she says impatiently.

"What?" Webb says in mock surprise. "You don't like it here?" He has hardly said a word all afternoon, except to greet Jordan's friends.

"It hasn't improved any," Cass says. She stretches and takes a step down toward the field, only to find that Jordan's face has turned white and that she looks as though she might cry. "What is it?" Cass asks, feeling her pockets frantically to see if she has dropped something unforgivable onto her seat, a joint or a flask or a pair of underpants. Her pockets are clean; her fly is zipped. "Honey," she says. "What's the matter?" She could swear that Jordan was smiling only a minute ago.

"It's only *half*time," Jordan blurts. "We can't go yet." Her hands are clenched stiffly at her sides, and a furrow rises between her eyebrows.

"I thought the game was over," Cass says. "I heard the whistle, and then all your friends took off . . ."

"It's halftime," Jordan repeats fiercely. "That's all. We have to stay."

Later, Cass will wonder why she didn't talk Jordan into going. She'd met all of Jordan's friends, seen Amy and Frank and the school, but instead of suggesting they go for ice cream and then head on home, she said, "Of course we'll stay," and then sat through the long third quarter while the wind blew down the back of her neck and Webb fell asleep beside her; sat through most of the fourth quarter, her feet transformed into stones, until the moment when Jordan, who had been looking anxiously over her shoulder, froze in place as if she'd been pinned. Jordan's face took on a strange expression, a blend of emotions too complicated for Cass to read, and Cass was just about to ask Jordan what it was when she heard Ben's voice.

"Hi, baby!" she heard Ben call happily. "Sorry I'm late—better late than never, though. Right?"

Cass twirled around toward him, watching his face change into a mask as complicated as Jordan's as he caught sight of her, Cass, with Webb asleep beside her. And now Cass is afraid to wake Webb, because Webb may say something terrible. Despite herself, something passes through the bleachers that wakes Webb up anyway, snaps him bolt upright with a frown on his face and his eyes locked dead on Ben's. "Shit," he mutters, his hand inching over to Cass's.

Cass can feel the cloak of their invisibility shredding into streamers in the wind, turning into something glaring, something loud. All around them heads turn, faces seeming to stare at them and at the long, crackling lines passing between them and their father, between Jordan and them. "I don't believe this," she says.

Jordan clears her throat and pleads, "Wait, just wait. Please?" Then she calls clearly down to Ben, "Dad? Come on up here."

Cass stares at Jordan. She planned it, she thinks, Jordan's whole scheme suddenly apparent to her. Cass is just about to tell Webb to relax, it's just a mistake, they'll get through it, when the woman standing behind Ben turns away from her conversation with Mrs. Jaspers and begins to follow Ben up the bleachers. It's Jill, of course, and Webb rises with a garbled groan of dismay as Jordan's face collapses completely. The ruin of her plans is written there, as clear to Cass as if Cass had made the plans herself. Jordan invited Ben, Cass sees, but Ben alone, Ben without Jill, in the hopes that they'd all make up. And Jordan didn't tell Ben that Cass and Webb would be there, because she wanted to surprise him the way she surprised them, and so Ben hadn't thought to come by himself. It would be sad, Cass thinks, if it weren't so ridiculous. Here I'm dreaming about these negatives, about this family of mine all together, and Jordan's dreaming *her* family together, but they're not even the same family and we can't either of us win without the other losing. Jordan shoots her such a startled look that she realizes she is mumbling to herself.

"Sit, please," Jordan begs Cass and Webb. "Please? You'll ruin everything, if it isn't already ruined—just for a minute? Just to say hello?" They can't say no to me now, she thinks, her mind working frantically even as she slides into Ben's hug and extends one cool hand toward her new stepmother, her stepmother who should have stayed back in that blue apartment, where she belongs. A few yards away, Amy and Iris are staring at Jill's red hair and black jeans and the boat-necked emerald sweater that brings out her eyes. Could I pass her off as a sister? Jordan wonders. She pokes Cass, who croaks out a stilted hello. Webb does no more than grunt before he unfolds his thin legs completely and strides down the bleachers between the startled shoulders of her classmates and friends. One down, Jordan thinks. Already. Before her eyes, her brother and sister are transformed into a pair of gawky, graceless creatures, their beaky noses reddened in the cold. Jordan turns toward her father for help.

The wind has risen, and the sky has turned as gray as if Ben had brought clouds in his pockets. Now he shoves his hands into his lime-green corduroys and thrusts his small, hard stomach out awkwardly. "Cass," he says, clearing his throat dryly. "I don't think you've met Jill."

"Not formally," Cass says coolly. "Of course we've seen each other around town."

Jill stands behind Ben, where only Cass can see her face. Cass nods at her curtly and Jill, in response, holds a hand in front of her lovely mouth, pulling down the corners of her eyes with her thumb and little finger and pushing up on her nose with her middle finger to make a pig's snout. Despite herself, Cass laughs.

Ben whirls around, too late to catch anything more than Jill's bland smile. "What's so funny?" he says. "What's going on?"

"Nothing's funny," Cass tells him. "Listen, why don't you stay for the rest of the game and bring Jordan home afterward? I've got to find Webb and then get going."

"No!" Jordan says, pounding her small fist on the seat above her. "You sit here and talk!"

The three adults turn to stare at her. Like I'm a bug, Jordan thinks miserably. Like I'm a baby. They don't have to act as if she's done something terrible—it was a good idea, it could have worked. Ben might have come earlier, alone; he might have brought the picnic lunch he promised and they all, her and Cass and Webb and him, might have sat here eating sausage rolls and talking to each other. Now Webb has vanished, probably sulking in the car, and Cass and Jill are giving each other the strangest looks, their chins tucked back and their necks curved and tensed in the way of two cats meeting each other, and Ben is just standing there, one knee bent and his belly out, smiling his public smile as if this has nothing whatsoever to do with him.

"Sit!" Jordan commands, the way she'd talk to Willie. Ben plumps down obligingly on the wooden seat. Cass rises as soon as Ben sits and ends up standing next to Jill. They lean away from each other then, but only from the waist up, their feet polite. It will never work, Jordan thinks. Never, never—I'll never get them together. I'll always have to see them in little groups. She tugs Cass's hand, prepared to plead with her, but Cass shakes her head and pulls away. What am I supposed to do now? Jordan wonders. Go home with Cass and Webb? With Ben and Jill? Sprout wings and fly?

"How's your mother?" Jordan hears Ben ask Cass. At least he's trying.

"Fine," Cass says. "Traveling."

"Uh-huh," Ben grunts. "And Otis and Cindy?"

"All fine," Cass repeats.

Jordan is about to say something, anything, to ease this conversation, when from the corner of her eye she catches sight of Sal, crossing the field below them like a spirit. Jordan shakes her head and looks again—perhaps she is mistaken. But no, Sal makes a beeline for them until, at the foot of the bleachers, she stops and calls, "Hi there!" gaily. She's wearing a purple wool poncho that hangs in crisp, regal folds, and with her she has Willie, who strains against his leash and sniffs at the shoes of the spectators. He looks up and bolts for Jordan, bouncing back at Sal's firm jerk on his leash. "We just came out for a walk!" Sal calls. "Isn't this fun?"

Jordan groans and, behind her back, pounds one fist against the other. This is all she needs, just what she should have expected—it was that picture, that stupid picture in her back pocket, that brought Sal here. She has never fooled her grandmother for long. That picture of her and Willie that she meant to give to Ben but which she can't ever give him now, not with Jill here and Webb gone and Cass so angry . . . "Shit," she whispers, echoing Webb.

"Quite a party," Sal continues cheerily. "I saw Webb out in the parking lot, drinking beer on the hood of the car, and here's Cass and your father and—would that be Jill?"

"That's right," Jill says.

"Nice to meet you, dear. I'm your husband's second ex-wife's mother."

"Lovely," Jill murmurs, just loud enough for both Cass and Jordan to hear.

"May I come up?" Sal calls.

"Sure," Jordan says with a sigh. "Why not?"

Sal clambers up the bleachers, with Willie loping beside her. Her shoes are bright red and laced around her ankles, and she seems to admire them as she sets down each tiny foot. "Really," she says, when she reaches them. "What a nice surprise to find you all here." She waves her arm out over the field, where the boys are still playing. "And isn't this nice," she says. "All those little boys dressed in Pegasus suits—who do you suppose thought of that?"

"They're called the Flying Feet," Jordan says faintly. "It's sort of a pun, you know?"

Sal laughs her silvery laugh. "How lovely!" she says. "You know how Pegasus rescued Andromeda and carried her off, and of course he did all sorts of good deeds for Perseus after he sprang full-grown from the Medusa's blood, and then there's the story about the water he made come out of the rocks and the way he got fixed in the sky as a reward and . . ."

"Really," Cass says firmly, just as Sal is getting warmed up and explaining how significant this constellation is even though it's not part of the zodiac. "Really, I have to go." She touches Sal's shoulder, so Sal will understand that this is nothing personal. "You'll take care of things here?"

"Oh, of course," Sal says. "Of course."

Cass pats Willie's head on her way down. She could swear that Willie smiles at her, because she has not taken two steps down the bleachers before her retreat is cut off by Ben's garbled scream. She spins around to find Willie clinging firmly to Ben's calf, his teeth sunk deep into the corduroy pants and the flesh below.

"Get him off, get him off!" Ben shouts.

Willie growls louder at the sound of Ben's voice, but he unclenches his jaws when Sal jerks at his leash. "Bad dog!" Sal says, and taps his nose. But instead of yelling at Willie she turns to Ben and says firmly, "You never should have kicked him like that. Willie, sit."

Willie sits. Ben says, "I was just pushing him out of the way before he tipped me over—it was a fucking *tap*! I didn't expect the son of a bitch to *bite*!" He bends down and rolls up his trousers to reveal two small, red holes in his calf, each leaking a trickle of blood. Jordan, her hands raised before her chest, is backing slowly away from everyone. And so when Cass calls, "Watch out! He always faints when there's blood . . ." there is only Jill beside him to ease him down onto the seat and stuff his head between his knees. His face is the color of chalk.

"What else?" Cass mutters. She turns to ask Sal what they should do, but Sal has vanished as quickly as she arrived and is halfway across the field already, Willie prancing before her with his plumed tail bouncing in the wind. The game has ended somewhere during all this, and the boys have left the playing field. The bleachers empty slowly, an occasional person shooting curious glances at Ben. No one stops to help.

Surprisingly, Jill has things more or less under control. She cups the back of Ben's head with her hand, keeping him bent between his knees, and she croons to him while finding time to say to Jordan, who is hunched in a tight ball nearby, "Don't feel bad. It wasn't your fault."

"He's *my* dog," Jordan mutters despairingly. How did this happen? Everything's ruined, again. No matter what she does, she can't seem to keep these people together.

"Your father's fine," Jill says calmly, still pressing down on Ben's head. To Cass she says, "He'll be fine in a minute, but I think I'll drive him over to the emergency room and see if they want to put a few stitches in."

"You'll be all right?" Cass says awkwardly. "I could come, if you needed the help . . ."

"We'll be fine," Jill says.

Ben sits up slowly, still very pale. "Jordan," he says thickly, "you come with me. Come with me to the hospital."

His words freeze the four of them in the air. Cass's feet feel nailed to the seat. Jordan can't move her eyes. Ben hunches into himself, only his neck craning slightly, furtively, in Jordan's direction, perhaps to see how she'll respond. Jill's hand pauses partway through a gesture.

"Come on," he orders, almost in the old way that Cass remembers. "Come take care of your dad."

Cass unfreezes first. Ben hasn't asked her and won't even look at her, but still she says to Jordan, "Go ahead if you want." She doesn't want to be responsible for cutting Jordan off from Ben. She thinks that maybe, if

she had not always been so aware of how much Penny
hated Ben, she might not have drifted so far away herself. They might all be together, her and Webb and
Penny and Ben, and she might not be where she is right
now, unable to help her own father. "Really," she says
softly to Jordan. "It's okay. Jill will bring you home."

Jill makes an odd face at Cass, but then nods.

They're all waiting for Jordan to make a decision, but
Jordan's too cold to concentrate. I should have worn a
coat, she thinks. The wind blows down her neck, up
under her sweater, around her ankles; the cold gray
light makes her family look as though they've been
carved from rocks. Don't look at me, she thinks frantically, as Ben slides his gaze over to her. I can't decide.
It's only a ride to the hospital he's asking for, but his
eyes are cool as he makes his request and some part of
her whispers that he wants more than that. He looks
like a bird, like a heron perhaps, slyly watching to see if
he can lure her over to his side. His wounds have
stopped bleeding and the color's returned to his face,
but still he holds his hand over his calf as if he's in great
pain. Jordan knows that these are, after all, tiny punc-
tures. Ben groans as if he's reading her thoughts.

"We should go," he says. "Before I get any worse.
Suppose I get rabies?"

"You won't get *rabies*, Dad," Jordan tells him. "Willie's not sick."

"He could be," Ben says. "He bit me, didn't he? After
I didn't do anything."

Jordan is silent. She knows for a fact that Willie came
up to sniff Ben's leg and that Ben, busy saying something to Jill, put his foot against the side of Willie's
stomach and pushed him firmly away. Not a kick, exactly, but awful close, and she's not so sure she wouldn't
have bitten him herself, if she'd been Willie.

"Did I?" Ben asks, turning to Jill for confirmation. "I

was just standing there, perfectly innocent, when he rushed up and bit me . . ."

"Dad," Cass says impatiently, still watching all this from a few feet below. "You know that's not what happened."

"It is," he says stubbornly.

Cass tosses her head in disgust and turns to leave.

"Wait," Jordan says, surprised at the sudden jolt of panic in her chest. "I'll come with you. Dad'll be all right without me." She turns her head when she says this, so she doesn't have to see her father's stricken look. She catches Jill's eye instead, but Jill smiles coolly and says, "Don't worry—I'll take care of him."

"I know," Jordan says, the foolishness of her dreams suddenly clear to her. He'll be fine, she thinks. He doesn't need me or Cass or anyone but Jill, and he's never coming home again. And although she knows she could go live with him and Jill if she wanted, that she has only to say the word, she can't imagine that life. He's always gone; she'd spend all her time with Jill. And besides, she thinks, startled at herself. Besides, he lies. "Well, he does," she mutters aloud, ignoring Jill's sharp look. He does. He always has. Perhaps this is why Cass and Penny and Diane are always so mad at him.

"You all right?" Cass whispers.

"Fine," Jordan says. She turns and kisses Ben good-bye, brushing his cheek lightly with her lips. Cass holds out her hand and Jordan takes it as together they walk down the bleachers and out across the field. In the distance they see Sal appear from behind a clump of hawthorns. Sal bends down to unsnap Willie's leash, since everyone has gone home by now. I lie too, Jordan thinks as she looks at Sal. I lied to her. Willie bounds across to them.

"You sure you don't want to stay with Dad?" Cass says. "We could go back." She can't quite believe that Jordan is walking here with her, any more than she can believe Sal's cryptic smile as she comes to greet them. It is almost, Cass thinks, as if Sal had planned this whole thing. Cass pauses, remembering the times in her life when Sal seemed to have planned everything, times when she had this same idea and then dismissed it. Perhaps she should have paid more attention. Perhaps it has always been Sal who engineered everything, from Cass's own departure from home to her return. She looks at Sal, but Sal's face is perfectly cheerful, perfectly bland.

Sal bends down to hug Jordan. "Well," she says. "You suppose your grandmother could ride home with you? Paine dropped me off and I don't have a ride home."

Jordan hugs her back fiercely. "Sure," she says. She doesn't ask how Sal knew she was here, but she takes the picture, so useless now, from her back pocket. Then, with Sal watching her curiously, she holds it out to Cass and says, "I brought this for you. Uncle Paine took it and I thought you might like it."

Cass looks at the picture, an eerie shot of Jordan and Willie transformed into airborne creatures. Jordan's braid streams out behind her, and her hands float before her as if she is reaching for something beyond the boundaries of the picture. Willie, his tail held high and his feet tucked up as if he's a horse, grins directly into the camera. It's a picture Cass never would have seen if Jordan hadn't brought it, a picture as strange to her as the negatives that sit in her purse. She takes the picture from Jordan, thanks her, and almost gives Jordan one of the negatives in return before she remembers. Wrong Ben, she thinks. Wrong time. Wrong life. She hands her sister the Rapidograph that her fingers happen on instead. Jordan smiles as if Cass has given her the world.

Stars Whose Cause Is All Unknown
(August 1978)

★   ★   ★   ★   ★   ★

Penny, home from the islands these past six months, lights the last of the candles dotting the smooth cedar platform that juts out from her roof. The platform straddles the peak, open to the sky above her neighbors' houses. She can see clear to the Canal from here—the lights on the passing ships, the lamps on the railroad bridge, the markers at the channel's mouth—but her gaze usually strays upward to the circling stars, guided by her telescope. Tonight the telescope's covered and her viewing stool is gone; instead, six soft pillows cluster around the low table she and Walker dragged up the stairs and out through the dormer they converted to a door. Candles gleam on the table, at the four corners of the platform, and along the platform's edge. The night is warm and clear, and the quarter moon shines beautiful but not too bright.

She hears the clump of Walker's boots on the attic stairs, and then the door opens upward toward her.

Walker's head pops through, framed in the square opening. "All set?" he asks.

His wiry hair, still red in places, is striped with
white, and his beard is white all over. He's tied a ban-
danna around his neck for the party, and with that and
the whorls of hair springing up above his collar he looks
more like a pirate than like the gentle, steady soul he is.

"All set," she says, and smiles at him, glad to find
after all these years that her instincts were right. He
hasn't changed much—he's the Walker she chose years
ago, the soft glow of a moon rather than a supernova's
last flare.

"Looks great up here," he says, passing out a platter
of rolls that she sets on a warming tray. The coffee pot
bubbles behind her, and a tiny black head pops through
the door and bats at Walker's beard. "Mizar!" he says,
snatching the kitten from his face. "Give me a break,
huh?" Another cat pops out at Walker's waist and he
shouts, "Alcor!" as he grabs it. The kittens—Penny's
third set, granddaughters of her original Mizar—struggle against Walker's big hands.

"Let them out if you want," Penny says. "They're
smart enough not to jump."

Walker tosses the kittens out and watches them fly
onto the platform, where they streak immediately for
the bowl of chicken salad on the table.

"No!" Penny says. "Bad!" She pries their claws from
the cellophane and taps each black nose lightly. Mizar
decides to eat a candle instead and sticks her nose so
close to the flame that she singes a whisker and leaps
away in panic. Penny watches Alcor closely to see if
she'll be as dumb, but Alcor trots demurely away. Below them, the doorbell rings. Walker thunders down to
answer it and opens the door with a flourish that brings
a giggle from Jordan.

"Come in, come in," he booms. "Penny's on the roof
already."

Jordan shyly hands him the fruit salad she's made. Cass and Diane and Webb crowd in behind her, bearing wine and a cake and a pair of cedar candlesticks that Webb has carved. Cass presses her cheek to Walker's beard and looks around, thinking how it never changes here. A skinny Chihuahua—not Chuck, but another, smaller dog named Fay—leaps at her legs, and swarms of neon tetras and angelfish fill the aquariums lining the porch. Inside, the house is still a mess. On the walls hang maps and nautical charts scored with the red routes of Penny's voyages, along with astrophotographs snipped from magazines and tacked up carelessly, a cartoon depicting four versions of sailing in four parallel universes, and, grouped together in a black mat, the prints Cass had made from her mystery negatives, which she gave to Penny for Christmas last year. Penny hung them to remind her, she said, of the worth of previous lives. Stacked in corners and piled under tables are life preservers and depth finders and other equipment from Walker's boat in various stages of repair.

Cass turns to Walker, gestures at the things on the floor, and says, "Looks like you've been busy."

Walker grins shyly. "Getting ready for another cruise," he says. "Come September. We're eating on the roof—want to head up?"

"Sure," Diane says, poking her head around Cass's shoulder. "Should we bring the food?"

Walker nods and leads them all to the back bedroom closet, where the stairs climb up to the roof. "Jordan first," he says. "Cass, you go behind her, then Webb, and then Diane. I'll follow in case anyone trips."

"Funny," Diane says. "Ha."

Jordan climbs up the narrow stairs, ducks her head to clear the attic beams, and pushes open the door. For a minute she thinks the roof is on fire. There are candles everywhere, in dishes and little bowls, and in the midst of them stands Penny, one hand on her covered telescope and her grizzled hair streaming over her shoulders. A teal-colored shirt floats over her pants and gleams in the gentle light. Mizar and Alcor dash for Jordan's feet and pounce on her sneakers.

"They're getting big," Jordan says, as she shakes the kittens from her feet.

"Aren't they? Come give your Aunt Penny a hug."

Jordan squeezes Penny's narrow hips, and Penny bends down to plant a kiss in Jordan's hair. It smells like ferns; the ends move in the flickering candlelight like the fins of her angelfish. Like I used to dream of Cass, Penny thinks, remembering the dream she had on her honeymoon, before Cass was born. She thinks again, as she often has recently, how there'd be no Cass without Ben; no Jordan, no Webb; no trace of this life she loves, without the young man whose only existence now is in the framed pictures downstairs. Caught in the black mat, rendered harmless after all—and she left her children with him, a man who might have been the sun's faint companion star, which, on its eccentric orbit, extinguishes life on earth periodically. The star's orbit lurches; comets fly; meteorites hail down to earth. Cass and Webb could have vanished like dinosaurs. Leaving them could have been such a mistake; for a while she thought it was. And yet she and her children, separated, only toughened and grew strong. The bonds between them held while they formed new ones, more mysterious ones, to Diane and Sal and Paine and Jordan, to Otis and Walker. Stellar chemistry, she thinks, imagining her family as atoms stripped to their component parts in a star's hot core, only to be remade.

Someone coughs and she straightens, realizing she's been silent too long. "Where's everyone else?" she asks.

"Right behind me," Jordan says.

Cass and Webb step out onto the platform. They've cut their hair again, into matching curly caps; they're both burnt brown. Cass hands two bottles to Webb and reaches back for a white cake studded with candles. She sets the cake on the table and kisses Penny's cheek. "You look great," she says.

"Mom," Webb says, draping his long arm around her as he surveys the decorations. "You're cruising for a fire with all these candles. But I guess you know that."

Penny laughs and says, "You worry too much." She untangles herself from her children and goes to greet Diane, who's been a frequent visitor here this past year. Diane has pierced her ears and taken to wearing large earrings, which she sometimes exchanges with Cass. Tonight she has a big silver disk in one ear—a moon? Penny wonders—and a dangling chain of jade spheres in the other. Cass wears an identical mismatched set. "Pretty," Penny says.

"The moons are Cass's," Diane says. "The jade ones are mine."

Walker closes the door behind him, takes the bottles from Webb, and uncorks them. "Good stuff," he says, sniffing deeply.

"From Paine," Cass tells him. "He gave me a few bottles as a present for Mom, since he and Sal couldn't come tonight." She smiles, thinking of Paine and Sal curled in their matching armchairs, bowls of popcorn and Willie at their feet, *The Magic Flute*, which they wouldn't miss for anything, on their TV.

"Sit, everyone," Walker says.

They lower themselves to the cool wooden floor around the table. Jordan feels a little thrill at being included in this—it's late, almost ten, and the party's just beginning. She's brought a warm sweater for later, in case the night grows cold; Cass wears hers already, a big spill of blue that hides her from shoulders to knees. Penny leans over and pours the wine, smiling so that the deep grooves from her nose to her mouth are hardly visible. She looks like a bird, Jordan thinks. Like a huge white owl.

"Let's have a toast," Penny says. "To Maria Mitchell, born one hundred fifty-nine years ago today."

"To Maria Mitchell," her family responds. Walker hugs Penny as if it's her own birthday they're celebrating, and Jordan asks Penny who Maria Mitchell was.

Penny pulls at her bottom lip, wondering where to begin. "She was our first woman astronomer," she says finally. "She spent most of her life looking at the stars and teaching other people what was there, and she discovered a comet."

Jordan looks up at the sky. So? she thinks. She's never seen a comet except in books, where they're painted as huge white streaks across the sky that anyone could spot. But because she knows Maria Mitchell is important to Penny, she asks politely, "How do you find a comet?"

"Not so easily," Penny says. "Especially not without a good telescope, and especially not if you're a woman who's not supposed to know these things. They look like stars, sort of. The only way you can find one is to know the positions of all the other stars so well that you can spot something new moving through them."

"Did she get famous, then?" Jordan asks.

"Mm-hmm."

"Mom's taking astronomy now," Jordan says proudly. "In school."

"I know," Penny says. She smiles at Diane, who's been in school full-time since January.

"You'll be able to see Halley's comet in eight years," Diane tells Jordan. "If you want to see a comet that's really a comet." She raises her hands above her head and holds them, palms out, toward the sky. "Glory, glory, glory," she rumbles, in a put-on Southern preacher's voice. "Get down on your knees all you sinners and pray, for the end of the world is upon us."

Then she laughs, and Jordan giggles. A year ago, Jordan thinks, her mother wouldn't have said that. Sal might have, or Penny or Paine, but her mother wouldn't have known it to begin with and wouldn't have found it funny if she did. It's because we study together at night, Jordan thinks. It helps.

"Halley's, 1910?" Penny asks. "Somewhere in Arkansas?"

"Tennessee," Diane says. "But otherwise yes."

Jordan lifts her water glass again and says, "Well, hurray for Maria Mitchell!"

Hurray indeed, Penny thinks. In the dark nights, with her children away and her husband gone and Walker off on his boat where she'd sent him, it was the vision of Maria sweeping the skies that kept Penny going. Not that she's ever expected to discover something new—she's strictly an amateur. But each night these past ten years and more she's found something new to her, and this seems to her to be worth celebrating.

"Can we look through your telescope?" Jordan asks.

"After supper," Penny says. "Let's eat."

She peels the cellophane from the chicken salad, and the cats, alerted by the crinkling sound, spring into the air.

Later, Cass pats her stomach and burps quietly. They've had chicken salad tucked in warm rolls, Jordan's fruit salad, wine and nuts and soft cheese spread on Walker's home-baked sesame crackers. The remnants of the birthday cake litter the plates on the table. Cass has had two pieces, and now she sips her coffee gratefully. Webb echoes her ladylike burp with a loud, rolling belch. He sits with Walker against the railing, where they've propped their pillows. They're talking man-talk there—some deep conversation about bogs and boats and tools—and they're drinking beer. Webb's eyelid droops just a bit.

"I don't know," Cass can hear Webb say. "I think a slow drying, myself. First outside, maybe over the win-

ter, and then in an unheated shed. Once you bring a
chunk inside, you're setting up stresses."

Wood? Cass wonders. Is that what they're talking
about? Walker listens attentively, and Cass can see from
the tilt of his head that he finds Webb worth listening
to. He's like a father to Webb, she thinks. The way Otis
was with me. All those dinners, all those late nights
hunched over models and plans while we imagined
mountains—I wouldn't have known squat without him,
wouldn't have been anything. Does Walker do the same
for Webb? She remembers how Otis gave her her first
set of drawing pens, her first drafting table, her first
good advice. Walker gave Webb his first woodworking
tools, and she wonders if that was the same. Were they
both that lucky?

Walker says, "How's the dulcimer coming?" and
Webb says, "Fine," spreading his callused fingers as he
describes the way he fixed a tuning peg. Cass sips at her
wine and then at her coffee, thinking how she ought to
stick to one or the other. She'll be up all night the way
she's going, her head wandering free from the wine and
her heart pounding from the caffeine. Across the table
Penny and Diane huddle their heads together, deep in
talk. Diane, whom Penny persuaded to go back to
school, is now trying to get Penny to join her.

"You'd love it," Cass hears Diane say. "I'm learning
so much."

Cass can't hear Penny's reply, but she knows what it
is: I'd rather teach myself. Penny believes in college, but
only for others—for herself she'd rather carry home
piles of books and swoop through them at her own pace,
in her own remarkable way. Perhaps, Cass thinks, she
imagines herself another Maria Mitchell. She's seen
Penny reading in bed, with her books and papers
strewn across the covers. One month she'll decide to
learn Latin and the other Greek, and then she'll toss
those both aside to browse through twenty years of *Sci-*

entific American back issues. She'll read about black holes and decide she needs to learn math, and then when she gets stuck on math she'll read about the origin of the universe, skipping Kepler and Galileo to read Pythagoras and the Bible. She has no logic, Cass thinks. Her mind is like some great sea, strewn with shining fish. And now, as if to confirm Cass's thoughts, Penny says to Diane, "You should take math. I've always wished I knew more." She sounds wistful when she says this, but Cass knows she doesn't mean it. The things Penny knows connect in a way that doesn't work in school.

Jordan plucks Cass's sleeve. "You asleep?"

Cass smiles down at her sister's soft blond head. "Nope," she says. "Just dreaming with my eyes open. Want to lean up against me?"

Jordan props her pillow against Cass's shoulder and lies back on it. "Nice," she says. "What were you dreaming about?"

"I don't know—this and that. What about you?" Cass tucks a strand of Jordan's hair back and thinks, No doubt about it, she's going to be beautiful. Jordan's hair hasn't dulled and her huge green eyes haven't been lost in her changing face. Her nose promises to be small and straight, without the little bump at the bridge that marks Ben's and Cass's and Webb's. What did she get from Ben? Cass wonders, scanning Jordan's face. I got the nose and an eye for land and some of the canniness. Webb seems to have gotten away with just the nose. Jordan has Ben's coloring, but it is also Diane's. Perhaps Jordan has gotten away clean.

"I was thinking how nice it is up here. And about winter, and how much I used to like skiing with Dad and Webb—do you think we might ever go skiing? Just you and me?"

"You want to ski?" Cass asks, surprised. She's never skied with Jordan—she was away from home by then, and she avoided the Nelsons' house when her family was there. "What can you do?"

"Stem turns," Jordan replies. "I was just beginning parallel when Daddy left, but now I've forgotten how."

"That's not so bad," Cass says, not mentioning how, at Jordan's age, she was already skiing like a pro. We were lucky, Cass thinks. Me and Webb. At least we got a little of the good part of Dad. She can still see him on the bleachers at Jordan's school, his hand clutched to his bleeding leg as she and Jordan walked away. She hasn't seen him since, and as for Jordan—well, Jordan can hardly ski and sees him and Jill only every fourth Sunday afternoon. "I could teach you," Cass says. "We could go for some weekends this winter, and I could give you lessons. Would you like that?"

"Sure," Jordan says. "I'd love it."

Cass nods. "Then it's settled. The first big snowfall after Christmas, we're in the Volkswagen and on our way to the slopes."

"Where will we stay?"

"With Otis and Cindy, I guess. Remember them?" She feels a sudden stab of homesickness for the Nelsons' house. Although she still does some drafting for Otis, she's picked up work here on the Cape and now it's hard for her to visit them.

"A little," Jordan says, Cass's words stirring in her a faint memory of a house shaped like a triangle, a man with thick glasses, a friendly woman, and a little boy a few years older than her, whose bedroom she shared. She heard the grown-ups talking downstairs at night and later, much later, her mother and father arguing next door, their low, sharp voices slicing through the wall. Was I five then? she thinks. Maybe six. That was the winter Webb got so sick, when his eyelid started to droop and no one would tell her anything. Her father came in after the argument and pressed his cheek to her face, and she asked him if they were getting divorced.

Webb had taught her that—that fighting meant a divorce—but her father said no, they were just disagreeing. Was he lying? she wonders now, thinking of the things she herself has concealed. Did he already know?

"I remember," she says. "I haven't been there in a while."

"Me neither," Cass says. "It'd be nice."

Walker tips his head against the railing and roars at something Webb has said. "That's good," he says, wiping his eyes. "That's funny. Where'd you hear that?"

"Some bar," Webb says with a shrug. He scoops up Mizar and Alcor, who are slinking past his legs in search of moths. "Catch," he says, tossing Mizar and Alcor to Walker. Cass holds her breath as Alcor arcs through the air near the platform's edge, but Walker catches the kitten easily, in a hand as big as a baseball mitt. Men, Cass thinks. Even the good ones. They're so strange.

"Remember stem turns?" Jordan is saying. "I was thinking about skiing just the other night, and I couldn't even remember where my weight was supposed to be. Uphill ski, downhill ski . . ." Thinking, as she says this, that she can't even remember what it felt like to be in that family, which she hasn't tried to reconstruct since the soccer game. This is my family now, she thinks. Even if none of us live in the same place. There's Penny here, Webb in his bog house, Walker on his boat; Sal and Paine next door and Cass a few miles away in her apartment over the grocery store, where she moved six months ago.

"Look," Cass says. She rummages in her purse for a pen and the little sketchbook she always carries around, and then she flips past the pages where she's sketched her old house from several angles, the island across from it, her new apartment, Webb's bog house. With a few swift strokes she draws a stick figure, knees bent and poles grasped in a two-fingered hand. "This is you," she says. "Okay?"

"Okay," Jordan says. "But at least give me some hair."

Cass adds a few curly wisps and a pair of thick lines for skis. "You're traversing a slope," she says. "Heading to the left. You want to go right." She sketches another quick figure with its skis open in a V. "What do you do?"

Jordan closes her eyes. It's cold, she thinks. Packed snow, lots of people . . . she moves her arm, plants an imaginary pole, shifts her weight—where?

Cass feels Jordan's slight frame shifting against her shoulder. "What are you doing?" she asks.

"Trying to feel it," Jordan says. "Plant my pole, stem my uphill ski, shift my weight—*down*hill. Right?"

"Right," Cass says. She pulls a candle closer and draws a series of stick figures making their way around a turn. "See?" she says. "Like this. You'll remember as soon as you get on the snow." From the corner of her eye she catches a flicker that could be a bat.

Jordan traces the figures with her finger. "I wish I could draw like you," she says. "I've been using my Rapidograph, but nothing ever comes out the way I see it."

"You'll learn, " Cass says. "Look how well you learned the stars."

The men have blown out the candles near them and their corner is dark. "Water line needs work," Cass hears Webb say. She'd like to wave them over, but she knows they're happy where they are. Walker's lit his pipe and fills the air with the smell of cherry tobacco. Webb's foot, sticking into the light, taps out some melody inside his head. "We ought to replace a few sections," he says. "Before we flood the bog."

"Get me an estimate," Walker says. A smoke ring floats into the light.

Webb nods. He's stretched out full-length with only his head propped up; in a few minutes, Cass knows, he'll be asleep. He still sleeps as deeply and easily as he did when he was small. In the middle of a party, the middle of a sentence, he'll drop off and sleep until morning. Mizar sneaks up to him and buries her head in his shirt.

"Cass!" Webb calls sleepily. "Toss me another pillow. You staying up all night?"

"All night," she says. She tosses a pillow at his head, and Jordan yawns and drops down onto Cass's lap.

"Can we look through the telescope now?" Jordan asks. "I'm sleepy."

"Later," Cass says. "You'll get your second wind." Across the table from them, Diane and Penny are still chattering. Penny has her star charts near her knee, but she shows no sign of moving to her telescope.

"Name what you see up there," Cass says to Jordan. "It'll keep you awake."

Jordan shifts her head so that it's cradled on Cass's thigh. "Big Dipper," she says, "Little Dipper, Draco, Hercules, Boötes, Corona Borealis, Cygnus, Lyra . . ." I know this, she thinks. I do. Even without the star dome, she can trace her way across the sky. Cass was right—it's all in how the constellations are related. From the Big Dipper, she can find her way anywhere.

"That's right," Cass says when Jordan pauses for breath. "Fantastic."

Jordan continues to recite. Cass picks up her pen, flips her sketchbook to a clean page, and begins to draw her sister's delicate profile.

"Can you believe it?" Diane is saying. "Another baby, at his age . . ."

Penny listens to her with one ear and listens to the soft murmur of Jordan's voice with the other. Like a litany, like a chant, Jordan picks her way through the

tapestry above her. Cass taught her that, Penny thinks.
Cass taught her, the way I taught Cass and Gram taught
me, back behind her house in Brattleboro. Always one
person passing it on to another.

"I saw her on the street in Hyannis," Diane says.
"She looked bad."

"Who?" Penny asks, because she has not, or not really, been paying attention to Diane. The sky tonight is
very beautiful.

"*Jill*," Diane says impatiently, flicking back her
newly cut hair with a gesture Penny has seen in a hundred other students. "I'll bet it's another girl," Diane
continues. "Forty-seven years old, and running for state
representative this year, and I bet he gets himself another feisty daughter."

"I don't know," Penny says. "He's due for a son."

"Girl," Diane says decidedly. "I can feel it. If we can
find out when she delivers, I'm going to get my mother
to cast her a horoscope."

Penny wrinkles her peeling nose. "You're still in-
volved with that?"

Diane shrugs and then laughs. "I've still got horoscopes in with my ice cubes," she says, unembarrassed
by these relics. "I put them in the freezer years ago, and
they're still there—mine and Jordan's and Cass's and
Webb's, sealed in tinfoil. I took them out when I was
defrosting, and I got to thinking how I ought to get Jill's
and the new baby's to complete the set. And yours, really."

"I'll pass," Penny says quickly. "I don't want to know
what's coming. What you really need is one for Ben—
you might've learned something from that."

She says this absently, half jokingly, because even after all these years around Sal and Diane she still can't
believe anyone takes astrology seriously. But Diane
says, "Right," so bitterly that Penny is forced to pay
attention. "Sure," Diane continues. "You can't learn

shit from men, except maybe how to understand other men, and that's no help at all. We learn the world from women."

"That's not completely true," Penny says quietly. She usually lets Diane bumble through the new ideas she picks up at school each week and discards the week after, but this unreflecting dislike of men disturbs her. We learn the world from women, Penny thinks, echoing Diane. Of course. But we learn ourselves and other women in part from men and from how we react to them. She'd like to show Diane the pictures downstairs, which Diane has always passed with averted eyes. If she could see them, Penny thinks, really see them, and then go home and dig through the attic for her own, and look at those . . . "Look what you're learning at school," Penny says, picking the least true but least offensive example. "Astronomy and geology and literature, most of it done by men. Look at Kepler. Look at Galileo."

"I meant *living* men," Diane says.

Penny pours more wine. "Ben," she says.

"Oh, sure, Ben," Diane snorts. "Mr. Teacher."

Penny shrugs. "Just because you can't choose what you learn from someone doesn't mean you don't learn."

Diane says nothing for a minute. She can't talk about Ben now without a sneer, can't think about him without hating him for what he's done, and sometimes this embarrasses her. She sits in the cafeteria with all the other middle-aged women who've shed their husbands and gone back to school, and when she leans back in the midst of their conversations, those tales of who did what to whom and how, she's astonished at their viciousness. So much hate, she thinks then. Hate that, like gravity, seems to act over a distance, so that the farther they get from their former lives the more they all reject them. And yet on the horizon, years away, perhaps, when she is Penny's age or older, she can just glimpse a time when she might let her anger go. She can just admit that Penny's attitude toward Ben is not a weakness.

Penny watches her, smiling as if she can read her thoughts. "Anyway," Penny says. "I just meant you shouldn't waste so much energy pushing that part of your life away. He's happy about the baby?"

"Hard to say—you know Ben. I don't think he really feels married until he gets his wives pregnant. As soon as we start to show he knows he's got us, got a home. But then he has to start pushing us away."

Penny laughs. "Too bad we didn't figure that out sooner," she says. "But then look what we would have missed." She nods at their daughters, one looking up at the sky and the other sketching with soft, swift strokes. They might almost be mother and child.

"True," Diane says. "And I wouldn't change things, not really, except I wish I'd been a little smarter. Maybe Jill's girl will fit in with ours."

"That'd be something," Penny says. She turns her head, meaning to ask Walker to bring up more coffee, but Walker is sleeping and so is Webb. "Look," Penny whispers to Diane. "After midnight they turn into pumpkins."

"Men," Diane says, unable to stop herself. "No stamina."

"They're morning people, both of them. I can't figure it out." Penny gets up, takes an old gray blanket from the pile near the door, and drapes it over the two men. Webb's mouth opens a little and Penny worries that she's woken him, but he is only dreaming. Of fish, perhaps? When he was little, he used to dream about fish. She doesn't know what he dreams about now. His new girlfriend, his bog house, the bats in the trees—it could be anything, and Penny knows that she'll never be sure. He's as separate from her as Walker is. That's what I learn from them, she thinks. The ways I have to stretch to guess what's in their minds. She bends, takes Walker's pipe from his hand, and sticks it in her mouth for a minute. Her tongue curls at the unfamiliar, bitter taste. Alcor lies in the crook of Walker's arm; Mizar, in the crook of Webb's. The men look as soft and helpless as snails without their shells.

With the men asleep, the women gather more closely about the candlelit table. Jordan, done naming the stars, lies quietly on Cass's leg and listens to her sister's pen scratching the paper. Her eyes are open but she's dreaming anyway, imagining that the sky is water and that she hangs upside down in it, not breathing. Paine bought her a kayak this spring for her birthday present, and she's spent the summer trying to learn how to roll it. The motions she needs to make underwater are backward from those Paine demonstrates right side up, and she hasn't yet learned how to translate them. It all seems clear until Paine tips her over. Then, hanging weightless below the boat, she gets to watching the crabs and weeds and forgets what she's supposed to do until Paine's nervous, hollow rap on the bottom of her boat reminds her. But she has lost all sense of direction by then. Everything's reversed, and she holds her paddle over her head instead of at her waist. In the water, up is down and down is up.

"Aunt Penny?" she says, aware of a lull in the conversation.

"Mmm?"

"I named all the constellations right."

"That's great."

"Make Mom do it—I want to see if she remembers as well as me."

Diane laughs and says, "Bet you a dollar I can."

"You're on," Jordan tells her.

Diane tilts her head back, but for an instant the stars seem to form no patterns at all. She sees bright points, duller ones, fires, flares—where is north? Where is south? North is New Hampshire, south is the ocean, east is Ben and Jill and their new family. East is Pegasus. She finds the Great Square with a sigh of relief and works her way around from there. It all falls into place.

Jordan nods when she's finished and says, "Not bad for an old Mom. But where did they all come from?"

"All what?"

"All the stars."

"That's so complicated," Diane says, shaking her head. "Maybe your Aunt Penny will explain it."

"Not me," Penny says. "You're the one taking classes —you do it."

Diane tries to recall the lecture she heard last spring on the origin of the universe. It confused her then and confuses her still. "In the beginning," she says hesitantly, "there was nothing." That's what her teacher had said—that there was just nothing. No time, no space, no matter.

"Nothing at all?" Jordan asks.

"Nothing," Diane says. "And then, somehow, there was something, and the something exploded and made space, and time—"

Penny shakes her head and says, "You can't explain it that way . . . who could understand?" She turns to Jordan. "Think about it this way. Imagine a long time ago, when all the stars up there were like snowflakes crammed into this incredibly hard, heavy snowball. The snowball exploded, and all the flakes rushed out and turned into stars that gave off heat and light and made elements that went into new stars, and those stars made new elements and other stars, and that's still happening. The stars get born and grow old and die, and when they die their parts go out into other things."

"So where are the parts?" Jordan asks.

Penny shrugs and waves her arm over the platform, over the village below. "Everywhere," she says. "In everything. We're made of stars."

"We're made of stars," Jordan echoes. "So who made the snowball that made the stars?"

"Who knows?" Penny says. In the candlelight, Jordan's face is so radiant that it really does seem made of stars. Who makes beginnings? Penny wonders. The point, the speck, the instant in time that started the stars; the point, more than two decades ago, where she and Ben met and started these elements joining and separating and recombining into changing patterns. She tries to remember what she was doing in the bitter cold outside Harry's bar the night that she met Ben, but she's no longer sure. It was hot inside, and stuffy, she remembers, and she was tired of waiting on rude men, and she went outside for just a glimpse of the stars her grandmother left her. All I had left of her then, she thinks. Or all I thought I had. And yet from her, from that moment, everything else has come. Bless Gram.

Jordan yawns loudly, startling Penny. "Wait," Penny tells this almost-daughter. "Don't go to sleep yet—it's almost time." She checks her watch, scans the sky, and then points over the platform railing toward the moon. Two bright dots have risen with the shining crescent and form a close pair above it, a luminous chain that resembles one of Diane's earrings. "Sit up," she says.

Jordan straightens, and Diane and Cass turn to where Penny points. "A conjunction," Penny says. "See above the moon? Those are two planets. There, right in line with it."

"Pretty," Jordan says.

"Pretty," Diane echoes, wondering what the planets are. Venus and Mars? Jupiter and Saturn? Sal would know—if she cast a horoscope for a child born here and now, she'd read all sorts of things into this alignment. The moon, two planets, the constellations nearby—it's as if their loose-linked family hangs in the sky, joined for a few minutes by the wandering moon. It's the moon that ties this group together, but the moon moves quickly and in half an hour, an hour at most, the pattern will disappear.

"I wanted you to see that," Penny says.

"Should we wake Walker and Webb?" Jordan asks. "So they can see?"

"Let them sleep," Penny says. "It's not important to them."

Cass bends over her sketchbook, drawing the sleeping men, the moon and two planets, her mother and Diane and Jordan, all joined for an instant. With her pen she renders black as white and white as black, as if she draws a negative. At the corner of the page, where she'd be if this were a photograph, she draws the tip of the pen from which this picture flows. This is what I want to do someday, she thinks. When I've had my fill of drafting. Jordan says, "Can I look at the planets through the telescope?"

"If you want," Penny says. "But you won't be able to see the group together. You can see only one thing at a time through it."

Jordan's face falls. "But . . ." she says.

She looks so disappointed that Penny relents. "I'll show you something else," she says. "If you'd like."

Jordan nods.

"What do you see up there?" Penny asks. "Besides the moon and the planets?"

"Stars, of course."

"Ah," Penny says. "Not of course." She looks up, remembering how she tried to explain this to Ben so long ago. "The stars you see with your eyes are called lucid stars," she tells Jordan. "Or naked-eye stars. There aren't as many of them as you'd think." She gets up and holds her hand out to Jordan, leading her to the telescope. She uncovers it and focuses on the double cluster in Perseus. Before she lets Jordan look she points over something and says, "What's that constellation?"

"Perseus," Jordan says promptly.

"Right. Now see the two stars off the tip, pointing to Cassiopeia?"

"Uh-huh."

"Stars, right?"

Cass smiles at Diane. This is an old trick, one they've both seen.

"Right," Jordan says.

"Now look at them through here."

Jordan leans over the eyepiece and gasps in surprise. The stars aren't stars at all but vast clusters of stars, each one resolving into thousands of points. More than she can count—more, in these two clusters, than are scattered over all the sky when she looks with just her eyes. Her throat goes dry. "Are they all like that?" she whispers.

"Like what?" Penny says.

"Each star I can see by myself—is each one really a cluster?"

"No," Penny says gently. "Some are really stars. But others are clusters, and others are galaxies, and others are groups of galaxies. You can see maybe two thousand stars by yourself, on a clear night. But you can see millions through a little telescope—billions through a big one. Most of the light in the sky comes from the stars you can't see."

"Is there any black sky?" Jordan asks. "Really?"

"Not much."

"Can I move the telescope?"

"If you want."

Jordan nudges the telescope past the double cluster to a dark patch in the sky. The field fills with faint stars. "Everywhere," she murmurs.

"That's right," Penny says.

And Jordan is just about to ask how this can be, how the sky so spare with lucid stars can be packed with secret galaxies, when something brilliant streaks across her field of view.

"Comet!" she says.

"Shooting star," Penny tells her. "Make a wish."

Cass's hand flies across her sketchbook, adding these last details. Three heads, upturned, wishing on a star; two cats asleep in the crooked arms of two unconscious men; and the moon, on its solitary course.